The
Girls

ALSO BY LORI LANSENS

Rush Home Road

The
Girls

A Novel

Lori Lansens

 LITTLE, BROWN AND COMPANY

New York ∾ Boston

Little, Brown and Company
Time Warner Book Group
1271 Avenue of the Americas, New York, NY 10020
Visit our Web site at www.twbookmark.com

First United States Edition: May 2006

First published in 2005 by Alfred A. Knopf Canada

The excerpt from the poem "To Bring the Dead to Life" by Robert Graves is
from *Robert Graves: The Complete Poems in One Volume* and is reprinted
by permission of Carcanet Press Limited.

Library of Congress Cataloging-in-Publication Data

Lansens, Lori.
    The girls : a novel / Lori Lansens. — 1st U.S. ed.
       p. cm.
    ISBN-10: 0-316-06903-5
    ISBN-13: 978-0-316-06903-8
    1. Conjoined twins — Fiction.   2. Abandoned children — Fiction.   3. Young
women — Fiction.   4. Adoptees — Fiction.   5. Sisters — Fiction.   I. Title.

PR9199.4.L36G57 2005
813'.6 — dc22   2005024510

10   9   8   7   6   5   4   3

Q-MB

Book designed by Paula Szafranski
Printed in the United States of America

For my mother and father

The
Girls

Ruby & Me

I have never looked into my sister's eyes. I have never bathed alone. I have never stood in the grass at night and raised my arms to a beguiling moon. I've never used an airplane bathroom. Or worn a hat. Or been kissed like that. I've never driven a car. Or slept through the night. Never a private talk. Or solo walk. I've never climbed a tree. Or faded into a crowd. So many things I've never done, but oh, how I've been loved. And, if such things were to be, I'd live a thousand lives as me, to be loved so exponentially.

My sister, Ruby, and I, by mishap or miracle, having intended to divide from a single fertilized egg, remained joined instead, by a spot the size of a bread plate on the sides of our twin heads. We're known to the world medical community as the oldest surviving craniopagus twins (we are twenty-nine years old) and to millions around the globe, those whose interest in people like us is more than just passing, as conjoined craniopagus twins Rose and Ruby Darlen of Baldoon County. We've been called many things: freaks, horrors, monsters, devils, witches, retards, wonders, marvels. To most, we're a curiosity. In small-town Leaford, where we live and work, we're just "The Girls."

Raise your right hand. Press the base of your palm to the lobe of your right ear. Cover your ear and fan out your fingers — that's where my sister and I are affixed, our faces not quite side by side, our skulls fused together in a circular pattern running up the temple and curving around the frontal lobe. If you glance at us, you might think we're two women embracing, leaning against the other tête-à-tête, the way sisters do.

Ruby and I are identical twins and would be identical looking, having high foreheads like our mother and wide, full mouths, except that Ruby's face is arranged quite nicely (in fact, Ruby is very beautiful), whereas my features are misshapen and frankly grotesque. My right eye slants steeply toward the place my right ear would have been if my sister's head had not grown there instead. My nose is longer than Ruby's, one nostril wider than the other, pulled to the right of my brown slanted eye. My lower jaw shifts to the left, slurring my speech and giving a husky quality to my voice. Patches of eczema rouge my cheeks, while Ruby's complexion is fair and flawless. Our scalps marry in the middle of our conjoined heads, but my frizzy hair has a glint of auburn, while my sister is a swingy brunette. Ruby has a deep cleft in her chin, which people find endearing.

I'm five feet five inches tall. When we were born, my limbs were symmetrical, in proportion to my body. Presently, my right leg is a full three inches shorter than my left, my spine compressed, my right hip cocked, and all because I have carried my sister like an infant since I was a baby myself, Ruby's tiny thighs astride my hip, my arm supporting her posterior, her arm forever around my neck. Ruby is my sister. And strangely, undeniably, my child.

There is some discomfort in our conjoinment. Ruby and I experience mild to severe neck, jaw, and shoulder pain, for which we take physiotherapy three times a week. The strain on my body is constant, as I bear Ruby's weight, as I tote Ruby on my hip, as I struggle to turn Ruby over in our bed or perch on my stool beside the toilet for what seems like hours. (Ruby has a multitude of bowel and urinary tract problems.) We are challenged, certainly, and uncomfortable, sometimes, but neither Ruby nor I would describe our conjoinment as painful.

It's difficult to explain our locomotion as conjoined twins or how it developed from birth using grunts and gestures and what I suppose must be telepathy. There are days when, like a normal person, we're clumsy and uncoordinated. We have less natural symbiosis when one of us (usually Ruby) is sick, but mostly our dance is a smooth one. We hate doing things in unison, such as answering yes or no at the same time. We never finish each other's sentences. We can't shake our heads at once or nod (and wouldn't if we could — see above). We have an unspoken, even unconscious, system of checks and balances to determine who'll lead the way at any given moment. There is conflict. There is compromise.

Ruby and I share a common blood supply. My blood flows normally in the left side of my brain, but the blood in my right (the connected side) flows to my sister's left, and vice versa for her. It's estimated that we share a web of one hundred veins as well as our skull bones. Our cerebral tissue is fully enmeshed, our vascular systems snarled like briar bushes, but our brains themselves are separate and functioning. Our thoughts are distinctly our own. Our selves have struggled fiercely to be unique, and in fact we're more different than most identical twins. I like sports, but I'm also bookish, while Ruby is girlie and prefers television. When Ruby is tired, I'm hardly ever ready for bed. We're rarely hungry together and our tastes are poles apart: I prefer spicy fare, while my sister has a disturbing fondness for eggs.

Ruby believes in God and ghosts and reincarnation. (Ruby won't speculate on her next incarnation though, as if imagining something different from what she is now would betray us both.) I believe the best the dead can hope for is to be conjured from time to time, through a note of haunting music or a passage in a book.

I've never set eyes on my sister, except in mirror images and photographs, but I know Ruby's gestures as my own, through the movement of her muscles and bone. I love my sister as I love myself. I hate her that way too.

This is the story of *my* life. I'm calling it *Autobiography of a Conjoined Twin*. But since my sister claims that it can't technically ("technically" is Ruby's current favorite word) be considered an *auto*biography and is opposed to my telling what she considers *our* story, I have agreed that she should write some chapters from her point of view. I will strive to tell my story honestly, allowing that my truth will be colored a shade different from my sister's and acknowledging that it's sometimes necessary for the writer to connect the dots.

What I know about writing I've learned mostly from reading books and from Aunt Lovey, who, along with Uncle Stash (born Stanislaus Darlensky in Grozovo, Slovakia, in 1924), raised Ruby and me from birth. I was accepted into the English program at a nearby university, but Ruby wouldn't agree to go. I knew she'd refuse, but I'd applied to the school anyway, so I could be aggrieved and excused. With Ruby sulking at my side, I'd handed the acceptance letter to Aunt Lovey. "How can I ever be a writer if I don't study writing? How can I be a writer if I don't even have a degree?" I cried.

Aunt Lovey hated self-pity. "Don't blame your sister if you don't become a writer. I don't know how pistons piss, but I can sure as hell drive a car." She gave me a look and strode away.

The next day Aunt Lovey presented me with a book called *Aspects of the Novel* by E. M. Forster. She wrapped it in leftover Christmas paper and taped a daisy from the garden to the top, even though it was a library book, due back in two weeks. Then she drove me to the Kmart to purchase a ten-pack of pencils and a stack of yellow legal pads. Ruby threw up out the car window when we pulled into the parking lot, somewhat ruining the excursion. As Aunt Lovey cleaned the side of the Impala, I opened *Aspects of the Novel* to a random page and read aloud from a long, tedious paragraph on the subject of death and the treatment of death in the novel. Aunt Lovey beamed at me as though I'd written the passage myself. Ruby groaned, but I don't know if it was illness or envy.

From the very beginning, Ruby hated my writing. She didn't see the point of my character sketches and accused me of cheating when my poems didn't rhyme. One time, after reading one of my short stories, she asked me, "Who are you writing this for anyway, Rose?" I was stung. Because I didn't know. And thought I should. My love of reading has distanced my sister and me. Ruby has never enjoyed books, unless you count children's books and the Hollywood magazines she drools over in doctors' waiting rooms.

I inherited my love of books from Aunt Lovey, though I like to think my birth mother was bookish too. Aunt Lovey was seldom without a book in her hands or one splayed on the arm of her brown vinyl La-Z-Boy in the den. She made the sunporch beside the pantry at the back of the old farmhouse where we grew up into a storage room filled with books. We called the room "the library," though there wasn't a bookcase in sight — just stacks and stacks of paperbacks, 784 in all, keeping the cold in the plaster-and-lath walls. When Aunt Lovey died, we donated her books to the Leaford Library, which happens to be where we are currently employed. I sort and shelve, and Ruby reads to school groups, though obviously not at the same time. (In case you're wondering, we are each paid a salary for our individual hours worked.) Aunt Lovey used to tell me that if I wanted to be a writer, I needed a writer's voice. "Read," she'd say, "and if you have a writer's voice, one day it will shout out, 'I can do that too!'"

My voice did shout out, but I'm not sure it said, "I can do that too." I don't ever recall being that confident. I think my voice said, "I *must* do that too." When I was in eighth grade, one of my poems, called "Lawrence," was selected for the yearbook's Poetry Corner. I submitted the poem anonymously, pleased to know that when the yearbook staff chose it, it wasn't out of pity for one of The Girls. After "Lawrence" was published (even if I was just a kid, and it was only the yearbook), I announced (at fourteen years old) that my next work would be an autobiography. Aunt Lovey snapped her fingers and said, "Call it *Two for One.* Wouldn't that be cute? Or *Double Duty.*"

I've sent sixty-seven short stories out for review (one has been published in *Prairie Fire*) and several hundred poems (eleven published in the *Leaford Mirror,* one in the *Wascana Review,* and a fifth

of one — don't ask — in *Fiddlehead*). I've been composing this autobiography in my mind for fifteen years, but these are the first words
I've put down. If someone asks how long it took to write, I won't
know how to answer.

MY SISTER AND I knew from early on that we were rare and
unusual, although I can't recall any single moment of clarity, as in
"Ahh," she thought, "not all people are attached to their siblings." I
do remember a struggle. We must have been around three years
old — I've played it over and over in my head.

It goes like this. . . . There are the burnt-orange fibers of the shag
carpet in the den at the old farmhouse. My small hand disappears
completely in the thick deep pile. The room smells of Lysol and
Aunt Lovey's lavender powder. Aunt Lovey has placed Ruby and
me in the middle of the room. I'm sitting on my bottom. Ruby is
clinging to me, alternately balancing herself on her curious little legs
and wrapping them around my waist as I shift to accommodate her
weight. Ruby is forever beside me. I understand that I am *me,* but
that I am also *we.*

Aunt Lovey wades through the carpet in her worn pink house
slippers and places a Baby Tenderlove doll on the other side of the
playroom in front of the silver radiator. Baby Tenderlove is mine.
Aunt Lovey gave her to me in the morning when she gave Ruby her
Kitty Talks a Little. She let us play with the dolls for a few minutes,
then took them away. Aunt Lovey was deaf to our sobs. Here's the
doll again. Only she's so far away. I lift my arms. And stretch. I
know I can't reach the baby doll this way, but this is my language. It
means "I want it." I kick my feet and cry. I see Aunt Lovey and Uncle Stash watching from the doorway. Aunt Lovey says, "Go on,
Rosie. You go get your baby. You go get your baby doll." I look into
Uncle Stash's eyes. *Please. Please, Uncle Stash. Please.* He's a pushover
for Ruby and me. He starts forward to get my baby doll, but Aunt
Lovey holds him back. I scream again. And kick the floor. Ruby
whimpers, frustrated and annoyed and wondering what became of

her doll. I kick the floor again, bumping myself up and down in protest, and suddenly, without intending to, I move forward. I pause. I bump up and down again. Nothing. I kick and bump at the same time. I move forward. I stop crying and kick and bump again. I grip my sister around the waist and kick and bump, and bump and kick, and drag her along with me. We advance. Refining my alignment and the rhythm of my kick and bump, using my free hand to push, I go faster and faster across the fuzzy orange carpet. Ruby squeals in protest, her legs gripping my middle, her arm yanking my neck, tugging me back because she's not ready for this. But I'm ready. I reach the doll.

The next day, Aunt Lovey placed us in the middle of the floor again. This time she didn't put my Baby Tenderlove doll in front of the silver radiator but Ruby's Kitty Talks a Little. And it was Ruby's turn to learn how to get what she wanted. Ruby's challenge was greater than mine, though. According to Aunt Lovey, it took Ruby six months to coax me across the room. Some time after that, Aunt Lovey put my doll and Ruby's doll at separate ends of the room. A casual observer might have thought she was being cruel, but Aunt Lovey wanted more for us than just survival.

When Ruby and I were nine years old, Aunt Lovey drove us to the Leaford Library to look for books about our condition. (What books did she think we would find there? *Welcome to the Wonderful World of Craniopagy?*) Ruby had, and still has, severe motion sickness. She doesn't always tolerate antinausea medication, and more than half the time we travel, even short trips, she gets sick. Sometimes very sick. Ruby's motion sickness has further limited our already profoundly restricted lives. My travel bags, even for day trips, contain several changes of clothes for us both. Under most of my travel memories is the shaker-cheese smell of Ruby's breath.

On the way to the Leaford Library, Ruby threw up twice, and by the time we arrived I was wearing the last of my clean clothes. Even though it was normal for my sister to be carsick, I knew that it was more than Aunt Lovey's driving. (The next day Ruby was covered in chicken pox, which I, incidentally, did not get.)

Aunt Lovey had been disappointed to find that there were no books about cranial conjoinment, or any kind of conjoinment, in the children's section upstairs. On our way to the elevator she stopped to tell the older woman at the desk that Leaford Library needed to look at its children's collection and include a book or two about *birth defects and whatnot*. "Especially," she'd added, "since you have a set of craniopagus twins living right here in your own community."

The old woman, whose name tag said ROZ and who was wearing a young woman's purple angora sweater, stared at me and my sister. Like most of Baldoon County, she'd only heard of the rare conjoined twins. She seemed less astonished than most people on first meeting Ruby and me. Maybe it was because she knew someone not similarly, but equally, exceptional. She agreed that the children of Leaford needed to be enlightened, and then she escorted us to the elevator. I felt Ruby go limp on the quick ride down and I knew that she'd fallen asleep. I could feel the heat from her fever and considered informing Aunt Lovey that we should go home, but the old woman in the angora sweater had directed us to a book of photographs (from the Mütter Museum in Philadelphia) on one of the high shelves in the adult section. I could not leave without looking inside.

On the front of the huge book was a daguerreotype of Chang and Eng Bunker, twins from old Siam, the original Siamese twins who were famous for doing circus acrobatics while being joined at the chest. After entertaining the courts of Europe, the brothers settled in North Carolina in the mid-1800s, married nontwin sisters, and fathered a total of twenty-one children! (This is absolutely true.) In the photograph the twins look distinguished, wearing identical dark suits tailored to cover the band of flesh that bound them at the thorax. They lived to be sixty-three years old. Chang died in the night of a ruptured spleen. His brother's parting words are said to be, "I'll go now too."

Aunt Lovey carried that big picture book, and a few smaller books, to a large quiet table at the back of the reading area. Ruby's sleeping body was heavy. Hot. I settled down carefully on a narrow bench and held my breath as Aunt Lovey's freckled hand (you would never have known by looking at her that my Aunt Lovey had Native Indian blood) opened the book. The first photograph, in black and white, was a graphic shot of a severely deformed human skeleton. Aunt Lovey read the small print out loud — "Skeleton of a seven-month-old fetus with spina bifida and anencephaly" — before she cleared her throat and turned the page. On the next page was a photograph of a nude woman, surprising not because of her white nakedness but because of a curvature of the spine that caused her to bend sharply at the middle, like a walking letter *r*. I asked Aunt Lovey to read the small print on that page, but she turned it instead. The next photograph was of a middle-aged man dressed in a starched white shirt and cravat. An enormous plum-colored tumor appeared to have frightened the man's right eye into his forehead and chased the nose off the center of his face. I would have liked to linger on the photo, but Aunt Lovey turned the page. There, on the next page, against a velvet background, incredibly and spectacularly, were the pickled remains of infant craniopagus twins, joined not at the *side* of the head, like Ruby and me, but at the *back* of the head, so that one looked forward and one behind. The babies were afloat in a massive glass jar, eyes wide, mouths open, a tooth bud visible in the larger one's lower gums. Back to back. Bum to bum. Flotsam in fluid. Tiny elements of metal visible here and there. The babies had been posed before being sunken in the jar. They were holding hands. A sob rushed out of Ruby's throat and startled me because I hadn't felt her wake. Aunt Lovey slammed the book shut. Her cheeks were scarlet. She rose to return the book to the shelf.

Ruby sniffed into the plaid handkerchief she kept, as old ladies do, tucked up in her sleeve. I opened a small red book with no pictures and read a story that haunts me, like music. The story of Minnie and Marie. Minnie and Marie were born joined at the chest (that would be a thorapagus conjoinment) in Wales in 1959. The combined weight of the girls at birth was only seven pounds. By the time they were eighteen months old, they'd spent more time in the hospital than out. Minnie and Marie were physically beautiful babies with porcelain complexions and thick black curls, and they laughed more than they cried. The babies embraced and kissed each other often, but they also fought viciously and sometimes had to be restrained by the nurses. They were slow developing language skills but communicated easily with each other. For some reason, they each called the other "Marie," which they pronounced "Me." Their adoring nurses and doctors called both babies "Me" too. Minnie and Marie were normal in all aspects except that they shared one heart, which began to fail as they neared their second birthday.

Specialists were brought in on the case, thoracic and vascular and cardiac surgeons, all of whom proposed sacrificing the sicklier baby, Marie, and giving the shared heart to the stronger twin, Minnie. Their mother, panicked by the ticking clock and the doctors' insistence that both girls would die if something wasn't done, agreed to the surgery. She kissed baby Marie good-bye forever while she prayed that the shared heart would work in baby Minnie. The heart did work in Minnie, better than the doctors had dared hope. When little Minnie opened her eyes a few days following the surgery, the roomful of doctors and nurses erupted with applause. The baby clapped too, then reached out to embrace her sister, frightened and confused to find her twin gone. Minnie searched the room for the face of Marie. "Me?" she whispered. The doctors and nurses fell silent. The baby looked around again. "Me?" she begged. "Me?" Then she looked down and, suddenly, seemed to understand that her sister had been amputated from her chest. "Hurts," she whimpered, touching the white bandages. She found the eyes of her mother, who by this time was awash in tears. *"Me,"* Minnie said once more, then closed her eyes and died too.

AUNT LOVEY TOLD me way back then to write my story fearlessly, a little how it is, a little how I wish it could be, not just as a conjoined twin but as a human being and a woman, and all these years later, that's what I'm going to do. "Write," she said, "as if you'll never be read. That way you'll be sure to tell the truth." But I *do* want to be read. I want to share this true story of my life — with you.

Mother's Nature

Atornado touched down in Baldoon County on the day Ruby and I were born. According to eyewitness accounts, after hovering over twenty acres of seed corn near Jeanette's Creek, the fury suddenly drove to the earth, plucked four-year-old Larry Merkel and his blue bike from his gravel driveway, and, cutting a swath through the seed corn and sugar beets, stole south toward the lake with its trophy. The tornado never reached the lake but veered sharply at Cadot's Corners as if just having remembered the way. There were sightings in three more townships, then nothing. The Merkel boy was lost, but his blue bike was found on the roof of a house three concessions over, more or less intact.

The little bike, with its slightly bent front frame, once sat behind a rope in the Leaford Museum, flanked to the left by a display of antique farming implements and to the right by a congregation of monarch butterflies straight-pinned to cork. The museum was across the road from our farmhouse on Rural Route One, so Ruby and I were frequent visitors. We knew the exhibits well, and Ruby even became a valuable contributor. In addition to the butterflies, there were cases of musket shot from the War of 1812, and a tobacco

pouch said to have belonged to the great Chief Tecumseh. What began as a small display of Neutral Indian artifacts grew, as each year
my sister searched for and found dozens more objects in the fields
around our home. Across from the Indian exhibit in the Leaford
Museum were two larger-than-life photographs of my sister and
me, taken when we were three and a half years old.

I loved listening to our Aunt Lovey, or sometimes Uncle Stash,
read the handwritten signs describing Leaford's riches and rarities.
Beneath our picture the placard read: "Rose and Ruby Darlen. Born
joined at the head on the day of the tornado — July 30, 1974 — at
St. Jude's Hospital, Leaford. Rose and Ruby are one of the rarest
forms of conjoined twins — craniopagus. They share an essential
vein and can never be separated. In spite of their situation, the girls
enjoy a normal and productive life here in Leaford. Picture taken by
Stash Darlen, the girls' uncle." (Aunt Lovey told me they'd originally used the word "predicament" to describe our conjoinment.
She'd made them change it to "situation.") Beneath Larry Merkel's
bent blue bike the placard read: "Child's bike. Found on Don Char-
boneau's roof after the tornado, July 30, 1974. The tornado devas-
tated Baldoon and the surrounding counties, wounding dozens of
people and killing two. Property damage was estimated at over
$300,000. Ninety-mile-an-hour winds carried this child's bike al-
most four miles." The dead boy (whose body was never found) was
not named. And there was no mention of his poor grieving mother.

St. Jude's Hospital, the place where we were born, was not
equipped for disaster, and the staff didn't know where to start after
the tornado had come and gone and taken Larry Merkel with it.
Most of the injured were seasonal workers from the Caribbean, and
many of them had been stranded in the field, unwisely seeking shelter in a derelict barn when the wind began to wail. There were
eighteen rooms in the squat brown medical building, and by four-
thirty in the afternoon, a half an hour after the tornado hit, all the
rooms were occupied. Several dozen bruised and bleeding men
were crammed into the musty waiting room, a few more spilling out
onto the slippery floor in the hall. The less serious cases waited out-

side, smoking and joking in their island patois, glad for the excuse to be away from the farm. Pale and white-haired Cathy Merkel, mother of little lost Larry, walked among the wounded, searching the halls for her swept-away son, standing shocked and still from time to time, like one of the lengths of birch scattered across the township.

I should stop here and make it clear that all I know of the details of the tornado, and of our birth, was told to me by Aunt Lovey, who was "Nurse Darlen" to her coworkers at St. Jude's Hospital and everything to Ruby and me. Aunt Lovey was in attendance when we were born, benignly plump back then, her mop of curls more blond than gray, her freckled face hardly lined. You might have guessed she was forty. She was fifty-two.

My recollections of Aunt Lovey's recollections of our birth will differ, of course, the story having been combed by my memory and set by imagination. And my sister's recollections of Aunt Lovey's recollections of our birth, or her own memories of any of the things that have happened in our lives, are very different from mine.

Back to our story: Aunt Lovey said that on the day of the tornado, Dr. Richard Ruttle Jr., on seeing his hospital crowded with injured migrant workers, called his elderly doctor-father, Dr. Richard Ruttle Sr., out of retirement to help. Nurses from several neighboring communities appeared with boxes of supplies, and a few Catholic League ladies brought food: mushroom soup casserole, Kraft slices on white bread, chicken salad with celery chunks, and Cocoa Krispies from the fridge.

Aunt Lovey was paged on the intercom. There was a call from Uncle Stash, but she couldn't take the phone. The message had been scribbled by a harried staffer in blotchy blue pen on the back of a Kentucky Fried Chicken napkin. It said simply, "You." Uncle Stash was in Ohio visiting his elderly mother and had missed the bad weather altogether. He'd heard about the storm and called St. Jude's, relieved to learn that his wife was unharmed. "Please, just to tell my wife, 'You,'" he'd said in his thick Slovak accent, then spelled it y-o-u, when the staffer thought she'd misheard. "You." It's what

Uncle Stash and Aunt Lovey said to each other, perfect in its singu-
larity, throughout their whole married life. It meant "I love you,"
and other such powerful clichés. *You* are everything to me. I've been
so worried about *you.* I'd die if anything happened to *you.* I'm sorry
if I've hurt *you. You* have made my life. Uncle Stash also called Aunt
Lovey *"moja mila,"* which means "my darling" in Slovak. Aunt
Lovey would laugh and say, "I'm everyone's darlin', Darlen." She
said you had to have a sense of humor about names when you were
born with the name "Lovonia Tremblay," then married to become
"Lovey Darlen." Being a craniopagus twin, I understood what she
meant about needing a sense of humor.

After tucking the napkin with its precious blue code into the
cleavage of her damp brassiere, Aunt Lovey took a moment to wonder at the chaos around her. She'd scratched her blond head, feeling
ridiculous for the gesture, thinking that Leaford hadn't seen a tornado in more than forty years, and never one as vicious as this.
When the public alarm siren behind the water tower in the park by
the Thames River sounded off, Aunt Lovey just assumed (though
she knew, of course, that our country was not at war) that Leaford
was being bombed. She'd been shocked by news of the tornado and
perversely disappointed not to have felt the lash of the killer storm
more directly.

Aunt Lovey felt the napkin shift in her brassiere. Then a pregnant patient lurched through the Emergency Room doors. And the
electricity went out.

The sun had yet to dip, so the degree of panic in the room did not
increase noticeably. Everyone assumed the lights would be quickly
restored, and for the moment they could see well enough. Aunt
Lovey instructed a fellow nurse to bring water to an old man with a
superficial scalp wound, then hurried to attend to the frightened
pregnant woman contracting in the hall.

The woman, our mother, was eighteen years old, petite and
pretty, with long wavy brown hair and a wide, full mouth. On her
bottom, she wore a pair of men's boxer-style underwear swung low
under the hill of her belly, and on top, a pink, not-quite-long-

enough, smocked maternity dress with no bra. A purple Popsicle had melted down the front of her pink dress and stained her lips and tongue. Her hair was tangled from the wind. Her eyes, smudged with black mascara, were terrified. She was large, as pregnancies go, one of the largest Aunt Lovey had ever seen.

"Twins?" Aunt Lovey guessed, smelling cigarettes on the young woman's heaving breath.

Our young mother suddenly noticed the wounded black men spilling out of the waiting room. A hollow, haunted, white-haired woman (Mrs. Merkel) watched her from the far end of the hall. Our mother bit her cheek, trying not to cry, but she was afraid, and she was in pain, and she was really just a kid herself. Aunt Lovey drew the pregnant girl from the twilight of the hallway into the large closet she used as an office. After fondling the light switch and hoping for a miracle, she asked, "Where you from, hon?"

Our mother couldn't answer. She tried to catch her breath as the pain from a contraction chugged up her spine.

Aunt Lovey already knew that our mother wasn't from Leaford or anywhere nearby. "I'd say you were from Windsor," Aunt Lovey said, sizing her up.

Our mother, having earned a reprieve from the contractions, tore the plastic off a fresh package of cigarettes she'd found in her dirty macramé bag. "I'm having a nic fit," she explained, then checked the darkening sky. "Aren't hospitals supposed to have generators?"

Aunt Lovey pointed to a NO SMOKING sign on the wall, bristling, "We have a generator. Of course we have a generator."

Our mother seemed reassured, if annoyed about the smoking. She chewed on a strand of damp hair. "One doctor said twins early on, I guess, but I haven't really been to see him in a while, so . . ." She descended into a yellow swivel chair. "I parked my car in Reserved. Are they gonna tow?"

The window was open full and the wind was still fierce, coaxing the papers on Aunt Lovey's bulletin board to flap out a beat. Our mother kept time with her jangling legs as Aunt Lovey looked into her eyes, thinking they seemed too large, like a borrowed boot or an older sister's sweater. "What's your name?" Aunt Lovey asked, as she held our mother's wrist and counted the beats of her heart.

"Liiiizzzz," she answered, so slow and uncertain it had to be a lie.

"Well then, Liiiizzzz," Aunt Lovey said, reaching for the blood-pressure cuff, "I'm gonna take a wild one and say this is your first baby? Or likely babies."

Our mother nodded glumly.

Aunt Lovey checked the lights in the corridor. Still nothing. She looked at the sky. There'd be an hour's more light, at best. There must be a problem with the generator, she thought. We do *have* a generator.

"Do you know your due date, dear?" Aunt Lovey asked.

Our mother shrugged.

Aunt Lovey gave our mother a clipboard and pen, asking that she fill out her own admittance form, then the nurse wheeled a sleeping leg-wound patient back to triage, so the pregnant girl could labor privately in Room One. When Aunt Lovey later found the clipboard and read it in the light from a candle, she saw that, under "Name," our mother had written "Elizabeth Taylor." And under "Address," she'd put "Hollywood, California." The rest of the form was obliterated by spiral and box doodles.

Our mother was sweating severely, straddling a chair and smoking a cigarette out the window when Aunt Lovey and Dr. Ruttle Jr. entered her room. Aunt Lovey marched across the checkerboard floor, jerked the cigarette from her hand, and threw it out the window. (The room being on the first floor made the gesture somewhat less effective.) Our mother didn't, or couldn't, protest. She let Dr. Ruttle Jr. and Aunt Lovey lift her from the chair and heft her up to the hospital bed, where she lay frightened and craving nicotine.

Aunt Lovey pulled the curtains back as far as they would go. There was just enough light to see. In twenty minutes they'd need candles and flashlights. "I couldn't find your admittance form," Aunt Lovey said, clucking her tongue. "You'll have to fill out another."

Our mother nodded, watching the undulations of her babies beneath her blue hospital gown. Dr. Ruttle Jr. bent to pull the gown up, but it was stuck under her sweaty bottom, and there were some embarrassing maneuvers before Liz Taylor's stretched-raw skin was finally exposed.

"What's your name?" Dr. Ruttle Jr. asked. "Where's her chart?"

"Chart's in the hall," Aunt Lovey answered. "Her name is . . ." She waited to see if our mother would introduce herself, but she just stared off, stroking the *linea negra* on her swollen stomach. "Her name is Elizabeth. Elizabeth Taylor, just like the old movie star. Isn't that cute, Dr. Ruttle?"

"Yes, Nurse Darlen. That's cute." Then, for the first time, the doctor looked directly into his patient's eyes. He smiled kindly. "Who brought you in, Miz Taylor?"

Our mother began to cry.

"The father couldn't get here because of the tornado," Aunt Lovey lied.

"It's just stupid that you won't let me smoke," our mother sobbed.

Dr. Ruttle Jr. laid his small palms on the huge lump and submitted us to some forceful palpitations. "Twins. They're both engaged."

"Engaged?" Our mother sniffed and blinked.

"The babies' heads are down," Aunt Lovey explained. "It's good."

The doctor snapped on a latex glove, pried apart our mother's knees, and stabbed between her gooseflesh legs. After a moment he extricated himself and, letting the strain of the day creep onto his face, pinched the bridge of his nose with his lubricated fingers. Quickly realizing his mistake, he reached for a tissue. "Four," he said.

"Four?" Our mother looked horrified. "Twins are *two*."

"Centimeters. You're four centimeters dilated, dear." Aunt Lovey patted our mother's shoulder. "First delivery. Twins. It'll be a while yet."

I like to think our mother knew what "dilated" meant. I like to think she was not terrorized by the invasion of Dr. Ruttle's fingers. I like to think that, before he breezed out of the room, he assured her that he'd delivered hundreds of babies and dozens of twins and all would go well. It's more likely that our mysterious mother just lay there contracting in the darkness, dying for a smoke.

The electricity was not restored. The generator, if there was one, did not kick in. The streetlights did not come on, nor any other light in the whole town of Leaford. Our mother, young and afraid and sweating beneath her blue gown, labored alone. She asked for some movie magazines but couldn't read them with only two candles to light the room. Aunt Lovey, or one of the other nurses, stopped by each quarter hour with a sip of some swampy-tasting water, apologizing that there were no ice chips to suck on, assuring her that when it was time to deliver, the nurses would bring in kerosene lamps.

By ten o'clock that night most of the migrant workers had been treated and sent back to the farm to slumber in their makeshift barracks. A few of the men had been rushed to Chatham by ambulance. Three near-drowning victims, teenage boys whose stolen fishing boat had capsized on the choppy lake, had been collected by their fathers and brought home for a thrashing. And the talk of the hospital (before we arrived anyway) was that Dr. Ruttle Sr., in a feat some called heroic, had removed the shard of wood from a split-rail fence that had impaled a young autoworker with four children. Assisting as his father removed the giant splinter from the poor man's chest, Dr. Ruttle Jr. would recall a day when he was six years old, double-riding a bike down Rondeau Road, clinging to his father's back and thinking the man a giant.

White-haired Mrs. Merkel sat alone on an orange vinyl chair where she could watch people coming and going from both the front doors and the Emergency entrance. She was clutching Larry's picture (shorn white hair, slit gray eyes, fretful brows), dreaming of his little blue bike spinning without a rider in the vortex of the storm. In the dark, there were soft steps and whispers. Down the hall, dancing circles from a flashlight.

At 11:33 p.m. the Stones, a family of Mennonites from the Eleventh Concession, staggered through the Emergency doors into the dark hospital. Fifteen of them, with injuries from mild to severe, had spent hours digging out from the rubble of their collapsed cellar. Their horses were lost, so they'd stumbled the five muddy miles from farm to hospital. Two of the men, though bleeding and limping badly, carried a third, who appeared to be dead. Six small children, bits of wood clinging to their hot wool caps, floated behind the others. Aunt Lovey was relieved to see that the children seemed mostly unharmed, until the little girl in the center fell to the ground and stopped breathing. Dr. Ruttle Sr. dropped to his knees to begin cardiopulmonary resuscitation.

Most of the volunteers had already been sent home, and with them had gone the extra lanterns and flashlights. In the dark there were cries for light, and water, and light, and bandages, and light, and saline, and light and light and light. The man who'd been carried in dead had been revived by the commotion and, on seeing the fallen child, began to wail. There was so much noise in the Emergency Room, with trying to revive the little girl and administering care to the rest of the family, that no one could hear our mother moaning, or maybe yowling, some sort of deep, throaty, animal sound. No one except Mrs. Merkel, who, steeped as she was in worry, prepared as she was to grieve, followed the river of cries from Room One, groping through the blackness until she found our mother, on her knees, leaning over a chair with her forehead flat on the windowsill. (Aunt Lovey thinks she was trying to climb out the window to retrieve her cigarette.) The candles that had been in the room were dead on the ground outside. (Presumably she was trying to cast light on the grass to see if she could find that smoke.) Whatever brought our mother to the window, she'd been overcome by searing pain from her longest, strongest contraction yet, and before she could right herself, let alone make it back to the bed, another wave of pain had come, and then another and another.

Even in the pitch black it was obvious to Mrs. Merkel, who unintentionally set her hands on the woman's pulsing stomach, that this was the pregnant woman she'd seen before. "Help me," our mother begged. "Please, God, help me."

Mrs. Merkel shouted down the hall, "Nurse! Doctor! There's a woman having a baby! It's coming! The baby's coming! Please! *Please!*"

But no one came. Mrs. Merkel (who only had the one child) knew nothing of midwifery but had the presence of mind to offer some comforting words, find the sink in the dark, and soap up fast. There was a sound from our mother, a spine-chilling scream, as if she'd just had her arms amputated in a horrible sneak attack. And then another scream, the legs gone now too. Mrs. Merkel started out of the room, but circled and returned.

With her sleeves pulled up to her elbows, Mrs. Merkel reached down to feel the slick hair moon that was my (our) head between our mother's legs. "Good Lord," Mrs. Merkel whispered. "Good Lord in heaven." Of course, being conjoined, our head was nearly twice the size of a normal baby's head. Our mother grunted and pushed.

From anus. To clitoris. Her tissue tore.

One would assume that the birthing mother would be screaming, but she was not. "Oh my God," Mrs. Merkel whispered. "The head's out." She could hear the faucet dripping in the corner. Her hand on our bloody scalps, unable to see the two-faced twin that we were, Mrs. Merkel drew a deep, thrilled breath.

Suddenly Aunt Lovey was in the doorway with a kerosene lamp. The flickering lamp lit the scene at the window just enough for the nurse to see that an enormous head had emerged from young Elizabeth Taylor and that it had two distinct faces. Pinched faces not quite side by side, sharing a crop of thick dark hair. Aunt Lovey cocked her head and drew closer, not shocked or repulsed but utterly entranced.

Cathy Merkel screamed.

Within seconds, Doctors Jr. and Sr., followed by a passel of female nurses, appeared, all clutching some source of emergency light — a candle, a kerosene lamp, a flashlight, shining their lights upon the thing, the thing that was *us*.

It was a full minute before someone thought to remove the screaming Mrs. Merkel from the room.

The Doctors Ruttle quickly agreed not to try to move the patient from her all fours, acknowledging that hands and knees was, in fact, a fine posture to birth what appeared to be the first case of conjoined twins in Leaford and, possibly, the whole country. Dr. Ruttle Sr. at her left flank, Dr. Ruttle Jr. at her right, using two pairs of obstetric forceps, wrenched us from our mother's body, our internment with her ended, ours with each other about to begin.

Our entry into the world was greeted not with gasps but with the quiet reverence of professionals. Someone scooped us up and carried us, uncovered, to the examination table. We were slippery with creamy vernix, blotchy, purple, trembling. The doctors and nurses moved as one to watch us wriggle on the crinkling paper blanket. How long must they have stared before someone spoke?

Our combined weight at birth was ten pounds seven ounces. I was the longer one, my legs perfectly formed, my torso somewhat shorter than normal, making my arms appear somewhat longer. My sister's legs hung limply from her hips, two clubfeet annexed by her shortened femur bones. Ruby's upper body was normal, but very petite. I can imagine what the silent staff at St. Jude's Hospital saw as they looked down upon us: our heads welded together, my crooked face looking this way, and Ruby's pretty one looking that.

I've heard a number of versions of what happened next, but I'm sticking with Aunt Lovey's. There was a hushed round of "Oh my Gods" and "Lord in heavens" and "Holy mackerels." Then Aunt Lovey whispered, "The little one looks like the big one's doll." Dr. Ruttle Jr., never taking his eyes from us, called for a camera, then told Aunt Lovey to get on the phone with the Children's Hospital in Toronto. Before Aunt Lovey could turn to go, an instrument cart crashed near the door. People did not instantly spin to look, as they would in normal circumstances. And when they did turn, one by one, with their lamps and candles and flashlights, they were not shocked (after what they'd just seen, nothing would ever seem shocking again) to see Dr. Ruttle Sr. sprawled on the linoleum, a scalpel resting comically on his forehead, dead of a heart attack at age seventy-eight.

I abruptly stopped crying and led the room in a moment of silence. Heads twisted and swiveled, wondering at the extraordinary birth, conceding the timely death. Dr. Ruttle Jr. moved to his father's side. He did not attempt resuscitation. His father was already gone. He returned a rogue white hair to its dignified place on the old doctor's head, then set the instrument cart back on its feet. Quietly, calmly, he retrieved the bag of saline, the forceps, the clamps, and the other things strewn about the floor, straightening and revising the exact position of the scalpels twice while he considered that his beloved father had died on what had likely been the best day of his life. My newborn cries recommenced.

Finally, Dr. Ruttle Jr. turned his attention back to the craniopagus twins as Aunt Lovey and the other two men in the room (the custodian and one of the Mennonite men who'd been drawn by all the commotion) hoisted the elderly doctor's body onto a gurney and ferried him away.

Our mother, exhausted by her labor and likely reassured by the sound of my mewling (Ruby was still mute), did not make inquiries. She did not confirm, "Twins?" She did not question, "Boys or girls?" She did not even ask for a smoke. She allowed the attending nurses to roll her toward the bed, where Aunt Lovey helped to deliver the afterbirth. But there was a hemorrhage with this second delivery and enough blood to severely deplete the poor young girl, if not quite enough to require a transfusion.

Within two hours of our arrival, Ruby and I were on our way to the Children's Hospital in Toronto, in the back of an ambulance with head nurse Lovey Darlen. Our mother, Elizabeth Taylor, lay silent and staring but conscious for a full week following our birth. She would not divulge her real name (Mary-Ann Taylor) or eat, but she did manage to obtain some cigarettes. Aunt Lovey was in Toronto with us, and the rest of the staff, feeling sorry for the wretched new mother, didn't have the heart to enforce Aunt Lovey's no-smoking rule. On the morning of the tenth day, our mother accidentally or intentionally started a fire in Room One. Before the smoke was cleared, someone reported having seen her wobble toward the beat-up yellow Mustang parked in the tow zone. She was not seen again.

It is my opinion that our mother lost her mind when she delivered us. I think any normal woman would come unhinged giving birth to conjoined babies, and our mother was still just a girl, and an unmarried girl, in 1974, in southern Ontario. Ruby thinks it wasn't giving birth to us that drove our mother away but having her twin girls taken from her with so little regard. Ruby has deified our mother somewhat. I don't have the same illusions.

Nature's Mother

L arry Merkel was the first casualty of the tornado. Missing, presumed dead. Leaford also blamed Dr. Ruttle Sr.'s death on the storm. It was said that stress from the tornado caused his massive heart attack. The third death, the one that is not counted in any official records, might be blamed on the tornado a little too. Perhaps if our mother hadn't been caught in the storm, maybe if she'd delivered us in another town, her married lover waiting anxiously in the hall, the event would have materialized for her in a different way. Maybe she would have kept us. At least it's possible.

Contrary to some Web site information, our mother did not jump out the window when she saw that Ruby and I were joined at the head. (The room *was* on the first floor, after all.) She died alone in Toronto, in her dusty fourth-floor walk-up, of sepsis, eight weeks postpartum. Aunt Lovey said our mother must have been mentally deficient to have suffered the infection without seeking treatment. Uncle Stash said you didn't have to be crazy to do something stupid, just young.

We spoke of our dead mother often when we were children, less as we grew older. Aunt Lovey tolerated our adulation for the woman who'd abandoned us, but only because she was dead. She encouraged Ruby to draw pictures of her (Ruby is quite the talented artist) with diamond tiaras and angel wings, wearing white robes and riding on clouds. I wrote poems and short stories about our mother, keeping the unflattering portraits to myself. When we grew bored with drawing and writing, one of us (usually Ruby) would say, "Let's play that game," and the other knew it meant the game where we called our mother *Liz* and intentionally mixed her up with the real Elizabeth Taylor. It was the game where Ruby pretended we lived in Hollywood and people found us more interesting than freakish.

When we were twelve years old and pestering Aunt Lovey with questions about our birth mother, Uncle Stash had the idea to hire a private investigator. It was an incredibly exciting week for Ruby and me as, each day, Uncle Stash brought another tidbit of information home to the orange brick farmhouse on Rural Route One. Our mother's name, as I said, was Mary-Ann, not Elizabeth. She lived in Toronto but had friends in Windsor. She'd once had a part-time job in a secondhand bookstore, where she was well liked by the staff. A coworker told the investigator that she was a voracious reader and was saving money to go to college (I loved knowing that). She had been very interested in all things Native (Ruby loved knowing that), and she had belonged to a church youth group (which my sister and I could never picture).

Just before our fourteenth birthday, Uncle Stash took a day off from his job as butcher at Vanderhagen's Meat (where the other men called him Stan) so he and Aunt Lovey could drive us to Toronto for a doctor's appointment for Ruby's gastrointestinal problems — and to learn a little more about our birth mother. In Toronto we parked the old red Duster in front of the apartment building where our mother had lived on Sherbourne Street, across from a park and near a hospital. We sat in front of the unremarkable brick building (Uncle Stash bought a fat Saturday newspaper to read) for a full hour before Ruby finally said we could go. Where I'd found my attention drifting toward the beautiful, dangerous young people in the park, my sister had never taken her eyes from the red-brick building, imagining that each stranger going in or out had been our mother's trusted confidant and had some important story to tell. Ruby had sulked when Uncle Stash said we could not approach the strangers for questioning, and then she refused to eat the picnic lunch (honey ham sandwiches and date squares) that Aunt Lovey had packed that morning. "Don't be cute, Ruby. You are going to eat," Aunt Lovey had promised.

After lunch in the hot car (because Aunt Lovey would not expose my sister and me to those beautiful, dangerous young people in the park), we drove to Mount Pleasant Cemetery to put pink carnations (Ruby's favorite) on our mother's grave. The gravestone, which we'd found on the map given to Uncle Stash by the private investigator, was pink granite with specks of scarlet and amber. The stone read: MARY-ANN TAYLOR. BELOVED DAUGHTER. BORN, JANUARY 10, 1956. DIED, SEPTEMBER 21, 1974. My sister and I found comfort in seeing the grave, just as Aunt Lovey had told Uncle Stash we would when I overheard them arguing about it one night.

While standing in front of the pink granite gravestone, I sensed Ruby mouthing our mother's name, *Mary-Ann Mary-Ann Mary-Ann.* I felt sorry for my sister, at the same time curious as to why she was mouthing *Mary-Ann Mary-Ann* and not *Mother Mother.* Ruby urged me to kneel so we could be closer to the grave. I consented, though it was incredibly uncomfortable squatting on the grass that covered the dirt that covered the coffin that covered the body of Mary-Ann Taylor, and I was embarrassed. There were only a few people nearby in the cemetery (none of them squatting on their loved ones' plots), and they were all staring at us. Of course, they were staring because we are conjoined, but they were also staring because we were a spectacle.

After five or ten minutes of Ruby moaning *Mary-Ann Mary-Ann,* I began to feel really irritated. I didn't have the same longing for our mother that my sister did, and I felt guilty and confused by my lack of emotion. I asked Ruby if we could go and waited patiently each time she said, "A few more minutes." Soon Ruby began to weep with abandon, *Mary-Ann, Mary-Ann, oh Mary-Ann.* A family from several rows over drew closer.

I can count the number of times I've physically dominated my sister — the number of times that I have carried her away against her will — but at this point, with the gawking family closing in and my sister bellowing *Mary-Ann,* it was all I could think to do. I stood, gathering my sister in my right arm, feeling Ruby shake with shock and protest, and marched us back to the family car. After a moment, Uncle Stash appeared with the keys. His hands were trembling and he wouldn't look at me. I knew that whatever Uncle Stash was thinking, it went triple for Aunt Lovey.

On the way to dinner no one spoke, except Ruby, to declare that she would not be eating. My sister hadn't eaten lunch (in spite of Aunt Lovey's promise that she would), and she'd be sick if she skipped dinner too. This made me anxious (when Ruby gets sick my life is severely restricted), and I could see it worried Aunt Lovey too. She shared a look with Uncle Stash, after which he suddenly pulled out his notes from the private investigator and announced that we'd be having dinner at Lindy's Steak House on Yonge Street, "where your mother worked as a waitress!" Ruby clapped her hands — like a three-year-old. Gullible. Vulnerable. I loved her beyond comprehension in that moment, though we were not yet back on speaking terms.

Aunt Lovey and Uncle Stash had a chef's salad and a T-bone steak. I had a banquet burger, and Ruby had the fish. (She had a psychic feeling that fish had been our mother's favorite. Groan.) Of course there was staring. Whenever we go out in public there is staring, even in Leaford, where we grew up, and went to school, and hold jobs, and where we've been described in the local paper (Ruby and I *hate* this) as the town's mascot. (Being called a mascot is bad enough, but to singularize us — that's the worst.) We've been stared at so much in our lives we find it normal, and only really notice when we *haven't* been noticed. (I've wondered if beautiful women process staring the same way that Ruby and I do. Oh yes, they're *looking. Of course,* they're looking. Why *aren't* they looking?)

My sister remembers little about that pilgrimage to our mother's grave. She doesn't remember the dinner at Lindy's or the cemetery, or that we stayed in a cramped Lakeshore hotel and saw our first and only cockroach.

Back to the day of our birth. Since it was not possible for our mother to travel with us to the hospital in Toronto, Aunt Lovey volunteered, or rather begged, to go. With the Emergency Room still attending to the injured Mennonites, St. Jude's could not spare more than two of its staff, the driver and Aunt Lovey. As the ambulance hit the on-ramp to Highway 401, my sister began to cry, then so did I. Aunt Lovey scooped us out of the incubator and juggled us until she found a comfortable hold. She rocked us until we stopped crying and fell asleep. The weight of wonder, she thought, and then, the weight of worry.

Alone with my sister and me in the back of the ambulance for the full four-hour drive, Aunt Lovey determined that we were alert, responsive, and, surprisingly, more different than the same. ("From the moment you were born you had such opposite demeanors," she'd once said, and I later wondered if she'd read that term in a poem and forgotten she'd read it, then claimed it as her own.)

That was all it took — four hours — for Aunt Lovey to fall in love, the way you do with babies, deeply and without effort. She fed us infant formula and sang a song she made up about two chicken sisters. (When I was sixteen, on the eve of a violent acne eruption, I broke Aunt Lovey's heart by asking that she never, ever, sing that stupid song again.) Ruby does pretty fair vocal impressions. She sings the song with a little tremolo, just like Aunt Lovey used to. It makes me sad, but I never ask her to stop. (What is it about sadness that can be so fulfilling?) "Two little chicks just sleeping in the sun. First chick peeped and woke the other one. 'Who are you?' said the one to the two. 'Who am I? I'm your sis-ter!'"

Aunt Lovey named my sister "Ruby" because she shone like a gem. And she named me "Rose" to carry on the tradition of her eccentric mother, Verbeena (and hers before her), who named their girls after places or plants. As rain pelted the ambulance roof, Aunt

Lovey found herself thinking of Verbeena and of her own childhood in the old orange farmhouse. She thought of Stash and his upbringing in distant Slovakia (once known as Czechoslovakia: the Slovaks separated from the Czechs in 1993). She also thought of the conjoined South Asian twins she'd read about who'd been raised in the basement of an institution for the criminally insane but were found to have genius IQs. What would life be like for Rose and Ruby if Elizabeth Taylor wanted to raise us? I think Aunt Lovey knew, though, even before our mother ran away, that Elizabeth Taylor could not, would not, raise us. (I'm not bitter. I don't blame her.) Aunt Lovey believed that God had sent my sister and me to her, in answer to a prayer.

The July sky offered a cleansing rain for most of the journey down the flat, gray Highway 401. Aunt Lovey fretted that the ambulance would spin out on the slick black roads. When finally we approached the Emergency bay at the Toronto hospital, she saw that there were dozens of doctors and nurses waiting on the dock and imagined there must have been a terrible accident and a load of injured on the way.

"Pull up!" she'd called to the Leaford ambulance driver. "Pull up, for Pete's sake! They've got accident victims coming in."

The driver pulled the vehicle forward, and the doctors and nurses, led by a small, rather attractive, middle-aged Asian man, followed. They had not been waiting for accident victims. They'd been waiting for *us*.

Aunt Lovey was not prepared for the hungry way Dr. Mau (the eminent craniofacial surgeon) and the others set upon her babies, or the way they seemed not to notice or care when they yanked us from her and we began to wail. One of them called us "it." One of them let out a whoop, like he was at a *bucking rodeo roundup* (Aunt Lovey's words, not mine). Aunt Lovey said Dr. Mau reminded her of a large black spider descending upon two little fruit flies.

The press came; television reporters, newspapermen, and, of course, the sleazy tabloid guys. Aunt Lovey, as our self-appointed guardian, kept them all away. She'd been horrified to turn on the news that first night and see the Polaroid snapshot that was taken of Ruby and me shortly after our birth, and she'd been furious with Dr. Ruttle Jr. for releasing the photo to the media. (Newborn babies seem more alien than human to begin with, so you can only imagine what Ruby and I looked like through that awful Polaroid lens. Our Nonna calls newborns *"creatura."*) Aunt Lovey was determined that no unauthorized photos would ever find their way to the media again.

Fearing for our emotional development, Aunt Lovey made sure it was she, and not one of the other nurses, who fed us our bottles, gave us our bath, and sang the chicken sister song as she rocked us to sleep each night. Ruby preferred a cuddle against the chest, while I liked to be held higher up on the shoulder. "You had to be *Give* when you were *Take,*" she told Ruby. "And visie versie for you, Rosie."

Doctors from all over the world came to Toronto to confer with Dr. Mau and to examine the rare craniopagus twins. Newspapers around the globe carried the story (accompanied by that awful Polaroid photo) of our miraculous birth and its concurrence with the freak tornado in Baldoon County. For a short time, anyway, we put Leaford on the map. Channel Seven featured daily progress reports on the six and eleven o'clock news. Viewers were rapt, especially because there was fear early on that Ruby was too feeble to survive. A team of twenty surgeons was standing by, prepared to assist Dr. Mau in slicing my sister and me apart in the event she perished, so I might be saved. People prayed for Ruby's death, thinking it would have been kinder to both of us.

Wearing a crisp white nurse's uniform even though she was not officially on duty, Aunt Lovey sat next to our hospital crib, reading books or calmly looping wool from the pink yarn in the basket at her side. Doctors came and went with foreign germs and disregard. Aunt Lovey read, and looped, and prayed to God that Elizabeth Taylor would not return to claim us. When the children's welfare people had given her temporary guardianship of Ruby and me, Aunt Lovey hated the way they thanked her for taking on such a "tragic case." She held us when she could and promised us the moon. "I'm your Aunt Lovey," she whispered, nuzzling our soft cheeks, "and you are my family."

Aunt Lovey and Uncle Stash had never been separated for longer than a few days before, and these separations, when Uncle Stash went to see his elderly mother in Ohio, were rare — not even yearly (only when Mother Darlensky called to say she was dying, then didn't). As much as Uncle Stash missed Aunt Lovey, he was delighting in his solitude. The World Series was on Channel Two. His beloved Tigers (if you lived in Leaford you were a Detroit Tigers fan) hadn't made the play-offs, but the Los Angeles Dodgers were playing the Oakland A's (the A's were Uncle Stash's second-favorite team) in Game Five in Oakland. (The Athletics were not a team in the seventies; they were a dynasty, winning three consecutive World Series!) Not only could Uncle Stash watch his baseball in peace but he could smoke his forbidden pipe in the house and eat supper in his underwear in front of the TV.

(An aside: In some strange way I can celebrate the unlikelihood of Ruby and me through the game of baseball. Maybe that's why I love it. The controlled chaos. The trillions of possibilities. And millions of improbabilities. The home run. The pop fly. The double play. The shocking outcomes. Not to mention the simple thrill of watching a mere mortal launch that little white ball into the stands. Uncle Stash would clap his hands, shouting, "Vack dat ball, Kirk Gibson! Vack dat ball, Gibby!")

(Another aside: I didn't know that Uncle Stash had a thick Slovak accent until Ruby and I were in fourth grade attending a parent-teacher meeting about Ruby's inability to focus. Mrs. Hern, whom Ruby disliked but I adored, seemed not to understand a single word Uncle Stash was saying. Aunt Lovey said Uncle Stash's ear didn't hear his own accent. At his workplace, except for the sound of the saws, there was quiet. The other butchers didn't have much to say — which is just as well with all the bad tempers and sharp knives. We lived in the country, where the nearest neighbors were across the field and over the creek. Before that, Aunt Lovey and Uncle Stash had lived in a little bungalow beside Nonna, an old woman whose Italian accent was as thick as Uncle Stash's Slovak one. Uncle Stash didn't hear his accent, so he assumed people who couldn't understand him were either stupid or deliberately trying to irritate him. *"Picovina,"* he would mutter under his breath — the Slovak word for "Bullshit.")

(Ruby hated — still hates — baseball. Ruby hates all sports, preferring just about any mindless garbage on the television: *Bewitched* and *I Dream of Jeannie* reruns from the 1960s or one of her endless movies taped from TV, neatly labeled and stacked in a room, like Aunt Lovey with her books. Our conflicting taste in entertainment causes conflict between us during the hockey play-offs, and the basketball play-offs, and the Olympics, and especially the World Series.)

All that to say that Uncle Stash was enjoying being alone, smoking his pipe in the living room, watching Game Five in his underwear, and he had not been paying enough attention to Aunt Lovey's voice on the phone or her face when he was visiting the hospital on the weekends. He didn't suspect that his wife was falling in love with the conjoined twin girls. Her phone call about guardianship came from the proverbial left field.

"I have to *tink* about it, Lovey."

"What do you have to *think* about?"

"Lovey . . ." His tone was a warning. She was already being unreasonable. He watched the tobacco smolder in his pipe.

"Have you got the baseball on, Stash?"

"It's Game Five."

"Well, for the love of Pete, turn it down."

"Rollie Fingers is at pitching."

"You say, *on the mound,* or *is the pitcher,* or just *is pitching,* Stash — you know that." Aunt Lovey had been correcting her husband's English for nearly thirty years, but he never seemed to mind. "Please turn it down, Stash. This is important."

Uncle Stash left the phone to lower the volume. Steve Garvey singled to first.

"What if they are not finding the mother?" he asked when he picked up the receiver.

Aunt Lovey had one of her feelings (Aunt Lovey's big on premonitions) that our mother would not reappear, but didn't share it with Uncle Stash. "She'll turn up, but if she doesn't, I s'ppose we could try to make it permanent."

"We're old, Lovonia," Uncle Stash said, sounding old. He was fifty, exactly two years younger than his wife.

"Speak for yourself."

"Twins." He paused. "Joined twins." Another pause. "I don't know," he muttered, badly wanting to put his pipe in his mouth, afraid his wife would recognize the clicking sound of the stem hitting his teeth.

"Stash . . ."

"First I see her, okay?" Uncle Stash drove to Toronto each Saturday to spend a few hours with Aunt Lovey, then drove back the same night (neither would have dreamed of wasting money on a hotel), but he hadn't been allowed in our room and hadn't yet set eyes on us.

"Not *her,* Stash, *them*. Why?"

"It's reason to want to see her, Lovey."

"Reason*able*. And not *her. Them*." She was exhausted. "Twin girls. Not one girl with two heads. Two girls with two heads that happen to be joined together. Stash?"

"Lovey," he continued, "I don't know if it's the right thing. On Saturday, take me to see her. Take me to *see* her, Lovey. Then I decide."

"Well, it's pretty terrible. I mean, it's horrible but beautiful. You have to get used to it," Aunt Lovey told him.

Uncle Stash was silent, watching the baseball. For a moment he forgot he was on the phone. "Stash?"

"I'm watching."

"Listening. You mean you're *listening*. It's horrible, but they're beautiful too. There's nobody else, Stash."

"The doctor says it's all right to go from the hospital? Before you say the little one is no good."

"She's not *the little one,* she's *Ruby*. And I did not say she was *no good*. 'No good' is *not* what I said. I said she has a few *problems*. It's nothing I can't handle. Have you forgotten I'm a nurse? Stash?"

He was silent again, his eyes on the muted baseball.

"They need somebody."

"But Lovey, to be attached . . ."

She could barely speak. "They're *attached* to *me*."

Stash sighed and absently settled the pipe on his bottom lip.

"You should get the floors done, Stash, just in case those children's welfare people make a surprise visit. And make sure the sink isn't piled up with dishes. And for Pete's sake take that pipe outside!" She knew for certain that her husband was smoking his Amphora Red in the living room — and the toilet too, no doubt.

"Stash?" Aunt Lovey paused, so he'd hear it right. "You."

Uncle Stash paused too, but it was because he felt powerless, and he'd just missed Joe Rudi's home run. He hung up the phone, turned up the volume, and pulled the vacuum out of the hall closet.

"*Hovno,*" he cursed in Slovak. *Shit.*

Country Mice

Aunt Lovey knew, as everyone knows, that it's better to raise children in the country than in the city, even if the city in question is only Leaford, population 3,502. The city, no matter how small, is corrupt and unrepentant, while the sun shines brighter in the country, making people more wholesome. When Ruby and I were only five months old, Aunt Lovey and Uncle Stash bid a tearful good-bye to their widowed Italian neighbor, Mrs. Todino (Nonna), and their tidy bungalow on Chippewa Drive and moved us into the old orange farmhouse that Aunt Lovey had inherited (as the eldest child and the only one of five sisters still in Leaford) ten years earlier.

The sturdy two-story farmhouse had been built in 1807 by Aunt Lovey's great-great-great-great-grandfather, Rosaire, a carpenter by trade. Although he'd been trained to appreciate such things, there wasn't time for moldings or cornices, or urging tongues into grooves. In order to plant in the spring, Rosaire had to reclaim his land from the ravenous river. In order to survive the following winter, Rosaire had to find a wife.

He found a wife and had eight live children in as many years. The winter that Rosaire's ninth child was born, a terrible storm uprooted one of the huge pine trees that shaded the west-facing windows and flung it aside like a rogue hair. Rosaire decided to craft an enormous table from it, one that could fit his entire beloved family at one seating. He and his eldest boys whittled the pine tower into an eight-foot table with turned legs and scalloped edges. The table would barely fit the dimensions of the original kitchen.

Rosaire died of consumption (that's what they used to call tuberculosis because of the way the disease *consumes* you) before the table was finished. Rosaire's wife and three of his children died of TB the same year as he, and rest in a horizontal plot at the eastern edge of our cornfield, kitty-corner to the rural Leaford Museum, under a row of white gravestones, on a grade from large to small. I used to think they looked like the nesting dolls we brought home from Slovakia. Or stairs to heaven.

Aunt Lovey and Uncle Stash had never planned to live in the country. (They had been renting the farmhouse and surrounding land to Sherman and Cathy Merkel for nearly a decade.) In spite of the sunshine and the promise of virtue, the nurse and the butcher were not eager to abandon their jobs to become farmers, for whom disaster was expected, if not foreseen: a glut of grasshoppers to chomp the leaves, a dearth of bees to pollinate, potato bugs, army worms, wheat rust, too much rain, not enough rain, frost too early, snow too late, droughts that shriveled the crops and withered the wells. The only sure thing was a flood each spring. Their compromise was to live in the farmhouse, which was vacant anyway, Sherman and Cathy having moved into what we called "the cottage" on the other side of the creek after Larry disappeared, and to let the Merkels continue working the land. Aunt Lovey ignored the fact that the Merkels' four-year-old son had been swept up by the killer tornado in the driveway where Uncle Stash would be parking the family car. She'd decided that the Tremblay family farmhouse was the *only* safe place for we Darlen girls to live.

It's been years since I saw the old house. At that time I noticed it had shifted and lists to the left. Eight pine trees still towered over the vast front lawn. The apple tree near the driveway had ceased to blossom, but the willows wept as always. The maples that gave dappled shade to our wading pool obliterated the sun. The long pine table was still in the kitchen, the soft wood blurred by burns and blemishes, the impression of numbers and letters from a thousand homework pages swirling through the grain, a row of four tiny holes near the scalloped edge where I stabbed it once with my fork.

By the time our little family moved into the old farmhouse, the place was already dilapidated. All manner of bugs and rodents had made themselves at home. There were some problems with the plumbing, and the driveway needed to be regraveled. (Along with Larry Merkel's body and Cathy Merkel's soul, the tornado had taken all the paving stones.) Aunt Lovey cleaned the walls and floors with Lysol and ordered the burnt-orange shag carpet for the den. Uncle Stash caught twenty-eight mice in the first week. (He had Aunt Lovey take a photograph of him with two mice caught in one trap, holding them aloft the way a fisherman would "the big one.")

Of the three square bedrooms on the second floor, two of them were closed off and unheated in winter to save money. Aunt Lovey and Uncle Stash slept in the third room, the smallest, whose window had been bricked in because of the terrible winter drafts, but the only room from which they could hear Ruby and me if we called them in the night. Aunt Lovey attempted to brighten the grim room with daisy wallpaper and hung a pair of coordinated yellow drapes over the bricked-in window. Uncle Stash looked into the cost of a skylight but could never find the money in our tight family budget. The walls crumbled when you brushed against them or looked at them too hard. Bits of plaster and dust fell behind with the mouse shit and the ancient black wires. You could almost feel the joists heaving at night, steady and rhythmic, like breath. There were several loose floorboards in all the rooms and tiny ragged nails on which we all (but Ruby) ripped the soles of our feet, until Aunt Lovey filled every square inch (including the bathroom) with mismatched carpet remnants. There was a broken windowpane in the bathroom that, though plugged with a balled-up pillowcase, still let in flies. Even with all that, no one ever spoke of repairs. Not Aunt

Lovey to nag (which is kind of amazing considering she was a *nurse,* but then, she did contain multitudes), and not Uncle Stash. Not Ruby. Never me. We all must have sensed the same thing — that the soundness of the structure relied on its delicate balance of decay.

There was a big red barn behind the orange brick house that sheltered a few dozen chickens and the tractors and some antique tools, which are probably valuable today. Painted in large white letters on the slats of the barn, letters that made Uncle Stash glower each time he chanced to glance, was the name Tremblay. The word, he told me once, was like a scream. "No *Polack* son of a bitch is gonna marry a *Tremblay!*" The name on the barn was just another imperfection we didn't dare repair.

The Merkels' cash crops were seed corn and soybeans, and winter wheat when we were young. Telling Aunt Lovey we were going to pick lilies from the ditch, Ruby and I would take the handle from the stable broom and head for the wheat field. There, we'd flatten the stems of the wheat and sit down inside our crop circles, awaiting an alien encounter. One time Cathy Merkel walked by with her big black dog — a Bouvier she called Cyrus. The dog barked like crazy, so we knew that she knew we were there, but she never said a word.

Aunt Lovey's father, and his father, and his, had grown everything from peanuts and peppermint to sugar beets and tobacco. Of the crops Sherman Merkel grew, I loved the corn the best. Mr. Merkel grew sweet corn in a small plot out back of the barn, just enough for our two families to share. We harvested the fat ears in the first few weeks of August, or a little before, or a little after (farming isn't an exact science), then boiled them for thirteen minutes and slathered them in butter, *never* margarine. Aunt Lovey cut the kernels off for Ruby, and to this day she won't eat it any other way.

Most of our fields were planted with seed corn. I loved to watch the corn grow knee-high by the Fourth of July (or a little before, or a little after), then in two weeks' time it was higher than me, then higher than Mr. Merkel, who was a very tall man. Aunt Lovey used to say the corn looked "gussied up" with her golden tassels and her green plumage. Corn syrup, corn oil, cornmeal, cosmetics, explosives, detergents, *peevo* (the Slovak word for "beer") — corn is in all of these. I loved the way the smell of the corn could climb up my nose after a good rain, and the feel of the silk before it dried up and went brown. We used to tear the leaves and make small woven carpets for our dollhouse.

Sometime in mid-July the corn detasselers, a busload of teenage girls in tube tops, would arrive to work Mr. Merkel's seed-corn fields. If you were a teenager in Baldoon County, you worked as a corn detasseler, walking the mile-long rows in the blistering sun, pulling the quivering tassels from the female plants so their ears could be fertilized by the adjoining rows of male plants. Our fields were always done by the girl crews. Maybe Sherman Merkel arranged it that way, hoping teenage girls would remind his wife less of Larry. Or maybe it was the tube tops.

For three weeks or so each summer the detasseling girls, with their bloodred faces and sliced white legs, their short shorts and potty mouths, thrilled and terrified Ruby and me.

(An aside: My sister and I did not have many friends while we were growing up. Children spoke to us at school and on the bus, but no one ever came to our home, even though Aunt Lovey used to whisper invitations when she thought we couldn't hear. I consider Roz and Rupert, and Whiffer and Lutie from the library our friends, but we don't really see them socially. Rupert doesn't do well veering from routine, and after a couple of disastrous dinners with Roz and him, Ruby and I stopped trying. Whiffer keeps saying he's gonna take me to a Red Wings game, but I'll believe it when I see it. There is some alienation, of course, in being so different, but it's also been fascinating, and a unique opportunity, I think, to have *observed* our generation without fully *participating* in it.)

The best days were when the detasselers hit their lunch break at our end of the mile-long row and we could watch from the window as the girls spread their blankets on the lawn. It encouraged me somewhat to see that the teenagers were as cruel to one another as they ever were to Ruby and me. I mocked and derided the detasseling girls to Ruby, and I did genuinely find them mean, but I would have loved, just one time, to join them.

(Ruby and I were not allowed near the detasselers. Aunt Lovey found a condom and a marijuana joint after the bus left one day. In fact, we were not allowed near the corn at all after mid-July, which was when it grew so high and dense a child could get lost for days and die from exposure and dehydration. Death by corn.)

We were encouraged, as long as we were careful, to pick the blue-berries that grew wild around the creek, and the apples and peaches from the low branches. An acre of land was reserved for the family's needs (we referred to the acre as the "family field"), where we also planted rows of snap beans and baby cucumbers and tomatoes and parsnips. What we didn't eat in season we canned for the winter. We called it "putting up," as in "Aunt Lovey put up thirty cans of beets today." Aunt Lovey and Cathy Merkel never put up the same thing. If Aunt Lovey did a relish, Cathy Merkel did a jam. If Aunt Lovey put up the peaches, Cathy Merkel put up the pickles. They passed the jars back and forth, until both their pantries were full and even, care-fully complimenting the other on an especially good batch, noticing the extra pinch of this or dash of that. Still, they weren't friends.

The Merkels never once had an evening at our house, and we were never invited to theirs. Mr. Merkel was like Uncle Stash — when the day was done, he liked to flip on the tube and watch sports. And Mrs. Merkel spent her free time walking the country roads with her dogs. (Mrs. Merkel has had three dogs since we've known her. Funny how you can measure time by pets that were not even your own. Her dog until we went to grade school was a shih tzu she called Cutie Pie, or sometimes just Pie. Pie had a problem with his anal gland and used to drag his scratchy bum all over Mrs. Merkel's kitchen floor. Her next dog was Cyrus. And the last, because Mrs. Merkel hasn't kept dogs for a few years, was that barking mutt Scruffy.)

Aunt Lovey sighed one night, after we'd seen Mrs. Merkel walk-ing with Cyrus the Bouvier along the dark country roads, "She needs to bury that child. That poor woman needs to bury that poor child."

———

ON THE FARM, in our first-floor bedroom with the queen-size bed and the entwined-hearts comforter and the shelf for Ruby's stuffed animals and the rack for my baseball cards and library books, my sister and I were sheltered in the essence of normal. We were not hidden, but unseen. The orange farmhouse was our castle, our kingdom the fields around, and the shallow creek that bisected our property the sea we crossed to find adventure.

Aunt Lovey had been right about the country. Ruby and I watched kittens being born under the porch out back and meteor showers in the blackest sky. We trod the rock-hard furrows in spring, searching for Indian arrowheads churned up by Sherman Merkel's tractor. We learned the names of trees and plants. (Ruby could tell you the names of dozens of edible plants that grow wild near the creek on our farm where the Neutral Indians foraged. Aunt Lovey showed us where to find the bitter cress, the Solomon's seal, and the sorrel, which were all eaten raw, but some of the wilder weeds would be boiled for teas and broths.) We ate sun-hot apples and wormy peaches, and we strung necklaces from Indian corn.

Each year on our birthday Ruby and I remembered Larry Merkel. Under the apple tree near the driveway, the place from which he'd disappeared, we'd say a prayer (though we were not officially baptized and were never really clear on our status with God) for his lost soul. We'd been told that Larry Merkel was dead, but in our imaginations he was very much alive. When Ruby and I were young he was our secret friend, a wild boy who didn't wash and couldn't talk, who lived deep in the bush at the edge of the property, not hidden, but *unseen,* like Ruby and me.

When it got cold we made a shelter of twigs for our wild friend, with a corn-husk roof and a bed of scratchy horse blankets from the barn. We brought tumblers of milk and raisin cookies that we knew he ate in the night because they were always gone by morning, the milk spilled and lapped clean from the ground. We left books with interesting pictures and poems (drawn with symbols) under a damp old pillow. I secretly hoped he liked me better than Ruby.

In later years, as my sister and I were becoming pubescent girls, who, in spite of being attached at the head, were normal, Larry Merkel became our boyfriend. Sometimes he was mine; sometimes he was Ruby's. Once in a while, when we couldn't agree on whose turn it was, we'd make him our protective older brother.

Once a week when the weather was fine, my sister and I went to the Merkels' place on the other side of the creek to deliver the eggs (feeding the chickens and packing the eggs was Aunt Lovey and Uncle Stash's single concession to farming). Even though Mrs. Merkel wasn't very friendly or kind, we loved her, because she loved Larry. There wasn't much to the walk (we could be seen by either house the entire way there and back), but it was still exciting to cross the rickety bridge over the creek and find Sherman Merkel aiming his shotgun at the crows. Once, we sat on the bridge for a full hour and watched a fat green tobacco worm stuck on its back. Ruby wanted to put him right. I believed in nature. Or I was cruel. One summer we made a race out of the trip with the eggs, pretending that Cathy Merkel would die if we didn't get there in time.

Mrs. Merkel never offered us cookies or bread and jam. In the summer, if we looked very thirsty, she gave us cloudy water from the tap. With mud-caked paws and jowly jaws, her big black Cyrus watched us from his post at her side. Aunt Lovey used to call him "the mutt from hell." But I liked Cyrus. (I hadn't cared for Cutie Pie, the shih tzu. The butt-dragging was disgusting.) And I was sure that if he liked Ruby and me, Mrs. Merkel would like us too. I used to stare at Cyrus to communicate my sincerity.

On Saturdays Uncle Stash came with us to the Merkels', the heavy camera swinging from his neck, threatening to thump Ruby or me if we got too close. He loved to take pictures of the landscape, the people, the details, us, even Mrs. Merkel, though she'd scowl at him afterward and call him by his full name, Stanislaus, which even Aunt Lovey never did.

Uncle Stash had a way of taking a picture that made photography art. Aunt Lovey put together a photo album for our birthday one year of all his best shots. She arranged the pictures thematically, by season. There were the wonderful landscapes of the farm, and candid snaps of Ruby and me, our life to date. At some point in putting the album together, Aunt Lovey must have realized there was not a single picture of Uncle Stash: he took the pictures, so he was never in them. The final picture in the album was of Aunt Lovey and Uncle Stash, their black-and-white wedding photo. I hated that their picture came last, because it felt like they were saying good-bye.

On a rainy Tuesday last week, Ruby and I looked through the album together for the first time. (If we can do something alone, we usually do, and so it was with the photo album.) I enjoyed the little journey with my sister, and we both admired anew the way Uncle Stash had captured our farm with his camera, verdant in summer with rich black loam and mile-high corn behind our home — King Grain baseball caps skimming dusty gold tassels; brawny field hands blocking sugar beets; straw hats; black arms; one old man's eyes so distant he looks dead. Ruby and I, at about three, in our wading pool in the shade, wearing identical swimsuits with a ruffle at the bum. (Ruby's legs don't look real. I'm already strong.) The fall photographs: a wall of leaves, stippled scarlet with saffron striations; Ruby and me at night, eating roasted pumpkin seeds on the picnic table near the creek — Merkels' cottage in the background, lamplight in Mrs. Merkel's sewing room. Another close-up picture of Aunt Lovey resting her cheek on our heads; it's cold enough to see our breath. Then the winter shots: one photograph so white there appears to be no separation of earth or sky, just brilliant snow with a sun flare in the corner. Another picture spots the ragged flag on our fence post in the distance and a leafless tree so filled with black crows it looks alive — and sinister.

Ruby and I have often said, "Imagine if we hadn't grown up in Leaford but somewhere else." Or imagine if we'd grown up with someone else. Or imagine if we'd grown up in another time, when

people like us were *exhibited* or *killed*. How isolating — and strange!
Which is not to say that our lives haven't been, at times, isolated and
strange.

Aunt Lovey would scold Ruby and me, those times we whined
that the world was unfair. "You're lucky to be you," she'd say, looking from me to my sister. "You girls are remarkable. Most people
can't say that."

Writing & Deadlines

My laptop sits on a pillow at my left. I type quickly with my wrong hand. I sense that I'm naturally a right-handed person, but my right arm belongs to Ruby for all intents and purposes (when I was little I thought the term was "intensive purposes"), so I'm a reluctant lefty. My clumsiness annoys Ruby, who is both responsible and blameless.

I started to write this book only a short time ago, and already my wrist begs a rest. But I can't rest because I'm afraid that if I stop writing Leaford will vaporize, and with it all my memories. I thought my story's path would be a straight one. A simple one. After all, it is the true story of my life, to the point I have already lived it, and for which I know even the most incidental detail. But the story isn't straight. Or simple. And I see now, as I begin to think of the next chapter, that even the truth can spin out of control. My story. Ruby's story. The story of Aunt Lovey and Uncle Stash. The story of me, and we, and us, and them. The story of then. And the story of now. How can the story of *me* exist without all of it?

Ruby feels alienated and like an outcast and hates this book already, though she hasn't read a word. My sister doesn't know how to use a computer (she's so afraid of technology she won't let me retire our VCR and buy a DVD player), so I'm not worried she might do something sneaky with my laptop, but it's killing her not to know what I'm writing. She pretends to fall asleep at night, then tries to peek at my screen in her left periphery, her breath purposeful and wheezy, following none of the true pattern of whistle and pause and sigh and repeat beside which I've slumbered for twenty-nine years.

We've promised each other that we won't read what the other has written.

Presuming that my sister is going to include chapters at all (I'll believe it when I see it), Ruby's work will be written in longhand and we'll get Whiffer (our friend from the Leaford Library) or somebody to transcribe her pages. (Ruby thinks I'm infatuated with Whiffer, but Ruby is mistaken.) When and *if* Ruby writes her chapters, we'll have a third party insert them where they might best be read. Maybe Dr. Ruttle will help us. I've been encouraging Ruby to write something. I gave her some yellow pads. But Ruby is somewhat lazy and would rather object than make amends.

I'm writing in the evenings. With Ruby asleep and the night still around us, with the stars in the sky, the wind kissed by leaf fires, and a chill from the open window, it's a good time to conjure. I'm filled with confidence when I begin, but by the end of a writing night I'm left to wonder if other writers feel the way I do — that with each letter, word, phrase, sentence, paragraph, I'm digging a toehold, gripping a rock, a fool on a mountainside, alone and ill-equipped, a disastrous fall more likely than a gloried ascent. Why did I start climbing? Where am I now? Who gives a shit if I reach the summit?

I've given myself a deadline. Although I know it's unusual to write a book, any book, quickly, I've calculated that, writing at my current pace of four pages a day, I could finish what I speculate will be a four-hundred-page book in approximately 113 working days. Adding some time for revising and a day off here and there for exhaustion or illness (or writer's block — can you get that with an autobiography?), I believe I can complete this story of my life by Christmas, about seven months away. This thought comforts and inspires me.

Ruby stirs. I know she's cold, so I use my feet to kick the cover over her hopeless little legs. Ruby's always cold. Even when we were children, we fought about the quilt. As I grew older, I found I could surrender my own comfort so effortlessly it didn't qualify as sacrifice. The old patchwork quilt, with the entwined blue and red paisley hearts on a cream background, which covered our bed up until a few years ago, is threadbare from washing now, folded into a tattered square and crammed into the cupboard in the laundry room. I can't bear to throw it out, knowing how Aunt Lovey suffered to make it, not being as skilled with needle and thread as her own mother had been. She'd designed the quilt for her marriage bed, the hearts representing her and Uncle Stash, joining forever as one. But on the eve of her wedding, Mother Darlensky presented Aunt Lovey with a white, lacy, old-fashioned bedspread, which her mother in Slovakia had made as a wedding gift to her, and Lovey felt obliged to use it instead. The day after Aunt Lovey and Uncle Stash had settled into their little bungalow on Chippewa Drive, the Slovak in-laws (who had been second cousins and should *never* have married, Aunt Lovey told us confidentially one night) came to inspect. When Mother Darlensky saw that Aunt Lovey had made the bed with the lacy white bedspread, she flew into a rage, telling her son that her daughter-in-law knew the heirloom was too precious to *use*. Out of spite for the miserable woman, Aunt Lovey made her bed with that god-awful bedspread for a full seven years. When Uncle Stash's father died, Mother Darlensky moved to Ohio to live with her widowed sister, and Aunt Lovey drove to the Kmart to purchase a comforter with matching curtains that she could have sewn for half the money.

When Ruby and I were four years old and beginning to master our *situation,* Aunt Lovey moved us to a "big girl's bed." She'd remembered the quilt with the entwined hearts and retrieved it from her cedar chest, realizing the quilt had never been meant for her and Stash but for me and Ruby. If she'd only known about us years ago, she'd say, she would have been spared the pain of thinking she'd never be a mother. After a thousand washings, I swear you can still smell cedar in the fabric of that old quilt.

There has never been a possibility of my being separated from Ruby. We have known that it could not be, and declared that even if we could, we wouldn't. Still, I have an elaborate fantasy life in which I am a singular woman. My right arm belongs to me. My right leg is the exact length of my left, and I tote nothing on my hip but a funky leather bag. My features have been surgically corrected and I have my sister's pretty face. I am mysterious. I live alone in a small but chic apartment in Toronto with a view of the lake. I take long bubble baths with dozens of candles. I am a well-known author and I have a poet boyfriend (actually many boyfriends — not *all* poets) for whom I dress provocatively. (Oh yes, in this fantasy I also have large, shapely breasts.)

I know that even if a surgical separation had been possible, the truth of being an individual would be somewhat less dazzling. I suppose I would move to Toronto, though I'd likely never afford an apartment near the lake. I would try to get a job as a writer, any kind of writer, even in advertising. I would like to have my face cosmetically corrected. I could conceivably lead a normal life. Just to be clear — my fantasy is not so much the product of burning desire but a distraction from reality.

I was thinking of when Ruby and I were children, sleeping under the entwined-hearts quilt in the old orange farmhouse on Rural Route One. I was thinking of the soft bed beneath the open window. The lowing of livestock. The stinking sweet air. The mice in the corner under our chair. The crows in the field. The kittens wet born. And the world beyond the whispering corn.

In sleep, my sister and I found a common breath. In dreams, we knew the moon.

I'VE DECIDED TO proceed by telling this autobiographical story more or less chronologically. (That is a more difficult decision, and more complicated task, than you might imagine.)

Holy Ghosts

Holy Cross Church, at the intersection of Chippewa Drive and Tecumseh Road, was the first Catholic church in Leaford, built by the French settlers. The aisle measures ninety feet from door to altar. The honey oak floors and darker oak pews were carved from the trees cleared to make space for the small church cemetery on the sunny west side. There are six spires, two cupolas, gold-leaf frames, and enough precious icons that the doors need to be locked before and after Mass. One hundred fifty years ago Aunt Lovey's ancestors drove a horse and buggy to worship at Holy Cross. Men prayed to be led from temptation. Women prayed for better men.

Aunt Lovey and Uncle Stash had both been raised Catholic, and they dutifully, eagerly, made the pilgrimage to Holy Cross each Sunday to hear Father Pardo invoke the Holy Ghost in his slurry old-man voice. It was widely known that Pardo took sacramental wine for breakfast and had a nip on nights he couldn't sleep, but he was agreeable enough and not often *noticeably* drunk. Aunt Lovey and Uncle Stash had been pillars of Holy Cross for years before Father Pardo was transferred (or *banished*) to Leaford. Aunt Lovey was president of the Women's League, organizing day trips to nursing homes and craft shows. Uncle Stash passed the collection plate and knew how to linger without appearing to beg. They would share a glance when Father Pardo stumbled up the steps or when he snickered or snorted at some inappropriate moment, but Aunt Lovey and Uncle Stash would not desert their church.

After Mass one day, when Ruby and I were nearing our first birthday, Aunt Lovey cornered Father Pardo at the rusty gate by the lilac bushes and asked, as she had been asking repeatedly for weeks, about a date for our baptism. It was a detail Aunt Lovey had overlooked during those intense early months of parenthood — one that suddenly consumed her after Ruby had mysteriously stopped breathing one night and my frightened cries had awoken Uncle Stash.

(Some people think that Ruby and I are cursed to live conjoined. But think of how blessed we are to be so connected that we can and did and do cry out, "There's something wrong! Help!" Imagine if a husband knew the instant his wife stopped loving him and could bring the marriage back to life before it was too late. If a mother could see the second her child took the wrong path and call while he was still close enough to hear "Come back! You're going the wrong way!" Ruby and I endure *because* of our connectedness. Maybe we all do. How can that be a curse?)

The old priest hesitated, frowning at having to state the obvious. "It's not for me to judge. But some of the older parishioners, a few of the older parishioners think that she" — he cast a glare at Ruby and me wriggling in the oversize pram nearby — "is . . ." He pulled Aunt Lovey farther from the crowd, and from us, into the quiet of the gated church garden. "It might be better if we wait until after her surgery," he said, patting her arm. "I'm sure things will go well."

Aunt Lovey informed Father Pardo that there would be no surgery, could be no surgery, no matter what he thought or what rumors he'd heard. She'd been proud of her restraint. "Let's talk again when you're sober, Father," she'd said. "I'm sure you'll see that my girls are perfect the way they are. God made them, after all."

Under the influence of several rather large goblets of wine, Father Pardo told Aunt Lovey, regrettably, "God makes bowel movements too, but I wouldn't baptize one."

Aunt Lovey and Uncle Stash considered firing off letters to the cardinal and the pope, but their faith in the Church was too completely destroyed. Not so their faith in God. Ruby and I were taught about God as we were growing up, using the basic constructs of Christianity — Love one another, Do unto others, Don't sleep with your neighbor's wife — though we never again set foot in a church. Uncle Stash would always add to our lessons in faith that we should question authority and follow our own instincts, and that even the Bible is mostly fiction. Aunt Lovey would wag her finger and say, "Don't believe God's some old man with a beard. God could be a woman. Or Chinese." It was all very confusing. Still is.

Ruby and I would perch on the side of the bed, where our entwined-hearts quilt had been neatly folded back, to say our nighttime prayers. (It was Aunt Lovey's job to put us to bed. Uncle Stash was old-fashioned that way. Ruby and I kissed his whiskery chin as he lounged on the La-Z-Boy, then we joined Aunt Lovey in our room after we'd brushed our teeth.) I don't know how many prayers God heard, but Aunt Lovey heard every one — except one — until the day she died. And in all that time, and the thousands of prayers, she never suggested an edit or a correction beyond "More gratefulness. Fewer requests."

(An aside: If Aunt Lovey hated self-pity, she hated ingratitude worse. One summer day when we were children, Ruby complained about being bored: "I'm bored. It's so boring here. There's nothing to do." Aunt Lovey reminded Ruby of her many blessings, but Ruby kept it up. "It's boring, boring, boring on the farm." Aunt Lovey didn't respond directly but disappeared down the cobwebbed stairs and hauled the camping cooler up out of the basement. She filled the cooler with Popsicles and Oreos and instructed Ruby and me to get in the car. Ruby thought we were going to the lake for a picnic and was delighted that lunch would be her two favorite foods. Even when we turned away from the lake instead of toward it, Ruby was hopeful, thinking that Aunt Lovey had planned a picnic at the conservation area instead of the lake. But we sped past the gates to the conservation area and drove on farther, and when we finally stopped it was near a stinky ditch beside a field of high corn. Aunt Lovey got out of the car. She went around to the back and took the cooler from the trunk. Then she passed by our door without stopping to let us out. Ruby and I watched as she gazed out over the cornfield. She brought her hand to her mouth and whistled shrilly, using two fingers. That woman could whistle! Ruby wanted to get out of the car. She knocked on the passenger window, calling, "Let us out, Aunt Lovey! Let us out!" But Aunt Lovey shook her head. My sister and I watched as one, then two, then four, then ten, then more Mennonite children than I could count emerged from the shadowy rows of corn, with sunburned faces and shining eyes, smiling shyly at Aunt Lovey, moving toward the cooler, not like animals, not like the children at school would have acted over a cooler full of treats, but slowly, each child taking one Popsicle and one cookie, before disappearing back into the corn. At the end, when the children were gone, Aunt Lovey had one Popsicle left, which she broke in half for Ruby and me. It was banana-flavored, not Ruby's favorite, but she didn't *dare* complain.)

Every other night I went first with my prayers. "God bless Ruby. And Aunt Lovey and Uncle Stash. And Nonna. And Mr. Merkel. And Mrs. Merkel. And Larry. And our birth mother. God, please make Ruby not have to have a colostomy bag. Ever. Please make peace in the world. Please help me find my green-and-yellow speller." (We'd been cut down to three postscripts one night after Ruby asked God to please give the poppies more sun in the backyard and make the strawberries ripen faster, then launched into a litany of requests regarding the well-being of the remainder of the family farm, the seed-corn crop, the weather, and finally concluded with hope for someone to dust the displays at the Leaford Museum.) After Aunt Lovey died, Ruby and I stopped praying out loud, and somewhere along the line I stopped praying altogether. I wonder if it was then that I stopped believing in God. If only I'd been connected to Him the way I am to my sister, God might have called out to me that I'd gone too far away.

Maybe He did. Maybe I just heard Him.

I was thinking of those childhood prayers, Aunt Lovey's soft cheek, Ruby's quick road to slumber. In those dark, quiet moments when only I was awake, my prayers private and real, crickets courting in the weeds under our window, the smell of fish coming from the river not awful like it can be but glorious, I'd notice things: how Ruby smelled different because she was on a certain medication, or how smooth her hair felt when it fell between us, or how lovely the weight of her hand resting on my collarbone. It would occur to me how deeply I loved my sister, and how profoundly I was loved by her. I think I found something of God in that. And in the way Aunt Lovey kissed me. And in the sound of Uncle Stash's voice when he said, "My girls."

And then there was Sunday school with Nonna.

On Sunday mornings, while Aunt Lovey and Uncle Stash tended the bungalow they rented out in town, our Nonna (Mrs. Todino) fed us Lune Moons and taught us about God. Nonna's God was not female or Chinese, and His authority was absolute. He was old and bearded and vengeful, meting out punishment like the judge on *People's Court,* sentencing masturbators to arthritis and sending a scourge of termites to the porch of a local man who sold Nonna a vacuum she didn't want or need. (Nonna refused to take responsibility for being sucked in — so to speak — by the vacuum salesman.)

"Say again why Jesus came to earth," I would ask.

Nonna was impatient. "He come to *suffer.*"

"I know, but why again?"

"To teach the *lesson,* Rose. He come to save the *people.*"

"But what's the lesson in suffering?"

"The lesson is to be *Christian,* Rose. You gonna live the way Jesus live. To be Christian is mean to love everybody."

Except, apparently, the vacuum guy.

"To be Christian is to go to church. You take Christ body. You take Christ blood. Then he gonna be inside. Inside you heart."

Ruby was alarmed by the discrepancies between Uncle Stash and Aunt Lovey's lessons and Nonna's on Chippewa Drive, eventually deciding that because Nonna was Italian, and the pope lived in Rome, she must be deferred to as the expert in all matters of God.

"Can't God be in our heart if we don't go to church?" Ruby asked her once, fretfully. "Can't God be with us even if the priest don't make us the baptize?" (Ruby said it the way Nonna did.)

Nonna shook her head sadly. We'd had numerous discussions on the topic of baptism, which Nonna explained like this: "The priest put the water on you head. It gonna glow like the Holy Spirit for all you life and even when you dead. If you don't gonna get baptize you don't gonna glow, then God is don't gonna see you in heaven."

Some Sunday mornings we were stopped at the traffic light on Tecumseh and could catch a glimpse through the double-glass doors of Father Pardo in his purple satin robes squinting from the glare of his marble altar, his bulbous nose gobbling the smaller features of his face. Aunt Lovey would clear her throat when the light turned. "Go, Stash. It's green, Stash. Honey. Go."

I LOST MY first tooth just days before our eighth birthday. (Most things have happened slightly later than normal for Ruby and me.) I had pushed with my tongue till it stung and ripped the ragged edge that still clung to my gums, then spit the tooth out on the floor. I put it under my pillow, delighted to find four quarters in its place the following morning. I was proud of my slippery speech and eager to show Nonna my quarters, and my gap, when she came to our birthday party that Saturday afternoon. Ruby didn't yet have one loose tooth, and I knew she burned with envy.

For the party, I had chosen a purple blouse with jeans, and Ruby was wearing a white shirt and a sky-blue skirt over altered black tights — a sort of uniform, which she still wears, even in summer, to conceal her deformed legs and clubfeet. We used clothespins to secure a plastic cloth to the table in the backyard, where we set out lemonade and barbecue chips (plain corn chips for Ruby) in plastic bowls. Uncle Stash had driven into town to collect Nonna, so there was no doorbell to signal her arrival, no warning that she was near, and certainly no portent whatsoever that she was bringing someone with her.

My sister saw him first. Adrenaline coursed through my body as Ruby's flight instinct sparked. My sister shifted swiftly so I could turn and I saw him too, alone and small at the end of the hall, resplendent in the amber light from the pantry's tinted window. There was something odd about him — not in the physical way that Ruby and I are an oddity, but something in his torn little eyes — that said he floated above it all in some universe of his own. At first I thought he might be a ghost, though I'd never seen one before, and in fact don't believe they exist. Then Nonna appeared behind the boy, shoving two brightly wrapped packages into his arms, swatting him gently on the side of his head, urging, "Say happy birthday to the girls!"

The boy, Mrs. Todino's only son's only son, had been told about us, but seemed quite unprepared for such a face-to-face-to-face. He did not say happy birthday. He did not speak at all but stared at us, openmouthed, appearing to grow smaller instead of larger as Nonna pushed him toward us down the hall. Aunt Lovey seemed as surprised as we were to see the boy. She shared a look with Uncle Stash.

Ryan Todino was tiny for nine, with inchworm bald patches leeching his shorn blond head and eyes that were barely slits with a strange changing color. He wore too-big cutoff shorts and a T-shirt with ironing marks. His lips were flaky, his skin pink.

"This my grandson, Ryan." Nonna beamed, patting the boy's head. "This my Nick's boy."

The boy, close enough that we could smell he'd eaten maple syrup at Nonna's, stared at us, still and strange and quiet.

Uncle Stash and Aunt Lovey looked confused, for they knew that Nonna's son, Nick, lived in Windsor and that Nick was estranged from his wife (who'd moved to Ipperwash), and they also knew that Nonna hadn't seen or heard anything of her grandson since Ryan was two years old. Plus, this boy looked nothing like the curly-haired cherub in the pictures on Mrs. Todino's TV.

Nonna repeated, "It's Ryan. He come from the Ipperwash. It's Nick's boy!"

(In all the years they lived on Chippewa Drive, and all the years they didn't, Uncle Stash and Aunt Lovey never set eyes on Nick Todino. Uncle Stash drove Nonna to the train station several times a year to board the VIA to Windsor to visit *him,* but he never once made the trip to Leaford, though he worked at Chrysler's then and most surely had a car of his own.)

Uncle Stash began to perspire and suggested everyone step outside to catch a breeze. At first there was none to be caught. But then the wheat trembled a little, and a sudden gust tipped the plastic chip bowl onto the table. Ruby and I moved to put it right, unsure whether to return the fallen chips to the bowl or brush them onto the grass. Glancing up, I noticed Ryan Todino staring, maybe not so much staring as studying Ruby and me, looking at the area of our conjoinment not furtively, the way most people do, but boldly and with what seemed like admiration. I felt Ruby shudder.

Ryan looked at me, then shifted to look at Ruby. "You have different hair," he said accusingly. His voice was high but croaky. "You're reddish. And you're darker and straighter."

"So?" Ruby spit, thinking the boy meant to be cruel.

"The old lady said you were *identical* twins."

Ruby was horrified. "That's not an *old lady;* that's your *Nonna.*"

Ryan shrugged. "How can you be identical if your hair's not identical? Identical is identical."

I was secretly pleased he'd noticed. "Why do you care?"

"I don't care."

The adults were whispering about Ryan's estranged parents in maddeningly inaudible tones. (I find scandal irresistible.) Punctuating the conversation, sounding more like a refusal than a name, *Nick, Nick, Nick.* There was no suggestion of opening our birthday gifts, tossed carelessly on a dirty plastic chair, and no mooning over the birthday cake, which was a layer of chocolate and a layer of white. I ate the chips that had fallen out of the bowl. Ruby simmered with indignation that Ryan Todino, who would not stop staring at our joined heads, was ruining our eighth birthday.

Ruby tried calling to Aunt Lovey a couple of times, but she waved us off. "Go play for a bit, girls. Show Ryan the bridge over the creek."

The rickety bridge over the shallow creek was where my sister and I spent a good part of our childhood. We'd sit for hours, watching the mud fish and tadpoles, Ruby chattering about the girls at school, me a million miles away, skywriting a poem for future consideration. The bridge was our special place. We did not want to bring Ryan Todino to our bridge.

Ruby and I walked the ledge of the creek, where Aunt Lovey encouraged a small wildflower meadow to grow, and where bloomed the asters and foxglove and purple field thistle and pinweed and goldenrod, and where fluttered the dragonflies and damselflies, and where, if we stayed too long, the chiggers bit us silly. We listened to the frogs croak among cattails. We didn't stop to turn and look for Ryan until we reached the bridge.

I noticed Mrs. Merkel in her garden and waved, but she pretended not to see me. My sister and I sat on the side of the bridge, where we could spy on the orange farmhouse and the adults in the distance. Uncle Stash had said he'd call when the hot dogs were ready, but he hadn't even lit the charcoal in the barbecue yet. In a moment we felt the bridge shake. Ryan settled down behind us, dangling his legs the opposite way, facing Merkels' cottage.

The wind had kicked up again. There was a loud noise from the direction of Merkels', like something big had fallen down. We couldn't see if Mrs. Merkel was still in her garden. Ruby and I wondered if we should head back, the reality of tornadoes never far from our thoughts, but the adults just waved from the yard, Nonna delighted to see we'd made friends with her grandson.

Ryan didn't turn to look at us. For a long time no one said a thing. We watched the creek from our separate sides of the bridge, seeing much the same thing but not the same thing at all. There were skitter bugs racing on top of the brown water, and some underwing moths resting on cowbane nearby. Then, suddenly, a yellow warbler fluttered and burst from a tall patch of ironweed and came to rest on the edge of our side of the bridge. Had Ruby and I been alone, we would have shrieked over the sighting. The warblers came from Mexico and South America. It was rare to see one, and rarer to see one up close.

No one spoke until Ryan asked softly, so softly at first that we had to ask him to repeat.

"Could I touch it?"

Ruby and I knew instantly what Ryan meant and were shocked dumb.

"Could I? For a sec?"

There was something obscene in the request.

"No," Ruby and I said in unison.

"I just want to touch it."

"No," I repeated.

"I'm not gonna hurt you."

We felt Ryan's slitty eyes on the backs of our skulls. "Just for one sec?"

"Why?"

"I just want to."

"Why?"

"'Cause I'm gonna be a doctor."

I was unconvinced.

"I like bones," he added hopefully.

We three stared down at the rippling water. Ruby motioned at the house and I shifted so she could see. "Have they started the barbecue yet?"

Uncle Stash was stirring a pitcher of fruit punch. There was nothing on the grill.

"We're dying of starvation here!" Ryan suddenly shouted.

The adults, who hadn't heard exactly, just waved and nodded, which made Ruby and me giggle.

"We're dyyyying," Ryan cried, sending Ruby and me into peals of laughter.

"I'm never gonna make it!" Ryan fell back onto the bridge, pretending to be dead. Ruby and I laughed about that, surprised when the boy rose and was instantly petulant. "They can't wait forever. We gotta go to church."

"Can't you miss it one night?"

"I can't miss it ever. I'm gonna be a priest." Ryan huffed, as if it was something we should have known.

"Thought you were gonna be a doctor."

"Why doesn't she go to church Sunday morning, like a normal person?" Ryan wondered aloud.

"Nonna likes the folk mass," I replied, though it wasn't quite the truth.

"Nonna doesn't want to hear Mass from Father Pardo because he's the one that won't make us the baptize," Ruby added.

"Plus, she's addicted to *Coronation Street,*" I said, which was true.

"You're not baptized?" Ryan's horror frightened me. "What if you die?"

(On the subject of our dying unbaptized, Aunt Lovey had always said, "If God stops two good girls like you from entering heaven just because some drunk old priest wouldn't sprinkle water on your head, well then, God is just not who I thought She was. I most certainly wouldn't want to spend eternity in a place a whole lot of perfectly nice people were turned away from. You girls shouldn't either.")

"If we die," I told him, "Aunt Lovey said there's another heaven, one like the Catholics have, only more tolerant."

"That's a lie! There's no tolerant heaven!" he said, leaning over Ruby to see me. "There's just purgatory. And you don't want to go there."

We watched the wind chase some chipmunks through the weeds. I could feel Ruby holding back a flood of tears. I followed an impulse: "Bet you've seen a million baptisms."

Ryan shrugged.

"You probably know the words. Do you know any of the words?"

He shrugged again.

"You are gonna be a priest."

"Or a doctor," Ryan countered.

"Probably a priest though," I insisted. "You remember the words to say for a baptism?"

"Yeah, I don't know, it's all stuff about the Holy Ghost." Ryan craned to check on the adults.

"You could do it. You could baptize us."

"No way."

"We could do it down there." I pointed to a shallow place under the rickety bridge. "Come on, they won't see us."

Ryan was resolute. "I'm not doing it."

Ruby shifted. "Do it. You could do it."

Ryan shook his head again.

"We'll let you touch it." I shifted, grasping my sister's thigh. "Right, Ruby? We'll let you touch it if you baptize us."

Ruby inhaled. "For one second."

Ryan moved so he could see the adults in the distance. They were too involved in their discussion to notice us. Ruby and I sat perfectly still as the boy's hands found our scalps. He used his fingertips to probe our fused skulls slowly and with very little pressure. He was tender like Aunt Lovey, the way no doctor had ever been. I felt the heat from Ryan's breath as he shifted to investigate our faces, the separation of our jaws, our missing ears, my pulled eye, Ruby's pretty nose.

I swallowed hard, unprepared for my sudden swell of emotion. Ruby felt my tears impending.

"That's enough," Ruby said, though I would have let Ryan Todino touch me forever.

Ryan said nothing as he sat down beside Ruby, dangling his legs from the bridge. I didn't know any other nine-year-old boys very well, but I didn't think they could all be as strange as he was.

"Now," I said, "let's go." I had a sudden craving for this union with God's spirit, this Holy Ghost that could grant me passage to the real heaven. I badly wanted to glow with the power of God's love.

Ryan scrambled down the slope near the bridge and found a shallow spot (the water was only ten inches deep) beside which we could kneel. I followed, Ruby riding my hip.

Ryan cleared his throat a little and glanced at the sky. "I'm just gonna say 'I baptize you in the name of the Father and Son and Holy Ghost.'"

"All right."

"I'm not saying anything else."

"All right."

I kneeled in the mud, formulating a lie for Aunt Lovey about how I got dirty. Ruby gripped my neck and whined because the bottoms of her stockings got wet.

Ryan made the sign of the cross and cupped his palm, preparing to scoop the brackish water collected by the pool beneath the bridge, cautioning that if we died before he became a priest, or if he did not become a priest at all, the sacrament would not likely be valid.

The wind began to blow like an oscillating fan. Little gusts on a two-four beat. "I baptize you," Ryan whispered to us as he bent to dip his palm in the water. He sprinkled the water on my sister's head, then mine. "In the name of the Father and the Son and the Holy —"

Suddenly a voice in the distance boomed, "Ryan . . . ?"

Ryan bolted like a fugitive. We heard the swish of weeds as he scurried up the bank of the creek. I started to rise, so we could see where Ryan had gone, but I slipped on the mud and lost my balance. I tried to break our fall, but I came down hard on my arm and heard my bone snap clean a couple of inches above my wrist.

There was mud in my nose, my teeth, my eyes. My arm felt hot. I didn't dare gasp for air until I could push us clear of the water. But I couldn't push us with my broken arm. I couldn't lift us an inch. And my other arm, having grown around my sister as it has, was useless to me too. Our joined heads and our particular anatomy make Ruby and me top-heavy. I could not, using any muscles or the fulcrum of our bodies, raise us from the creek. I knew, given the depth of the water, that Ruby's face was submerged too. We were drowning.

Pressure in my lungs and my throat and my sinuses and behind my eyes. It's said that your life flashes before you when you're about to die, but it wasn't like that for me. (Ruby claims to have seen a tunnel and some light, but she told me about that memory two years later, after she'd watched a show about near-death experiences.) I did not see any life but the present, and I saw it from somewhere above — perhaps it was a view from the rickety bridge — of me and my eight-year-old sister drowning in ten inches of water.

I felt my body, though I was certain I did not have one, flushing with a strange, thrilling calm, and I knew that Ruby was experiencing it too. Ruby and I do not fully understand what happened next. I think it'll remain one of the mysteries of our life. Ruby's right arm, though a normal arm, is a beam in the structure of our connected selves more than it is a tool. Her arm is limber, but not strong, and though it must be assumed, because there was no one else around, that Ruby was the one who pushed us out of the water with her thin and fragile arms, she has no memory whatsoever of doing it. Ruby thinks it was a ghost, and given the date (our birthday/Larry's death day) and that we were so near Merkels', she's pretty sure it was Larry who saved us.

One moment we were drowning, the next we were rising and gasping, and Ruby was pointing to the mud near my knees at a half-submerged toy fire truck, which had to have been Larry's and therefore was a sign.

The adults found Ryan sobbing behind a tree, a few yards away from Merkels', with Cyrus snarling at his heels. Ryan pointed out Ruby and me, panting beside the creek, mud packed in our eyes and nostrils, kneeling perilously close to the water. We were rushed to the hospital, where my broken arm was set, and Dr. Ruttle cleaned our nostrils and examined our craniums. Aunt Lovey and Uncle Stash would never know about the attempted baptism or exactly how close my sister and I came to drowning. Still, we were punished for playing near the creek, never saw a slice of birthday cake, and had to wait a full week to open our presents. My arm took forever to heal. We never showed anyone the little toy truck.

We wouldn't see Ryan Todino again for nearly fifteen years until he appeared at the front door of Nonna's bungalow one Sunday morning out of the clear blue asking to borrow money. He looked not unlike his nine-year-old self, except for some scruff on his chin and some muscle in his chest. If he had a memory of having baptized us in the creek near Merkels' that July when we turned eight years old, he did not show it. Instead, Ryan glanced at us furtively, or not at all, and declined the tuna *sang*wiches Nonna made us all for lunch. "You're not eating your *sang*wich," Nonna had cried.

Father Pardo was transferred (or banished) from Holy Cross many years ago. Nonna experiences dementia from Alzheimer's now. She has good days and bad days, but more often than not doesn't recognize Ruby and me when we visit and seems not to understand that we are two women. Nick (Ryan's father) has been living with Nonna on Chippewa Drive for four years, and though he hardly ever cuts the lawn and hasn't pruned a bush or tree since we've known him, Nonna seems well fed and the house is always tidy, even when Ruby and I do our surprise inspections. Ruby hates Nick, but I think he's fine. Just sort of sad. He's lost a lot in his life. You can see it in his eyes.

I've thought often about that day of our eighth birthday when we were baptized and nearly drowned, and I've wondered about the Holy Ghost Ryan called upon. Sometimes I feel possessed by it, and other times I hope to hell Aunt Lovey was right about heaven.

It's Ruby Darlen writing now.

Let me start by saying I'm not the greatest writer in the world. Books are not my thing. And I haven't really written anything but a couple of letters since we graduated from Leaford Collegiate. I tend to avoid doing things I'm not good at, like writing, so it's taken me a while to get to this. I'm not even sure what this is. My sister says it's her autobiography. I asked her how a conjoined twin can write the story of her life when she hasn't lived her life alone. Rose said if I really feel that way I should write some chapters from my point of view.

So here I am writing from my point of view. The problem is Rose won't tell me what she's writing beyond saying her life. Kind of a broad topic. So I don't know what I should be agreeing with or what I should be disputing.

Rose said just write like I'm writing to a friend.

So, Hi friend.

And she said use quotation marks if it's dialogue. I'm thinking — Dialogue? In an autobiography? What's she gonna do — quote herself? I don't plan on using dialogue, as in she said this and I said that, just so you know. But I do feel it's important to have some say in the story of my sister's life because although we're conjoined twins, and technically have parallel vision, we don't always see eye to eye.

I'm not allowed to read Rose's chapters (not like I know how to use her computer anyway), so I said if I couldn't read her chapters she couldn't read mine. We made a deal that when the book's done we'll make a copy and read the whole thing together. She'll read my chapters out loud. And I'll read hers. (There's a party you don't want to miss.)

Rose has high hopes of having this thing published. She won't admit it, but she does. She says if no publisher wants it she'll do it on the Internet, which I don't understand, but she says it's possible.

I'm being realistic about Rosie's odds. Who wants to read about a couple of sisters who work at the library in a boring small town, even if we are joined at the head? If you spend an hour with us, you get over the physical weirdness of our being conjoined and see that my sister and I are just two normal women. I've never seen any book written by a conjoined twin before. And working in the library, I've seen lots of books. The reading public wants mysteries, and crime dramas, and hysterical romance, and glamour, and dirt (by that I mean celebrity gossip). Rose and I are not mysterious or criminals. We have been hysterical once or twice, but we're not glamorous. We're sort of celebrities, though. To people in Baldoon County. Personally, I'm as well known for my Indian artifact discoveries as I am for being conjoined. I was invited to join the Baldoon County Historical Society. And I have had many telephone conversations with professors and museum guys about where I found artifacts on our farm, and how the things were positioned in the ground. A couple of guys came out to the farm so I could lead them on a tour of my finds. A picture of Rose and me standing alongside Errol Osler, a real expert on the Neutral Indians, was in the *Chatham Daily News*. Errol Osler is a volunteer at the Museum of Indian Archaeology in London. The London museum is the re-creation of the Indian village that stood on its site four hundred years ago. Rose and I have been going there since we were kids. Aunt Lovey and Uncle Stash used to take us there after my specialist appointments.

Rose is not interested in the Neutrals the way I am, but she never complained about going to the museum. She's done some online research for me too. We are completely supportive of each other, even though we have different interests. But I don't necessarily think it's because we're conjoined. I think it's mostly just because we're sisters.

I'm writing my chapters in longhand on a yellow legal pad, which is at my side and which Rose can't see because she's a bit nearsighted. Doesn't really matter. Rose can read my mind. She's done it since we were little. And even though I can't read her mind, I know she's probably writing embarrassing things about me — which, personally, I think if someone wants to call their story an autobiography, they should write embarrassing things about themselves and leave it at that.

Rosie tends to exaggerate things so there's a warning for you.

She also tends to round things off. Know what I mean?

Rose said I should start by saying what it's like to be conjoined. I've thought about that one for a long time. Maybe that's why it's taken me so long to write, because I can't imagine how even the most brilliant author could describe to a stranger what it's like to take your life's journey with your sister attached to your head.

When I told Rose I was stuck on what to write about our conjoinment, she said I should share my interests and hobbies. Well, my hobby, since I was about eight years old, has been searching for Indian artifacts. Specifically artifacts from a large band of Neutral Indians who had a fishing camp spread out on our farm hundreds of years ago. Our farm isn't right on the Thames like you'd expect, but a ways away, on higher ground that doesn't flood.

Ninety percent of the Neutral Indian artifacts at the Leaford Museum, which is almost right across the street from our old farmhouse on Rural Route One, were found on our land, by me. The bone handle with the engraved decoration, the bird effigy pipe, the bone-bead necklace, the dozens of arrowheads, the flanged cooking pot. I have a list somewhere of the rest of the things I found. I'm not an Indian expert or anything, and I don't get how writing about my interest in the Neutral Indians tells you anything about me and my sister and what it's like to be conjoined, but Rose says all that stuff will fall out between the lines.

After we met with Dr. Singh in Toronto last month, Rose and I took a short taxi ride to the beach, and we found a quiet spot where we wouldn't be stared at or interrupted, and we talked about what we'd like to do with whatever time we have left.

That night Rose started to write this book, which she calls *Autobiography of a Conjoined Twin*. I told her I think that's the worst title I've ever heard. She already thought of a book jacket design. She says the design is very important.

She said our prognosis gave her inspiration and a deadline in two words. She can joke about it all she wants. I know she's scared.

I think that's why she's so obsessed with writing so much so fast. The tapping of her computer keys drives me nuts when I'm trying to fall asleep. I don't know how she stands it. Banging on the keys. Looking at the computer screen for hours and hours. Remembering. Thinking. Rose has always been reflective. She's the in-love-with-learning type. I guess that's why she's a writer. I don't really like to learn. I just like to know.

When I first started getting headaches it was once every few days and they weren't bad. But the headaches have gotten worse and they've been more frequent and last week my left eye started to blur. Obviously that's not good. There's no MRI machine in Leaford or Chatham so we had to go to Toronto. The train was sold out. The bus is cheaper, so that was a bonus, but I get sick on the bus more than the train because of the fumes. All the way to Toronto I'm thinking, Don't puke — brain tumor — don't puke — brain tumor — don't puke — brain tumor. Then a man got on at Woodstock and sat downwind of Rose and me and the guy was wearing so much aftershave I did puke. I'd forgotten to bring a clean shirt, and Rose wouldn't let me borrow her spare blouse. Fair enough, because she knew I'd probably puke at least one more time and next time it might be on her shirt. But at the time I was mad. So we didn't talk the rest of the way there. The taxi driver in Toronto took us the long way to the hospital, and the cafeteria was closed for renovation. Then the prognosis from Dr. Singh. Inoperable aneurysm. All in all a fun-filled day.

I don't know what to say. Maybe that's why I haven't written.

I imagine Rose has already said it all. So she's already told you about seeing Dr. Singh and finding out that my sister was having headaches too. Really, really bad ones. And then finding out about the aneurysm. And that it's in her brain. Not mine.

Rose never calls it by the right name: aneurysm. She calls it her "thing" when she talks about it at all, which is only when I bring it up. When I asked her to go on her computer and get as much information as she could find about brain aneurysms, she came back with two pages and said there wasn't much information out there. I couldn't believe that, so I thought about slipping Whiffer a note, but we've agreed not to tell anyone at the library that we are dying.

I don't want to ask Dr. Singh for information beyond what he's already given us because he seemed bugged when I said I thought we should get a second opinion. But then again maybe he wasn't bugged. Maybe I read him wrong. Rosie's better at reading people and she says I'm paranoid. I wonder if anyone else thinks that.

I call it our aneurysm. Six months ago I didn't know exactly what an aneurysm was. An aneurysm is a weakened vein, which can be in your head or your heart or your stomach, which stretches like a balloon. It can stretch to the point where it leaks a little blood or it can stretch till it bursts open all the way and you can die. It can also put pressure on vital areas and cause other problems.

Usually these things are operable but in our case the aneurysm is not operable. That's the second opinion too, which we got yesterday. But I'm sure Rose has already written about that too.

I expected to have Dr. Singh's diagnosis confirmed, but I think Rose was hoping for a miracle. She hardly said a word all the way home. She gripped me tight, which she always does when she's mad (whether she'll admit it or not), and didn't want to talk.

When we got home from that first diagnosis, Rose wanted to go to bed. She always brings her laptop to bed so that wasn't unusual. I fell asleep and woke up a few hours later and she was still on her computer. I'll bet Rose wrote about a hundred pages that night. The next day she told me she had started to write her autobiography. Which is when I said that technically I didn't think she could. In some ways that seems like a year ago, but it was really only a few weeks.

If I look up from where I'm writing on my yellow legal pad I can see

Rose in the mirror. She's reading a book. I can't read the title from here. It's got leather binding. Shakespeare or a classic. She is frowning, which means she loves it.

We have a lot of mirrors in our house. About ten times the mirrors that an average person would have. We have at least six mirrors in each room. Rose and I can't see each other, so we use the mirrors to look at the other when we want to. Sometimes we even feel like we need to. Sometimes, but not often. Mostly, we don't need the mirrors to know what the other is thinking. I know if Rose is angry because of the way her eyebrows tighten and pull at the skin of my temple.

We fight more when we don't look at each other, even if it is only through the mirror. Sometimes I catch myself staring at Rose, forgetting that we're joined.

Staring is a fact of life when you are a conjoined twin. I think especially when you're joined at the head, because that's when people really go Oh my God! Imagine that! It's not as weird to Rose and me as you'd think. Aunt Lovey used to tell us that we were lucky because we were rare, and we shouldn't mind when people stare.

Dr. Kitigan (the second opinion) said the same thing Singh said. The aneurysm could erupt virtually any time. In Rose's next breath or in our sleep tonight or in a month. Or two months or three or six months. But likely not seven. And most certainly not eight. That's what Singh says. Most certainly. Most certainly not eight. I asked him point-blank, Are you saying we only have six months left? He didn't answer right away because, even for a doctor, these things are hard to say. Then he said yes. Six months. At the most.

Rose reminded me it's the same for everyone. No one knows the precise moment of his or her death. That's why we should carpe diem (enjoy today because who knows about tomorrow). We don't know what to expect with the aneurysm. Most of the symptoms will be Rose's. But we share a major vein, so there are issues of fluid and pressure. I'll experience more headaches. And continue to have some blurring vision. Or loss of smell. Or worse things, like blindness and loss of motor control. Or we could go on with mild symptoms, then just suddenly drop dead.

We have three months to go till our thirtieth birthday. I never expected to see thirty, so I'm not gonna say I feel cheated about the length of my life. Still, it would mean something to me to turn thirty years old. The longest-surviving craniopagus twins next to us died at twenty-nine. Just being alive has sometimes felt like an accomplishment. I would like to reach a milestone like thirty years old. I would very much like to have that distinction.

I've been praying lately. We didn't go to church when we were growing up, but Uncle Stash and Aunt Lovey taught us about God. Rose says she's undecided, but I believe, and I've been praying that God will please let us celebrate turning the big 3–0.

Rose said that I should remember, when I'm writing, to write about my life, not just our life, and to share my own thoughts and memories of the past.

So, here's something. Like I said, Rosie and I grew up in the country in an old farmhouse on land near the river where the Neutral Indians had a fishing camp hundreds of years ago. After the earth was tilled each spring, we'd walk through the fields. (Just so you know, even though I don't walk with my feet, I still think of myself as a walking person. Obviously I'm not in a wheelchair or anything. The best way I could explain it is to say that I feel like I borrow Rose's legs when it's my turn to lead. There have been times when Rose has stubbed her toe or stepped on something sharp where I swear to God I felt it.)

Anyway, we'd walk through the fields after Mr. Merkel'd been through with the plow, when the earth was really black and clean. You hardly ever saw rocks in it. So when you did see something gray or flinty or clay-colored, one out of ten times it was a very good arrowhead or a bit of pottery. On our side of the creek I found twenty-seven partial pieces, and one full piece, of clay pottery, hundreds of flints of all sizes, a dozen grooved stones and fluted points and ax heads, a traveling kit, and three pipes with animal effigies — two turtle heads and a bird. I also found a large bone sucking tube, which is really cool. It's all under lock and key at the Leaford Museum (which closed its doors a few months ago because of no funds. I telephoned the lady from the Historical Society three times saying how I'd love to go visit the collection, but she hasn't returned my calls). I wanted to keep the bone sucking tube. I loved the way it felt in my hand. It had a vibration. All the things I've found do. You hold this old thing in your hand, this stone or arrowhead or mortar and pestle, which was an everyday tool for a person from hundreds of years ago, and there's something warm in it. Something alive. I wanted to keep the bone sucking tube, but Aunt Lovey lectured about how history doesn't belong only to me. Uncle Stash was slightly more sympathetic, but he still made a call to the Historical Society and said we'd bring it to the museum.

Rose and I were not allowed to look for artifacts on Merkels' side of the creek where Mrs. Merkel might look out the window and see us searching. Aunt Lovey said it would remind the poor woman of when the whole town was out looking for Larry.

Rose's eyes aren't as sharp as mine. She hardly ever found anything good. Sometimes I'd make her stop right in front of a piece of pottery or an arrowhead and pretend not to see it myself, so that she could be the lucky one. Rose is so blind. Or maybe she didn't really care.

(I just realized you might not know what a bone sucking tube is. It's a tube made of hollowed-out bone, and the medicine men in the tribe would use it to suck the illness from whatever part of a person's body it was in.)

One time I found the top of a skull in the field. I didn't know it was a skull at first. I was actually pretty excited, thinking it might be a ceremonial bowl. But then I saw the suture joints on the bone. Rose moved the dirt away with her foot so we could get a better look. It was pretty shocking to realize it was a human skull. There was this huge hole in it. When Rose and I saw the hole we both screamed, and Aunt Lovey and Uncle Stash came running.

Aunt Lovey was a nurse and she knew right away it was a skull. She got down on her knees in the dirt to examine it and saw that it was fractured. Uncle Stash bent down to have a look too, and he pointed at something inside the skull. Finger bones. Inside the hole in the skull. Aunt Lovey looked puzzled. Uncle Stash thought for a minute, then raised his hand to shield himself from an imaginary ax or hatchet, demonstrating how a person's finger bones could end up in his or her skull. He was clever like that.

We buried the skull very deep, six feet under, so the plow couldn't turn him up again next year.

I never did very well in school except in art, but I got an A on the project I did about the local Indians. Aunt Lovey had Native blood in her, which you would not have guessed in a million years. She was so fair. If someone had said she was Irish or Scottish or Welsh or one of those, you would have believed it. But, really, she was French, with an Indian great-great-great-great-grandmother. So my interest comes from two places. From my Aunt Lovey and from my home where we grew up.

Rose and I went to school with a boy named Frankie Foyle. He lived a few concessions away from us. There was this huge mound in the middle of Foyle's corn, about the size of a swimming pool. The mound was grown over with grass and had been for years. It was too much money to bulldoze it, so I guess Frankie's father, Berb, didn't think about the mound much one way or another. He just fenced it in and left it be. Then one day one of his big dogs dug up a bone. The dog brought this bone to Berb's wife, and she got suspicious.

Somehow Mrs. Merkel heard about the bone, and she thought maybe it was Larry. The police went out to Foyles' and found more bones, all of them human, dug up from the grassy mound in the middle of Berb's corn. So the police kept digging, and the forces from London and Windsor came and took over. The local police tried to tell the others that the mound on Berb's property had been there ever since anyone could remember. But no one paid attention. More men came to dig, and more, and trucks and whatnot, and in the end they counted more than seventy skulls.

They took Berb to jail while they investigated, and they discovered that the bones were similar to the skeletons found in a Neutral Indian camp near Rondeau. When they realized the hill in Berb's farm was an Indian burial mound, they dug a deep hole and put the skeletons back in the ground and covered the hole with earth. The government and other groups got involved. And they even put up a commemorative plaque. But no one's very interested in looking at a patch of weeds in the middle of a cornfield. And Berb's known as a crazy, so you don't necessarily want to find yourself alone in a field with him either.

I don't know if people were suspicious of Berb before the thing happened with the human bones, but after he got out of jail, his wife left him, and the whole town kept looking at him weird. Even Aunt Lovey and Uncle Stash. And Frankie (his son who is around our age and who there is a whole huge story about which I don't want to get into, but Rose will I'm sure) split his time between his father's farm and his mother's rented house, which just happens to be the bungalow on Chippewa Drive that Aunt Lovey and Uncle Stash owned at the time. And where we live now. After a while Frankie started spending more time at his mother's than his father's. Even though Berb did not really kill anyone.

Rose said to write about things that have been important to us. Aunt Lovey and Uncle Stash. The museum. The library has been important. Our family history has been important. How boring!

When Rose and I talked about what we wanted to do in the time we have left, I said I wanted to go to the Museum of Indian Archaeology in London. We haven't been there since Uncle Stash and Aunt Lovey passed away.

The museum has a huge collection of artifacts, and an exact replica of a longhouse that you can go inside. If Errol Osler is there, he'll let Rose and me have a minute in the longhouse alone. That's about the closest thing we get to a church. I think even Rose finds the longhouse to be a spiritual place. She never says no when I ask if she wants to go.

Over the years of our going there, Errol Osler sort of became a friend. He's a very interesting person who has clocked thousands of volunteer hours for the museum and he's quite an archival genius, even though he never went to school for it. I love talking to Errol about my recent finds. He has a different way of looking at things. Even at me.

It was Errol Osler who first told me about reincarnation. He was explaining how the Neutrals sometimes buried their dead children in the middle of the longhouse or along the busiest village paths because they thought the children's souls could rise up into the belly of pregnant women and be reborn. Somehow that made sense to me. I talked to Aunt Lovey about it later, and she said she believed in reincarnation too. Aunt Lovey and I were a lot alike in that we believed our souls could be reborn. And we both thought dreams had significance if you could just figure them out.

I have a recurring dream about losing my sister. I wake up relieved to feel her breath (even though it's usually rank with garlic) on my cheek. Relieved like when I wake up from one of my shattered-teeth dreams and find they're still in my mouth.

I never dream about being separated from Rose. Never.

When I was little, the only way I could fall asleep was if my sister touched my earlobe. I used to cry for her to do it. I called it Lolo for some reason. So I used to cry, Do Lolo, Rose, until Rose would rub my earlobe. Some nights she was too mad at me. Some nights she was tired herself and just didn't want to. I would cry, or Aunt Lovey would persuade her, and Rose would do Lolo and I would fall asleep. But after a while, Aunt Lovey said, No more Lolo. She said it just wasn't fair to make Rose responsible for helping me get to sleep, and I cried and cried and cried. Rose couldn't stand it and she gave in almost right away, but Aunt Lovey threatened to duct tape her hand to her leg to stop her from reaching for my ear. Hearing that made me stop crying, and I didn't ask for it anymore because I didn't want Rose to get in trouble. Rose would do it anyway. Not for half an hour the way I liked it, but just a little tug on my earlobe after Aunt Lovey left the room. Just a little tug to say I love you. We also had this thing where I would put my freezing hands on her warm skin, and she'd say, Don't take my warm. And I'd say, I'm taking your warm. I'm taking all your warm. It's not as weird as it sounds.

Dr. Singh said it will happen like this. The aneurysm will likely burst and kill Rose instantly. My death will be a little slower. My body will continue to pump blood into Rose's, but hers will not respond and I will bleed out, into her. I'll be conscious for a while. If I want to be. I have two syringes of Tatranax, one for my purse and one for beside the bed, in case I want to expiate my death following my sister's. I don't think "expiate" is the right word, but you know what I mean.

Tatranax will make me sleepy, then unconscious, then stop my heart. I can't imagine it's possible that my heart could continue to beat after Rose's has stopped. (Rose said I should never say which doctor gave us the Tatranax syringe because technically it's not legal.)

I was going to write about Uncle Stash taking us to Slovakia after graduation, because Rose said to write about some of the things we've done and places we've been. That trip was a big one. Huge. Then again, I don't know if I want to remember Slovakia. Actually, I don't. And plus, it won't even make sense without telling all the details of Grozovo, where Uncle Stash grew up, and the Slovak saints' festivals and their culture, and how they are different from North Americans in a million ways.

Rose said I could write the story about Aunt Lovey's wedding dress, which is a simpler story to tell. I can't write anything more now, though. I find this writing thing exhausting. This was my first time, and it probably will get easier, but if it doesn't I'll just do little updates or something.

If I'm supposed to be writing to a friend it seems weird not to say good-bye.

So good-bye.

Birds & Feathers

I have a clear memory of a trip to Philadelphia to see Dr. Mau when Ruby and I were about six years old. (Dr. Mau, the cranio-facial specialist who examined us in Toronto shortly after our birth, had transferred to the Children's Hospital of Philadelphia.) Ruby says she has no recollection of going to Philadelphia. She claims not to remember the awful car trip and throwing up in my lap. She doesn't remember being frightened by the strange albino woman who screamed when she saw us in the parking garage or our first taste of Greek food, because nothing else was open.

Ruby remembers nothing. I recall it all — the black and aquamarine tiles in the reception room at the hospital, the greasy vending machine with mostly Clark bars that we'd begged quarters from Uncle Stash to buy, the smell of ammonia in the screeching elevator. The staring in the waiting room — staring at the others staring at us. A small girl with a ledge of white tumors over both eyes. A baby with a severely cleft palate. A limbless toddler throwing a fit in the hall. St. Francis on the wall, pitying.

We are accustomed to being examined. My sister always falls asleep. Maybe it's true Ruby doesn't remember Philadelphia. Maybe she slept through the whole thing. Ruby, with her frequent digestive and bladder problems, had us to Leaford weekly when we were young to see Dr. Ruttle Jr. (and later, when he retired, his son, whom we call Richie or Rich), but our examination in Philadelphia was different. We endured dozens of X-rays, and needle pricks, and electrodes, and swabs, and other procedures I wasn't familiar with, and after several hours we were taken to a large operating theater where Dr. Mau and a group of ten other doctors waited.

The whole operating room must have been chrome, for all the reflections I could see. The reflection of the hot white lights, of Dr. Mau and me and my conjoined sleeping sister. We were lying naked on two large gurneys that had been pushed together. Aunt Lovey was worried because I was perspiring so heavily. I was irritated by Dr. Mau's poking fingers, and though I was too well raised to protest directly, I was shooting him some evil looks.

I had no idea who Dr. Mau was, or why Aunt Lovey and Uncle Stash had brought us to see him, or why they seemed so anxious when he didn't want to let them into the examination room. Aunt Lovey's tone had been respectful, but her refusal to be left outside was absolute. I remember that, after an hour or so of Dr. Mau's picking and prodding and talking to the other doctors in a foreign language, his black eyes had found mine. If he understood that I was glaring at him, he didn't seem to mind. He'd studied me, smiling warmly as he dragged a large white duck feather back and forth over my sleeping sister's clubfeet. He was wearing cologne. I had never smelled such a scent, sharp and spicy, before. (Uncle Stash smelled of beef blood and Amphora Red tobacco. Aunt Lovey smelled of lilacs and Palmolive.)

Watching my eyes, Dr. Mau continued dusting Ruby with his ridiculous white feather and whispered, so as not to wake her, "Rose? Can you feel this?"

I'd responded with what I thought was politeness, whispering back, "No, Dr. Mau. Can you?"

I hadn't meant to be funny or clever, but Dr. Mau had laughed and turned to Aunt Lovey, asking, "Is the parasitic twin clever too?"

In my memory, Aunt Lovey jerked the doctor off his feet like a rag doll and yanked him out of earshot. I know she more likely tugged at his sleeve or merely urged him over to the door, raising her voice somewhat, too angry to remember her place. I couldn't turn my head to watch, but I heard the sound of Aunt Lovey hissing like a snake and the obscene word "parasitic, parasitic" whispered by one and then the other, again and again.

When Dr. Mau returned to the table with his watery dark eyes, he seemed different. Maybe he was contrite after Aunt Lovey's dressing down. Ruby woke up when the doctor accidentally jabbed her with the sharp end of the feather. She was groggy and seemed to have no idea where she was. Dr. Mau smiled at her, explaining that he was an old friend, an old doctor friend, just making sure she was in good shape. Ruby must have smiled back because he looked past me, at Aunt Lovey and Uncle Stash, and the other doctors, and said, "This one's *quite* pretty."

Aunt Lovey did not jerk the doctor off his feet or even urge him out of earshot when he said that. Instead, she and Uncle Stash moved closer to have a look at Ruby themselves, and they smiled too, because it was true.

Coots

Smelling of motor oil and buttered turnip, and speaking no English, thirteen-year-old Callula Crezda was enrolled in our fourth-grade class at Leaford Public School. The principal brought her to our room, and Miss May, frowning, found a seat for her in the front. She was two years older than the oldest fourth graders, Ruby and me. She had crossed black eyes and straight black hair and a single large mole on her right cheek. She wore a brown tunic, a white blouse with a coffee stain, and boys' black rubber boots with a stripe of red at the top. The class of fourth graders (who tolerated Ruby and me because we were locals, and because they'd been threatened to death by their parents) were starving for a target, and they found it in the cross-eyed immigrant. It was clear to everyone, within minutes of her arrival, that Callula Crezda had "the coots."

Callula lived in a tiny rented house beside the railroad tracks with her father, who was huge and savage, and who walked with a limp and did not work, and her mother, a doughy, grinning woman who wore a black babushka. Her mother got a job cleaning vats at the canning factory, and soon after that Callula came to school wearing a black pirate patch to train her lazy eye. I begged Aunt Lovey for a pirate patch, but Ruby said she would not go to school if I wore one.

My sister and I talked about Callula incessantly. Not between each other (never between each other), but at the supper table with Uncle Stash and Aunt Lovey, when they asked us about our day. Ruby did most of the telling. I revised and edited as she went along. There was the story about how a boy dropped his spelling book and it hit Callula's head. Callula thought he did it on purpose, so she smacked him on the head with *her* spelling book. There was one incident when a disposable razor fell out of Callula's purse at recess, and she used it to threaten another girl. Ruby even told about Callula climbing to the top of the monkey bars and letting everyone see her dirty underwear. Aunt Lovey and Uncle Stash winced and shook their heads upon hearing our Callula Crezda stories. "That *poor* girl," Aunt Lovey would say, though she never sounded so piteous about Ruby or me.

One day, during fall flu season, Callula threw up porridge. The sight of the mess made my delicate sister puke too, and we'd ended up in the nurse's office at the same time. Callula was sitting at the far end of the room. She was glassy-eyed and silent and didn't notice when we slipped through the door. As Ruby whimpered behind me, I studied Callula. Her sweater was badly pilled. There was dirt in her raggedy nails. A yellow crust around her nose. Her stockings filthy with ladders and holes.

"Hi, Callula," I whispered, knowing she couldn't hear.

Ruby pinched me hard. She was terrified of Callula, and of other things I didn't understand.

That night, after our brief interlude in the nurse's office, a derailed freight train slammed into the back of Crezdas' little rented house by the tracks. At four o'clock in the morning a freight train hauling grain went rumbling past Leaford, its wheels screaming on the wet rails, challenging the thunderstorm overhead. The last car of the train, which was loaded with seed corn, came unhitched and jumped the track, skiing down the embankment and shearing off the back half of the Crezdas' house, before flipping and rolling and finally coming to rest against the hill at the end of the road.

By six o'clock that morning all of Leaford, including Aunt Lovey and Uncle Stash and Ruby and me, were standing in the pouring rain, staring at the remains of the poor little house. (The London newspaper carried a photograph of the immigrant family huddled together in the front seat of their old car, the scowling Crezda father, the grinning Crezda mother, Callula with her pirate patch, arms crisscrossed over her breast buds under thin cotton pajamas.) Uncle Stash shook his head, looking at the house and the train beyond. "Nothing to do." He shrugged mournfully. "We go."

Aunt Lovey nodded.

"No one else is leaving," Ruby complained.

"This is tragedy, Ruby," said Uncle Stash. "This is not for entertainment."

Aunt Lovey nodded but didn't make a move.

I could see Callula at a distance, shivering in the car between her mother and father. She looked waxy and white, not angry so much as defeated. I was confused by my urge to flee.

Aunt Lovey suggested that Ruby and I go talk to our classmate. When I asked what we would say, Aunt Lovey seemed surprised. "Just tell the poor girl you're sorry about what happened to her house."

I was afraid Callula Crezda would understand "sorry" as an *apology,* and thought Aunt Lovey was giving me bad advice. Why would I want Callula Crezda to think I had something to do with the train wreck? "I don't want to," I said.

The interior walls of the Crezdas' house, the ones that separated the two front bedrooms and living room from the kitchen, laundry, and bathroom at the back, had crumpled after the train crashed, and the contents were laid bare. In the living room, a scratched coffee table between two torn red chairs, a sunken sofa, and, beside it, stacks of books — not like Aunt Lovey's paperbacks, but large hardcover volumes with rich navy spines and gold-leaf titles. A small mattress on the floor of each bedroom, several garbage bags in the corner for clothes. A few crooked Christian icons on the shocked yellow walls.

The Crezdas — the father, the mother, and Callula in her cotton pajamas — sat silently. The rain stopped. More people came. Gawkers from Raleigh County and Harwich brought lawn chairs and binoculars. Behind the steering wheel in the unmoving car, Mr. Crezda's eyes grew darker.

Then the crows came. A black cloud that stole over our heads and descended like a cloak upon the seed corn spilled from the wreckage.

(Leaford is the crow capital of the world. An army of several thousand sleek black crows makes Baldoon County home, dining splendidly in farmers' fields, fighting for turf on trash day. Every year someone has some brilliant idea about how to drive the crows away. Mayors in Leaford have been elected on their crow-eradicating platforms. When Ruby and I were fifteen years old, a falconer was hired to scare the birds off. There were so many crows that year, Zimmer's single-engine crop dusters couldn't fly safely in or out of the Leaford Airfield. The most seasoned farmers in the crowd had never seen the crows like this, so many at once, maybe a thousand, turbulent and hostile, flying as a collective, swooping too close to the crowds, battling one another in midair.)

A few of the onlookers opened up their umbrellas as the crows continued to circle and dive. Other people returned to their cars. Still others, determined to stay with the carnage, climbed into the remains of the Crezdas' house and made themselves at home, with their muddy boots on the mattresses and their fat asses on the torn red chairs, as focus shifted from the derailed train to the black winged beasts.

I could not have been the only person to watch Callula's father catapult from his car and lunge toward the bisected house. Of course no one inside understood his screaming, since it was in Yugoslavian, but it was impossible not to know his intention. He hoisted himself up over the foundation and into his half-house and ran at the people, swatting them with his open hand and kicking at them with his boots. Uncle Stash made us leave before we could see any more.

The next morning, my boots sucking the muck of the unpaved lane, the warm air stinking of pig from Lapiere's to the south, and with the crows cawing loudly in the cornfield behind the barn, Ruby and I made our way down to the road and to the shelter of our weather shed. (Uncle Stash had fashioned the shed of corrugated aluminum, with a silver domed top and a boat's portal window. It took him eight full days to construct. All the country kids had such enclosures to shelter them while they waited for the school bus, but most were boxy sheds slapped together with incidental scraps of wood, uninspired, hardly ever even painted. No one in the county had a shed like ours: a spaceship; an alien shuttle; an upturned submarine. Now that I think of it, it was actually rather phallic — which may account for at least some of the laughter from the back of the bus. Oh my God, what must Frankie Foyle have thought, watching Ruby and me emerge from our giant silver penis?)

As we waited in our silver stalk for the yellow bus that would ferry us to Leaford PS, I thought about asking Callula what it felt like when the train sliced through her house, but wondered if my interest would be misunderstood. The bus was buzzing with talk of the train wreck and Crezdas' misfortune. I had a twinge of anxiety, fearing that Callula might gain status because of the accident and be too high ranking to consider a friendship with the likes of Ruby and me. We arrived in our classroom to find Callula Crezda's chair vacant. She had been moved to grade five. I knew it would be worse for her there with the older, bolder children, but I shared Ruby's relief. "Coots. Coots. Coots. Coots." They'd chant it whenever the halls were teacher-free. The boys would tease Callula into chasing them into the green field at recess. Someone taught Callula a few English swearwords. "Eat me out!" she'd scream at her tormentors, though she couldn't have known what it meant.

Her family moved away from Leaford before high school started. I thought I saw Callula Crezda amid the throng of people at Aunt Lovey's funeral, but of course it wasn't her.

It's Ruby again.

Rose hasn't been eating. I can feel in her hips that she's getting thinner. Lately I've had to fight to get us into the shower. That's not like Rose.

All she wants to do is write. Or think about writing, or talk about writing. She says a good day is when she writes eight pages instead of four. She's says it's like losing ten pounds, which I can't relate to because I've never had a weight issue. But if I ask Rose what she's writing, she won't say. I don't know what she thinks is going to happen to this book, even if it is published, and like I said before, I am truly doubtful that will happen because who, besides other conjoined twins, is going to want to read it? I hate to think my sister's wasting her time. Especially now.

Plus, I don't get it. She's on her computer for hours at a time and she only writes four pages?

I have the headache tonight. We joke that we pass it back and forth, but the truth is Rose usually has it and it's usually a bad one. She told Dr. Singh that, by evening, her head is a cave of pain. A cave of pain. That's how she really talks. (She can be very embarrassing.) She has taken a leave of absence from work, which, because of our circumstances, may sound weird as I did not take a leave of absence and Rose is obviously still at the library when I'm doing reading circle with the school groups. But her job, which was shelving the books — reaching and leaning and lifting more weight than just me (which is enough) — could strain Rose and cause a premature eruption of the aneurysm.

Rose still participates in the questions and answers with the kids, thank God.

When we first started at the library (seven years ago this fall), I read books from the kiddie shelves to the school groups from the surrounding counties. *Goodnight Moon* and *Where the Wild Things Are* and *The Cat in the Hat,* plus anything that's won a Caldecott Medal and has a silver seal on the cover. But the kids have read these books a million times with their parents and teachers. Really, they want to know about me and Rosie and what it's like to be joined at the head. So I got some photocopies blown up of other conjoined twins. Famous ones like Chang and Eng Bunker, who were real Siamese twins. (Just so you know, they were called Siamese twins because they were from Siam. North American twins like Rose and me think it's so weird to be called Siamese because we are obviously from Leaford and we are obviously not cats!) I have pictures of Millie and Christine McCoy, who were joined at the base of their spines and born into slavery in North Carolina. They were brought to Europe to sing for kings and queens. In their pictures they're always wearing beautiful costumes. Violet and Daisy Hilton were joined at the lower spine too, and they became even more famous. They were really beautiful, and they were in Hollywood movies and everything. My favorite are the Italian twins Giacomo and Giovanni Tocci, who were born in Turin (like the Shroud of Turin) in the late 1800s. They're called Deicephalous twins (not sure of that spelling), which basically means they were born with normal upper bodies, but, somewhere around the stomach, they were connected. So they had one stomach and one penis and two legs, but each of the legs belonged to the other and they could never learn how to walk. I don't know which boy the penis belonged to. Their father went insane when he saw them after birth, but later he toured them for big bucks, which is what happened to Chang and Eng and Millie and Christine and most of the conjoined twins you read about in history. The Tocci brothers were blond and adorable. They were called the Two-Headed Boy, which they must have hated.

I used to show pictures of Laleh and Ladan Bijani, who were Iranian women and joined at the head like Rose and me. These girls were brilliant and accomplished — one a journalist and the other a lawyer — and every time Rose heard something about them she got an inferiority complex because she didn't go to university and, more than anything, I think, she would have liked to do that. But a year or so ago, the Bijani twins decided on surgery to separate them, and even though many leading doctors told them it wouldn't work, they wanted to do it anyway. They both died, so of course I don't show the children their pictures anymore.

Yesterday an eight-year-old boy from the Chatham Dutch School asked Rose and me if we pooped at the same time. It's not the first time we've heard that one. We explained to the boy that our heads are joined but that our bodies are not, so we eat different foods at different times and we defecate (Rose likes to teach the kids vocabulary) separately. Then a little girl asked if we pee together. It's very difficult for children to understand that we don't share a brain or body, no matter how many different ways we say it. It seems difficult for some adults to understand too. Our boss, an older lady named Roz who's been at the library for about 130 years, sewed twin dolls joined at the head by Velcro to help illustrate the separateness of our bodies and functions to the children. Roz has a boy with multiple sclerosis. Well, technically he's not a boy because he's nearly fifty years old, but she calls him her boy. He can't talk. He can't walk. He can't feed himself or dress himself, and he uses adult diapers. His name is Rupert, and he works at the library too. At least, we say he works there, but really he just hangs out in the staff room because Roz can't afford home care and because he would die of loneliness if he wasn't close to his mother, who is his best friend and the only one who understands him. Rupert's mind is not deteriorating. Roz says he's smart as a whip. He likes me more than he likes Rose. You can just tell these things.

I'm glad Rose hasn't asked me to take a leave of absence from the library. I would miss Roz and Rupert and Whiffer and Lutie and everyone. And I would miss the kids very much. And I think we'd be missed too. We will be missed. Rose and I haven't told Roz or anyone about the aneurysm. We don't want to be pitied or worried over.

Since she started to write her book, Rose has been asking me, Do you remember this? Do you remember that? She asked if I remembered the chocolate-chip thing when we were twelve years old, and the hair thing when we were in high school. I asked if she was writing about the chocolate-chip thing and the hair thing, and she said she wouldn't discuss what she was writing, and that I shouldn't either. I said, Then stop asking me, Do you remember this? Do you remember that?

Okay — so I thought I was nibbling chocolate sprinkles that had fallen behind the fruit bowl on the big table in the kitchen. It turned out it wasn't chocolate sprinkles but mouse shit. I had a bad cold and couldn't taste it. Anyway, I did not scream that I needed to have my stomach pumped out, and I did not pretend to fall unconscious so that Aunt Lovey would take me to the hospital. I really did fall unconscious, and though it sounds funny, it was not at the time. At all.

And the hair thing. Just in case that one comes up. Rose was the one who wanted to straighten her hair to look more like mine. We know it was not the smartest thing to use a product for black people's hair that we found in a torn package in the bargain bin. I still say I set the timer right. Anyway, it grew back slightly less frizzy, which is what she wanted in the first place.

Because we work at the library and have access to so many books (well, actually, I guess everyone has access to all those books, don't they?), we have read about dying and all the emotional stages that we should be or will be going through. (I'm not the biggest reader. Rose says I'm intellectually lazy, and I guess it's true because what else do you call it when you'd rather watch bad TV shows than read a good book?) Maybe I'm going through the stages backward, but I've been pretty much in the accepting stage since we got the news.

Aunt Lovey took us to the library when we were young and showed us a huge picture book full of people with deformities. The pictures came from the Mütter Museum, which is in Philadelphia and is basically a place where human specimens are on display. It's used for teaching medical students, and it's also for the public who like freakish things. On the way home, Rose wanted to talk about the pictures and the deformities, but I had the mumps coming on, or something, and her talking was making me carsick. Rose wanted to know if all deformed people had their pictures taken for that book and if we would when we died. Aunt Lovey said it was up to each person to decide what to do with their earthly remains. (That book is still on the top shelf, and Rose still looks at it sometimes. I do not understand why.)

Aunt Lovey was sorry she'd shown us the book, because the same night we saw those pictures, Rose was still going on about it. And she was asking a lot of questions about dying. Aunt Lovey had already told us that if one of us died, the other would die too. We were young, but we understood. She had also already told us that we might never grow old. She said that we might reach adulthood, but the tangled veins in our heads would likely give us trouble at some point (which they have), and I also have some gastrointestinal troubles that have threatened my life — and so Rose's life too. (I was this close to having a full colostomy, but the medication finally started to work.) The doctors we've seen throughout the years have not always been truthful with us, but we could always count on Aunt Lovey. She believed a patient should make informed choices. I suppose some people might have thought she was being cruel for being honest.

Rose and I are the oldest surviving craniopagus twins in the world, and we're only twenty-nine. There are many things that an average person would have done by the age of twenty-nine (university, marriage, career, children, travel) that we haven't done, making twenty-nine seem younger than it is. On the other hand, we've learned things about life that an average person would not have the chance to learn until they were much older. Rose says we shouldn't kid ourselves, that we are really very naive. But I think we can be naive and wise at the same time. Aunt Lovey was like that.

(Aunt Lovey believed people could be separated into three categories. People who love children. People who love their own children.

And people who don't even like children but have pets they call Baby. Thinking about that now, I'd have to add a category for Mrs. Merkel. People who treat their pets like children because a tornado took their only son.)

When we were little girls, Aunt Lovey would put Rose and me in the middle of the bathtub. We each had a set of stacking cups to play with. We liked to pour water over each other and ourselves, and Aunt Lovey says it was interesting to watch how often we stacked our cups working together, and how little we did it alone. She said even though we were so different in our personalities, our instinct was usually to cooperate. She said cooperation made us efficient and ensured our survival.

Aunt Lovey had a big green plastic watering can from the garden that she'd fill with warm water, and after she shampooed our hair she'd say, Close your eyes, girls, because the sky sure looks like rain. And she would tip the watering can, and the warm drops would fall on our heads and over our faces and wash away the shampoo. It seemed to take an hour, but it still wasn't long enough. When I think of Aunt Lovey, I feel warm water rushing down my head and my back and I can smell that herbal stuff for Rose's dandruff.

After the bath, Aunt Lovey'd lay us on the bed and unwrap us from the sewn-together towel and we'd say Gobble us up, Aunt Lovey! Gobble us up! And she'd kiss our tummies until we screamed for her to stop. Then she'd spread olive oil on Rose's flaky skin and dab cortisone on her red spots, and she'd dry and style my hair in a side ponytail (the only kind that really works for me) or clip it back with my butterfly barrettes. (Rosie said the hair dryer made her hair frizzier, so Aunt Lovey had to be careful directing the nozzle.)

Last week we discussed our upcoming birthday. Neither of us said if we turn thirty, which I think is good because I believe in the power of positive thinking. But we are so far apart on how we might celebrate our birthday I think we might have to go to the coin. This is something that we don't often do because we can usually work it out (which means I usually give in). But sometimes I feel like being as stubborn as Rose, and we have to toss a coin. Like when we were going to the prom and Rose thought it would be funny if she wore a tuxedo instead of a dress. (I won — Rose wore an ugly navy gramma dress just to be a spoilsport, and I wore a vintage sea green taffeta that Aunt Lovey cut down for me and gathered at the waist with a cluster of tucks.) And the time Rose wanted to write to the Children's Wish Foundation, even though Aunt Lovey had forbidden it because it was stealing an opportunity from a child who was really sick, which we weren't. (I lost that one — Rose wrote the letter anyway and sent a picture of us and everything, but we never heard back — which was proof Aunt Lovey had been right. But maybe it was because Rose wrote that our wish was to meet the queen of England, and that is not the most believable of wishes, if you think about it.)

Get this. To celebrate turning thirty, to celebrate defying the odds against us, especially the recent ones, Rose wants to call in for pizza and drink a bottle of expensive champagne in bed. I can't stand alcohol, and she knows it. Our blood crisscrosses the joined sides of our brains, so if alcohol is in her bloodstream it's in mine too. We can't and shouldn't drink because it's dangerous. If Rose loses her balance and falls, it can be serious for us both. That's why she wants to drink the champagne in bed. But I made the point that eventually she'd have to get up and pee.

My idea is a surprise party, but I'm telling Rose that it's a taxi ride and a dinner at a fancy restaurant on the river road. First I'll say I forgot my purse at the library. I'll have to go and get it from the staff room, and that's where the surprise party will be! The guest list is Roz and Rupert and Whiffer and Lutie, Dr. Ruttle and Richie, and Mrs. Todino from next door (if she's up to it), and because he lives with her we'll have to invite her son, Nick. I'll invite the Merkels, but they won't come.

I've always wanted a surprise party. That the surprise will be on Rose makes it even sweeter. I have to remember to get Roz to bring in a few mirrors and get Whiffer to bring his video camera because, for sure, I want to see Rose's face!

I just thought of something. If we don't celebrate this birthday (her way or mine), no one will be reading this. Because our birthday is now only eight weeks away, and there's no way Rose could write her whole autobiography in eight weeks, and who would want to read the story of a life if the person died before it's fully told? I've never heard of that before.

We are both dealing with dying in different ways. I guess Rose wants to write about it. I want to talk about it. With her. Because no one else could understand. And because I want her to know how sorry I am about certain things that have happened. And I'm afraid she won't let me say it.

The Secret Life of Crows

Last week of June, just before our sixteenth birthday. My hair was growing back in dark, kinky puffs after my sister's botched attempt to straighten it with the wrong kind of product. I was pitiful — and miserable. Leaford was in the fifth day of an extreme heat wave, and Ruby and I were on our way out of the school gym, where our eleventh-grade math exam had just been canceled because of the crows. A battalion of crows had descended upon the grub-studded turf of the football field and could not be scared off. The symphony of caws was so distracting that the principal scheduled a makeup exam for the following day.

This day, expecting to see Aunt Lovey waiting for us on the school steps as usual, Ruby and I left the musty gym to find bony little Nonna, dressed as always in tea-length black, dabbing her eyes with a stark white hankie and wringing her hands like a bad actor. Nonna spotted us as we walked down the hall. "Your Uncle Stash," she called out, choking, "has the heart attack."

Without a car of her own, our trembling Nonna drove us in Uncle Stash's old red Duster (I suspect she didn't have a driver's license either) to St. Jude's Hospital, where we found Aunt Lovey conferring with Dr. Ruttle Jr. (who by this time was Sr. to his recently graduated doctor son, Richie). I didn't recognize Aunt Lovey when we first got to St. Jude's Emergency. She was wearing a borrowed black sweater, and her gray curls were combed out because she'd been at the hairdresser's for a wash and set when she got a call from Vanderhagen's. "Girls," she'd breathed upon seeing us. "Girls."

"The next twenty-four hours," Dr. Ruttle Jr. said, then raised his palms heavenward to remind his best ex-nurse "It's not up to me." We went home to the farmhouse with Nonna that night, the only night we spent away from our Aunt Lovey until the day she died. We three said little to one another when we got back to the house. Ruby and I were excused from chores and went out front to lounge under the willow for the rest of that deadly hot afternoon. I reviewed *Grapes of Wrath* for the literature exam scheduled for the next day, even though I felt sure I'd be missing it due to a death in the family. Ruby listened to soft music on Uncle Stash's portable radio, even though she'd be taking the same exam and had yet to read *Grapes of Wrath,* let alone review it.

At dinnertime, Nonna called us into the house. She looked inside our refrigerator and, deciding there was nothing fit to eat, announced, "I be back." She climbed into the old Duster and sped off, weaving down the country road, returning after what seemed like hours with a tinfoil pyramid of mortadella on Wonder Bread, a giant bag of Humpty Dumpty chips, and something in cellophane for dessert. Ruby and I were delighted, then remembered Uncle Stash and couldn't eat a thing.

I needed to know the details of what had happened to Uncle Stash. When? Where? Did he call in the emergency himself? If not, who'd found him? I imagined what had happened must have been horrible, because I wasn't being told, and no one else was asking. Finally, I begged the story from Nonna, who hesitated until Ruby said, "I want to know too."

THAT MORNING, UPON hearing from the radio that the extreme heat conditions would be torturing Leaford for yet another day, Uncle Stash had almost called in sick, a thing he had never, in twenty-seven years with Vanderhagen's, done before. He was scheduled to drive out to Harwich for a face-to-face with a cattle farmer named Berb Foyle, a local man regarded as a nut and a hothead. Berb had been held by police on suspicion of murder years ago, and though he was never charged, and was not guilty, people stayed away. The more people stayed away, the crazier Berb got. He'd threatened the gas man with a hoe. And chased the quality-control guy from Vanderhagen's when he'd knocked on the door a week before. Management had asked Uncle Stash to have a talk with Berb, because Berb's elderly mother was Slovak and used to come into the butcher shop, where she found Uncle Stash to be especially kind. The boss at Vanderhagen's thought if anyone could talk to Berb, Uncle Stash could. Uncle Stash couldn't say no. Now his stomach roiled at the thought of the confrontation with the abnormally tall, wild-eyed farmer.

Uncle Stash hadn't been feeling well for a few days and had complained to Aunt Lovey as he was leaving for work that morning. She'd thumped his hard ball stomach and joked, "Lay off the sausage, Pork Chop." Uncle Stash climbed into the old work truck (which he parked in the driveway behind the Duster each night) and headed for Harwich County. The truck's refurbished engine had started to smoke several miles from the Foyle property. Cursing, Uncle Stash abandoned the overheated vehicle. He took to the dusty road muttering in Slovak, and by the time he had walked to the edge of Foyle's, he was roasted.

Uncle Stash could see the old farmer, erect among his tomato beds, propped up by a hoe like a scarecrow, not looking admiringly upon his young plants but darkly, even suspiciously, into the dense canopy of maple trees, which rose up on either side of the wide, deep ditch, with their long branches entwined so completely they seemed more like one tree than two. Uncle Stash knew that Berb Foyle was not a murderer (there was a big misunderstanding about some bones found on his property), but he *looked* crazy, and that was frightening enough. Only a crazy person would look at the trees the way he did. Like they were alive. Like they wanted something from him. In the distance, behind old Berb, Uncle Stash could see a dozen underfed cows. He walked closer, nauseated from the heat.

Though his eyes never left the towering maples, Foyle shouted from across the ditch, "You seen my shepherd, Darlen?"

Uncle Stash shook his head. He knew Foyle was referring to his farm dog, a German shepherd, and he hadn't met any dogs on the road.

"You know my boy?" Foyle called, his eyes still on the trees.

Uncle Stash nodded. Foyle's teenage son, Frankie, was a year ahead of Ruby and me at Leaford Collegiate. He lived half the time with his father at the farm and the other half in Leaford, on Chippewa Drive, in the little bungalow Mrs. Foyle was renting from Aunt Lovey and Uncle Stash (the same house where we live now). Frankie Foyle was the only person in our school to have an insane father and separated parents.

Old Berb Foyle kept his eyes on the maple trees. "I hit the dog. I hit the guldarn dog."

Uncle Stash waited, then asked, "With the hoe?"

Berb let his eyes leave the trees to find Uncle Stash, ashen by the road. "With the tractor, Darlen."

"Oh."

"I hit the guldarn dog with the guldarn tractor, and he just run off into the bush."

Uncle Stash felt a stab of sympathy, for the dog and for Berb.

The old farmer lifted his left hand and pointed at the distant figure of his teenage son. "Boy's looking out the back."

Uncle Stash nodded. The dog had to be found.

"He's got the rifle."

Uncle Stash nodded again.

Berb Foyle swiveled his head. "You got no truck, Darlen? You walk all the way out from town? Come on in the house. I'll get you some water, and we'll talk about my cattle."

Uncle Stash felt weak walking up to the farmhouse and didn't know what to make of the crazy farmer's hospitality. Once inside the stifling kitchen, he helped himself to a glass of cloudy tap water while the farmer went, presumably, to wash his hands. Uncle Stash drank the first glass of water in a single swallow. Then he drank another quickly and two more, and another and one more, and felt better. When the farmer returned with an ice-cold Molson Golden, Uncle Stash accepted the beer (even though it was before noon, and he was on the job) and decided he'd misjudged the old man.

The fellows were drinking their cold beers, trading Tiger baseball trivia, when a shot rang out in the field beside them. They were quiet for a moment, then Uncle Stash, uncharacteristically gentle in his approach, said, "You know we have problem with the beef."

The old farmer pushed himself back from the table, walked to the kitchen door, opened it to the heat, and held it for his guest. "Get the hell outta here, Darlen." His invitation to exit the house was as surprising as the one to enter. The farmer was shaking. "I said, get the hell off my property."

An unbalanced farmer. An uncased rifle. Uncle Stash had no choice but to leave, and swiftly. It occurred to him, however, as he staggered down the farmhouse lane, that he'd drunk a gallon of water, and the beer of course, and was badly in need of a bathroom. He made his way to the road at the edge of the property, then hunkered down in the ditch. Sweating and panting, he unzipped his trousers, letting them fall to his ankles. He pissed a steady stream and sighed, and was about to hoist up his trousers when he was shocked by the sudden sting of sharp claws piercing, then seizing and squeezing the muscle of his heart. He clutched his chest and stumbled back, falling bare-assed into the wild lily ditch, under the canopy of conjoined maples.

A moment passed. And another moment. And another, each moment's passing a miracle, for Uncle Stash thought he was dead and that moments should be passing no more, but ceasing altogether. The pressure continued to crush Uncle Stash's chest and make ragged his breath. He opened his eyes. Another moment. And another. There were black spots in his field of vision, which, when he managed to focus, revealed themselves as a massive assemblage of black crows in the maples. The crows, Stash thought through his pain. Old Berb had been staring at the crows.

One curious crow descended to the ditch, flapping brashly and landing within inches of Uncle Stash's feet. He tried to kick the bird away but did not have the strength to move his smallest toe. A second crow joined the first, and another and another, no longer silent but calling to their fellows about the man in the ditch with his trousers at his ankles. Uncle Stash was suddenly, horribly aware of his exposure and, afraid he might be found this way, or, worse, that he would not be found at all, attempted to rise. He attempted to pull up his trousers. He attempted to call out. He wished he had his camera and could take a picture. He cursed the crows in Slovak. "*Metrovy kokot do tvojeje riti,* you little crow shits." (Loosely translated: "Shove a meter-long stick up your arses, you little crow shits.")

As Uncle Stash struggled to stay conscious, several dozen of the black birds swooped down from the branches and joined him in the ditch. One of the crows stood on his chest, strutting like a champion, which seemed to make the others laugh. Another pair of crows tugged at his laces, trying to steal his old shoes. The ones to his left were sizing up his wedding ring, arguing about how to get it off. There were no more black spots in the trees. The crows had him surrounded.

Of course Uncle Stash knew, even as he was slipping into blackness, that he was hallucinating about the crows. They were there, of course, but not with motive or intent, just *there,* the way crows are always there when something bad happens in Baldoon County.

Then it wasn't the crows anymore causing Uncle Stash to swallow his fear. It was Berb Foyle, who had appeared suddenly over the ridge of the ditch, aiming a rifle at Uncle Stash's head. The blast from the rifle erupted in Uncle Stash's ear. He let go of consciousness. He let go of fear.

Of course Nonna didn't describe the story exactly that way because she didn't know then, no one knew then, the events preceding Uncle Stash's heart attack. But she did say that when Uncle Stash was found, he was in Berb Foyle's ditch surrounded by crows. The rest I pieced together as the years went by and the secrets of that day were, one by one, unveiled.

One of the things I learned, a thing that shocked me (because I could picture so easily Berb Foyle, his crazy eye exaggerated by the scope of his rifle, about to shoot Uncle Stash), was that it wasn't Berb, but *Frankie* Foyle standing there with the gun. He'd been drawn to the spot by the crows and by a sound he described as "howling." He'd been aiming his rifle because he thought his wounded dog was in the ditch, and he was gonna do what he had to do as quick as he could do it. His bullet hit a cattail about fourteen inches from Uncle Stash's head.

Frankie laughed about the cattail and described the way it had exploded when he told Ruby and me that story a few months later, riding down the snowy Fourth Concession in the rickety yellow school bus. Ruby and I both instinctively acted as if we already knew about Frankie's involvement, even though we'd never been told and would never have guessed. (I was pleased — more pleased than I should have been under the circumstances — that it was Frankie Foyle who had found, and nearly shot, my Uncle Stash.)

Back to the night of Uncle Stash's heart attack. When the telephone rang, Nonna raced from the kitchen to take the call. I watched her in the mirror. With each phrase that Aunt Lovey uttered on the other end of the line, Nonna's face revised its forecast from bleak to bleaker. There'd been an episode. Uncle Stash had flatlined. The doctors had shocked his heart back to life, but he wasn't expected to survive the night. I heard all of this, repeated in heavily accented English by Nonna, but, as much as I knew it was all true, I couldn't believe a word. Most of all, it seemed impossible that Aunt Lovey hadn't asked to speak to *me*. I was her second-in-command. I was *the strong one*.

Ruby slept that night. But I was too angry to sleep. Or too afraid to dream. When I opened my eyes at dawn, there was a black crow on the windowsill. His feathers were mottled and his beak looked rusty. He regarded my sleeping sister and me with his right eye, then his left, then his right again. He bobbed his head up and down for a time, then cawed and flew away. I felt oddly insulted.

I was startled when the telephone rang. I lay with my arm around my sister, helpless, and desperate to hear Aunt Lovey's voice. In a moment, Nonna came into the room wearing the woolly black bathrobe she'd brought from home. She was smiling.

By the time we got to the hospital, Uncle Stash had opened his eyes, though he wasn't quite strong enough to sit up and not ready to speak. I couldn't lean down to kiss him, of course, so I squeezed his fingers as hard as I could. Then I urged Ruby to the window because I didn't want him to see me cry.

"Leaford is the crow capital of the world," Ruby said, though she had not seen the crow on the windowsill that morning and could not know that I had been thinking about the bird at that very moment.

Heaven's Door

Aunt Lovey had so many stories to tell. When we were children, they were made-up stories about Ruby and me, but as we grew older the stories became memories, extrapolated upon and polished, and they began to stretch beyond Ruby and me to Aunt Lovey and Uncle Stash, their courtship and their youth, then further back to stories about her mother, and hers. After a while, I sensed that Aunt Lovey was not telling me the stories so much as entrusting them to me.

It was Aunt Lovey's belief that all ordinary people led extraordinary lives, but just didn't notice. She said her favorite books were about average people and their everyday existence, and she didn't go in much for crime drama or murder mysteries. She'd read a bumper sticker once that said, "God is in the details." She had nodded solemnly, but couldn't answer when Ruby asked what it meant. I didn't write for a full year after Aunt Lovey died. Not even in my journal. Ruby took it worse. Dr. Ruttle considered putting Ruby on antidepressants, but was unsure how they might affect me. (I've had some terrible side effects from Ruby's medication.) Ruby wasn't eating much and wasn't sleeping at all. Time would not ease her sorrow. I felt her awake at night, praying that heaven was true and that

Aunt Lovey and Uncle Stash were there riding clouds in white robes. There were times I felt Ruby imagining she was riding the clouds with them. But I had the strangest sense she was there without me.

We decided to visit the graves. Ruby's idea. I was reluctant; my graveside experience with Ruby being what it was, I was terrified she'd make a scene. We took the Leaford bus to the cemetery, where we said good-bye to the driver, Joey, after promising twice that we'd be at the stop when he returned in an hour. (Ruby and I cannot and never will live anonymously. Because of our situation, people treat us like children, or the elderly. Can you imagine a city bus driver extracting a promise of return from any other twenty-two-year-old passengers — as we were at the time?)

I felt guilty and responsible that the place wasn't better tended, but I liked the feel of the long soft grass tickling my calves, and the smell of the black earth and the ragged cedar hedges that hid the barren field to the east. It was the middle of the day in the middle of the week, and, to my relief, we were the only two people in the cemetery.

We had to pass through the old cemetery (some graves dating back to the early 1800s) to get to the new cemetery, and, in the maze of weathered white crosses and headstones inscribed by verse describing deaths from childbirth and influenza and old age, I found myself slowing down. I sensed behind each ordinary grave an extraordinary tale, just as Aunt Lovey had said. I wanted to read all the inscriptions and imagine the stories of these dead people's lives. Ruby was impatient and unaffected by the strangers' graves. "It's up there past the catalpa tree, Rose."

The headstones grew larger as we moved toward the new section, gray and clay and pink and polished, some with hand-painted pictures, some with lavishly landscaped plots, neat beds of annuals, and frothy perennials. A few of the headstones were dwarfed by bushes planted long ago and forgotten. We'd brought two wilting pink peonies from Nonna's thorny bush out back.

A sweat bee buzzed around my ear as we searched and found the green double granite Uncle Stash and Aunt Lovey had chosen for themselves when they long ago wrote their wills. We set the two fragrant pink peonies, entwined, on top of the double headstone and said a few private words to them both.

Ruby began to cry. Not to sob but, worse, a tight little whimper that stretched her cheeks, and mine, and was no release at all.

"Aunt Lovey would call this a waste of time," I said.

"I know," Ruby sniffed.

"She'd say our time was better spent cleaning out the silverware drawer," I said.

"I know," she sniffed again.

"They're not *here,* Ruby."

"I know."

"What can I do, Ruby?"

"Nothing."

"Let's go wait for the bus."

"Okay."

As I turned to move, Ruby's hand, the hand that lives on my neck and shoulder and is so much a part of me I imagine its pulse linked to my heart, not hers, suddenly lost its grip and, as had only ever happened when my sister was very sick, my balance shifted and the two of us nearly careened headfirst into the sharp edge of Aunt Lovey and Uncle Stash's stone.

The deadweight of my fainted sister forced me to my knees. "Ruby. Ruby. Ruby," I whispered and shook her, but she didn't wake up.

"Help," I whispered in the direction of Aunt Lovey and Uncle Stash.

I felt Ruby's lids lift. "Did I faint?" she asked.

I was afraid to rise. I knew our blood pressure was low and that I'd be dizzy. There was an ant, or some other small insect (I couldn't turn to look), biting the back of my knee. I took some pleasure in the irritation. I think it helped me focus. "What can we do, Ruby? I want to help you."

"Is it time for the bus?"

I made Ruby drink all the water we'd packed in the knapsack, and we each ate a raisin cookie (made from Aunt Lovey's mother's recipe, which I thought was nice). After a short time we rose and started for the road. The long grass sliced at my bare legs. The sweat bee that had followed me before returned with some friends. I must have looked strange from a distance, swatting the air near our heads. Just before Ruby and I reached the bus stop, with only ten minutes to spare before Joey's next run, I realized we'd forgotten the knapsack at the gravestone. We walked back to retrieve the bag from the grass where we'd left it. I used my foot to catch the strap and lift the thing closer to my hand. We turned to go, but Ruby stopped me with a gasp. She squeezed my shoulder and gestured at the top of Aunt Lovey and Uncle Stash's double headstone. The entwined peonies were gone.

We searched the surrounding area, then checked the nearby gravestones in case there was a vandal or an animal that might have swiped the flowers. The air hardly stirred, so the wind couldn't have blown them away. And there wasn't a squirrel in sight. We were stumped. Then Ruby decided, by process of elimination, that if it wasn't an animal or a vandal or the wind that took the peonies, it must have been a ghost (or ghosts). It was obviously a sign from Aunt Lovey and Uncle Stash. They wanted us to know that they were all right. And together.

That night, Ruby slept for the first time in months. I stayed awake and wrote a short story about a sister's kind deception, encouraging myself that I'd done the right thing tricking Ruby about the disappearing flowers.

As Ruby's sadness lifted, so did mine.

Mysterious Ways

Our cinder-block bungalow sits in the middle of Chippewa Drive, a short straight street lined with identical cinder-block bungalows, each with a small window on either side of a solid wood door. The kind of house a child will draw when she's still in her stick-people phase. The houses are architecturally the same, but their owners have changed them so that, except for being identifiable as bungalows, they are as different as any two people. Back then Mrs. Foyle (Berb's estranged wife), even though she was just a renter, had painted the little home in forest green, with a lemon-yellow trim. The lawn ornaments — an elf on a toadstool, a frog couple in wedding apparel, a large fairy with pointed ears and butterfly wings — were hers too. Mrs. Foyle caught Ruby and me staring at the ornaments one day and remarked, "Aren't they a hoot?" On a particular weekend, when Frankie was ripped on lemon gin, he swung a golf club at the frog couple and kicked the shit out of the elf.

Frankie Foyle was crude. And rude. And dangerous. And a hero of sorts. He had saved Uncle Stash's life (and nearly shot him in the ditch after his heart attack) and was a current object of obsession for Ruby and me. ("Desire" is too tepid to describe our crushes.) We'd known Frankie since first grade. Then he was a chubby, scowling boy with wiry blond hair who sat with us at the back of the bus and talked nonstop about hockey and basketball and baseball. Now he was tall and broad, with smoldering eyes and pouting lips and locks that shone gold in the sun. He was a natural athlete (much too cool for team sports, but he dazzled with a Frisbee) and had reportedly outrun the Leaford police on three separate occasions. He was popular and infamous, a druggie, and a dog with the girls.

I argued about sports with Frankie. (We both liked the Tigers and the Pistons, but for some inexplicable reason he liked the Maple Leafs! The *Leafs?* If you live in Leaford, your team's gotta be the Red Wings!) Ruby and Frankie commiserated about their grades. They both failed math and went to summer school nearly every year. I got straight As in every subject except math, where I got an A+. Still, I had to go to summer school with Ruby, who could not fathom functions or equations or algebra or geometry. When I groaned about it to Aunt Lovey, she'd said, "Ruby's going to summer school for the math, but you'll be learning a valuable lesson too, Rose."

I'd have stomped, if I were a stomper. "It's just not fair," I whined.

"Yep." She'd nodded. "That's the lesson."

Having learned that life wasn't always fair, and even less so for a girl attached to her sister, I took some comfort in knowing that Frankie Foyle would be at summer school and that Ruby and I could worship him from our pushed-together desks at the back of the room. Ruby insisted Frankie was disgusting, but I knew, the way I knew everything about Ruby, that she was infatuated with him too.

We were eager to accompany Uncle Stash and Aunt Lovey to the house on Chippewa Drive each Sunday afternoon, which is when they did maintenance inside and out. Uncle Stash raked the leaves, shoveled the snow, cut the grass, and watered the flowers while Aunt Lovey sat in the kitchen with Mrs. Foyle, pouring sympathy, drinking tea. Once in a while Frankie was home, dribbling his basketball idly in the driveway or lying facedown on the broken lounge chair in the backyard. (He had angry red pimples all over his back.) We spied on him from behind curtains. When Frankie came inside, we went out. We inhaled when he shifted, gasped when he moved, hoped he'd see us, died when he did.

Sometimes he wore gym shorts.

On one particular Saturday, we were to accompany our aunt and uncle to the Chippewa house to see about a leaky pipe that couldn't wait a day. Aunt Lovey thought it was something Frankie could have looked after. He was seventeen years old, after all. But Uncle Stash wanted to take care of the leak. After his heart attack, he'd taken a leave of absence from Vanderhagen's. But he hated being idle. He even, disastrously, took up golf. "I am only Slovak on whole golf course," he told us, winking. *"Hovno!"*

They were going to bring separate vehicles. Aunt Lovey would be getting groceries after what needed doing was done. Uncle Stash would drive himself home in the truck. I wanted to go with Uncle Stash. Ruby wanted to go with Aunt Lovey. It was always like that, and we laughed.

When we discovered that Frankie and his mother were not at home, we'd gone over to see Nonna, disappointed to find that she was gone too. (She'd gotten to the train station herself and rushed off to Windsor when her son, Nick, called to say he needed money.) Ruby and I wandered back to the rented house, entering unnoticed through the side door. I saw that the door to the basement, which was usually locked from one side or the other, was open a crack. We had never been down in the basement before. We were not under any circumstances allowed to go down in the basement. Here I saw a unique opportunity.

Ruby whispered, "No way, Rose," when I reached for the door but didn't object further when I pulled it open all the way. Her heart was thudding, and mine was too, because this was not a regular basement — this was where Frankie Foyle slept. And that's why we weren't allowed down.

Ruby and I knew about Frankie's basement room. Everyone at Leaford Collegiate knew about Frankie's room. It was a place of fable and legend where Frankie had sex with a married woman from Chatham, and French girls from across the river, and college girls home from Windsor and London for the weekend. It was where the senior boys got stoned and the cool kids pulled *all-nighters*. Frankie had a full bar with imported beer and liquor, a tray of glow-in-the-dark condoms, and a stereo system worth six thousand dollars.

Ruby and I didn't discuss it as we inched down the stairs, but decided that to see this room just once would be worth the consequences if we got caught. The truth is we never expected we'd get caught.

As I found the first stair with my foot, we were hit by a deadly stench. Ruby buried her nose in my neck. "Gross."

I can close my eyes and still smell the mingling of musk and skunk and mildew, an odor so pungent I felt it invade my pores. We'd forgotten to switch on the light at the top of the stairs, and halfway down it was too late. I made my way slowly, clutching the banister, relieved to reach the bottom. (Stairs are a challenge for Ruby and me — especially the narrow ones. We need to edge down sideways, plus, our situation prevents me from looking down at my feet, so navigating stairs in the dark can be frightening.)

It took a moment for our eyes to focus in the dim light from a small window over the furnace. There was a paint-spattered laundry basket full of dirty clothes on the floor near an old wringer washer. Beside the washer was a broken dryer, and on top of the dryer was a large plastic pitcher filled with amber fluid, which I mistook at first for gasoline. I lifted the pitcher and sniffed. Urine.

Beyond the washer and dryer was a room that we could see had been framed and drywalled, but not taped or painted. The room had a door, and the door had two locks. Secrets in. People out. Right now, the door was unlocked and open a crack. Ruby sneezed from the dust. I stopped, pinching her hard. We heard the sound of the screen door upstairs and the purr of the car starting up in the driveway. Then we heard the sound of the wrench on the pipes under the kitchen sink, and we knew Aunt Lovey had gone to get groceries while Uncle Stash continued with his plumbing.

We approached Frankie's room and, pushing the door wide open, stood blinking in the light from two high filthy windows. In the corner, on the damp cement floor, a blue bedspread snaked across a badly stained mattress. Next to the mattress was a stack of pornographic magazines, which kept company with a second plastic pitcher full of pee and a mountain of cigarette butts on a yolk-smeared bread plate. Across from the bed was a high-end vintage turntable, and two enormous speakers and several dozen vinyl albums in milk crates: Jimi Hendrix, Stevie Ray Vaughan, the Stones, David Bowie, the Clash. Ruby turned up her nose at the music, but I thought the albums were things of beauty. I sifted through them — *Ziggy Stardust,* and *London Calling,* and early Elvis Costello. I wondered if it was true that no compact disc could match the sound produced by that silver needle in the vinyl groove.

On one of the speakers there was a half-smoked marijuana joint beside a half-drunk bottle of Southern Comfort. This fabled room of Frankie Foyle's was really just a stinky boy's room. And it was really time to go.

There was another sound upstairs — a door opening. Then voices dripping through the floorboards.

I froze. Ruby began to buck as if I were her hesitant horse. (Something she does that I *hate.*) I pinched her.

"Boy," Uncle Stash said, and we knew he was talking to Frankie.

"Where's my mother?" Frankie Foyle demanded.

Uncle Stash did not like Frankie's tone. "I don't know where is your mother, *boy.*" We didn't hear any more words, just something that sounded like growling. Frankie had saved his life, but Uncle Stash didn't tolerate disrespect. Or maybe there was another dimension to their hostility that I didn't yet imagine.

The screen door banged open and screeched closed. We knew it was Uncle Stash who'd left. I didn't have to see Ruby's face. She was scared shitless. I moved toward the door. Ruby pressed against it slowly and gently. The door to the basement opened. We could barely breathe as Frankie's boots started clomping down the stairs.

We knew we couldn't hold the door shut. So we stood in the middle of the room. And waited.

In a moment the door was thrown open. And he was there, in the fading Saturday afternoon light, Frankie Foyle, shirtless, in green gym shorts. It occurred to me that his waist was so tapered it almost seemed girlish, and his hips so slender they were hardly hips at all. His gluteus muscles, hard and round, like half of a weight, like half of a wheel. There were dark curly hairs encircling his nipples, and a thatch of it beneath his belly button. Frankie Foyle was beautiful.

What a silhouette Ruby and I must have been, there against the glare from those high windows. Frankie reared back with a quick intake of breath and some words that sounded like "What-the-fuck?" He looked from my face to my sister's, his mouth hanging open, exposing his fine white teeth.

Ruby smiled at him and offered, "Hi," at the exact moment I raised my hand. (We feel like a freakin' sideshow. I can't *stand* it when we do that. Worse, I irrationally blame Ruby, who irrationally blames me.) It occurred to me that we were trespassing. What if he called the cops?

"We weren't gonna steal anything," I offered.

Frankie Foyle closed his mouth. His black eyes were red-rimmed and heavy. He moved past us into the room. I could smell his armpits. Burned pizza. I wondered if he was drunk or stoned or both.

"Our uncle was fixing the pipes," Ruby chirped. "We just came for the ride."

"In my bedroom?"

"What?"

"He was fixing the pipes in my bedroom?"

Ruby mistook his lack of menace for friendliness. "No," she laughed falsely. "In the *kitchen,* noodlehead."

"If I was you I wouldn't call anybody anything *head,*" Frankie said.

Ruby laughed hard, but I could feel tears in her chest.

I pinched her.

"Ouch!" Ruby cried and twisted a mole on my neck.

"Don't," I warned quietly.

Frankie gestured at the albums, which he could see had been moved. "Did you touch my music?"

"Well, *I* didn't touch them," my sister sang.

Frankie Foyle was looking straight at Ruby. "So why are you in my bedroom?"

Ruby's throat seized. And where seconds ago I'd been thinking, My sister's too stupid to live, I was now the mother bear and Ruby my threatened cub.

"Uncle Stash said to go down and look for leaks. We didn't know your bedroom was down here," I shot.

"*Everyone* knows my bedroom is down here." Frankie glared at me from behind his bangs.

"Well, we're not exactly everyone, in case you hadn't noticed, and we didn't know what everyone knew."

He seemed to have trouble processing what I said, then gave up altogether. He did not ask us to leave.

"Uncle Stash would probably help you finish it," I offered, gesturing at the bare walls. "Help you mud it and paint."

He grinned. "What are you, a contractor now?"

"I watched Uncle Stash do the drywall when he renovated the kitchen for Aunt Lovey."

"Don't tell him I got a room down here, all right?"

"I won't."

"He might make me tear it down."

"I won't," I repeated. "Anyway, he's just the landlord, not the cops."

Ruby laughed nervously. "Yeah, he's not the cops."

I pinched Ruby hard, again.

"Ouch!" Ruby twisted the mole on my neck, again.

"Don't," I warned quietly.

"You guys are freaking me out," Frankie said. He settled on the floor beside his stereo and began to sift through his albums. None of us spoke, which was fine with me, but Ruby couldn't bear the silence.

"Does your mom ever come down here?" Ruby asked, though

she already knew the answer. Ruby and I had overheard Aunt Lovey and Nonna wondering about Mrs. Foyle's new boyfriend from the Tim Hortons.

Frankie shrugged. "She's busy."

I shifted, feeling his loneliness. He didn't want us to go.

"My uncle might not come back for a while," I said.

"Your uncle can kiss my ass," he said.

Ruby grew quiet, but I laughed nervously. Then, to make my betrayal of Uncle Stash complete, I joked, "Uncle Stash might have benefited from a larger gene pool."

Neither Ruby nor Frankie understood the joke, but I felt bad anyway.

"You can hang out or whatever," Frankie said.

"Here?" I wasn't sure I wanted to stay in the basement, trapped by the layers of urine and cigarettes and another worse smell I wasn't sure of. "Did something die down here?"

Frankie roared with laughter.

I felt emboldened. "Seriously. It stinks really bad."

He stopped laughing. "I know," he said. "My weed is so fuckin' skunky." He opened a gym bag on the floor nearby and showed us several large plastic bags with dry bundles of olive-green pot.

"Wow. You gonna smoke all that?" Ruby breathed.

"Smoke some. Sell some."

I felt thrilled by the illicit gym bag and Frankie's nearness. "Can we sit on the bed?"

"Whatever."

Ruby and I settled down on the mattress, leaning against some pillows near the wall. I was grateful to rest my back. Frankie grabbed for the half-smoked marijuana joint we'd seen before and lit the end with a match. The smell of the skunk weed filled the room. He offered the joint to Ruby and me. We declined simultaneously, waving our hands in the exact same way, feeling once again like the worst kind of circus act. "We should go," I said, suddenly afraid of the smoke, afraid it would get into my clothes, my hair, infiltrate my mind. Aunt Lovey said drugs make you wild.

Frankie Foyle smiled. "You don't have to go. Shit, I bet you two don't do shit. You're not babies anymore."

"We do lots of shit," I said. "It's just, Aunt Lovey and Uncle Stash don't know where we are and I'm worried they'll worry." I was just being responsible. Wasn't I?

Frankie Foyle smiled again. "Come on, you can hang out for twenty minutes."

Ruby gushed, "Yeah, Rose, we can hang out for twenty minutes."

Ruby was right. We could hang out. I relaxed, and when Frankie passed me the bottle of Southern Comfort, I took it and drank a little, surprised how sweet the liquor tasted. I'd only ever had sips of Uncle Stash's cold Pilsners before. I liked the hard stuff better. Frankie offered the bottle to Ruby, but she would not, could not, drink the alcohol. She didn't want to vomit on the mattress where the object of our obsession laid his head.

"It's so, like, weird . . ." Frankie spoke through the smoke in his lungs. I noticed that he was making more eye contact with Ruby than me and felt jealous.

"It's so weird . . ." Frankie said again, holding the smoke in his lungs. "I've known you guys for so long that you don't really seem all that weird. And that's weird." He thought for a moment, then busted up with laughter. Finally he caught his breath. "Or maybe I'm just really fuckin' high."

"We're not weird," I whispered.

"That's what I'm saying."

"*That's* what he's saying, Rose."

"We're not weird. We just have a weird condition."

"I know."

"He *knows,* Rose! That's what he's *saying.*"

Frankie took a long swig from the bottle, then, like a big dog we'd had all our lives, he bounded from the floor to the bed. Ruby and I squealed as the mattress caved in and we three sank to the middle. Frankie grabbed a remote unit from the tangle of blue bedspread and aimed it at his stereo. The arm on the turntable lifted and found the groove with a click. Bob Dylan's "Knockin' on

Heaven's Door." I knew all the words. Frankie joined in, singing softly and soulfully. I sipped from the bottle of booze when Frankie passed it again. His knee was touching mine.

Ruby hated that Frankie Foyle was smiling at me. And that we were sharing the Southern Comfort. And the music. "Where'd you get that?" Ruby asked, gesturing at the leather bracelet tied around Frankie's wrist.

Frankie lifted his arm to admire the thing himself. "Goat leather."

"From a girl?" Ruby asked.

Frankie grunted.

"Is she pretty?" Ruby asked.

I pinched my sister as hard as I could, thinking she sounded like an idiot, worried that Frankie might send us away, but she didn't even flinch. Instead she blurted, "Do you think *I'm* pretty, Frankie?"

"You're a mutt," he said, laughing.

"Seriously," Ruby said.

I hummed beside her.

Frankie sat up a little, appraising her. "You're . . . I don't know . . . I mean, you'd be, you know, you'd be . . . if, you weren't like *that,* you'd be all right I guess."

I felt Ruby's blood rush to her cheeks. "Ya think?"

"Sure."

"If I wasn't like this?"

"Yeah."

"All right enough to kiss?" Ruby asked, shocking me, and herself (not to mention that Frankie Foyle couldn't have seen *that* coming). I glimpsed Frankie's distorted reflection in the smooth plastic lid of the turntable. His mouth was hanging open again.

"Well?"

"I don't know," he said. "I guess."

"Kiss me," Ruby said.

I had never met this bold sister, this brave Ruby, this sister who desired a kiss so badly she risked the cruelest of rejections.

"Fuck that." Frankie laughed.

"Afraid?" she taunted.

"Yeah, I'm afraid."

"You won't turn into a frog."

"What'll I turn into?"

"Kiss me and see."

There was a pause in which Ruby must have convinced Frankie with her eyes, or with her lips, or in some other mysterious way that women convince men to do surprising things because, in a moment, I heard a wet sound and knew that Frankie Foyle was kissing my twin sister. I felt sick from the booze, and the smoke, and the envy.

Frankie pulled away from Ruby's lips. "Too fuckin' weird," he said, swinging his head from side to side.

"Aren't I a good kisser?" Ruby was asking frankly.

"You're all right. It's just weird."

"Once more. Come on," Ruby said. "I won't tell."

Frankie Foyle gestured my way without actually looking at me. "What about her?"

I closed my eyes.

"She won't either. She *won't*," Ruby promised.

Bob Dylan sang. Frankie kissed Ruby. I could not see but only hear the sound of their kisses as the needle on the stereo arm popped and snapped with dust. They kissed as the next track played. They kissed and kissed as that song finished and another began. I could hear from within the sound of Ruby swallowing. I thought I could feel Frankie's tongue.

I wondered if Uncle Stash or Aunt Lovey had realized their mistake by now. I hoped they hadn't. I wanted Frankie Foyle to kiss me too and didn't want to miss my turn.

But Frankie didn't kiss me. My turn never came. Frankie kept kissing Ruby. Even when his fingers crept spiderlike onto my shoulder and dropped down inside my blouse to find the nipple of my right breast. And even when his hand slid lower, traversing my flat stomach and thighs. And even when he shifted me, because he wasn't quite comfortable, and even when he parted my long legs, Frankie kept kissing my sister.

And even when . . .

Even then.

I didn't protest. Neither did my sister. I believe we were struck by the strangeness of the moment. We've never discussed it directly, but the kissing must have been amazing for Ruby to have endured my part in the affair.

After. Shivering. Ashamed. I asked Frankie for a tissue.

"Use the bedspread," he said.

UNCLE STASH ARRIVED to find Ruby and me standing quietly by the living-room window. No harm done, he thought.

The following Monday, when Aunt Lovey was at the hospital, we found our seat on the bus. We had practiced how we'd say hello, casually, in different ways at different times. Frankie Foyle barely grunted and would not meet our eyes. We never spoke another word to each other. I hated his regret.

That's how it ended.

And yet, that wasn't the end.

It's Ruby writing.

At a time when Rose and I should be closer than ever, we're more distant than we've ever been. She's preoccupied by her writing. She also claims that I'm jealous of her book, and I can't deny that's true.

Rose thinks my jealousy is because her book takes her attention away from me, but that's not it at all. I'm jealous because I'm not a writer. Because I'm not anything. As the days and weeks race past I have this sinking feeling, like when I've heard a joke I didn't get, or spent a night watching a movie I didn't like, or done something the hard way that could have been done easy. What was the point?

We've danced around the subject of our birthday and we still haven't technically agreed on what to do, though I've convinced her to ditch the idea of getting drunk and at least agree to go out. I can let her decide about where to go because no matter where, I can have forgotten my purse at the library and I can bring her to the staff room and there it is. Surprise.

Roz is making that spinach dip you put in the hollowed-out bread. Whiffer's bringing drinks, which likely means a keg of draft beer and no-name cola, which I hate, but I don't want to insult him. All of this planning and preparation has been done with a series of notes from me to the guests and back, and it's been frustrating because I don't always get answers when I need them and I have to make up excuses about why I need to see this person or that person. I have not spoken one single word out loud about this party and it's killing me. I hope Rose appreciates all this trouble.

I asked for another thing of Tatranax because I like to change purses and I've left the house twice without my syringe.

I asked Rosie if we should go back to church. I think it's important that she connect with something on a spiritual level. Rose says that writing about her life is giving it meaning. I wish it was giving her hope.

I wonder if the fatigue I'm feeling is because of Rose's aneurysm.

Maybe I'm just tired because of planning the party.

I'll feel better when I get to work tomorrow. I always feel better at work. We've got a senior biology class from Leaford Collegiate coming in. They're learning about cell division, and we're the next case study. The teacher told me on the phone that the students had really enjoyed meeting a thalidomide man the week before. *A thalidomide man.* I bet he just loved being called that.

Last night I dreamed I was at a pig roast, like the one Aunt Poppy had before we left Michigan. In my dream Uncle Stash was turning the huge pig on the spit. He tore a few pieces from the sizzling pig and asked Rose and me if we wanted some crackle. Rose pointed at the spit, and I saw there was a baby turning over the fire, perfect and white, with big sad eyes, but Uncle Stash told us not to look and that it'll just kill him if we turn vegetarian. How's that for dream symbolism?

I know what people mean when they say they feel weighed down by guilt. I feel like that now. Heavy. When Rose lifts me she struggles and grunts like when she's doing free weights in physio. I think it used to be easier for her.

A long time ago we were examined by this famous brain doctor called Dr. Mau at this hospital in Philadelphia. I think Aunt Lovey and Uncle Stash were investigating the possibility of having us separated, but I don't really know that for sure. One of the interns there that day asked something about me and called me the parasitic twin, and Dr.

Mau was furious because that was not the correct term and the intern was obviously an idiot. There have been instances of parasitic twins, like this boy called Laloo, who had a pair of legs sticking out of his stomach, but that was not the case with Rose and me, as I am a whole person with a brain, and not just some appendage that only exists courtesy of my sibling.

I think we should make an appointment with Randy Togood, whom we went to Leaford Public School and Leaford Collegiate with, and who is a lawyer with an office near the library. We need to make a will. We're not the Rockefellers, but there'll be some money from the sale of the farm and the house on Chippewa. Nonna is in her eighties and she'd only leave it to her son, Nick, who is fifty-five and a pig, so forget that, but we have to leave it to someone. And, also, we should talk about what we want done with our remains.

Rose and I always talked openly about death when it wasn't just a few months away. It never mattered before that we could not agree on our remains. I want to be cremated. I like the thought of becoming smoke and floating in the air, returning on a raindrop or something. Rose thinks we should donate our bodies to science. She likes the idea of hanging in glass at the Mütter Museum, which is a thought that actually makes me sick to my stomach.

So we made some headway with the birthday plans, but Rose keeps putting me off when I want to talk about our arrangements. She keeps saying, When I'm done with the book, when I'm done with the book. When I reminded Rose that we could die tomorrow, she said we could not die tomorrow (and why would I want to curse us like that anyway?) because she still has hundreds of pages to write and hasn't even written the story of how Uncle Stash and Aunt Lovey met yet.

I'll just say that the story of how Uncle Stash and Aunt Lovey met is one of my favorite stories, but I don't get why it's in Rose's autobiography. She said the story of Aunt Lovey and Uncle Stash is a parallel to the story of her and me. And that our story doesn't even exist without theirs. And that I would know that stories about different people can exist together if I ever picked up a book that was about something other than Neutrals on the Thames.

If the book is torturing her so much, she should let it go. She said when the book is done, so is she. That kind of drama-queen stuff is really, really, really annoying. Also, how am I supposed to feel about that? When her book is done, so am I? And what about my contribution to all of this?

Rose says that leaving something artistic behind, like a story or a painting or a sculpture, is the closest thing you can get to immortality. I like to draw, but I don't see how a few lines on a page are going to make me feel better about dying. Still, you often hear about writers who have strangers begging them to write the story of their life (or at least to help them get published), so there must be something to it. Aunt Lovey used to say that everyone has a story to tell and that even ordinary people have wild things happen. Maybe she was right.

I wish Aunt Lovey was here. I miss her and Uncle Stash so much.

I am not enjoying the things I used to, like scrambled eggs with cheddar cheese or wearing my salmon-colored cashmere that Rose bought me last Christmas. When I ask myself what I'm living for, the answer is my sister. But Rose is so far away.

Yesterday I asked Rose if she ever felt bad about Mrs. Merkel. She acted like she didn't know what I was talking about. Bad about what with Mrs. Merkel? I reminded her how Larry Merkel's bike used to be in the Leaford Museum beside the huge pictures of us. I reminded her of the poem about Larry Merkel that she wrote for composition class and how Mrs. Merkel read it when it fell out of Rose's book bag when we went over to deliver the eggs.

After Mrs. Merkel read the poem, she looked at Rose like she'd stolen something. Then she folded the paper and put it in the pocket of her apron and said, This is mine.

Rose is one to stick up for herself, but she didn't know what to say, so I said, Well, it's Rose's poem, really, because Rose wrote it.

Mrs. Merkel stared at Rose, and she said really slow, as if Rose was an occupational student, she said, This is not yours. It is not yours.

Rose swallowed hard, then Mrs. Merkel started crying and Cyrus started barking and we left. Rose said she was okay, even though I knew she was shaken up. Then she made me recite the poem with her all the way home so she could remember it and write it down again. (I believe I must have said that poem 150 times, then many times after that, and even now the thing will not leave my head.)

Lawrence
I thought you'd find me over there,
when I was taken by the air,
flung against the earth awake,
where rocks engrave the silver lake.

Mother hear me I am nigh
and long to hear a lullaby.
Sing to me so I can dream
of dragons, knights, and soft ice cream.

Then bury me where I may rest
for here I am no longer guest
but ghost who wanders futilely
looking for my apple tree.

When Rose submitted it to the yearbook, she didn't sign her own name and she changed the title to something else. Rose and I did not agree on her submitting that poem to the yearbook. I thought, considering how Mrs. Merkel had reacted, she should have kept that poem to herself. She had at least twenty more poems in her scrapbook. She read them all to me at least once. But Rose said "Lawrence" was her best. I remember her saying Mrs. Merkel would never see it published in the yearbook, and, besides, she'd taken Larry's name from the title.

The day after the yearbooks came out, Larry Merkel's bike was stolen from the Leaford Museum. Everyone expected Mrs. Merkel to shatter because of it. Rose and I were the only ones who knew she was the thief. And we were the only ones who noticed that the huge rock under the apple tree had been moved and the earth dug up around it. Somehow we knew she'd moved the rock. Alone at night. And we admired her for that. She'd buried the bike under the apple tree. I always wondered if she thought Larry's spirit was speaking to her through Rose's poem. I'm not being sarcastic about that. I believe it.

Mrs. Merkel asked Uncle Stash to deliver the eggs from then on and we hardly ever saw her, except from a distance, out with her dog.

I was thinking about who would attend our funeral. Dr. Ruttle and Richie and his family. Nonna and Nick. Roz and Rupert. Whiffer and Lutie. I realized the birthday party guest list would be practically the same for the funeral. The Merkels would come to the funeral but not the birthday party. Crazy Berb Foyle would come. Berb's like that. Frankie Foyle? Would Frankie come? (Frankie moved to Toronto to be a cop after graduation, but I think he kept in touch with his dad.) Even though I imagine Berb would pass along the news, I doubt Frankie would come. Remember, he didn't know about Rose's baby, and I wouldn't be surprised if the thing that happened with us, which I'm sure Rose has gone into gory detail about, is a memory he'd sooner forget.

Our Michigan relations would likely just send an arrangement. And a chintzy arrangement, knowing them. We don't really have any close relations, except Rose's baby, of course. Taylor is around twelve now. Her name is only Taylor to Rose and me. To the people in her real world, she's whatever her adoptive parents named her. Hopefully it's something cute, like Courtney or Alisha.

She's not all that much younger than Rose was when she gave birth. (Aunt Lovey told Rose to go ahead and name her, though it was almost certain the adoptive parents would not choose to keep the name.) Rose named Taylor after our birth mother, which I think hurt Aunt Lovey, but you can understand not wanting to name a baby girl Lovey in this day and age. Aunt Lovey came from a family where girls were named after either flowers or places. Aunt Lovey was named after Livonia, Michigan. Her sisters' names were Poppy, Salle, Iris, and Daisy. Aunt Lovey's mother's name was Verbeena because the grandmother was addicted to Lemon Verbeena tea. (Rose said maybe she smoked it instead of drinking it.)

Aunt Lovey told a million stories about her mother, Verbeena, but in all of the stories she sounds more than just eccentric. She sounds like she was right off her rocker. Like, a long time ago when she was a young mother, Verbeena was trying to cure her second-oldest daughter (which is Aunt Lovey's sister Poppy) of fingernail biting. Poppy was around eight years old. Verbeena tried bitter herb paste on her fingers, and she even tried electrical tape on her fingernails, but nothing worked. She was going to ask the priest for advice one Sunday, but on their way to the church, Verbeena's father died. He was laid out in the parlor because that was the custom back then. Verbeena brought Poppy into the parlor to pay her respects to her grandfather, and while Poppy was standing there at the casket, Verbeena suddenly grabbed both the little girl's hands and stuffed them inside her own dead grandfather's mouth.

Poppy just shrugged when Rose and I asked if the story was true, like she didn't think what her mother did was so terrible. She said she never bit her fingernails again. Aunt Lovey used to say, What doesn't kill you makes you stronger, as if we didn't know.

I think Taylor is a cute name for a boy or girl.

We don't know who Taylor was adopted by, so we don't know where she lives. We went to stay with Aunt Poppy in Michigan so Rose could have the baby. No one in Leaford except Dr. Ruttle knew about the pregnancy. The adoption was arranged by Poppy's husband, who was Polish and worked at Ford. As far as we know, there are no records. Which Rose has probably already explained. Over the years Rose has talked about finding her daughter, but the part of her that doesn't want to must keep winning out. The part of her that knows it would completely flip out a preteen girl to learn that she's the daughter of one of the oldest surviving craniopagus twins. We talk about Taylor sometimes. Once I said, Wouldn't it be neat if Taylor grew up to be a writer like you? and Rose shocked me by saying, Maybe she'll grow up to be a singer like her Aunt Ruby. I like to sing, but I'm not a singer. Still, that was a sweet thing for my sister to say.

I never thought it was right that Rose didn't tell Frankie Foyle about the baby, but no one gave me a vote. Also, Aunt Lovey was dead set against Frankie's knowing, and she had the biggest influence of anyone. Rose has regrets, but I think she did the right thing. What kind of life could that little baby have had with us, especially with Rose only a kid herself? Aunt Lovey told us that God had a plan for Taylor, just like he had for us, which was to find the right parents, who were not always the birth parents. Rose knew in her heart that a family with a mother and a father, and brothers and sisters who were not conjoined, would be the best way for Taylor to grow up. I think her sacrifice showed a lot of courage and love. But you don't get over a loss like that. Maybe there are no losses you really get over. No matter how things play out in the end.

You

Stanislaus Darlensky was twenty-two years old, slender and movie-star handsome with a helmet of curly black hair, when his boat docked in Halifax in the summer of 1946. He, along with his mother and father, boarded a train bound west for Windsor, Ontario. In Windsor, the Darlensky family would have opportunities and a better life, and might begin to escape the unimaginable loss of Stash's two older brothers, who'd perished in the Grozovo mining disaster just six months earlier. The Darlenskys were to have their own apartment in a building owned by Mr. Lipsky, a family friend from the homeland. There was a job waiting for Stash's father as a meat cutter at a Slovak butcher shop downtown and an apprenticeship there for Stash too. The daughter of one of the church leaders (and, more important, a store owner), a raven-haired beauty by all accounts, had been tagged as a possible wife. There were many Slovak people in Windsor (that's why his father had chosen it), and they all wanted to help the Darlenskys.

The journey from Slovakia had been long, with frequent trials, and the ocean crossing hadn't been the worst of it. The trip from Halifax to Windsor, on a hot train with engine trouble, nearly killed his middle-aged parents. Gray and ill, not having eaten more than some dry black bread for two days, they had arrived at the station, disheartened to find there was no one to greet them. Stash was sent to the counter, since he knew the most English words, to inquire how they might get in touch with the relative, an uncle of his mother's, who was supposed to collect them.

Stash approached the counter, surprised to see a pretty blonde with a spray of freckles across her nose perspiring behind the wicket. The girl, who was about his age, was wearing a brown skirt and a yellow sweater so snug it made Stash warm. She was reading a book, licking the edge of a long thin straw, which she occasionally dipped into a glass of lemonade. In front of her sat a cookie on a cloth napkin. Young Stash, starving Stash, admittedly had as much interest in the cookie as the girl.

Leaning an elbow on the counter, Stash lifted the left corner of his mouth and narrowed his eyes, a somewhat menacing look, but one the girls in Grozovo had found irresistible. He waited for the pretty girl to look up, but so absorbed was the blonde in the book that she didn't notice Stash leaning there and was startled when he cleared his throat. She closed her book and looked at him, smiling broadly. "*You* gotta be *Stanislaus.*" (She'd even pronounced it correctly.) "Am I right? Am I saying your name right? But he said they call you something else."

Stash understood enough English to know that this girl was saying his name, and enough about facial expressions to be confused that she seemed to know him, when, of course, she did not. He nodded oafishly. "Stash. Me. I."

She saw how he was struggling with the language and spoke more slowly. "Well, your uncle — whose name I will not even attempt to say — has been here and gone and here, and at the moment he is gone again. He asked me to say that he would be back."

Stash liked this girl's confidence, and her curves.

She appraised the young foreigner, grinning. "Your uncle said there'd be a couple and a *boy.* I wouldn't exactly call you a boy."

He nodded, though he didn't understand, and glanced at the cookie on the napkin.

"It's got nuts. You want it?"

Stash took the proffered cookie and crammed it into his mouth, not wanting to let his mother see he'd taken food from a stranger.

"I like Pecan Sandies, which is what my Gram makes, but Gram's got the gallstones, so the neighbor lady did the baking this week and she made Wallys, which are fine and dandy if you like walnuts, which I don't."

Uncle Stash chewed and swallowed, having no idea what the blond vixen was saying but appreciating her smile and enjoying the quality of her voice. He wanted to hear more, but the swinging oak doors to the train station opened and his parents rushed to greet the miserly old man who hobbled in. "*Dobre den.* Thanks for coming. It's so good of you. You're so kind. We owe you so much," his parents gushed in Slovak, so grateful Stash wondered if they might drop to their knees and completely humiliate him in front of the blond girl.

The old Slovak man did not smile, but kissed Stash's mother on both cheeks and patted his father on the back. "That's your uncle," the girl said, crinkling her nose. "Guess you better go." She returned her attention to her book.

In the parking lot, the old Slovak uncle led the shrunken family to a shiny black Ford, which his mother and father quickly, effusively, pronounced the best car they had ever seen. Stash thought the car spectacular too, but didn't care to add his voice to the flurry of compliments. He climbed into the front passenger seat, hardly minding his mother's hand swatting the back of his head, hardly hearing her whisper, "Say, 'Thank you,' say, 'Thank you, Uncle.'" Stash prepared to drink in the New World.

The uncle didn't inquire about their awful trip, which was just as well because Stash didn't want to relive it through his mother's canned imagination. He cringed when his mother gestured at the busy city streets and sniped in Slovak, "The women here all paint their faces."

"What's that?" his father asked incredulously, pointing at the towering buildings across the wide black river.

"That's Detroit," the uncle answered in English. "Tiger base-ball." He took his hands off the steering wheel long enough to make a gesture of holding a baseball bat, then swung and clucked his tongue. "Another home run for Charlie Gehringer!" he said, show-ing off his North American accent. Then he launched into a sudden, surprising rant, not about Detroit or baseball, as Stash would have liked, but about how his youngest son wanted to abbreviate his Slo-vak name to something that sounded more English. (Uncle Stash would do the same thing within a few years, changing Darlensky to Darlen, an act for which his mother and father would have dis-owned him if he hadn't been their only surviving son.)

As they neared their destination, the Slovak neighborhood in the west end, Stash admired the two- and three-story brick houses with their sloping slate roofs, palaces compared to the squat stone huts they'd left in Grozovo. And there were hundreds of cars too, while in his hometown there had been just a dozen vehicles, and most of them trucks.

The Slovak uncle inched up to a stoplight. In the sleek auto next to them, three young men Stash's age laughed at some hilarious joke, then sped away, blasting the Ford with a plume of exhaust, fully intoxicating young Stanislaus. On the street, a group of young children were splashing in a spouting fountain, and a throng of beautiful, unescorted women poured out of a buzzing diner. Every-where there was activity. Everywhere there was laughter. And the stores, so many, with surprising and rich goods spilling onto the streets.

Soon the car stopped in front of a boxy, whitewashed, four-story building, and the Darlensky family was delivered to a mildew-scented basement apartment where a somber welcoming party awaited. Stash knew a few of the people, distant relations from Gro-zovo who'd immigrated before them, and those people he didn't know looked, and sounded, enough like relatives to fool him. Stash glanced around the smoky room, where everyone wore black be-cause, somewhere, someone they had loved was dead. He'd been hoping to see some more North American people, like the boys in the car and the blond girl from the train station, and not this gathering of taciturn crows. The food was a disappointment too, homey recipes from Grozovo: halushki and palacsinta and rice sausage, cabbage and more cabbage, when all he wanted was lemonade and another Walnut Wally.

A group of young Slovak men corralled Stash near the kitchen. They were contemptuous, like they resented having to break him in. The most arrogant of the boys, the one who'd been there longest and the son of the Slovak uncle, said with his excellent North American accent, "You wanna shot, Stash?"

Of course Stash didn't know what a "shot" was, gun or otherwise, and was surprised when one of the boys pressed a glass of clear fluid (three or even four ounces' worth) into his hand. He knew right away what it was. "Slivovitz?" It smelled like truck fuel. The boys nodded, waiting. Stash held the glass up, aware he was being tested. *"Nostrovia,"* he said, throwing the fluid into the back of his throat. When he finished, he restrained himself from holding both ears (something he later did to make Ruby and me laugh whenever he drank liquor. Just like he also said "whiskey" instead of "achoo" every time he sneezed).

The arrogant cousin stepped up again, overpronouncing, "Here we don't say *'Nostrovia.'* Here we say 'Down the hatch.'" The other boys laughed, and Stash, who did not understand the English words, could only assume that he was being ridiculed.

Woozy from the booze, young Stash lowered himself to a chair. He felt a lump at his back and reached around to find a baseball stuck between the cushions. Stash knew a little about the sport, though he'd never seen it played (in Grozovo they didn't play anything but soccer). He'd never held such a ball in his grip. The arrogant cousin happened to notice that Stash had the baseball. "That's my ball, chief," he said.

Suddenly afraid that his cousin would suggest he try a throw, or worse, a catch, Stash bolted from the chair, stumbling through the crowd, still clutching the baseball, moving from one cramped room to another, dizzy and not sure what he was looking for. He found his mother, arguing with a group of women over which of their husbands should go to the shop to buy more butter. (The women made their own sour cream and buttermilk, and some slaughtered chickens in the backyard, but a modern Slovak woman living in Windsor in the forties did *not* churn her own butter.) Stash volunteered, and his mother, informed by the other women that the shop was only a short distance down the road (and that the girl they were thinking of for Stash was working the counter that very afternoon), agreed to let him go.

On the street, alone, Stash began to further feel the effects of the double (triple?) shot of slivovitz. The sun was baking the top of his black head, and he wished he'd remembered to bring his hat. He wondered if he should find a place to sit down or turn around altogether. He was sober enough to understand that he had to walk toward the Detroit River, on the same road as the apartment building, cross two streets, and look for the shop on his left. But he was not sober enough, or perhaps he'd never be sober enough, to want to meet the girl these good Slovak strangers had decided he should marry. He remembered he still had the baseball in his hand only when it dropped to the dusty pavement and began to roll down a hill toward another street altogether.

Stash considered letting the ball go, then thought of how his arrogant cousin would mock him (and worse, in English) for his carelessness. Baseballs must be very costly. Maybe the cousin would expect compensation. His mother would be furious. This was no way to begin his new North American life. Stash ran after the baseball, which picked up speed as it rolled down the hill.

Dizzy from tracking the thing with his eyes, Stash nearly crashed headfirst to the pavement with each step. Finally he was on top of the ball and could pluck it from the ground. In leaning down, he stumbled, but recovered artfully. Feeling proud of his athleticism, enjoying the feel of the ball in his hand, young Stash was not paying attention when he stepped out from between two parked cars and was hit by a speeding bicycle.

The bike caught Stash on his left side and sent him crashing against a traffic sign standard, on which he smacked his forehead before falling to the concrete. The bicycle's rider gripped the hand brakes and skidded safely to a stop.

The bicycle rider was not hurt, but Stash was prostrate on the sidewalk, bleeding from his forehead and mouth. The bicycle rider, a young woman, rushed to his side, lifting his head to her lap, unconcerned that his blood might stain her skirt. Uncle Stash opened his eyes. His pupils dilated.

He had a nasty gash on his forehead and had bitten his tongue, but he was more drunk than hurt. Stash regarded the young woman on whom his head so comfortably rested — a pretty blonde with a spray of freckles wearing a yellow sweater so snug it made him warm. "You," he said.

"Me?" This pretty young girl was Aunt Lovey, riding home from her waitress job at the Bridge Diner.

"You," Uncle Stash repeated. He'd mistaken Aunt Lovey for the girl from the train station and thought that the coincidence of meeting her again, in this way, was serendipitous.

"Are you all right?" Lovey asked.

Stash took a moment to catch his breath and, looking into young Lovey's eyes, thinking she was someone she was not, said haltingly, using his best English accent, "I tink God vant bring us together."

Lovey, who'd never seen this handsome stranger in her life, was struck by the familiar way he was looking at her. She'd never, ever, heard God used in a pickup line before. She dabbed at the stranger's mouth with a hankie from her pocket. (She was going to be a nurse and liked the practice with blood.) "You smell like liquor," she said matter-of-factly.

Stash understood the English word "liquor." He nodded. "Slivovitz."

Aunt Lovey nodded back. "Same to you."

Stash raised himself up. The fall had sobered him a little, and after a moment he felt ready to stand. Aunt Lovey helped him to his feet, appraising him as he rose, thinking him swarthy and cute. She decided that she could overlook his foreignness but knew her father never would.

"You come from Windsor?" Stash queried politely.

"I'm from Leaford," she said. "My father's a Tremblay. My mom's a St. John. Verbeena St. John. She grew up on the other side of Chatham. Her father did sugar beets."

Stash nodded slowly.

"I'm staying at my Aunt Lily's for the summer. It's there." She pointed to a modest white clapboard house on the corner.

Stash realized he still had the baseball in his hand. "I am Slovak," he said, hoping to explain why his English wasn't good, and why he was in the middle of the street holding a baseball.

"I'm pleased to meet you, Slovak," she said, and curtsied to be cute. "I'm Lovonia Tremblay. I was born in Livonia, Michigan. But my father didn't want to name me Livonia because I'd have been called Livy, and he had an Aunt Olivia whom they called Livy, whom he despised, so they named me Lovonia. Just call me Lovey, though. Everyone calls me Lovey."

Stash smiled, impressed by the blond girl's confidence, just as he'd been at the train station.

Aunt Lovey returned his smile. "You like baseball? My Uncle Jerry goes over to Detroit to watch the Tigers play all the time. He has autographs from Stubby Overmire and Dizzy Trout and Pinky Higgins and Hoot Evers and Earl Webb and Cy Perkins and Goose Goslin and Charlie Gehringer and Steve Larkin."

Stash had understood only the first part. "Uncle Jerry go Detroit?"

"All the time." Her curls bounced as she nodded.

"Uncle Jerry have the boat?" He made a rowing gesture.

She giggled. "He drives the Dodge, of course. You're so cute."

"He drive the Dodge?"

"Sure. Across the bridge."

"I did not saw no bridge."

Lovey giggled again. "You don't know about the Ambassador Bridge? You really are cute. When did you come to Windsor?"

"Today."

"Today?"

"Now." Stash felt himself grinning stupidly.

"You're saying this is your first day in Windsor?" She screwed up her face. "And you're already drunk?!"

Stash nodded hard, his face mirroring her confusion.

"Well, anyway, I'm sorry I hit you with my bike. But you should have been looking where you were going. And" — she swung her hips a little — "if you want to come see Uncle Jerry's Tiger autographs, that there's the house." She pointed again at the white clapboard house on the corner.

"This one?" He pointed too, just to be sure.

She climbed up on her bike and headed for the house, turning once to make sure the handsome foreigner was watching, then again to call out, "If you come, don't say you're a Polack right off!"

Stash watched until Lovonia Tremblay had gone into the house, then hid behind the parked cars and vomited. Feeling better for relieving himself of the slivovitz, he set off to find the Slovak store, where he'd buy a cake of butter and tell the dark-haired girl behind the counter that he'd just met his future wife and her name was Lovey Tremblay.

Stash rose early the next day and ate a breakfast of cold palacsinta and blackberry jam. Then, with his parents arguing loudly in the bedroom, he opened the creaking door. He was closing the door when something hit his foot. The baseball from yesterday, which he'd completely forgotten about, rolled out after him. He picked the ball up, comforted by the feel of the stitching on his palm, and headed out to find the little white house on the corner and the pretty blond North American girl he believed God had sent to him.

That week, that first summer Stash was in North America, he found two of his best and most enduring loves, Lovonia Tremblay and baseball. Uncle Jerry would take him to Briggs Stadium when it became apparent he was serious in his intentions toward Lovey and appeared from the outset to be such a devoted Tigers fan, listening intently to all the older man's Tiger tales. He referred to

Stash, affectionately, as "the Polack," and just laughed when his niece tried to explain, as Stash had explained to her, that Poland and Czechoslovakia were completely separate countries with entirely different languages and customs. It would be several months before Uncle Jerry discovered how little English Stash really understood. It would also be several months before Stash would, having learned enough English words, and thinking she'd be amused, tell Lovey how he had mixed her up that first day in town with the girl from the train station. By that time they were already in love. By that time Aunt Lovey had moved back to Leaford, and Uncle Stash drove the family car from Windsor for dates on Saturday nights. By that time, Aunt Lovey's father had sealed the young lovers' fate by slamming his hand on the long pine table in the orange brick farmhouse and forbidding his daughter to marry that "no-good Polack."

I REMEMBER, WHEN I was young, asking Aunt Lovey how she could know the story of how she and Uncle Stash met, when she wasn't a witness to 90 percent of it. "Well, Stash told me most of it," she said. "And I filled some of it in, because I know him so well, and the rest, well . . ." She seemed to have uncovered this truth in the moment — "I guess I made it up."

It's Ruby.

I woke up last night to find Uncle Stash standing at the foot of my bed. He said everything was going to be fine, and he pulled the cover up over my legs. I knew it wasn't a dream because he was gone so fast my heart nearly stopped. And I had been cold, but then the blanket was on my legs and I couldn't have done that myself. I had that feeling of warm rain from Aunt Lovey's watering can as I drifted back to sleep.

Aunt Lovey and Uncle Stash haunt me. I know they haunt Rose too. She just uses different words to say she feels haunted. She'll talk about feeling sad all day, thinking about one of them or both of them. Or she'll play Uncle Stash's Ray Price tape over and over again. Or she'll say, Let's have a Slovak Night and make palacsinta. She'll write a sentimental poem about Aunt Lovey. Or a funny one about Uncle Stash.

Rose has written a lot of poems about grief. If she's writing a grief poem on a rainy day — watch out. I remember in one poem she called the drizzle dreary, and she got mad when I laughed about the dreary drizzle. Rose has never been good with criticism.

Lately, Rose's been frustrated by her writing. I don't understand why. She says she feels lost, like she's in a city she knows really well, trying to get to the street she's lived on all her life, but she keeps taking wrong paths and ending up back where she started. I don't understand that. She's writing the story of her life. How could she not know which way to go?

I don't feel frustrated from writing. Guess I just don't take it that seriously. I should write more often, though. It is a good way to make sense of the day.

So here's our typical day, leaving out the private stuff. We get to work by about ten-thirty. It's taking us slightly longer to get ready in the mornings. We take our various meds with juice. We eat something with fiber and get a taxi to work. Or Nick from next door drives us. I must admit he can be quite generous that way.

So, anyway, we go to work, we read to the kids, clean outdated notices off the bulletin board, that sort of thing, take a long break for lunch, usually resting on the big love seat in the staff room. Then we do more work, which sounds boring but it can really be a fun job. Then we go home. I like to cook, and Rose will eat just about anything except eggs. I draw the line at making two different meals. If Rose doesn't want what I'm making, she can make herself a peanut-butter sandwich. Tonight neither of us was very hungry, so we just made toast. Well, bagels, actually. And a bagel got stuck in the toaster and it burned like crazy. The First Alert went off, and Rose pulled the cord that releases the batteries, but one of them fell on her head, which stunned me, and must have really hurt her. Rose pulled the toaster cord out of the outlet and grabbed a knife and started stabbing the bagel that was stuck in the toaster. Pretty soon her knife started dragging up bits of wire and coil, and I knew we were never gonna use that toaster again. Rose realized she had ruined the toaster, so she threw the thing right through the screen door.

We were mad at each other because of the smell and the mess, and the huge hole in the screen door. We went to the living room, and Rose was reading and I was thinking about how mad I was that she ruined our toaster. Then we heard this scratching sound, so we got up to see if we had a mouse in the kitchen. Suddenly a pot crashed. Rose and

I were like, Holy shit! We went to the kitchen and opened the swinging door, and another pot crashed, and we looked on the stove and who's sitting there on the front burner but a squirrel. When the poor squirrel saw us, he started darting here and there, looking for the window, but all the mirrors confused him and he was just going crazy. Eventually he ended up in the cereal cupboard, and he's racing in circles and Raisin Bran is flying everywhere. Then, finally, he finds the hole in the screen door where Rose threw the toaster, which is how the squirrel got into the kitchen in the first place. Rose and I caught each other's expressions in the mirrors and burst out laughing. And we were laughing and laughing and we couldn't even catch our breath. After a while we stopped laughing and looked around at the mess. Then we just about cried. It took us two and a half hours to clean the kitchen. I blame Rosie's bad temper. Not the squirrel.

That wasn't a typical end to our day. But it was the end of this one. I'm sure Rose will write about it. Better than I just did.

It is a little more than two months since we got the diagnosis. Rose's headaches have been getting worse, but whatever pain reliever Dr. Singh put her on, it's not bothering me, and she's in slightly better spirits. Overall, our health is the same.

Rose asked me last night my opinion about contacting Aunt Poppy's daughters, Diane and Gail, and getting them to help us find Taylor, since they both still live in Michigan and we know the adoption was arranged there. We haven't stayed in touch with Aunt Lovey's family. Or really it's that they haven't stayed in touch with us. After the funeral, her sisters came back to the farmhouse for egg-salad sandwiches and left with a few mementos, taking the things with no regard for Rose and me. We wrote and phoned a few times after that, but they didn't return our calls. They pitied us but they never loved us, with the exception of Aunt Poppy maybe, but she died years ago, of ovarian cancer, which took her fast.

I don't think any of the relations in Michigan could help us find Taylor, and the truth is that, at this point, I don't think we should try. It's not that I don't understand how Rose feels. Of course she'd like to meet her daughter before she dies, but she must realize it's not the best thing for Taylor, or whatever her name really is. Rose even wondered about telling Frankie Foyle, who's a cop in Toronto with a wife and family, that he has a young daughter living somewhere in Michigan. Now she thinks he should know? Another case of What's the point? She thinks he could find her because he's on the police force. But I don't think he'd want to go down that road. I probably wouldn't if I were him. That's just being honest.

Of course I will do my best to try to talk her out of it, but if Rose really wants to try to find Taylor, I can't stop her. I do think it would be cruel, though. What would Rose say? Hi. I'm your mother. Rose Darlen. You might know me from the Internet. This woman attached to my head is your Aunt Ruby. We could die any day, so don't bother getting us tickets for your graduation. We just wanted to say Hi.

Still, there was this small part of me that fantasized about finding Taylor and having her show up at our surprise birthday party. Wouldn't that be amazing? Or maybe not.

Rose says that when she's writing, she tries to imagine that she's other people. When I imagine that I'm Taylor, I think I'd be split right in two. Half feeling so happy to meet my birth mother, and half wishing I hadn't, not because she's conjoined but because she's dying.

Anyway, Rose says it's ironic that I talk so much about the odds of this and that. Like I talked about the odds of publishing her book being slim, and the odds of finding Taylor even slimmer. She said the odds of twin girls not completely dividing is about the slimmest you can get, but here we are.

La Tranche

The summer we turned fourteen, Aunt Lovey and Uncle Stash took me to the zoo. It might sound strange, given my situation as a craniopagus twin, to say they took *me,* but the trip was mine. I'd gotten straight As in eighth grade. (Ruby had done poorly in school and was not putting forth her best effort.) The trip to the Detroit Zoo was a reward for me, just as the weekday ban on television was a restriction for Ruby.

We didn't (and don't) travel often. My sister's car sickness has made everyone think twice. Uncle Stash often worked weekends, and we had homework and summer school, and Aunt Lovey had her volunteering. Plus, there was the question of our comfort and safety in the backseat of the car, with the tangle of seat belts and the mountain of pillows Ruby sits on to level us out. We're high-maintenance travelers (though we do take the bus and the even roomier train with fair success), so our trips have been few but memorable.

I had always wanted to go to the Detroit Zoo. When I was a little girl, one of my favorite books in the Leaford Library was *A-nimal-Z.* The photographs in the book — the lion cub sniffing daisies, the wise silver wolf gazing beyond the horizon, the winsome bear lick-

ing her paw — had captivated me. I'd noted under many of the pictures a line that said "Courtesy of the Detroit Zoo," and I had
begged Uncle Stash and Aunt Lovey to take me there. Detroit
wasn't far away. We'd crossed the border on several occasions to go
to Hamtramck (a suburb of Detroit), which is where Aunt Lovey's
favorite sister, Poppy, lived, but the trip to the zoo had been put off.
Then it was made my reward for excellence in the eighth grade,
even though I hadn't looked at *A-nimal-Z* in years and had long
since outgrown my interest in the wolf or the bear.

Ruby tolerated two children's Dramamine tablets and slept the
full two-hour drive there. It wasn't really a two-hour drive, but Uncle Stash liked to take the long way, hugging the winding river road
near Chatham, where the homes were huge and the lawns tended,
and there were no cars on blocks in driveways or woodpiles in view
of the front porch. Then we'd cross the little bridge over the river
and pick up Number Two on our way to the border city. Along the
way Aunt Lovey would point out the sites of historical significance
because, as Ruby said, in Aunt Lovey's world a person was not allowed to breathe for more than thirty seconds without learning
something new or being reminded of a thing we already knew.

These are the kinds of things Aunt Lovey taught us back then,
when we were children in the car: the Neutral Indians who lived in
the county hundreds of years ago called the Thames River *"Eskinippsi,"* which translates to "deer's antlers," because of the way the
river curves and loops and winds around and comes back again.
Later, the French explorers called the wide, winding river *"La
Tranche,"* "the trench," because its banks were so steep and its magnificent trees — willow, chestnut, walnut, and birch — so lofty and
dense that it gave the French explorers the sense they were sailing
through a deep trench. *La Tranche.* (That would be a great last name
for a character — Monsieur LaTranche!) The land was swamp,
strewn with meadows of bergamot and thickets of trees, a refuge for
deer and raccoon, a distraction for rare migratory birds. Most of the
land where Ruby and I grew up was cleared by the earliest French
settlers from Quebec and Detroit.

There's a parcel of land on the road past the store where we would stop for Popsicles. We'd lick our treats (I got a space pop — Ruby always went for the cornet) while Aunt Lovey told us about the Oneida woman called Sally Ainse who fought for her right to keep 150 acres of land near the river and became one of the first settlers of the county. She had been a trader on the lakes. "A *woman*," Aunt Lovey would say, wagging her head in mock disbelief. "And a *Native* woman to boot."

"This community here," Aunt Lovey told us of the little village near the lake where we once drove to see a stock-car race, "was settled by fugitive slaves from the southern United States." The fact that some of the ancestors of those original settlers were still farming the land where their forebears had found freedom made Aunt Lovey shake her head all over again. "It just goes to show you," she'd say. Then, even though she'd told me a million times, she'd remind me, "As a point of interest, Rose, Fergie Jenkins's mother's people came to Chatham by way of the Underground Railroad."

I would sincerely, and unfailingly, respond, "Cool."

(Ferguson "Fergie" Jenkins was a phenomenal baseball player, a right-handed pitcher who threw fireballs and has a record of more than three thousand strikeouts. More than three thousand strikeouts! Anyone who knows baseball already knows that statistic, but you still want to let out a long, low whistle. Fergie pitched for the Phillies, the Rangers, the BoSox, and, best of all, the Chicago Cubs. Fergie Jenkins is the only Canadian in the Baseball Hall of Fame. How's that for a distinction? Fergie Jenkins is astonishing, and he is one of *us*. He lived and breathed this country air and trod these fields and walked these streets. And he was born just a ways from our old orange farmhouse. That just inspires the hell out of me.)

The roads we drove cut through lush acres of corn and beans, and gravel pits and scrap yards. We passed small red foxes chasing mice in meadows. Gaggles of geese skimming grass. One night, driving down a country road, catching a deer in our brights, Uncle Stash told the story of the forty-year-old father, a packer at Vanderhagen's, a German fellow everyone called Whitey because of his snowy white hair.

(Two years before, Whitey had chopped his left index finger off at the knuckle in an accident that was not work-related, but that's of no consequence to this particular story.) Whitey had been driving down a country road in the pouring rain when a large male deer leaped from the ditch and skidded onto the wet gravel. Whitey caught the deer's spindly legs on the bumper of his old Ford truck, unintentionally hoisting the beast up and rolling him onto the hood. The creature came crashing through the windshield, and Whitey saw a blur of fur and blood and antlers and glass. Then nothing. When Whitey came to, five or ten minutes after the collision, the rain had all but stopped. He felt a small deep gash on his forehead and was surprised to find that he was otherwise unhurt. He turned to look beside him where the deer had landed, ass-first in the passenger seat, front hooves on the dash like he was waiting at the drive-through, head back because it was taking too long. Whitey was about to laugh about the deer and how it had landed in his car looking so human and pissed off, but he suddenly remembered that he had not been driving alone. On closer examination, Whitey saw that his passenger, a petite young woman, remained strapped in her seat beneath the massive deer and was quite clearly dead. He tried to pull the dead animal off the dead woman, but the deer would not budge. Uncle Stash said that the moral of the story was, "Never drive in rain with mistress."

"What's 'mistress'?" Ruby asked.

Aunt Lovey had turned full circle to look at Ruby and me in the backseat. "A mistress is a woman who sleeps with a married man. A woman who has sexual relations with a married man." Her policy was, If you're old enough to ask the question you're old enough to be told the truth.

"What about a *man* who has sexual relations with a married woman?" I recall asking. "What's he called?"

Aunt Lovey had cleared her throat. "Depends. If he's married too, he's called an adulterer."

Uncle Stash pointed to his left at the restored Victorian house where the Doctors Ruttle had lived for generations. "Richie's building a new garage."

We passed orchards and ranches, and farmhouses like ours with orange brick edges worn by the wind. Those farmhouses seemed exotic from inside the car, just as the sky seemed bluer, and the sun larger, and the wind stronger, and the rain appeared not so much dismissed by the sky as drawn to the earth.

Uncle Stash had the opposite of lead foot, which would be what? Feather foot? He drove slowly, and he liked to stop at the historical markers on the side of the road, making Ruby or me read them out loud, twice if we stumbled a lot or if he was especially interested. Ruby learned the words on the marker about the famous Indian chief Tecumseh word for word. (She had this fantasy that we could be related to Tecumseh, but that's just because he was famous and she would love to have been famous, though not for being conjoined. Tecumseh was an Indian prophet who took sides with the British in the war against the Americans in 1812. He helped capture Detroit, but he was killed in Chatham in the great Battle of the Thames. There's a plaque in the park that Ruby used to like to grieve at, pretending he was our great-great-great-grandfather. Ruby could tell you more about Tecumseh.)

I liked it that, after twenty minutes or so of Uncle Stash's slow driving, Ruby usually fell asleep in the car and I could think my thoughts quietly and pretend to be alone.

Before that trip to the zoo, we'd crossed the border on exactly five previous occasions (one trip to the Henry Ford Museum and four visits to Aunt Poppy's in Hamtramck). I'd decided I much preferred the dark mile-long stretch of tunnel to the buzzing multilane Ambassador Bridge crossing, so in spite of its taking us out of our way, Uncle Stash always took the tunnel.

Uncle Stash pitched a few quarters into the metal mesh basket and, once the gate was lifted, drove from the hot white light of day into the black tunnel that joined Canada to America under the wide Detroit River. With Ruby asleep beside me, I listened to the purr of our tires on the smooth windless road and watched the pale yellow tiles rush by. At intervals I'd notice a tile was missing or a crack had formed, and thought I could detect the river dripping onto the passing cars. I worried that the weight of the water would collapse the tube altogether and we'd all be drowned.

(An aside: When I was a child I thought that the tunnel was suspended in the water like a large horizontal straw. I didn't learn until later that it was dug into the earth seventy-five feet under the mile-wide river. In high school I'd found a book about the tunnel on a field trip to the library, and I gave my oral book report on it that semester. Ruby did her oral on *Thirty Years of Barbie* and embarrassed herself by bringing her suitcase of Barbies from home as a visual aid. This is when we were sixteen years old. Amazing the things you remember. The tunnel was finished in 1930. President Herbert Hoover turned a key in Washington and bells rang on both sides of the border to mark the opening. The tunnel cost 23 million dollars and was finished a year ahead of schedule. I still look at that library book about the tunnel sometimes. I still look at the book from the Mütter Museum too. From time to time I read Beth's death scene in *Little Women,* and I still turn to the final page of *The Grapes of Wrath* and shiver with the last line about Rosasharn's mysterious smile. I feel, holding the books, accommodating their weight and breathing their dust, an abiding love. I trust them, in a way that I can't trust my computer, though I couldn't do without it. Books are matter. My books matter. What would I have done through these years without the Leaford Library and all its lovely books?)

Back to our story: As we emerged from the tunnel, Ruby woke with the sudden bright light, and I held the Tupperware tub so she could puke. Aunt Lovey covered the mess with a tight-fitting lid, prepared to clean it out in the parking lot later with a spray bottle full of bleachy water she'd brought from home. Such was our travel routine.

The huge border guard who loped out of the booth took our four passports in his big hands. (There had been some indecision on the part of the government as to whether Ruby and I should be issued two passports or one. Aunt Lovey had persuaded them we needed two by mailing a series of photographs that Uncle Stash had taken, some angles from my sister's side, and some from mine, and a note that read briefly, "Two girls. Two names. Two passports. If you please.")

Uncle Stash busied himself with a speck of dust on his dashboard. He would not look the border guard in the eye. Aunt Lovey said it was because Uncle Stash had bad memories of Slovakia. (So do I.)

Uncle Stash had not been born a Canadian citizen. He had an accent, and glinty eyes, and a bald head, and in his senior years looked like a perfect Russian villain, so the border guards were always suspicious of him. Add to this the fact that, in winter, he wore a black skullcap and that he always, always had a toothpick in his mouth, and you get the picture.

Uncle Stash had pulled his black cap off when the border guard asked sneeringly, "Where you off to today, chief?"

"The zoo."

"Zazoo?"

Uncle Stash stretched his lips over his teeth to overenunciate as he repeated, "The zoo."

Aunt Lovey was applying coral lipstick, praying into her compact mirror.

The border guard went on. "You carrying firearms?"

"No."

"Call him *sir*," Aunt Lovey whispered.

"No!" Uncle Stash responded.

"Beg your pardon, chief?"

"I was speaking to my wife."

"What's that, chief?"

"I was speaking to my wife."

"He was speaking to me, sir." Aunt Lovey smiled.

"You bringing any drugs into the United States?"

"No." Uncle Stash paused. "Sir."

"You bringing any plants or animals?"

"No, sir."

"You bringing —?"

"I'm bringing my daughters to the zoo. That's all."

At this the border guard closed Uncle Stash's passport. He opened the next, which was Ruby's, then he opened the next, which was mine. The head shots for the passports had been cropped, so that only the appropriate face appeared in each box. The brawny man leaned down and stared into the backseat. I saw his confusion. I felt his revulsion. I could tell Ruby thought he was cute.

The border guard straightened up and looked at the passport photos of me and my sister once more. He didn't say, "Drive on," the way the guards usually did. Instead he called one of his coworkers to have a look at the passports. The coworker, a small, thin black man, leaned down to look into the backseat. Ruby and I had already decided that she would smile politely, but I would not. The black man looked startled but did his best to smile back.

Uncle Stash grinned at the black man, who he knew would understand and appreciate his humor. "You caught me. Only one girl is real. The other is bomb." The small black man did not laugh. And neither did Aunt Lovey, when we were detained and questioned for a full two hours before we were given a warning about the serious crime of making jokes at the border, then sent on our way to the zoo.

The sun was hot that day, and I was sick. Waiting for Uncle Stash to finish his interview in the detention room, I'd rubbed my stomach and groaned, wondering if I was catching my sister's car sickness or, worse, her colitis. The Dramamine Aunt Lovey gave me had done nothing to help. I wanted chocolate from the vending machine, but Aunt Lovey claimed not to have change, and my sister and I were not yet in the habit of carrying our own money.

We went straight to the monkey cage. We'd seen the orangutans in the TV commercial for the zoo so many times we felt they were pets and expected them to know us too. The older female, the one who appeared to wave at the camera in the sixty-second TV spot, lounged on a log with her back to the glass. She wouldn't look at Ruby and me, not a glance, not a glimpse. Soon I felt myself wishing the rest of the zoo-goers felt the same lack of interest.

Next to the orangutan cage, two gibbon monkeys suddenly bounded out from an enclosure, one bouncing off the fence, then leaping at the glass, startling Ruby and me. We watched the young monkeys find a log, where they sat quietly, the little one grooming the larger one and snacking on the fleas. Disenchanted, we were about to leave when the larger one stood, stretched, squatted, and defecated directly beside his brother. Rather than feeling insulted, the smaller monkey began to paw at the poop, picking out whole seeds and, well, eating them. Aunt Lovey found the nature of their coexistence a marvelous thing. Uncle Stash compared it to politics.

The zoo was packed, and most of the animals were hiding in their little homes or sleeping under cool rock ledges in corners of their enclosures where we could barely see them. I had to wait several times for benches to become available so I could stop to take a rest. I kept shifting Ruby on my hip. Holding her too tight. I was hot and irritated. Aunt Lovey thought it might be heatstroke and scolded my sister and me for not wearing the stitched-together sun hat she'd made to match our outfits (our individual outfits — we never ever dress the same). I glared at anyone who dared stare for too long. Eating a frozen chocolate-covered banana made me feel somewhat better.

Ruby could not have known that the blood was mine, but I still can't quite forgive her for the way she screamed when we rose from the pine bench near the gorillas' cage and she saw the sticky red stain on the slats. "You sat in ketchup! You sat in ketchup!"

"Oh my," Aunt Lovey whispered, turning me around. "It's Aunt Flo, sweetie. It's your first visit from Aunt Flo." (The girls at school said "on the rag," but Aunt Lovey thought "Aunt Flo" sounded more genteel.)

When Ruby realized it was blood, my blood, from my first period, she fell quiet. Aunt Lovey accompanied us into the washroom, got a Kotex from the machine, dragged us into the large stall, and helped me stick the pad to my underwear. She smoothed my frizzing hair when I started to cry and said, "It's just hormones, sweetie. Menstruation doesn't hurt."

Aunt Lovey tied a sweater around my waist to hide the blood-stain on my tan shorts and said, "Well, welcome to womanhood,

Rose Darlen." Uncle Stash could not meet my eye. He patted my shoulder and muttered, "Sorry," as though it was his fault.

I was too miserable to appreciate the moment of transformation, and too aware of what I was to imagine my womanhood meant much more than further inconvenience. We watched an ailing tiger swat flies with his tail, then I asked quietly if we could go home.

Ruby cried in her dreams that night. I wanted to shake her awake and tell her that I'd give anything to be like her and have delinquent ovaries and never get my period, but it wasn't precisely true, and I said untrue things to Ruby only when I was sure she would believe them.

WITHIN FORTY-EIGHT hours of intercourse with Frankie Foyle, I knew I was pregnant. I awoke with a metallic taste in my mouth and a tingling in my breasts that was unlike the premenstrual tenderness I was used to. I sensed a fullness below my abdomen and an ache in my urethra. But most significantly, most vividly, I remember that my skin smelled different. A hint of mildew, a piss-sweet stink, something undercooked. Ruby noticed it too and asked me, "What have you been eating? You reek." I've read about other women who've experienced immediate recognition of pregnancy. How incredible it is to know that you have been occupied, in a most mysterious and sublime way. In my perfect youthful womb a perfect egg had joined with a perfect sperm and formed a cluster of beautiful cells, dividing completely to become a person who would be half me and half Frankie Foyle and all her own. A child who would not be joined to anyone but me, by a spongy cord and natural law.

I had imagined myself a mother many times in my private teenage fantasy life (not in the fantasies I shared with Ruby, though, because it would have hurt her). But I never, *never* pictured myself as a real mother, not like the ones Ruby and I watch in the library or at the grocery store, exhausted, harassed, peanut-butter and snot stains on their roomy errand clothes. My version of motherhood included upswept hair and white pants and perennial youth. I never expected to be a real mother. That is to say, I never expected to have intercourse. And I never expected to be pregnant. And I certainly never expected these two things to happen when I was only a teenager.

The nausea that plagued me in the first days disappeared, and during the first couple of months, it was easy to pretend that I was not profoundly changed. I began to write, each night, a letter to this perfect baby growing in my imperfect body whom I loved so well and deeply. Ruby punished me for writing, and for keeping a secret, by watching reruns and eating eggs, which were the only food whose odor I couldn't tolerate.

Initially I didn't gain much weight during the pregnancy, and hardly any that would have been noticeable in the first few months. But soon my sister began complaining about her difficulty in straddling my expanding middle, and sometime in my sixth month, Ruby glimpsed my body in one of the mirrors in the bathroom and, laughing, said, "I told you you're getting fat, Rose. God, you look pregnant!"

Ruby could not see my face in the mirror. There was a long pause.

I hid my face from the mirror's angles, knowing in that moment, as my sister made it real, that I would not, and could not, keep my baby.

I held Ruby's body tightly as she let go her grip on my neck. Slowly, leaning one leg on the edge of the vanity, she reached down to touch the swell of my womb. We found the other's reflection broken by the foggy mirror.

Where once we were two.

Now three.

Concentric Circles

Once a month, usually on a Sunday, Aunt Lovey would announce that it was Slovak Night, whereupon Ruby and I would stop what we were doing and follow her into the big steamy kitchen at the back of the old farmhouse. Uncle Stash would have already been put to work peeling potatoes at the long pine table or searing ham hocks in brown butter for Christmas Soup (an oily concoction made with sausage and barley that we — not Ruby — ate year-round). There would be the halushki to make (a dish of dumplings with cabbage and bacon and goat cheese). The cabbage rolls. Rice sausage. Horki. Apple strudel. And the palacsinta. We'd spend hours, our little family, together making the traditional Slovak dishes, which we kept in the freezer for nights when Aunt Lovey was working late at the hospital. We called them our "rations" and took their depletion seriously.

Ruby and I were in charge of the palacsinta, the Slovak version of crepes. We fried the thin eggy batter in a hot shallow pan, then spread the resulting pancake with a thin layer of black-currant jam and rolled it in the traditional way. The palacsinta weren't meant for the freezer. Instead, the little crepes sustained us while we cooked our Slovak freezer meals, in the thrall of one of Uncle Stash's stories (instead of Aunt Lovey's for a change). Nostalgic from the sauerkraut, Uncle Stash would talk about his boyhood village of Grozovo, describing the view from the church at the top of the hill, so that each time it seemed more wondrous and strange, like a place from one of Grimm's fairy tales. Uncle Stash talked endlessly about his cousins. Zuza had been the most beautiful, and Velika the best dancer. He talked about his cousin Marek, who was like a little brother. And Grigor and Milan, who were his boyhood chums. He told us all about the saints' days on the traditional Slovak calendar, St. Katarina, St. Ondrej, St. Lucia, and stories related to their superstitions, which we gobbled with our crepes. I could never remember if the Witches' Days began on the feast of St. Katarina or St. Lucia, and I couldn't keep straight which traditions made St. Ondrej's feast different from the others.

The fusion of cabbage and bacon, and our world and his. Even now, a whiff of paprika, and I'm transported to Slovak Night, licking jam from my fingers and listening to the story of how young Cousin Marek nearly drowned in the duck pond, weighted down, as he was, with pockets full of coal. Uncle Stash had saved the younger boy's life, dragging him from the water, pumping on his chest, and had basked in praise for the heroic deed. It was only when the village decided to hold a celebration to honor him that Uncle Stash's conscience stepped forward. It had been Uncle Stash's idea to steal the coal, after all, and to put the coal in Marek's pockets instead of his own, and his idea to swim across the pond too. He couldn't bear the guilt, and went to confess at the church on the hill. But Uncle Stash had forgotten that it was his grandmother's day to polish the pulpit, and when he finished telling the truth about what had happened at the pond, he drew the drapes of the confessional to find the old woman there, rag in her hand, rage in her eyes. She raised her arm and swatted Uncle Stash hard across the face, her hands so dry and rough he felt he'd been struck by five crooked asps. The priest didn't say a word. His grandmother, respecting the sanctity of the sacrament (though she'd eavesdropped on the confession), never told a soul the truth, and the celebration went on as planned. Uncle Stash ate all manner of sausage and too many pastries, and was sick for several days. He used to say that, if he looked hard enough, he could still see the imprint of his grandmother's hand.

One of my favorite stories, because it had mystery and intrigue (and no lessons in deceit), was about the time a man came to Uncle Stash's house wearing a military uniform and carrying a pistol. His mother let the man into the house and had a pleasant chat, then left Uncle Stash in the stranger's care while she went to fetch her husband. The stranger told Uncle Stash that he was his eldest brother and laughed when Uncle Stash insisted it couldn't be true. The man took his gun from its holster. "You want to hold it?" he asked casually. Uncle Stash nodded slowly. He took the gun from the man, stroking the black metal of the slim barrel. He'd dreamed all his young life of holding such a weapon. Uncle Stash raised the gun to his eye, steadying it on his forearm, the way he'd seen in pictures. But the stranger ruffled his hair, startling Uncle Stash, who pulled the trigger and fired out the window, which, thankfully, was open. Uncle Stash was paralyzed. The stranger cocked his ear and listened, waiting. But if the shot was heard by anyone nearby, it was ignored or credited to a hunter. Uncle Stash trembled, horrified, then thrilled. The man laughed, like a conspirator. The stranger took his pistol back from Uncle Stash and returned it to the holster. Glancing around, the man noticed the family Bible, the only book in the house, on a shelf above the stove. He picked the Bible off the shelf and looked through its pages. Glancing up at Uncle Stash, he grinned. An impulse appeared to strike him and he took from his pocket a fat roll of paper money (Slovak koruny), inserting the bills between the pages of the Old Testament, a few at first, then so many that the binding nearly ripped. Just as the man returned the Good Book to the shelf, the door opened and Uncle Stash's father appeared. He did not smile or embrace the stranger, or use the Slovak word for "son." Instead he began shouting and shaking his fists. The stranger cast his eyes down, not angry and not frightened, but something else. Uncle Stash couldn't bear his father's assault on the man who'd let him hold his gun, and he would have protested if the man hadn't turned on his heels and left. No one ever explained who the man was. It may have been his brother. Or not. When Uncle Stash gathered enough courage and had the opportunity to look in the Bible a day later, the money was gone. Poor as they were, Uncle Stash knew the koruny had been fed to the fire.

One day Uncle Stash's mother and father took him to visit the graves of his brothers in the cemetery. Then, with only a few relatives from the village aware of their plans, the Darlenskys climbed into the back of a wagon and set off for the airport at Kosice. Young Marek was supposed to go with the family to Canada, but, at the last moment, his drunken father had plucked him from the wagon, declaring he couldn't betray his homeland the way Uncle Stash was doing. Uncle Stash was heartsick, imagining he could hear the cries of his young cousin all the way down the mountain.

Slovak Night seemed as good a night as any to confess my pregnancy to my parents. Uncle Stash was stirring a pot of dumplings at the stove. Aunt Lovey was stuffing peppers at the long pine table. They looked up to see Ruby and me, struck by our grave faces.

Aunt Lovey sat behind her mountain of diced onions, quietly blaming herself, while Uncle Stash kept banging the pots and raging about the sicko, pervert, *hajzel, prdel, sračka,* who would do such a thing to his girls. Uncle Stash talked about killing the *kokot* bastard, while Aunt Lovey weighed the advantages of driving to see Mrs. Foyle over inviting Frankie and his mother to the farmhouse to discuss the matter. (No one mentioned Berb.)

I'd completely forgotten about Frankie Foyle. "He'll deny it," I said.

Aunt Lovey did not challenge me. Who would believe that a handsome young kid like Frankie Foyle would have sex with one (or was it both?) of The Girls? Aunt Lovey simply nodded several times and said, "We won't tell him."

Uncle Stash nodded faster, taking his wife's lead. "He will not ever know," Uncle Stash said. "The little *sračka* prick."

The matter of Frankie Foyle having been decided, Aunt Lovey

took a deep breath. "What do you want to do, then, Rose? You're nearly in your third trimester. You must have thought about what you want to do with the baby."

"I want to give the baby up for adoption," I whispered.

Aunt Lovey nodded, ignoring the quaver in my voice. "You're making the right decision."

"Okay."

"That is the greatest gift you could give that child, Rose."

"Okay."

"You're much too young to have a baby."

"I know."

"Your health is uncertain."

"I know."

"You're very courageous."

"Okay."

I felt Ruby tremble beside me.

Ruby was unexpectedly quiet about the whole thing, and though I don't officially believe in God (today), I'm thankful for the small mercy of my sister's silence about my baby and my choice.

Aunt Lovey didn't know, none of us knew, if what I was doing was the right thing. She knelt beside me, whispering close to my ear so Ruby couldn't hear. "But, Rose, if you want to keep the baby, I'll do anything to make sure that happens."

It hit me that Aunt Lovey was referring to a battle with the courts and child welfare agencies that might not consider a conjoined twin with elderly parents a suitable mother. I started to hum, and Aunt Lovey knew that I was gone, not physically of course, but that I had walked through a door and closed it behind me and could not be reached for comment. (Ruby has the same capacity to make a swift mental exit, and I've read about the phenomenon in other conjoined twins. Some people call it "wandering." It's a state of consciousness that is not quite here and not quite there, deeper than a daydream, not awake but not asleep. It is a technique Ruby and I discovered rather than learned, and I wonder if all people don't possess it in some measure. I've observed husbands wander from their wives while sitting thigh to thigh on the crowded Leaford bus. I saw a little boy wander while clutching his mother's hand, stabbing at a dead bird with a stick, though she'd said, "Stop it, Steven," eight times.) I wandered away a good deal after I told about my pregnancy because I couldn't bear the way Aunt Lovey was looking at me. And the way Uncle Stash was not.

Aunt Lovey let Uncle Stash have a pipe outside that night. Ruby and I quietly opened the window to let his Amphora Red smoke sneak into our bedroom. I listened to my uncle sniff, and exhale, and I knew he was crying, as men do, with hush and humiliation. I put my hand through the cloud of smoke that settled over my head. It was the nearest Uncle Stash and I ever came to talking about my baby.

IT WAS DECIDED that I could easily keep the pregnancy secret for another few weeks, until after Christmas, and then we'd make arrangements to go to Aunt Poppy's in Michigan for the final two months. Aunt Lovey would deliver the baby, and Aunt Poppy's husband knew someone from Ford who was looking to adopt a child. (The odds that my baby would have a birth defect were the same as those of the general population, but I had in the back of my mind, and still do, that my baby would not be average. In fact I'm quite sure that my daughter is extraordinary.)

Having been born, as Ruby and I were intended to be born, joined at the skull, we are normal to ourselves. It's normal for me and Ruby to be who we are and to live as we do. But being pregnant did not feel normal. For the first time in my life, I felt fully freakish and monstrously, hideously, deformed.

I remember my pregnancy in freeze-frame photos. There's the photograph of Ruby in her oversize navy blouse (which she wore in solidarity) and me in my stretched black pants and lime-green sweater set (from the plus-size department rather than maternity) hugging Nonna at her place on New Year's Day. I remember how Nonna kept touching my tummy, rubbing and thumping my bump, remarking on how fat I'd gotten, never suspecting I was expecting.

I was so afraid the baby was going to kick Nonna's hand and give her a heart attack. Nick was in jail that year. I remember Nonna crying because Nick had been wrongly accused of something unsaid (or unspeakable?). I remember Aunt Lovey crying too, and Nonna thinking it was empathy.

There's the photo Uncle Stash took the morning we left for Aunt Poppy's in Hamtramck. The fields were covered by a thick blanket of sharp white snow when we stepped outside. There were a few dozen crows in the distance, strutting on the icy crust. We were standing in the driveway waiting for the car to warm up. I was already having contractions then. Little tiny contractions, whose name I knew but have forgotten, preparing my uterus for the expulsion of this wondrous growth in my womb.

I'm not a vain person, not like my sister, and normally don't care how I look in pictures, but I hated to be photographed when I was pregnant. I was annoyed that Uncle Stash had insisted on going to fetch the camera before we left. Ruby and I froze as we watched Uncle Stash climb onto the picnic table to snap a picture of us two, careful to get the crows in the shot, saying that the crows in snow made the picture worth taking. I asked acidly why, if he wanted a picture of crows in snow, he'd made Ruby and me wait in the cold, to which he responded by muttering something in Slovak. When I saw the picture later, I had to admit it was interesting, with Ruby and me in the extreme foreground and the crows, sprinkled like pepper on a plate, in the back. I expected my face would look angry in the picture, or frustrated. Instead, I just look afraid.

There are many, many photographs of me, resting my new laptop computer on the hill of my pregnant stomach. (Aunt Lovey and Uncle Stash had discussed the wisdom of buying me the costly and rare computer. To Uncle Stash, it seemed like some sort of reward. But Aunt Lovey knew that writing would be my salvation.) I wrote a thousand poems when I was pregnant. Poems about connections, never feeling satisfied I had accurately described my delight and my horror, and my misery and my bliss, at the occupation of my body.

I shared the pregnancy with Ruby in surprising ways. She was affected by my hormones, of course, weepy and exhausted. She craved ketchup-flavored potato chips and black licorice, while I had no cravings at all. As my blood volume increased, so did hers, making her nose gush every time she sneezed, swelling her lips and other erogenous zones. One night I woke up because the bed was shaking. I was accustomed to night waking. Ruby shifts. I wake. Ruby snores. I wake. Ruby shivers. I kick the covers over her trembling legs. But on this night it was not Ruby's legs that were shaking, and she was not asleep. She was attempting to make the concentric circles I had described to her one night, when she'd tearfully questioned my disgusting new habit, and wondered why she never felt driven to do the same. Sex organs engorged with blood because of my pregnancy, Ruby had been awakened.

I encouraged my sister to put her hand over the mound of my stomach, to guess at the lumps: elbow, knee, tiny round bum. When the baby was moving, I guided her palm to the kicks. We talked to the baby, told her stories, and sang her songs. But I knew I would grieve, in a way Ruby could not, to lose this creature to whom I was mother.

I was content to be going to Aunt Poppy's to have the baby. We'd been to Hamtramck before for Tremblay family reunions, and I'd liked the way Aunt Poppy talked to Ruby and me separately, and the way she had gently grasped my shoulder when she leaned down to ask, "Are we having fun yet?" We would perch ourselves by a picnic table (me standing, Ruby balancing on her clubfeet so she didn't have to cling to me like an infant) and smile at the children shoved our way by pitying parents whose faces said, "There but for the grace of God go we."

Aunt Poppy was Aunt Lovey's favorite sister because they had both married Eastern European men against their French father's wishes and they'd both gone in for nursing. Aunt Poppy lived in a modest but sparkling new ranch-style house with an aboveground swimming pool in a neighborhood outlined by clean white curbs and putting-green lawns. She liked to tell stories too, especially stories about their mother, whom they referred to as "Mother," or even

"Verbeena," but never as "Mom" or "Mama." Aunt Poppy was not judgmental, but it was clear she thought I was doing the right thing giving up my baby.

Aunt Poppy's two daughters were grown and had children of their own. They lived a few miles on either side of Aunt Poppy in neighborhoods just like the one where they'd grown up, with husbands who worked at the Ford Plant alongside their aging fathers. The girls visited the house on several occasions in the time we were there, but never brought their husbands or kids. I understood that they didn't want to have to explain to their offspring how their conjoined teenage cousin, who was (thank God) no blood relation, had gotten herself in a family way.

Aunt Poppy's younger daughter, Diane, was beautiful, but Gail, the older girl, was homely, with a hawkish nose and jutting chin and hair that, like mine, tended to frizz. I thought we should have been friends, with all we had in common. But she and her sister stood apart from Ruby and me and looked at us too intently or not at all.

Aunt Poppy's husband, Uncle Yanno, was a frowning man with a floret of white hair at the top of his head and cheeks burned scarlet by his welding torch. He wore expensive fleece tracksuits and buffed his body on the rowing machine he kept on one side of the two-car garage. His biceps were poured concrete. He had no accent. Whatsoever.

When Uncle Yanno thought no one was looking, and even when he knew we were, he tickled the crack of Aunt Poppy's ass with his middle finger. She'd smack him hard, but she kind of seemed to like it, so I didn't understand when, one day, I overheard Aunt Poppy sobbing to Aunt Lovey about Uncle Yanno's much younger mistress.

Ruby and I slept in the back bedroom. Or, rather, Ruby slept. I shivered beside her, beneath two comforters, wondering why the forced air resisted the double grates in the room, though Uncle Yanno had checked it out twice. (It was the first and only time in our lives that I was the cold one.)

I ached from missing Uncle Stash. He crossed the border without incident (he claims) and came to see us at Aunt Poppy's three times a week, which I'd pouted about because I felt it was not often enough. Hurt and hormonally challenged, I'd suggested that if Ruby were the pregnant one, Uncle Stash would come every day. Aunt Lovey had sent me to my room for that. (Ingratitude was a grave sin in our world.) It was unbearably humiliating to be pregnant and sent to my room. Ruby, who had found my comment cruel and insensitive because she could not bear children at all, enjoyed my punishment, even if it meant her confinement too.

Our ground-floor room looked directly into the window of the adjoining garage. Ruby and I spied on Uncle Yanno on his rowing machine, tittering when he turned and caught us admiring him. We didn't talk with Uncle Yanno much but were conspirators in the game of look and hide. Livid with Aunt Lovey for sending me to my room, and annoyed with Ruby for perceiving her pain greater than mine, I looked out the window into the garage.

Uncle Yanno was there, as I'd hoped. He was dressed in his track pants and T-shirt, not sitting on his rowing machine but leaning against the garage's metal door, arms crossed. Ruby must have caught something move in her periphery. She shifted so that she could see Uncle Yanno too, and just as she did, Uncle Stash stepped into view. Maybe he had been there all along. Suddenly, without provocation (because Uncle Yanno did not move or speak), Uncle Stash rushed at the younger and fitter man, shoving him rudely. Uncle Yanno let himself be bounced against his own garage door and did not fight back, which was curious. Ruby and I both knew Uncle Yanno could have killed Uncle Stash if he wanted to.

When, later that night, I inquired about the nature of the fight between Uncle Stash and Uncle Yanno, Aunt Lovey told me I had enough to worry about. While she was helping Ruby and me bathe that evening (my girth had made washing extremely difficult), she reminded me how lucky I was to have Uncle Yanno's hospitality in this time of my great need. "It's not always good guys and bad guys, girls. It takes two to tango," she said. "You girls should understand that better than anyone."

I didn't understand. Not really. Not then.

"Well, I think Uncle Yanno's a bastard," I said.

"That so?"

"That's so. And I'm a good judge of character."

"A good judge?"

"I am," I said.

"Here's a riddle," Aunt Lovey began. "God says, 'Judge not.' So how can any judge be a *good* judge? Of character or anything else."

"Well, Uncle Stash hates him," I'd countered, loathing how she could so conveniently quote the smartest parts of the Bible.

"That goes back to the old country," she said, waving me off.

"Uncle Yanno knew Uncle Stash in Grozovo?" I asked, shocked that I'd never been told.

"No," Aunt Lovey answered. And somehow that sufficed.

Uncle Stash came less often after that, and he never stayed overnight. Each time he reached Hamtramck I sighed with relief, but his visits, much as we looked forward to them, made us fearful too. At first his weight loss gave us cause to applaud (Dr. Ruttle had been telling him to lose weight since long before his heart attack). But lean became slender and slender became gaunt and gaunt grew emaciated. Without Aunt Lovey, we saw that Uncle Stash wasn't eating anything at all. His teeth turned orange and his breath went foul. Of course he was smoking his pipe in the house. I think another month would have killed him.

(An aside: I have often wondered about the effect of Uncle Stash's job on his psyche. He slaughtered at Vanderhagen's longer than he should have. He was worried about our medical expenses, Ruby's and my future. So, for eight hours a day, five days a week, for decades, Uncle Stash was confined to a cold (or, God forbid, hot) antechamber where animal carcasses hung from hooks on a line. Scowling men. Clotted blood. Cigarette smoke. Glinting knives. Golden globules of fat making slippery the floor. My sister and I were not allowed in the slaughter room, but we'd glimpsed Uncle Stash there on occasion, through the smudged windows on the silver doors. He looked larger there, taller than he is, standing behind the massive wooden block wielding his cleaver. Holding the bloody leg of some poor creature, he would, in one quick motion, separate limb from body. Then he'd turn to hack at another joint, and chop at another, until the animal was body parts ready for Styrofoam and shrink-wrap. How awful it must have been for him to have been without his family for all that time we were in Hamtramck, and just the scowling men, and the dead animals, and his pipe to keep him company.)

Anxious as she was, Aunt Lovey was the only one who seemed certain that Uncle Stash would not die of starvation. "We're not long now," she'd say, patting my mound. "Any time, really."

I have not had full-blown insomnia since my pregnancy, so, on the rare occasion, like now, that I'm awake all night, too preoccupied or worried to sleep, I remember those nights in Hamtramck, listening to the neighbor's feet crunching through the snow at quarter past five. His old truck yawning to life, then warming up for five or ten while he made his mug of coffee for the drive. Then Uncle Yanno's van, not leaving early but returning late. The door creaking in the dark. Recriminations and denials from the kitchen. Aunt Lovey padding down the hall to dry her sister's tears. Ruby sleeping peacefully beside me as I looked out the window past the poofy gingham valance, nothing in view but the stars shivering in a cold black sky and a single leafless branch that broke off one night with the sudden weight of winter.

I couldn't imagine a life with my baby. I couldn't think of one without. I consoled myself that my baby and I would have something in common, in that neither of us would ever know our birth mothers. I called my baby Taylor (which I thought worked for a boy or girl).

So all that long winter month we spent cooped up at Aunt Poppy's, I thought about this book, this story of my life, which at that point was only half what it is now, and though I never put pen to paper, I thought of writing things down to help me understand my decision. Poetry. I did not know what else to do.

By the end of my pregnancy I was bedridden, and so was Ruby by proxy. I'd completely lost my sense of balance, and Ruby's legs could no longer straddle the balloon that was my waist. We spent that last month watching soap operas, eating cold noodle pudding and pierogies with grated cheese.

I had seen women give birth on television shows and in the films they showed in health class at school, but I'd never felt a contraction and had no idea when I had one that I was having my baby two weeks ahead of schedule. Aunt Lovey heard me cry out and hurried to the guest room. She and Aunt Poppy stripped the fancy spread from the bed and lay a protector (four plastic checkered tablecloths duct taped together) over the mattress. On top of the plastic they spread a floral print sheet. I was sure I recognized the floral sheet as the one that had been folded in the dog's bed, but Aunt Poppy denied it. Then, because I was somewhat hysterical, they took the thing away and spread out three beach towels that Aunt Poppy kept for her grandchildren on the narrow-for-us double bed.

Aunt Lovey had discussed with Ruby and me how difficult giving birth would be, primarily because I was about to surrender control of my body to the instincts of my unborn child and to the pain of labor and delivery. I would writhe. I would jerk. I would grunt. I would push. And so would Ruby. Therefore, because we risked serious injury to our necks and spinal columns, we needed an extra two people (nurse friends of Aunt Poppy whom we'd never met) to assist in the delivery. The nurses would help support us on the pillows, holding us level at the neck and shoulders to reduce our risk of injury, and Aunt Lovey and Aunt Poppy would attend to the birth. (Aunt Poppy had discovered that gently stretching the perineum with her index finger as the baby was crowning could greatly reduce tearing and the need for episiotomy.) Aunt Lovey had positioned one of the full-length mirrors so that Ruby and I could watch the birth.

The contractions came quickly, blistering pain that began in my lower back and radiated to my groin and thighs and up my spine to the base of my neck. "Back labor," Aunt Poppy said. "That's the worst."

There wasn't time for her nurse friends to drive all the way from

Oakland County, so Aunt Poppy called upon her daughters, who took their places reluctantly, cringing on either side of the bed. It would be their job to hold my legs apart and to ensure that Ruby's legs were out of the way. Lying in that bed with my knees up and spread, with five women encircling me, one of them attached to my head, I felt more afraid than I ever had before, and perfectly, utterly, alone.

"She wants some water, Diane," Ruby said. "She likes the bendy straw."

But I didn't want it and couldn't drink it when Diane put the straw to my lips.

Aunt Lovey had encouraged me, throughout my pregnancy, to read the books she'd brought home from the library (telling the staff she was teaching a class on obstetrics to some student nurses) about pregnancy and childbirth. I'd tried to read the books, randomly picking one or another from the stack, but those books were not written for women having babies. Those books were written for mothers. Of the few details I had read, I recalled a number — thirty-six — a story about a woman who'd had thirty-six hours of labor. The pain was exquisite. Too intense for tears. I could not survive thirty-six hours of such pain. My pain was killing Ruby too, I knew, though she couldn't feel it directly. She was confused. And helpless.

"Why isn't it coming?" Ruby cried to Aunt Lovey. "It's been nine hours!"

Aunt Lovey cleared her throat but didn't respond. She shared a look with Aunt Poppy.

"It hurts," I cried.

Ruby stroked the lobe of my ear and chanted *shh shh* over and over, like I was a toddler who needed a nap.

Aunt Lovey pushed Ruby's comforting hand away from my lobe. Then she leaned down, whispering in my ear, "You're going to do this, Rose Darlen. You need to concentrate. And you need to focus. Shut everything out. Can you do that?"

"I don't know," I cried.

"You've got to."

"Why?" I was afraid to do this alone.

"You have to, Rose. Shut me and Poppy and the cousins and Ruby, even Ruby, out of your mind."

"Okay."

"We'll be there when it counts, Rose. We'll be there when it matters, but for now you have to shut us out. You're not dilating, honey. It's not good."

"I can't control that," I whimpered.

"You *can*. You *have* to," she said, fighting to hold my gaze.

"I'll try," I whispered.

"Don't try, Rose. *Commit*," Aunt Lovey said.

"But —"

"Commit!"

I breathed through my next contraction.

"Picture your body, the baby inside. You know what you look like. You understand anatomically how you work. Your cervix isn't dilating and you need to dilate. Do you understand, Rose?"

"Yes."

"Imagine that your cervix is a flower bud."

"A flower bud."

"Visualize that bud opening, the petals unfolding. Spreading. Wider and wider and still wider. Visualize your beautiful baby emerging from the center of that perfect, open flower. Can you do that, Rose?"

"I can."

I did. And found myself amazed at what a person can will herself to do. My flower was a rose.

Ruby watched the baby crown in the full-length mirror. "Oh, Rose," she breathed. "Rose."

I listened to the commentary but couldn't watch my baby girl's head emerge with her thatch of auburn hair and her tiny angry face and her long kicking legs and balled-up fists. (That's how Ruby later described her to me.)

"A girl," Ruby sobbed. "Oh, my God." Aunt Lovey, still quietly in awe of birth, whispered, "She looks exactly like you." I wanted to scream and cry, until Aunt Poppy gushed, "She's just a perfect little princess," and I realized that Aunt Lovey meant that my daughter looked exactly like Ruby.

There was the sound of a ticking clock, and a kitten, but it wasn't a kitten, of course, it was my newborn baby's cry. Aunt Poppy cooed, "Hush, little one. Hush, little one."

I hadn't asked about the adoptive parents. I didn't want a portrait of them to carry around in my head. And I didn't look, even when Aunt Lovey said, "Rose, sweetie, it's your last chance to look," I didn't look.

"Aunt Poppy's taking the baby now. It's your last chance. Your *last chance,* Rosie."

"Taylor." I did not open my eyes.

"What's that, Rosie?"

"I'm naming her Taylor."

"Don't you want to hold her, Rose?"

"No."

"Rose?"

"No."

"You might —"

"No."

"You'll regret —"

"No."

I started to hum.

Ruby was utterly silent. I think she was pretending to sleep.

"All right." Aunt Lovey was crying. "All right, then."

Aunt Poppy and Aunt Lovey left the room. I don't know what became of the cousins. They certainly didn't stick around. Ruby was exhausted and drifted off to sleep. I waited until I heard the front door close and the car start up and back out of the driveway before I opened my eyes.

I took in the room as if I'd never seen it before. The flower pictures in white frames on the pale yellow walls. The shelf with the stacking babushka dolls lined up big to small. (I would never see that room again. Uncle Yanno left Aunt Poppy and she moved to an apartment close to her elder daughter. She died the following year of ovarian cancer.)

Aunt Lovey had given me a pill to stop my breasts from producing milk, but they were still hard and achy. I let my hand wander over my stomach, as I'd done a million times, stroking Taylor through my skin, declaring my love and rejoicing in my sin, shocked and alarmed to find the hump still there — not as large a hump, but a hump all the same — and it suddenly occurred to me there must be a second baby, a twin we'd somehow missed. I screamed for Aunt Lovey. Ruby woke up. I told Ruby about the hump and she began to cry. I knew my sister could not survive childbirth again.

Aunt Lovey raced into the room to find Ruby sobbing and me talking so fast she couldn't interpret. Finally she understood my fear that my womb, still big and hard and round and pushing my stomach out, held another baby.

"There's no twin, Rose," Aunt Lovey said sharply. Ruby stopped sobbing. I took a deep breath, for in all things medical I trusted and believed in Aunt Lovey. "It takes a while for the uterus to contract" — she demonstrated by clenching her fist — "from *this* back to *this*."

I was relieved, but dreamed that night that there really was a second baby. One my sister let me keep.

FOR THE NEXT few weeks I concentrated heavily on my physical pain because the other was so much worse. I tried to write, or rather rewrite, a poem called "Kiss." Even after all that had happened, I still wished Frankie Foyle had kissed me.

When I was walking well enough and able to carry my sister without risking a hemorrhage, Uncle Stash drove to Hamtramck to collect us. He was half the man we'd left in Leaford, wearing suspenders to hold up his too-big trousers. The flesh of his face had melted in those few final weeks. He looked old. And desiccated. I prayed for rain.

We eased into the backseat, Ruby fussing over her mound of pillows, I tired of being sore. It was early and I didn't want to go straight home to Leaford. Maybe I was afraid I'd see Frankie Foyle on the street and he'd suspect my secret if he saw my face, or maybe I just didn't want to go somewhere the same when I was so profoundly changed.

"Let's go to the zoo," I blurted.

Aunt Lovey and Uncle Stash did not respond right away. "What about if we go for Chinese in Windsor and head home?" Aunt Lovey asked hopefully.

"I don't want to go to the zoo," Ruby stated definitively, which made me furious. I was the injured party. *Me.*

"I *want* to go to the zoo."

Uncle Stash glanced at Aunt Lovey. "It's okay. We go to zoo."

Ruby pouted until the Dramamine kicked in.

The zoo was not crowded, and the day was not hot. We rode the train, which always gave me a thrill. I didn't care what animals we looked at, so Uncle Stash led the way. Bony and tired, he was so happy to be reunited with his family; he forgot we were not children and that I'd just given birth.

I didn't feel nostalgic about the orangutans. The polar bears left me cold. Watching amphibians in small glass enclosures in the wall, I wondered why I'd wanted to come at all. I thought the reason might reveal itself to me, the way reasons sometimes do. I ate a chocolate-covered frozen banana and felt somewhat better.

In the tunnel on the way home, I fell asleep. I dreamed that Ruby was clutching a pole and I was desperate to pull her away. I didn't know why I had to pull her away until I heard a splashing sound and saw that my baby was drowning in the bathtub, which I couldn't reach because Ruby was clutching the pole. I awoke with a start, to hear Uncle Stash saying, "Yes, sir. We just went for one day over to zoo for the day, sir," to the border guard on the Canadian side of the tunnel.

I have thought of my daughter every day since she was born. She is tall. She looks like Ruby. Beautiful, stylish, and original. Bit of a loner. In that awkward stage. Big reader. Smart. Athletic. Though of course Taylor will never know it, and I only just realized it myself, I am writing this book for her.

It's Ruby.

My sister's Red Wings choked this year. Whiffer and Rose were really counting on them to step it up in their final few games, but there you go. It was a disappointing end to an amazing season. (I don't care about sports so I'm being kinda sarcastic.)

The day after the Wings were knocked out, Whiffer came to work with a pennant for my sister. It was a souvenir from the game that he and his buddies were at the night before. Rose waved the flag like an idiot, and then, suddenly out of nowhere, she just started to sob. And she never cries. Even Whiffer said, God, Rose, it's only a game. Then he went on and on about how well the Pistons were doing in basketball. He said she needed to think positive.

I knew she wasn't crying about the hockey though. She was crying because it suddenly got to her the way it sometimes gets to me that she won't see another season or cheer another goal. You think about these words *final last never* a lot, and there are not many things, when you come right down to it, that you'll be happy to see the end of.

Whiffer promised Rose a long time ago that one day he'd take her (well, us, but her) to see a Red Wings game at Joe Louis Arena (which you can see from Windsor when you're standing on the bank of the Detroit River), but it never happened. I hated the idea of freezing my buns off in those uncomfortable seats anyway. Plus, what if they put the camera on us, and we showed up on the giant screen like some big joke? Something like that would kill Rose. It would have meant something to her, though, to see her Red Wings in person. It's too bad. (Now I'm not being sarcastic.)

Rose's second-favorite team, the Calgary Flames, made it to the finals but lost the Cup to Tampa Bay, which may or may not be because of a bad call by the referees in the game where a goal was not counted but, in the instant replay, you could tell for sure it was over the line. (Even I could see it was over the line!) I know it would have meant a lot to her to have one of her favorite teams win the Cup. Though I don't get why Calgary is her second-favorite team when it seems like it should be the Maple Leafs, because Toronto is closer than Calgary.

Rose says you choose your favorite team for proximity, but your second-favorite team can be anyone, as long as they're in your division or your country. She was getting emotional about the Flames bringing the Cup back to Canada. So I asked Rose where her national pride would be if her Detroit Red Wings were playing the Toronto Maple Leafs or the Edmonton Oilers. She said favorite-team loyalty, decided by proximity, presides over second-favorite-team loyalty, decided by country and division, so she'd still root for her Wings. That's how Rose explains it. But it still doesn't make sense to me.

Fair enough she was depressed about the hockey, but her Pistons are in the play-offs, and Whiffer says they're definitely gonna beat the Lakers because they've had solid leadership and coaching and they play like a team.

Yesterday Rose went on the Internet and found a list of celebrities who have had brain aneurysms and whatnot. She printed the list up and gave it to me. She hates talking about the aneurysm, so doing that was really quite a gesture. She acts like the aneurysm is hers, because it's in her brain, but the freakin' thing is gonna kill me too, so I say it's just as much mine. She still won't talk to me about future plans, and by that I mean the legal stuff. Basically, what happens to our money.

And our bodies. But I have to say that her giving me that list of celebrities just about made me cry.

Last week Rose and I were sitting on our big rocking chair on the porch and she started slapping at her legs, which was weird, and she said, God, these cucumbers are killing me. Cucumbers. She meant mosquitoes. Then yesterday she was pouring tea in her thermos for work, and I asked her the time and she said, Green. She tried to say something else, but it came out Blaymuth. Blaymuth. It's not even a word. I saw Rose in the mirror, and the look on her face upset me because it did not look like my sister. Rose is a person who never gets confused. When I asked her to tell me what was happening, she moved so I couldn't see her reflection. I said, Rose, please let me see you. But she took us right out of the kitchen and into the bedroom and got out her laptop with no regard for me. Like I was not even there. So we didn't speak to each other for about a day because I was so mad. And humiliated.

I have not been staying angry with Rose for as long as I used to, for obvious reasons. Eventually we started talking, and she admitted she's been having some weakness in her legs. It might be a sign that the aneurysm is getting bigger and putting more pressure on her brain. Our brains. Dr. Singh will say the same thing he says every time. It's getting bigger. We can't do anything.

It could be any moment, or you may still have a few days or weeks or months.

We joke about Dr. Singh a lot. I do his accent really well, but Rose says I shouldn't because it's racist.

Rose had this great idea that we should make a video for the kids at the library. It would be too sad to say good-bye, and what would we say anyway? We decided to tape ourselves reading some of the kids' favorite books instead.

I did *The Big Red Barn* and Rose did *Where the Wild Things Are* for the little kids. Then we did one of Rose's poems (which I drew hilarious pictures for). This is one we read to the grade threes and up, and they laugh like crazy. I would never tell Rose this, but I think it is one of her better poems.

(She'd hate me for that because it took her all of twenty minutes to write and she has taken hours and days to write shorter poems about more important things and she even took three weeks to write a six-line poem called "Kiss." But there you go.)

It's Not Snot
A little boy named Bobby Gadd
Was sent to bed for being bad.
His mother saw him once, then twice
Do a thing that isn't nice.
He stuffed his finger in his nose,
Found something that was not a rose
Then put it in his mouth he did!
His mother simply flipped her lid.
You just picked your nose! she said.
Bobby grinned and shook his head.
I saw you pick! I saw you chew!
I think just now you swallowed too!
Bobby! Son! Your gut will rot!
Don't worry, Mom. It's not snot.
Mother knew her boy had lied.
To your room right now! she cried.
The moral of the story is — Don't eat snot.

For the video, Rose read the poem while I flipped my drawings, which had dialogue bubbles for all the talking parts. We did it three times because Rose stumbled over some of the words, even though she knows them by heart. At the very end of the tape we say good-bye, but in a see-you-tomorrow kind of way instead of a forever kind of way. I asked Rose if she wanted to make a tape for anyone else, but she doesn't.

She is happy that Nick Todino is driving us to see Dr. Singh in Toronto tomorrow. I'd sooner go by bus, but Rose is worried about making bathroom stops and whatever. Last week my sister lost her balance (which is happening more and more and is obviously causing us concern) when we went to see Nonna, who doesn't usually recognize us now and doesn't always seem to understand that we are two girls. Anyway, Nick caught Rose and me and helped us to the couch. Even though he complained about how heavy we were, I guess it was still nice of him not to just let us fall. There are some people who would have panicked and been afraid to touch us. That's just how it is. Still, I'm not big on Nick. I think it's partially because his son Ryan tried to drown us when we were kids. That's a hard thing to forgive.

Our birthday is five weeks away. Today, which is June, was one of those strange days when the sun shines on one side of the street and it rains on the other. First there was no wind at all, then suddenly the sheers were blowing in the living room and a million green spinners were falling from the maple tree out back, and Rose and I had to hurry outside to get the garbage-can lid before it blew over to Todinos' and put it back on tight so the squirrels don't get into it later. If the squirrels do get at the garbage, then we have to ask Nick to come and clean it up for us, which is embarrassing, plus, I hate it when we have to ask Nick for favors. He's been living with Nonna for about five years. Uncle Stash and Aunt Lovey died before they ever met him, which still seems weird to me because it seems like Nick's been around forever. He has a second family in Windsor that he's court-ordered to stay away from. Nonna was happy when Nick got a job driving delivery for the Oakwood Bakery in Chatham, because that meant he wasn't a total loser, but he got fired the first day for having beer in the bread truck — which proved he was. That happened years ago, and I don't believe he's looked for another job to this day. He says he's on disability.

I've been writing my invitations on my yellow legal pad, so Rosie thinks I'm writing chapters for the book. I think I'm freaking her out a little, about how fast and how much I'm writing. I've put the invitations in little envelopes and given them to the guests when she's not paying attention. It is quite fun being sneaky, but I wish I'd done this surprise party thing years ago when there was no aneurysm and no worry that all this planning might be pointless. I've already paid for the cake, and Nonna has seven dozen meatballs in her freezer. Whiffer's bringing his stereo from home and a bunch of Rosie's favorite CDs.

Even if we don't make it to our birthday, people should dance.

I'm not much on traveling because I get really bad car sickness almost every time I get into a moving vehicle. Even watching television, certain shots of movement can make me dizzy. Rose has probably already written reams about how I've ruined a million opportunities because I don't travel well. I have tried sucking gingerroot and wearing acupressure wristbands, but nothing works. We went on a few family trips when we were kids, like to the zoo and to Aunt Poppy's in Hamtramck and to Niagara Falls, and the big one to Slovakia. And quite a few trips to the doctor too. But it was a big deal to get around because of my tricky tummy. It still is a big deal. We're going to the archaeology museum in London, though. Even if it kills me.

Uncle Stash used to drive to Ohio to visit his mother once a year. The drive was too much for me, so Rose and I couldn't go, and Aunt Lovey wouldn't leave us in anyone else's care. So Uncle Stash went alone. We had never met Mother Darlensky, though, technically, she was our only living grandmother.

Then one day Uncle Stash's mother called and said she was dying and wanted to see Uncle Stash one last time. Aunt Lovey said they'd been getting calls for twenty-five years about how Mother Darlensky had this fatal illness or that fatal illness and it never turned out to be anything. But Uncle Stash believed it. And he said that even if his mother didn't have a fatal illness, she probably was dying of old age and misery.

Aunt Lovey said we couldn't drive all the way to Ohio, which would have meant seven hours in the car for me and Rose, so Uncle Stash sent his mother bus fare to Chatham. She said she couldn't come because she was too sick, then she changed her mind, and there we were, on the way to pick her up at the bus depot — which was really a gas station/convenience store near the mall in Chatham.

Aunt Lovey and Uncle Stash had a big fight because Uncle Stash said we shouldn't call his mother Gramma, but the Slovak word, *Stara Mama.* And then he said that his mother should sit in the front seat because she was sick and old, which Aunt Lovey didn't seem very sympathetic about. Especially considering she spent most of her life as a nurse.

Aunt Lovey looked shocked when Mrs. Darlensky got off the bus because she really did look sick. She had thin white hair at the sides of her head and not much at all on the top. She was tiny and bony, and she wheezed when she climbed down the steps of the bus. I thought Uncle Stash would give her a big hug, but they didn't touch at all. Not even hands. He said something about her not looking very well, and she said something to him in Slovak that made him hide his eyes. Aunt Lovey had said, Hello, Mother Darlensky, we're so pleased you can finally meet our daughters. And then Rose and I stepped forward. We were probably smiling the same way at the same time, and we hate when we do that because it makes us feel stupid. Uncle Stash's mother looked scared.

Uncle Stash had sent his mother our school pictures each year and he sent the pictures that he took himself too, the ones he snapped with the huge lenses. The pictures Uncle Stash took were the best and looked the most like us, but I guess seeing us in person can be intense. Mrs. Darlensky fanned herself with her hands and said some Slovak words I'd never heard Uncle Stash say before, so I knew they were not swearwords, and she asked to sit down in the car.

Aunt Lovey took Mrs. Darlensky's elbow and helped her to the car and held the front door, like she'd never questioned that Uncle Stash's mother should sit there.

Mrs. Darlensky turned to look at us in the backseat and shook her head. Then she looked at Uncle Stash and said some more words in Slovak, but Uncle Stash acted like he hadn't heard a thing.

Oh, shit. The phone just rang. It's after ten o'clock!

Oh my God! Whiffer just called! He just about blew the whole surprise party!!! Rose answered because she had the remote phone on her side. She was shocked it was Whiffer because he's never called before. Let alone at ten o'clock!

Thank God he recognized her voice right away. He made up some lame excuse about wanting to borrow one of her CDs, but I'm worried now that she's gonna think he's interested in her, and I don't think Rose needs to deal with a broken heart with all the other stuff we have going on.

I'm too tired to keep writing. I don't know how Rose does it, but I'm starting to understand why.

Summer

Nonna used to make a pie that she called *"Quattro Stagione"* (four seasons). It was divided into four segments, separated by a crisscrossed pastry wall, and filled with seasonal representations. Strawberries for spring. Peaches for summer. Apples for fall. And black-currant preserves for winter. I always chose spring. The strawberries. Ruby went for the preserves.

Spring used to be my favorite season, but we hardly have spring anymore. Once there was a pause between the shiver of the crocus and the forsythia spray and the shy purple lilac and the chestnut bouquet. Now they shove and jostle in some rude rush to summer.

We are dying.

Ruby has already told you this. I know, because I know Ruby. I imagine it's the first sentence she wrote on the yellow legal pad I gave her. Knowing Ruby, she wouldn't have considered how to present that crucial bit of information about her main characters. Ruby's not a writer. She can afford to be honest, but I can't imagine beginning with such a confession. Wouldn't you be afraid to read on? To be left, bereft, by people you might grow to love, or like, or who you're just sort of curious about? Or maybe that's exactly how I should have begun.

Chapter One
We are dying. So are you. Some of you may even know it.

I have an aneurysm. A wall in a vein, in my brain, has stretched and ballooned, and is getting larger, and will eventually burst. My sister and I are going to die because of this aneurysm. This will happen tonight when I'm flossing my teeth. Or Wednesday afternoon, while Ruby is reading a Caldecott book to the kids. Or in two and a half months, on a sticky-hot afternoon when all I want to do is lose myself in John Irving while Ruby watches her TV. There won't be any miracle. The aneurysm isn't going away. But I hope it can contain itself for a while. Until our effects are sorted out. Until this book is done. Until, from our quiet place, in the lane beneath the window, we have the chance to listen once more to the Senior Chorus at Holy Cross and their glorious harmonies at Christmas.

My headaches have been getting worse. My vision is occasionally blurred, and I've had some weakness in my legs. There's a bizarre hallucination episode that I haven't told anyone about yet, but for a dying person I'm feeling surprisingly okay.

The aneurysm is inoperable. We've had three opinions on this matter. I have no wish to discuss the details, except to say that I've found some poetry in the medical language: saccular, fusiform, communicating artery, subarachnoid hemorrhage, pulsatile tinnitus ipsilateral, neoplasmic, granuloma, proteinaceous.

I am fearful that I'll lose control of my body. I'm terrified that I'll lose control of my mind. And through all of it I'm horrified to have to take Ruby with me when I go. And vexed and perplexed by her calm.

I've been struggling with the structure of this book. Originally I wanted to move onward from birth in the telling of my life story (*our* life story — maybe Ruby's right) and not mention my death until the end, or not at all, as if, like most people, I hadn't expected it and couldn't have known it was near. But the song of my past has been so altered — not the sequence of notes, exactly, but the pitch — that I find I can't go on writing about my past without sharing my present with you. Along with my fears. And my regrets. And my delight that you've cared to read this far.

I can't say exactly why I've chosen to write about the particular things I'm writing about. There are doubtless better stories from my life that I'm missing, events and escapades I'm not wise enough to know were important. If heaven is tolerant and writers are allowed (bunch of liars though they are), I wonder if they gather for coffee to ponder the prose they should have written instead.

MY BIZARRE HALLUCINATION occurred last week when Ruby and I were at Nonna's, next door. (I've never had a hallucination before, but, like a first orgasm, you know when it's the real deal.) I've been tiring more easily lately and I've lost a little weight. I'm often dizzy and I'm uncomfortable just standing still. Ruby has lost weight too but feels heavier than she ever has before.

I was leaning against the sofa watching Nonna watching *Coronation Street,* wondering how our dear Italian gramma could possibly understand what the characters were saying in their thick British accents, when I felt the heat of Nick Todino's body. I moved my eyes (by this time you know I can't swivel my head) too quickly, and the room began to spin. I felt blood rushing through my veins, a prickle in my brain. I was suddenly gripped by panic, reckoning that the aneurysm had erupted. The hot feeling spread through my head and made my lips wet and quivery. My hands and feet burned like spice does on the tongue.

My fear was such that I could not speak, though I wanted desperately to call out for Ruby. Not to warn her, though. I'll confess that my instinct at that moment was purely selfish. I wanted to tell Ruby I was going, so I didn't have to die alone.

I closed my eyes briefly, listening to my heart, somewhat shocked by its continued beating. I recalled that Dr. Singh had said that when my thing bursts, I will lose consciousness instantly, and I realized that I wasn't dying after all. I opened my eyes, surprised to see something moving in my periphery. And even more surprised to find that it was Ruby, coming down the hall. The hallucination was more brief than I could ever describe it; a flash frame from a day-dream. I can't remember the details of what she was wearing or the expression on her face, only that she was there without me and that it seemed perfectly natural. I felt myself slip away again. Quickly. Like a jump in the lake. Or from sleep to awake. Then, at the end of my nose I saw the dark curly hairs on Nick's strong forearm and I realized that I'd fainted, and fallen, and that he'd caught us. (Nick has offered to drive us to Toronto to see Dr. Singh again. He's al-ready driven us twice and says it's no big deal. He hates Toronto, so it *is* quite a big deal. He complains about the people and the traffic and the eight bucks an hour for hospital parking, even though Ruby and I pay for it! He remained sober the entire day last time and sat with us in the waiting room instead of his car. He read fashion mag-azines because there was nothing else. I found that sort of charming. On the way home we talked about the Pistons. He likes basketball better than hockey. He's in his fifties.)

UNCLE STASH MADE an oversize rocking chair for us when we moved from the farm to the bungalow. The callous winters on the porch have warped the soft pine, but there's a comforting dip when you rock forward and a little bump when you rock back. The chair seems to whisper, My Girls, My Girls, My Girls, as it dips and bumps. On summer evenings we like to rock until the mosquitoes invade. (They devour me, but they leave Ruby alone. Strange. Also strange is the fact that when Ruby eats asparagus, her pee has no smell of it.) The Chippewa Drive neighbors wave to us rocking on the porch, but they don't intrude. We say we like it that way, but I think both Ruby and I would like a little intruding. It would be nice to chat with the neighbors sometimes, especially now that Nonna's so out of it, and Nick (because of, or in spite of, his past) isn't much of a talker, or maybe he just doesn't trust us. The rocking chair makes Ruby drowsy. I feel the shift in her breathing and the heaviness of her body as her grip relaxes on my shoulder and she falls away from the world. The weight of wonder. The weight of worry. I hum some secret place into being, thinking of this other me, the one that only I can see, a girl called She, who is not We, a girl who I will never be.

One night last week we rocked and rocked, but Ruby did not fall asleep. The wind coming in from Mitchell's Bay grew cool. And rising from the rooftops, a black cloud to shroud the remainder of the day. Leaves shivered as lightning tore the sky to the east, and thunder crashed above us. My body vibrated with the violent eruption, in unison with Ruby's. We didn't speak of going inside. Neither of us made a move. Or a sound. Were we even breathing? Rain battered the porch's metal roof and quickly made rapids of the rocks in the garden. We were scared shitless. There was a moment of silence and stillness, then a gust of wind so strong it blew the lid off the garbage at the curb and threw us back in the rocking chair. I had the strangest sense that the tornado was coming, the very tornado that brought us, like he'd just realized it was all a big mistake. Still, we didn't leave the porch, or move at all, like animals afraid to be seen. The wind shook the curtains of rain as though it suspected we were hiding there. Furious it was, then frustrated, and gone.

The rain stopped and the clouds dispersed, and we watched the sun sink behind the Indian Crescent bungalows. We continued to rock as stars peered through the night, then we carefully left the front porch, inching across the short wet grass to retrieve the lid from our garbage can. In leaning to lift the lid, which I then hoisted up (using my leg like a winch the way I do), I got dizzy again, but not enough to faint or fall (or to have another hallucination), just dizzy enough to lose my place, like when you close a book by accident and have to flip through the pages to find your spot. In my moment of dizziness, I thought of Aunt Lovey and her mother, Verbeena, and the story of the wedding dress. I don't know why it came to me then. But I thought I should write it out because I know it means something.

The Story of the Wedding Dress

A long time ago, before Aunt Lovey even met Uncle Stash, Aunt Lovey's mother, Verbeena, was asked to sew a wedding gown for the mayor of Leaford's daughter. It was a wonderful opportunity for the skilled seamstress since the most important people in Baldoon County were invited to the wedding, and everyone would know who had sewn the bride's gown. Verbeena decided to ignore the mayor's daughter's reputation as a spoiled brat and happily took the job.

Verbeena quickly discovered that the mayor's daughter was worse than her reputation. Simpleminded and mean and impossible to please. To make matters worse, Verbeena'd made a tactical error in accepting payment early and buying the costly fabric herself out of the lump-sum fee. The bride had chosen snow-white satin, which any woman knows should never hang on any but the trimmest and straightest of forms (which the girl did not have), and with each fitting it seemed that the bride had added another five pounds to her hips, which meant a thousand stitches to rip and resew, but there were also the complicated alterations that required additional lengths of fabric. By the time of the wedding, Verbeena was paying richly to make the awful girl's gown.

Aunt Lovey, just a teenager then, had fondled the satin fabric as her mother cursed its slippery nature and tsked over the bride's excessive choice of one hundred pearl buttons down the back. The day before the wedding, Verbeena was blushing with pride. The dress was spectacular, and she knew the nasty bride could not help but be thrilled when she came by the farmhouse for her final fitting. But the mayor's daughter was not thrilled with the dress. She had grown fatter yet (on *what* is anyone's guess), and not one of the hundred buttons could be closed on the fitted satin bodice. The bride was furious. She threatened to sue the seamstress in court until Verbeena, sobbing, promised she could fix the dress.

Verbeena left the fat bride at the door and drove the farm truck to the dry-goods store in Leaford. But when she got there, she found not one scrap of white satin left on the fabric bolt. Verbeena felt dizzy and nearly fainted, but when she looked down she saw a beautiful spool of antique lace, which she bought on credit from the sympathetic shopkeeper. She went home to the farmhouse, sequestering herself in her sewing room with a pair of sharp scissors, the spool of lace, and a pot of mint tea, telling the children to slice ham for their supper and to remind their father to check the pump before bed.

Verbeena was still in her room when the rest of the family went to sleep. Aunt Lovey stopped to say good night, but Verbeena did not respond. When Aunt Lovey woke the following morning, she went to the door of her mother's sewing room. She listened, then knocked three times. And a louder knock. There was no answer. She opened the door and found her poor mother slumped in her sewing chair with three yards of white satin crumpled on her lap. Aunt Lovey shook her mother awake, aghast to see three huge bloodstains and what looked like a shriveled pink worm on the made-over bodice of the wedding gown. Aunt Lovey followed the blood trail from the dress, up to her mother's apron, and bosom, then all the way to her cleft chin. Gently urging Verbeena's lips apart, she found her mother's badly bitten tongue. Verbeena'd had seizures before, and Aunt Lovey knew she'd survive, even with a chunk out of her tongue. The dress, however, was ruined.

When the bride arrived unexpectedly early the morning of her wedding (there was no phone in the farmhouse back then), Aunt Lovey could not stop her at the door. She found Verbeena clutching the gown, saw the bloodstained satin, and screamed so shrilly she caused Verbeena to seize again. The mayor's daughter left the house cursing like a sailor. It was said she had to wear a wedding gown borrowed from the obese church organist. (And the gown must have been very ugly too, because there was no picture of the bride in the social pages of the *Leaford Mirror* and no description whatsoever of the dress.)

Needless to say, Verbeena was never hired to sew anything again, but after taking the bloodstained panels out of the bodice of the gown, she was able to make it over for Aunt Lovey's wedding to Uncle Stash a few years later. Aunt Lovey would never have had so beautiful and costly a gown, with a hundred pearl buttons down the back, if the mayor's daughter hadn't gotten so fat.

RUBY ASKED ME last night what will happen to these chapters, these pages and pages floating in my hard drive, and all Ruby's scribbles on her legal pad, if we die before the book's done. I explained that nothing would happen to the chapters because the chapters would never be read. Until it's completely done, I won't show this thing to a soul. (Whiffer's cousin is dating a guy, who's dating a guy who works in the publishing business in New York City. Whiffer is also a writer and has been complimentary about some of the poems I've shown him. He asked if he could use one of my poems called "Patty's Cake" as the lyrics for a song he's been working on. Whiffer's cousin's friend's friend read some of Whiffer's short stories and said he needed to find his voice. Currently, Whiffer's working on a screenplay. I don't think *Autobiography of a*

Conjoined Twin is the right title for this book, but I don't know what else to call it.)

OUR BIRTHDAY IS in three weeks. I know about the surprise party. All the notes passed back and forth — what did Ruby think I'd think? Did she really think I wouldn't notice? (Of course I'll act surprised, and she'll *never* know I knew.) I can think of many things I'd rather do for our birthday, though. In fact, I hate the idea of a surprise party. I know Ruby just means to be sweet. Ruby never expected to turn thirty, but I have expected to beat the odds. And I don't just want to make it to my surprise party. I want to live to see Christmas and Easter and spring and summer all over again.

Maybe I'm superstitious. I find that I'm reluctant to talk about what to do with our stuff, and I've been especially indisposed to discussing our effects and remains. I fear that once these things have been decided, my body will just quit. I have this strange sense that the thing in my brain has a mind of its own, and I imagine it's vindictive too. I don't want to make it angry. I don't want it to know I have my ducks in a row. I don't want it to think I'm ready to go.

I'm not.

Remains

I've been watching Ruby sort through her things, grouping and piling and discarding and wrapping and labeling. She calls these things her effects, which I find unnecessarily dramatic. (I don't understand her choices — why in the hell would she leave a bally old pink scarf to Roz? And does Rupert really want her VHS movie collection?) It reminds me of when we moved from the farmhouse to the bungalow on Chippewa Drive the summer after we returned from Slovakia. Uncle Stash had hurt his knee badly and was having trouble getting around. It was clear, watching Uncle Stash hobble on his cane, that we could not endure another winter on the farm. Frankie Foyle and his mother had relocated to Toronto, and suitable tenants had yet to be found for the bungalow. The time was right for a move to Chippewa Drive.

We were in the middle of a heat wave that August. The old windowsills in the orange farmhouse could not have withstood the weight of an air conditioner even if we'd had the resources to buy one. Between my overactive sweat glands and Ruby's colitis, we were miserable. Aunt Lovey'd come into the room (knocking first because she respected our privacy), handed us a box, and told us that we could not take everything with us to the compact little bungalow and that we had to be ruthless. She'd opened our closet. "Purge."

When Ruby and I complained that we couldn't possibly find a whole boxful of things to throw out, Aunt Lovey laughed and said, "Oh no, my funny girls, the box is for the things you want to *take*. I have five more boxes for the things you have to throw out."

Ruby and I labored that deadly hot afternoon over what to keep and what to chuck, arguing viciously about the value of this, the importance of that. Even when our quarrel became loud and physical (we pinched each other), Aunt Lovey did not intervene. As she knew we would, we grew weary from fighting and tired of our task. Our treasures became so burdensome that, in the end, we didn't even *fill* the box we'd labeled "things to take." My composition books. Ruby's maps and sketches of her artifact finds on the farm. Ruby and I noted that Aunt Lovey was not in the least ruthless with her own possessions. She didn't at any time consider her enormous collection of books to be dispensable. She packed them up lovingly, dusting each frayed jacket, promising herself to read each one again, though she never would — not one.

There were all kinds of benefits to living in town. From Chippewa Drive, Ruby and I could walk to the library and to downtown Leaford, and the city bus would take us anywhere else we could possibly want to go (though it would take some time before Ruby and I could fully appreciate our new independence). Our first day in town, Aunt Lovey walked us over to Brekkie Break, which was the unofficial head office for Leaford Transit. She introduced us to the drivers drinking coffee at the counter. (*That* wasn't embarrassing.) Then she bought us a day pass, gave us a Leaford route map, and said, "Be back by five-thirty or I will never let you out of my sight again." Ruby had been too excited to get motion sickness that day as we rode every route on the map, barely making it back to the bungalow for our curfew.

On Chippewa Drive we were steps away from Mrs. Todino, in case of emergencies (hers or ours). Flood or fire, we could be reached in time.

Before we moved, as much for himself as for me, Uncle Stash took a sledgehammer to the unfinished walls that had framed Frankie Foyle's basement room. On nights when I can't sleep, I lie in my bed, Ruby purring beside me, thinking of what happened that afternoon in the basement room. The smell of skunk weed begins to seep through the floorboards, and I taste sweet booze on the roof of my mouth. I close my eyes and watch Frankie Foyle shiver and shudder and arch like a cat — Do all men do that? — wondering what a relief such a release might be. I think of the moment Frankie abruptly stopped kissing my sister, and I thought he might kiss me. And when he didn't, how Ruby had quietly tugged the lobe of my ear, saying in the gesture that she loved me and that everything was going to be all right.

Many times in the years since Aunt Lovey and Uncle Stash passed away, I've considered that Ruby and I should sell the bungalow and get an apartment in the building next door to the library. I've been troubled by too many memories and that phantom smell of skunk. (I think of Taylor, the product of my brief union with Frankie, and wonder where she is now and what she's like. In spite of Ruby's insistence that it would be selfish and cruel, I want to meet my daughter before I die. Yet even as I write those words, I'm not sure it's right to even try to find her. How's that for confusion? I had an e-mail from Cousin Gail in Hamtramck today saying she doesn't know anything and can't help me, but I'm not sure I believe her.) There wouldn't be much sense in leaving the bungalow now, with so precious little time left. And what if Taylor came looking for me here? What if, by some miracle, she discovered her parentage and wanted to see me? What if she missed me by a day or an hour? You read about things like that happening. You read about things like that all the time. (Not in fiction books, though, where such coincidences would be sloppy writing.)

When we first moved to the city, I hated the sameness of the cinder-block homes, the awful squared-up gardens, the nosy neighbors (except Nonna, of course). There were no wildflowers on Chippewa Drive. No orchids. Or bergamot. No wild strawberries or yellow pimpernel. But I've come to appreciate the subtle shades of difference, the way people state their uniqueness with splotches of color, split-rail fences, garden gnomes, and craft-show mailboxes. I miss my wildflowers, but I've trained some gorgeous fluted ivy to climb up the bricks around the living-room window. And there's the trellis of pale yellow roses on the wall that faces Nonna's. (Aunt Lovey showed me how to pinch off the dead heads, a chore in which I find great satisfaction.)

Back then, after high school graduation, I'd been sad to leave the orange farmhouse. I'd miss the long pine table, and mourn the crumbling walls, and long for the corn and the creek and my childhood and Larry Merkel. My sister and I didn't talk about Larry so much then. He was a playmate we'd outgrown. But he sat like a lump in our throats as we packed up our box on that heat-wave summer day and prepared to say good-bye. We waited near the apple tree in the driveway for Uncle Stash to come around with the car. When Ruby asked if I thought Larry was there, I told her I didn't believe in ghosts anymore (I was twenty years old) and I didn't kid myself that Larry was alive. The truth is, I couldn't deny I felt him watching us from behind the goldenrod and through the black eyes of the crows. Ruby and I whispered good-bye out loud. I insisted we keep the little red fire truck (the one we'd found the day that Ryan Todino baptized us in the creek) instead of bringing it to Cathy Merkel. Ruby imagined the toy might bring her comfort. I was certain it would only revive her grief. And, selfishly, I didn't want to make that trip to Merkels' cottage, through the field and along the creek and over the little bridge. I didn't want that particular journey to be the last we took on the farm. There's a memory associated with that trip. A memory that I've managed to ignore most of my life. I saw something. And never told a soul — not even Ruby. I couldn't explain, and have never fully understood what I saw. Like most things unfathomable, I don't think about it much.

One day, on a trip to bring the eggs when Ruby and I were still in grade school — so we were just around twelve or thirteen years old — Ruby asked Mrs. Merkel if she thought Larry missed his blue bike. (To put this in context, Mrs. Merkel often spoke of Larry to us. She would talk about how Larry loved blackberry jam or how Larry was a natural on skates or how he could write his own name — first and last. She'd even shown us a picture he'd colored for her and signed on the back with two backward Rs.)

I saw immediately that Ruby had done the wrong thing asking Mrs. Merkel about Larry's missing his bike. Mrs. Merkel stood very still for a very long time, sorrow deepening the lines on her forehead. Her eyes were filled with the reflection of Ruby and me and the unmistakable flicker of revulsion. I've never exactly been fleet-footed, and I was wondering how I might dodge around the table if she raised her arm to strike Ruby or me, because it looked like she wanted to. But Cathy Merkel didn't raise her arm. Instead, she sank to a chair and said, "I'm going to throw up." Which she did. Causing Ruby to throw up too. Which would have been somewhat amusing had I not read Cathy Merkel's mind just then, had I not been sure that Mrs. Merkel was thinking exactly this: What kind of God takes my Larry and lets a monster like you live?

The following day Uncle Stash made some excuse about delivering the eggs himself, and we never delivered them again. We saw Cathy Merkel from time to time that year, a chance meeting at the grocery store in town or the library, where she copied recipes from cookbooks and rented action videos for Mr. Merkel. Or where she sometimes tore telephone-number tags from the bulletin board. She grinned tightly, the way she always did when she saw us. Aunt Lovey and she would exchange some brief pleasantry, and when Cathy Merkel was gone Aunt Lovey would sigh and say, "It's not about you girls. It's got nothing to do with you girls."

We saw Sherman Merkel daily in the fields. He stopped to chat every once in a while, but we usually made do with a wave from a distance. Except that I remember one spring when Ruby and I were searching for arrowheads out back and we stopped to watch Mr. Merkel test the soil for planting. Mr. Merkel knew that VanDyck had put in his corn the day before, and Zimmer had done his the previous week. It was Sherman Merkel's opinion that VanDyck and

Zimmer'd gone too early. He bent at the waist, reaching down with his big hands, and scooped a mound of earth, feeling it for moisture. He tossed a little of the dirt into the air and watched it ride the breeze. The rest of the dirt he licked from his palm, pressing it like peanut butter against the roof of his mouth. He gazed over the fields a moment, then stroked his stomach and said it was time for lunch. "Wife's making spaghetti and meatballs. You girls are welcome."

Ruby and I were sure that we would *not* be welcome in Cathy Merkel's kitchen. Though neither of us said a thing, the farmer must have known what we were thinking. After a long, thoughtful pause, he said, "She was different before Larry."

"Nice?" Ruby asked.

Mr. Merkel nodded slowly and walked home to his childless wife.

I would not have dreamed back then, could never have imagined, that one day I would be a childless mother too.

A few days later, curious about Sherman Merkel's arrowhead collection and drawn to Cathy Merkel in spite of her aversion to us, my sister and I decided to go to the cottage across the creek. But we needed an excuse. And that came in the form of the little red truck. Aunt Lovey was at the hospital for the day, and Uncle Stash was in the barn, sanding an old trough he was turning into a wildflower planter for her birthday. We stopped to tell Uncle Stash where we were going, but he wasn't there. Ruby and I weren't worried. (This happened before his heart attack, when we never questioned Uncle Stash's vigor.) We knew he was likely in the meadow taking photographs of spring thaw. Or had gotten distracted painting some milk cans instead of sanding the trough. I argued that it would take just as much time to go back in the house to write a note as it would to get to the Merkels' and back, which wasn't true.

Trudging through the field on the way to Merkels' cottage, a path grown over with briar and hedge, one we'd walked so many times and would never walk again, I clutched the little truck and said a prayer for Larry (or was it *to* Larry? I was never sure) when we stepped onto the bridge over the creek. I imagined that Mrs.

Merkel might think warmly of Ruby and me for having brought back something of Larry.

Then we saw the herons.

It never mattered to my sister and me that blue herons are not rare here in Leaford. They're so elegant in profile, so graceful in flight, that Ruby and I have always stopped to watch. And so it was that day when *two* herons appeared just as Ruby and I reached the gate to Merkels' cottage. The herons, iridescent, prehistoric, leggy, and cool, stopped at the edge of the creek, casting a backward glance at Ruby and me. The herons, with their heavy breasts and splinter legs and the fancy lash at either eye, didn't find us threatening.

"Herons," Ruby said quietly. "Stop."

I did stop, but I didn't turn around fully. "Beautiful," I said. Something in the window of Merkels' cottage had caught my attention. Flash. Flesh. Flash. Back. Flash. Buttocks. Flash. Thigh. I would not have guessed Mr. Merkel was so hairy. And I did not understand why Mr. Merkel was naked. Especially in the middle of the day. I knew a little about sex, but from what I had gleaned it was a lying-down-at-nighttime activity and not a standing-up-in-daytime one. I should have turned away. I should have walked away. But I stayed and watched the naked bodies thrusting behind the fluttering curtains. I could not see Sherman Merkel's face or his head at all, bent as he was over his wife's behind, but I imagined he had a somewhat sinister look. There was a gentle flapping sound as the herons lifted themselves into the air, a sigh from Ruby, and the birds were gone. Ruby nudged me. "Show's over. Let's go." But the show was not over, and I could *not* turn away. I wished I had a telephone so I could call the police. Surely, I thought, she must be tied up. And gagged.

Ruby sensed something was happening. "What? What's wrong?"

"Nothing," I replied. "Just be quiet and see if they come back."

I knew the herons wouldn't return. I stood watching Sherman Merkel reach down to wrap his arms around his wife's waist, pulling her against him, buttocks to groin, and back to torso. He bit her shoulder as he continued to thrust, and I saw their faces as the pair came fully into view. I was shocked to see that she was enjoying the rough invasion, but more shocked to see that the man behind Cathy Merkel was *not* her husband. So much time has passed since that day. Uncle Stash and Aunt Lovey are gone, and the Merkels are still on the farm. Ruby and I are dying, and I'm sure I will not shatter if I admit that the man behind Cathy Merkel was Uncle Stash.

Ruby is blissfully naive and emotionally rather fragile. I have a certain confidence that she will not read this book this far. (Ruby supports me completely, but Ruby's not a huge fan of my writing, which I guess is kind of funny, but I'm just not her proverbial cup of tea.) The truth about Uncle Stash could shatter Ruby, but I understand, and maybe I've always understood, that we humans are weak and complicated. And on the crest of judgment day I'm hard-pressed to be critical. Besides, what does it matter? Aunt Lovey dillied. Uncle Stash dallied. We are dying.

As for Larry Merkel's little red fire truck, after seeing what I saw in Cathy Merkel's window, and after telling myself that I had not seen what I saw, I convinced Ruby that going to Merkels' was a bad idea after all and that we should keep Larry's toy, because he'd meant it for us. She'd agreed, and that's what we did. And the strangest thing of all? The herons *did* return.

I'VE BEEN IRRITATED with Ruby for her preoccupation with her personal effects, but it occurs to me that this book, this autobiography, is just that. My effects are my stories, but I have the same obsession to group and pile and discard and wrap and label, to quantify and qualify, and even to bequeath. I've been surprised how little I care to discuss our estate. Ruby thinks I don't care about what we're leaving, but it's the opposite. I care so much I want to leave *myself,* so that, in the end, when Rose and Ruby Darlen are no longer, there will be a box with a bally pink scarf and a little red fire truck and this — this true story of us.

The surprise party was amazing! Happy Birthday to us!

ROSE AND RUBY DARLEN REACH
MILESTONE BIRTHDAY!

(The sound of cheering.)

There weren't really any headlines. We wanted to keep our birthday quiet and personal this year. Rose even called the *Leaford Mirror* to ask them not to post their annual birthday greetings to The Girls because, every year after the birthday message in the *Mirror,* newspapers and magazines from all over call to say they want to tell our story. Of course we know people want to exploit us. We've had a few calls this year even with no publicity, because so many people can find out so many things about us on the Internet. That's the biggest reason I don't like computers. There's too much information out there. And not enough smart people.

When Rose and I stepped into the staff room at the library, everyone screamed, Surprise! The look on Rose's face was hilarious —

and, believe me, she is no actress — so I knew for sure she never suspected a thing. All the hard work was worth it!

The tape deck and CD player on the portable stereo Whiffer brought didn't work so we had to make do with the radio, which was fine for Rose because Lutie found a Detroit station playing Motown. I was accused of pouting because I actually like music from the last ten years, but I have to admit the Motown stuff got the people dancing. It always does. Even in the movies, when there's a Motown montage, the characters dance and we all feel happy happy happy.

Rosie drank a glass of champagne and wanted more, but Nick said she should go easy. Drinking the champagne made her chatty, and Rose can be pretty funny, though I would say she has more of a guy sense of humor, which Whiffer and Nick seem to get more than the rest of us.

Lutie took a video of the whole night, and I have watched it four times already because it was one of the best nights of my life. It really was. Especially because of how I shared it with my best friend. And because I really love all the people who were there. (Except Nick.)

Rose got me a beautiful baby-blue raw silk blouse she ordered from her computer. It was delivered last week and I was going crazy to know what was in the box. It is so pretty, and I love the way the color looks with my complexion. I'm gonna save it for something special. Or, really, I was thinking I'd save it for laying out. I know that sounds extremely creepy, but if we decide to have a casket made and whatever, which I don't think we will, but if we do, I'll need something to wear. Wardrobe is a fact of death.

My sister doesn't care about clothes. Usually I buy her a book for her birthday. We go to the bookstore in Ridgetown, where the lady there is so used to us she doesn't stare. Rose picks out five books, and I buy one of them. The surprise is she never knows which one of the five she will get. But we can't really take the bus anymore because Rose is getting dizzy. I didn't feel like asking Nick to drive us to Ridgetown. I don't want people to get the wrong idea about Nick and us.

That glass of champagne Rosie drank had us stuck in the bathroom for half an hour trying to get rid of her hiccups! The whole time I'm thinking that each hiccup is going to rupture the aneurysm, and we haven't even cut the cake!

My sister wasn't just surprised about the birthday party, she was thrilled. People say they don't want something, but then, when it happens, they realize they've wanted it all along. And though she would have said she didn't want a party of any kind, and especially not a surprise one, she had the best time. The best.

Whiffer bought Rose a really cute charm bracelet. He gave me a gift certificate to the video store, which I thought was okay, but something more personal would have been nice.

At first I thought the whole party was going to happen without us. Rose hadn't been feeling well — headachy and weak — and she asked if I'd mind if we didn't go to Chatham in a taxi for supper, which is how we'd agreed we'd celebrate. She said she just wanted to go to bed and wake up to another day. I think she was feeling depressed. She did not care that turning thirty gave us the distinction of being the oldest living craniopagus twins in history. I'm very pleased about it, but not as pleased as I thought I'd be, because, in the end, there's still the end and it's coming way too soon.

(The way I got my sister out of the house was basically to freak out and cry so much that she'd rather have been anywhere than alone in the bungalow with me.)

The food was amazing. Nonna did eggplant Parmesan and the meatballs. Roz made sausage rolls and piped salmon spread on crackers and the spinach dip in the hollowed-out bread. Lutie brought a raspberry Jell-O with sliced banana that his mother made, and a dozen of the fresh cheese buns the Oakwood Bakery is famous for. I am having a bad time with my colitis lately and have been in some pain. I couldn't really indulge in our birthday spread, so I had some of the cheese bun but without butter, and I had to pick out the cheese, but I smelled the food and watched everyone (except Rose, whose appetite is getting worse) really really enjoy it.

Nonna was going to make the cakes but she got confused while she was baking and Nick had to finish.

I wanted a round chocolate layer cake for Rose, and to make it look

like a basketball by putting orange food coloring in the frosting and using black licorice to make the lines. And I wanted a movie clapboard for
me (just in case you don't know, a movie clapboard is used so the director knows how many times the actor has forgotten his lines). A
movie clapboard is black and white with slanted stripes at the top, and
Nick didn't put enough black color in the frosting so it just ended up
gray, and, basically, you could not tell what it was, even though he
tried to be cute and wrote THE SURPRISE PARTY STARRING ROSE AND RUBY
DARLEN on it. Nick put thirty candles — fifteen on each cake — which
technically isn't right. He also put the cakes on the wrong side so we
had to turn them around and the words didn't face us when we blew
out the candles — which everyone knows is bad luck.

There was a lot of laughing and talking, and we were playing the
music pretty loud. I think Rupert must have felt overwhelmed because
he started whining and Roz had to take him home. And Whiffer and
Lutie were going to meet girls or something. And Nonna was exhausted. She kept it together though. Or she did a good job of fooling
us. Sometimes she gets so confused she thinks that I'm Rose's infant
and she asks Rose, How's your little girl today?, which I find embarrassing. I do not play along even though Rose said I should. Anyway,
everybody was gone by about nine-thirty, but then Nick came back to
see if we needed help. I told him that we're perfectly capable of taking
a taxi home.

Rose said we should take a ride with Nick because we'd be stupid to
pay for a taxi when our neighbor was going our way. How could I argue?

On the way home, Nick said Nonna's confusion still comes and
goes. I'm surprised that Nick doesn't get more frustrated with her. I get
frustrated and I don't even live with her. Bet he has less patience behind closed doors. The night of the party she seemed totally like her
old self, but then, when Whiffer grabbed the spoon for the meatballs,
she smacked his hand and said, Wait until supper. Then she kept calling Whiffer "Fiodor," which was not the name of Nonna's husband,
Nick's father, who died before Nick was even born. It made Whiffer
and me laugh, but Rose pinched me because Nick wasn't laughing.
Then Nonna kinda went downhill from there.

Nick drove us home from the party, which is fine, though I have this funny feeling he's helping us out because he expects something in return. We haven't told him about the aneurysm or the prognosis, but we're going to see Dr. Singh in Toronto more often, and Nick must see from the look of us that we're not well, especially because Rose is getting so thin. I hope Nick's not being nice to us because he expects something in return. He won't be in our will. Not that I think Rose would want to put him in our will. Not that I know anything about what Rose wants to do.

Rose looked really pretty for our birthday, and I was glad she'd gone to some trouble because usually you can expect to have to nag her to comb her hair and change her shirt. She was wearing her new cream blouse from the sidewalk sale, and she even put on some of the pink lipstick I gave her as a present. I was wrong about the color. It did not suit her, but she got so many compliments on it I bet she'll want to wear it every day.

That night, when we were in bed, Rose squeezed me and said, We made it. I felt her shiver and she was probably thinking what I was thinking, which is, Okay, what now, God? Only with Rose, she'd just leave the God part out. Then we touched each other's earlobes to say I love you.

Aunt Lovey and Uncle Stash used to say You to each other. Before he left for work in the morning he'd kiss Rose and me and say, Be good, my girls, then he'd hold his heart and look into Aunt Lovey's eyes and say You. Just You. Sometimes she'd just smile and nod, and other times she'd do the same thing back. Hold her heart. Say You.

I remember when we were kids asking my sister why Aunt Lovey and Uncle Stash never said I love you. Only — You. Rose got out the dictionary and made me look up the word "redundant."

Last night she told me she was proud of how much I'm writing on my yellow legal pads because I've filled two pads already and I'm starting on my third. That made me feel good and quite annoyed at the same time, because I don't need her approval. But I do. You know?

She said she was halfway done with her book, and she asked me how close I was to being done. I can tell she's curious about what I've written, but she won't ask.

I'm not close to being finished at all. Or maybe I'm done right now. How the hell can you tell?

Rose still wants to find Taylor. She sent an e-mail to our cousins in Hamtramck to find out what they know about the private adoption, but they said they don't know anything. Uncle Yanno is the one who arranged it, but no one has seen or heard from him in years, and you can't even ask the cousins about their father because they'll bite your head off. Yanno left with another woman when Aunt Poppy lost her hair from the chemo. You wouldn't have believed the cursing Uncle Stash did about that. Uncle Stash punched Uncle Yanno out one time that we know of.

The only information we really have is that it was someone from the Ford Plant who adopted Taylor, and we're not even sure that's the truth, so Rose's idea of trying to get Ford to put a personal plea in the newsletter is obviously a lame idea. Rose said, Then why don't we get a private investigator to search for her like Aunt Lovey and Uncle Stash did to find Mary-Ann? Our birth mother.

I was thinking, Our birth mother. Oh my God. Our birth mother?

I looked at Rose in the reflection of the mirror and I could see she was serious and I realized that it hadn't ever once occurred to her that there was no private investigator. And that the grave we visited was not our mother's. I always thought it was just one of those things we thought about but didn't talk about. I told her I think Aunt Lovey and Uncle Stash lied to us because we were obsessed with finding our real mother, and they thought they were doing the right thing. I wasn't gonna say anything more, but she wanted me to, so I told Rose that I remember Aunt Lovey telling Uncle Stash we needed evidence. And closure. It wasn't long after that Uncle Stash had the idea about hiring the private investigator.

I can't believe Rose never thought about the fact that our family could not afford to heat the second floor of the farmhouse, and there's just no way Uncle Stash would have spent money on a private investigator unless there was some kind of guarantee. Then there's the fact that the mysterious guy never came to the farm, and we never heard his voice on the phone. Supposedly he'd found a trail from Leaford that led straight to our mother in Toronto. According to this private investigator's information, our mother was some perfect angel who worked in a bookstore and went to church and had a lot of things in common with Rose and me (like reading and writing and interest in the Neutral Indians — yeah, right) and conveniently died right after she had us. Her name was Mary-Ann instead of Elizabeth, and I figure that's because it was the only gravestone Uncle Stash could find with a female Taylor who died shortly after our birth.

Rose was really quiet after I said what I said. I told her she shouldn't be mad at Uncle Stash and Aunt Lovey, and she said she wasn't, but her reflection in the mirror was so sad I wished I'd never opened my mouth.

Rose really brooded about that. She likes a good brood. She does. But I choose to be happy. Aunt Lovey used to joke with Rose that she got her broodiness from her Slovak side. (The joke is that we're adopted, so we don't actually have any Slovak blood — that we know of.)

Later, when we were in bed, Rose talked about how she'd never in all this time considered that our mother might be alive, and how she needed some time with it. She wrote a lot of poems in that period. Then, after a few weeks, she brought up the idea of the private investigator again and said we should find Taylor and our birth mother and arrange for them to meet when we're gone. (And she says I'm the dreamer?)

I don't know if it's the aneurysm clouding Rose's thinking or if I'm the crazy one. I think it's a bad idea. If our mother is alive (and she probably is because she'd only be in her late forties), she knows who we are and could have had contact with us if she wanted. It's not like she's not gonna remember giving birth to craniopagus twins. Besides, if you wanted to know, one stroke of a computer key will tell you where we live. Everyone knows we're all over the Internet.

That night I dreamed that our mother and Taylor were eating blackberry jam in Mrs. Merkel's kitchen.

I woke up in the night because Rosie was crying. She said her head hurt really bad. I told her I was sorry. Then she said really quietly, so I knew she was serious, she said we should get two things of Tatranax and go. Just float off. Together. Right then in the night. She said let's do it now, Ruby. We can hold each other. It won't be scary.

I started shaking. I couldn't stop it. I didn't cry or anything. I just couldn't stop shaking. For the longest time. She kept saying, It's okay, it's okay, Ruby. She said she was just kidding, but she wasn't.

She wasn't.

Peevo

Aunt Lovey drank only on special occasions, and then only a little white wine, but Uncle Stash liked to sip a beer or two every
night — three if there was a sports event, four if his team was losing.
Uncle Stash never used the English word for beer. "Bring me the
peevo, Rose," he'd call. He said that, compared to slivovitz or Becherovka, the alcohol content in beer was so low it wasn't really *drinking*.
The *peevo* he bought at the beer store, but the Becherovka Uncle Stash
made himself from cloves and something that smelled like turpentine
(so it was really faux Becherovka). He said Becherovka was a magic
elixir, and he gave me a teaspoon for constipation if I promised not to
tell Aunt Lovey (who favored glycerin suppositories and strained
prunes). He wouldn't let Ruby touch the stuff, though. It would have
burned her to cinder. I think the Becherovka gave me a buzz. I know
it moved my bowels. The night before Mother Darlensky came to
Leaford, Uncle Stash drank half a bottle of the liquor, though I don't
believe it could cure his particular ill.

THE OLD FARMHOUSE had been withering in the weeks
leading up to Mother Darlensky's visit, from the scrubbing and

stress and the whispers and worry. Aunt Lovey scoured the wood floors raw. Ruby and I washed down the walls in the hall and sprayed Jean Naté on the burnt-orange carpet in the den where the miserable old woman would be sleeping. Uncle Stash vacuumed the car and raked forty-six bags of leaves.

It was October 31. Halloween, and Ruby and I were in our final year at Leaford Collegiate. (Halloween is a celebration that I fear and loathe, and one that my sister and I refused to participate in from the beginning.) Our bedroom in the old orange farmhouse on any given October morning was frosty, scented by corn husk and dry tobacco. But that Halloween morning, the day of Mother Darlensky's arrival, we woke to find the room damp and musty smelling, like a day in late July. We made our way to the window, and looked outside to see Sherman Merkel, in short sleeves, swatting at the crows with his stable broom, beyond him a field of dark orange pumpkins waiting for carving knives and piecrusts — and vandals. There were flies in the windowsill, confused, like us, as to whether it was the middle of summer or end of fall.

After dressing in our freshly ironed blouses and skirts, we went to the kitchen to find Aunt Lovey and Uncle Stash at opposite ends of the long pine table, something simmering between them. Aunt Lovey was wearing her coral lipstick, and Uncle Stash had used something slick to comb back his hair. He looked fairly ridiculous, and I wondered if that's what Aunt Lovey was frowning about, until she said, "I'm putting my foot down, Stash. She can sit in the *back* with the girls."

"She's old. It's too hard to get in back," Uncle Stash replied.

"If you hadn't noticed," Aunt Lovey began, "your two daughters get in the back of that car nearly every day!"

"It's one day, Lovey."

"Exactly. It's not too much to ask, Stash."

"It's not too much to ask to you too!"

Why Aunt Lovey was digging her heels in about the front seat was a mystery to me. Why Uncle Stash didn't just give it up was incomprehensible. The gulf created by the enormous table didn't help.

They were still not speaking to each other by the time we arrived at the bus station. Ruby and I watched the bus arrive. I could feel my sister's heart thudding when the doors were yanked open from within. But no one stepped off. Uncle Stash swallowed. Aunt Lovey looked somewhat relieved, hoping the old woman had changed her mind. After a longer moment, when *still* no one appeared, Uncle Stash went to investigate. He would tell us later how his mother was sitting pale and alarmed in her aisle seat while the driver tried to persuade her to leave. She'd looked up to see Uncle Stash, and smiled like a very young child.

Ruby and I watched Uncle Stash, holding his mother's two hands, help her down from the bus like a toddler not ready for stairs. She was puny and frail with hardly a hair. Her mouth was puckered. Her eyes were large and bewildered.

Uncle Stash didn't have to point Ruby and me out to his ailing mother. We were already the center of attention at the convenience store/gas station/bus depot. From the steps of the bus the old woman glanced our way. But she didn't quite seem to focus. And she didn't come close to a smile.

Aunt Lovey stood back, waiting to be recognized, but Mother Darlensky was intent on watching her feet, inching forward on her tiny white sneakers. There were stains on the old woman's blouse. And crinkles at the crotch of her polyester pants. Aunt Lovey took Mother Darlensky's elbow and said, "You're looking well, Mother Darlensky."

I almost laughed out loud.

The old woman nodded but said nothing, and didn't meet Aunt Lovey's eyes. Ruby and I were relieved when Aunt Lovey opened the front door of the car and helped the frail woman inside, before climbing into the backseat on Ruby's side. "I don't think she knows me," Aunt Lovey whispered, and the fact of not being recognized by her mother-in-law instantly disposed Aunt Lovey of her long-held resentment.

"I give you the tour of Leaford, Mother," Uncle Stash said.

"Take me home," Mother Darlensky said in Slovak.

"I drive past Vanderhagen's to show you my work."

"Home," the old woman repeated.

Uncle Stash turned the key in the ignition. Then he eased the car into gear and started out of the parking lot, saying, "We go the long way home. We have a good tour. You'll see." He drove toward downtown Chatham instead of heading home to Leaford.

After a time Uncle Stash opened his mouth but I stopped him. "Shh," I said. "She's asleep."

A momentary glance at his sleeping mother, then Uncle Stash returned his focus to the road and stepped on the gas.

As the car lurched forward Mother Darlensky's head fell back. Her mouth cranked open. Her neck crooked left.

Aunt Lovey leaned forward. "Mother Darlensky?"

Uncle Stash could see something wasn't right. He made a move to pull the car over, but didn't.

Aunt Lovey's fingers searched for a pulse in the old woman's neck.

"Stash?" Aunt Lovey said, when he did not turn down the road that would have taken us to the nearby Chatham Hospital but began to drive down the country road instead.

"Stash? Honey?"

A certain graceful turkey vulture soaring through the sky caught Uncle Stash's attention, and he slowed down to watch as it descended to pluck at some dead thing in a farmer's field. Uncle Stash slid a cassette into the tape deck, and I held my breath as music filled the car and we drove the road along the river, the one that curves and loops and seems to flow back into itself, the way I do my sister, and life does death.

Normally Aunt Lovey would have asked Uncle Stash to lower the volume. Instead she said, "Turn it up, hon. Turn it up a little."

We drove on past the river and headed for the bay, Ray Price crooning on the car stereo, Ruby sleepy from her Dramamine, me singing along (my sister says I have the singing voice of a male frog) to the songs I knew, Aunt Lovey sniffing into a handkerchief, deconstructing herself. Uncle Stash dry-eyed and silent, staring straight ahead. I wasn't sure what Uncle Stash was doing. Was he showing his mother's ghost our beautiful Baldoon? Was he unprepared to say good-bye? Or damned if she'd have the last word again?

At the bay we stopped to watch the birds and the boats and the cottagers and the couples heading to the Lighthouse Restaurant for a nice fish dinner. Not one of them had a dead body in their car. I was sure of that.

By the time the last song was playing on the tape, we had turned down Rural Route One, heading for home. Uncle Stash dropped Aunt Lovey and Ruby and me off at the laneway to the farmhouse, then stopped to light a pipe (the first and last that he would smoke inside the car) before he drove his mother's body to St. Jude's Hospital, to be pronounced dead on arrival by Dr. Richard Ruttle.

The strangest thing about strange things is that they're only strange when you hear about them or imagine them or think about them later, but never when you're living them. (I believe I can speak about that with some authority.) And it was like that with Mother Darlensky. It did not seem strange to be driving around Baldoon County with the music on loud and the old woman's corpse slumped in the front seat. At least not until Ruby and I were in bed that night, looking at the moon, pretending it was not Halloween.

Uncle Stash must have felt chilled by it too, because when we woke up the next morning, Ruby and I counted eight empty bottles of *peevo* in the carton beside the fridge. Uncle Stash entered the kitchen looking old and announced that he was taking his mother's ashes to his hometown of Grozovo, in Slovakia, to bury her in the hillside cemetery where his two older brothers rest.

"But what about burying her beside your father in Windsor?" Ruby asked innocently.

"She wants to go home, Ruby. I *know.*"

"You don't know that, Stash. The people in Ohio said there's no will," Aunt Lovey countered. "Besides, your mother and father had a joint plot. I saw it myself. I don't think you need more evidence than that of what your mother wanted. Her side of the headstone is already engraved!"

"She wants to go home, Lovey. That was her last word."

"But how do you know she didn't mean *our* home?" Ruby asked.

"How do you know she didn't mean Windsor?" Aunt Lovey added. "She was married to your father for forty years, Stash. They raised three children together. Traveled halfway across the world to start a new life in a new country. Surely she'd want to spend eternity in the plot next to his."

"She wants to go home. She wants to go to Slovakia. To my brothers. *That's* home. I *know. I* know."

A surprising thing for Uncle Stash to claim about a mother with whom he had little contact and for whom he had much contempt. And hurtful to Aunt Lovey, whose heart I thought he should have known best.

"I think a wife should be buried with her husband," Aunt Lovey said.

"Hmm," was all he said in response.

Aunt Lovey continued to argue with Uncle Stash about his mother's last wishes. It didn't really matter what Mother Darlensky wanted, though. It was Uncle Stash who wanted to go home, and we all, even he, knew it.

Deadlines & Writing

I stumbled. We fell. I told Nick not to tell. Then I started crying and confessed that we are dying.

This is my first day back at the computer after missing three straight days. I'm frustrated. It's the evil aneurysm, of course. (The little bastard wants to *ruin* my life before he takes it. And my sister's by proxy.)

Dr. Singh thinks the terrible headaches will most certainly subside, or get worse, or disappear altogether. It could mean the eruption is imminent or it could be days or weeks or months, but *most certainly* not four months — we most certainly won't be here for Christmas. I hate the way Singh says "most certainly," as if he's never wrong.

My sister has been incredible throughout these days of pain. Quiet and uncomplaining. If she's having headaches too, she has not said a word. I don't know this Ruby at all, who urged a bendy straw to my lips when she saw I was parched. This Ruby who warned, "If you pee the bed, I'll kill you, Rose Darlen." This Ruby who finally said, "I don't care if you hate me, I'm calling for help."

I have not allowed television. I have not allowed food except crackers and dry Cheerios. We've hardly even left the bed. When Ruby asked if she could write in her yellow legal pads, I said *no*. The scratching of her pen wouldn't have destroyed me, but my guilt and remorse about missing day after day of *my* writing, and my anxiety over what those missing days and missing pages would mean to my deadline, would have swallowed me whole. Of course it was only three days, but it's a question of flow. My flow has been dammed. My sentences have leaked from their chapters and changed from themselves into something unrecognizable and unnavigable. I am in deep shit.

For most of the time that we lay in the bed, I clung to Ruby with my eyes on the sky, whimpering, as Ruby sang softly. (Ruby's voice resonates for me because I don't just hear it, I feel it in our conjoined skulls.) I listened to her singing and looked through the window, the one near our bed, where bees tease pallid roses and the sun surrenders red. The few times we got up (because Ruby forced me to use the bathroom and made me stretch to avoid blood clots), both of us forgot to draw the drapes. We rose with the dawn, a length of day before us, with nothing to do and nothing to see but pain and its confusion, and even that was preferable to the alternative in all but my darkest moments, when I imagined death as a fairy, youthful and winged, on whose back we could cruise the clouds.

Ruby shook when I mentioned the Tatranax. It started as a tremble that I could feel in her jaw and chin. I tried to catch her in the mirror, but she resisted. The tremble became a shake and she couldn't talk. Did she shake because she wanted to take the Tatranax too but couldn't admit it? Is it possible she's never thought of such a clean, joint departure herself?

Although our view has been just sky, so many crows still fly by, I could easily imagine I was at the farm, Sherman Merkel calling from the barn, Ruby beside me soft and warm, our lives stretched out before us, instead of shriveling behind.

I ONCE READ some wise writer's advice that an author should clean his manuscript of blood and tears, then find the sentence that tickled him most when he wrote it down — the most lyrical line, the cleverest insight, the most potent image, the most profound conclusion — and promptly strike the words out. I feel confident, recalling my chapters, that my work is unburdened by any of those things. I have reached a peak, made an important discovery, and acknowledge that my book is what it is, rare and imperfect.

I IMAGINE RUBY is more a diarist, and she's writing about the day-to-day stuff, as though her chapters were to be inserted in a journal chronicling our final days. What a challenge to find the right place for Ruby's chapters, which she writes at one sitting, never returning, never revising. I imagine she's writing about the visits to see Dr. Singh in Toronto. My declining health (though I've begged her not to). I bet she wrote the full details of the surprise party. *Lutie brought a Jell-O salad* — that sort of thing.

When I was very sick, on the third day of our confinement, Ruby said she was going to call for help whether I liked it or not. I just assumed she'd call one of the Doctors Ruttle. But it was Nick Todino she thought to call. The second he saw us, he insisted he drive us up to see Dr. Singh in Toronto. He said, "Forget about Ruttle. We need the specialist." I liked the way he took charge. I think Ruby was relieved too. My head was pulsing and there were bright green spots flashing in my periphery. I couldn't think of a good argument why we shouldn't go with him.

On the way out to the car, I stumbled and fell against the porch railing. Ruby and I weren't badly hurt, but I suddenly found myself confessing about the aneurysm (because I didn't want him to think I was just clumsy). The details burbled out of my mouth like something carbonated and shaken. Nick didn't seem surprised about the aneurysm. I don't know how, but I think he already knew.

Nick owns an old Ford Thunderbird, which he keeps in cherry condition and puts in the garage when it snows. There's a bench seat in the front of Nick's car, and when I asked if Ruby and I could sit beside him he said sure, but on the way home.

It was a long day at the hospital, hours and hours of tests and taps and pricks and probes and waiting and waiting. I was relieved to be outdoors, even if it was a dusty downtown parking lot. (You can't see the stars in Toronto. That's reason enough not to live there. You look up. No sparkle. No twinkle. No glitter. You can't wish so well on overhead jet planes. And if you're looking for poetic inspiration, nothing rhymes with "helicopter.") I'd forgotten about asking to sit in the front seat until Nick came around the side to open the door for my sleepy sister and me. With Nick's help, Ruby and I were secured into the front seat, giggling like kids on a carousel. Nick said Ruby and I could sit in front anytime we wanted, as long as it was at night, when there was less risk someone might see us and cause a tragic accident.

Very quickly the thrill of the front seat wore off, and Ruby fell asleep as she always does in the car. I felt my stomach lurch, the way it always does, with the guilty pleasure of being without her.

I was sure that I hadn't brought up the subject of Ryan Todino with Nick, but maybe I had. I've been surprising myself with my candor. It could be the aneurysm affecting pressure, causing an imbalance, stimulating personality changes. Or it could be my personality as a narrator fusing with my personality as a person. I have always been a bit of a loner, which may sound surprising because I'm never alone, but where Ruby has been troubled by our exclusion from the normal, I haven't minded so much. I think Nick's like me in that way.

As Nick was speeding down the stretch of dark road, I had a flash of Ruby when we were little, sobbing because Aunt Lovey had promised a trip on the highway. "This isn't the *high*way," Ruby cried. "This is the *low* way." Aunt Lovey and Uncle Stash laughed when they understood what she meant, and that made her cry even harder. And then I had a flash of Ruby at about five years old, at the Jaycee Fair in Chatham. We'd gone on a child's ride (the race cars, I think), which, inexplicably, did not make Ruby queasy but did me. A crowd had gathered to watch us. I remember friendly faces for the most part, somewhat pitying, friendly faces, at least until we got off the ride and Ruby shouted, "That made my vagina tingle!"

Nick was talking about Ryan, and I was thinking of Ruby and her tingly vagina, when, as happens in daydreams, the image of my sister became that of my daughter, Taylor, and I was remembering moments with Ruby as though I'd lived them with my daughter. Then I thought of Ruby telling me her suspicions that the stories we were told about our mother weren't true, and that whoever she is, she's probably still alive. (Good God, she could live in Leaford for all we know! Or Chatham! Or Dresden!) I don't know if it was the aneurysm or the tension or the combination of the two, but I was suddenly very confused, and afraid, and somewhat panicked because I didn't know what was true. Ruby was asleep, so I blubbered and snorted and blew my nose and told Nick about my mother, and sex with Frankie Foyle, and giving birth to Taylor, and being afraid to die.

For a long time we just rode the dark, then Nick said, "I been in jail."

"I know."

"You know what for?"

I didn't know what Nick had gone to jail for. "Yes," I lied.

"You know I'm an asshole."

"Yes."

"You gotta tell people, Rose."

"That you're an asshole?"

He laughed, then said, "That you're dying."

Premonitions & Portents

Aunt Lovey was against the trip to Slovakia. She said she had a bad feeling, a premonition, but, as Uncle Stash pointed out, she'd been wrong before. (She'd had a bad feeling he was going to crash the Duster on a visit to Ohio one time and he did not, and she'd had a terrible nightmare where he hacked off his left hand at Vanderhagen's, but that never happened either. The things that did happen — his heart attack, the accident — those things she never saw coming.) In the end she was simply outvoted.

We set a departure date for late November after successfully arguing that missing a couple of weeks of our last year of school would be less difficult than trying to travel during the busy Christmas holidays. As we cleared dishes from the long pine table in the kitchen, Aunt Lovey was being an uncharacteristically poor sport.

"You'd think we were going to Paris, France, the way you girls are carrying on," she said. "You do realize there are no televisions in Grozovo. No Motown radio. And we'll have to go catheter on the plane."

(An aside: The flight promised a few horrors, as we would be badly cramped and, more disturbingly, catheterized for the longest leg of the journey because our particular anatomy does not config-ure with the teeny airplane bathrooms. We'd endured discomfort before. And we knew precisely what to expect regarding our fellow passengers. The staring. The questions. The staring. Still, this was the trip of a lifetime, and once the challenging air travel was com-plete, it was just a simple bus ride up the mountains to Grozovo and the welcoming arms of Uncle Stash's Slovak kin.)

"Good God, I hope they have running water," Aunt Lovey went on.

She walked toward the hallway and called into the den, "Do they have running water? Stash? I know you can hear me!"

Uncle Stash didn't respond.

Aunt Lovey went on grumbling. "I can't imagine how those people are going to feel when we just drop out of the sky." Once again she called into the den. "Isn't there an embassy? Can you call the embassy and get them to contact Velika or Marek somehow?"

Uncle Stash walked into the room slowly, frowning, impatient. "You're making too much. It's just visit to family."

"Visit from family they've never met before."

"Still family."

"What about Rose and Ruby?"

"It's okay with the girls."

"Grozovo is the backwoods, Stash. You told me that yourself."

"Still, they have seen things."

"But won't they be shocked to see *us*?" Ruby asked.

"It's Slovakia. Something is always shocking. Plus, they know my girls are conjoined girls. Every year we send the pictures from school."

(It was true. We sent off a row of school pictures, along with the cured meats and wax-coated cheeses, and plush toys for the chil-dren, and secondhand clothes in good condition, all taped up in a large cardboard box, each Christmas.)

"I have this feeling, Stash. I just have this awful feeling."

"The plane is not crashing."

"It's not that."

"I am not having another heart attack."

"No, you most certainly are not."

"My mother wants to be buried in Grozovo. It's my duty. And that is all." He turned on his heels and left the room.

Aunt Lovey sighed, for Uncle Stash rarely said "and that is all," but when he did, it was. She set the dishes in the sink and reminded us that, the following day, we were to collect Mother Darlensky's ashes from the crematorium.

(An aside: There was so much foreshadowing in the weeks leading up to our departure that, were I an editor and this not a true story, I would scratch "too many portents" in the margins — a magazine editor once did that to a short story I wrote about a little boy lost in a tornado. But I feel I must include portents because, in a true story, it's not exaggerated foretelling but just the shitty things that happened before the shittiest thing happened.)

I did not know there was a crematorium in Baldoon County. I assumed it was one of those things you had to travel to London or Toronto for, like the Hudson's Bay Company or a neurologist. I couldn't tell you now where the Baldoon County crematorium is, though I'm usually good with directions. I recall a short building, made of red bricks whose mortar was crumbling and repaired in places with something black and tarry. On the way there my head was swimming with travel plans, and on the way back I could not look away from the box that Aunt Lovey set to rattle on the dash.

The box was rectangular, like a miniature shoe box, and made of a heavy brown corrugated cardboard. (I thought something round and made of glass would have been somehow more appropriate.) It looked like a box you might send figs in. Or something in which to ship engraved invitations. Or a good place to keep instructions and warranties. It did not look like a receptacle for human remains. Aunt Lovey had reached out to take the box from the faceless man at the back door, glowering when she saw he'd left smudgy fingerprints on the lid.

Back at the farmhouse, Ruby and I watched Aunt Lovey clutching the cardboard box, looking around the huge kitchen for a place to put it. She set it in the middle of the long pine table, like a floral centerpiece, then whispered to herself (or was it to Mother Darlensky?), "No, no, not there, dear." She picked the box up and held it as though it were something alive. Something that might escape. Finally, Aunt Lovey dragged the step stool to the tall china cabinet at the far end of the long table and stretched to set the cardboard box on top of it, brushing aside the dry fern to make room.

After a moment, Uncle Stash came in the back door.

"I put her there, Stash." Aunt Lovey pointed, but Uncle Stash didn't look up at the box beside the dry fern. He didn't seem to care. He was juggling the bicycle pump and the air mattress with the duct-tape repairs that we were taking on our trip, intending to test it for leaks, cursing because the mattress was stiff and unyielding.

"Oh, Stash," Aunt Lovey started when she saw the pump. "Not in here. You're gonna break —"

Too late.

In trying to pull apart the stuck plastic of the air mattress, Uncle Stash elbowed the corner of the china cabinet and set it to rocking on its spindly Victorian legs. The corrugated box fell from the top of the cabinet onto Uncle Stash's head, covering his pate with Mother Darlensky's ashes.

I couldn't tell if Ruby had a giggle or a scream inside her throat, but whatever it was I was relieved that there it stayed. (Uncle Stash, being completely bald by then, was often the target of fouling crows, and he looked that way now.) Ruby and I were paralyzed. Aunt Lovey got the whisk broom and collected what she could of Mother Darlensky's ashes into the dustpan. She brushed a little ash off his shoulders, and the mound from his crown, and put that in the dustpan too. As to the rest, she said, "You're too oily, hon. You'll have to soap the rest off in the shower."

Less than one-third of the ashes survived the fall from atop the china cabinet. Practical person that she was, creative when it came to things like packing, Aunt Lovey took the ashes from the dustpan and shook them into a small white envelope, which she sealed not by licking but by dabbing spit on her finger to wet the glue on the flap.

Then Aunt Lovey folded the envelope and put it inside one of Uncle Stash's new white T-shirts.

"Do we have to declare her?" Aunt Lovey wondered when Uncle Stash was out of the shower and we'd gathered in the den.

Uncle Stash didn't understand.

"Your mother."

He still didn't understand.

"Should we say we're traveling with her ashes?"

"There's no rule to declare ashes, Lovey."

"I imagine there is, Stash. There might even be some charge."

Uncle Stash didn't have to think about it. "Don't declare. It's enough trouble we have with the girls." He grinned as he said this, assuring my sister and me that whatever trouble we were, we were worth it.

"What if they find the envelope?"

"It's only envelope, Lovey." Uncle Stash plopped into the La-Z-Boy.

"With your mother's ashes, honey. What about that?"

"Don't say it's mother's ashes."

"Say it's what, then? What kind of ashes should we say?"

"Cigarette."

"In an envelope? Plus, it doesn't look like —"

"Say it is ashes of animal, then. Family pet."

"Dog ashes?"

"Dog ashes. Fine."

"Why would we be traveling with the ashes of our dog? What are we gonna do with them? How should I say he died?"

"Say he asked too many questions and I killed him."

Aunt Lovey giggled as Uncle Stash pulled her onto his lap. He held her there, grinning, staring blankly at the wall. She leaned against him, staring at the same spot without even knowing it. When I was younger, I was afraid of these intimate moments between Aunt Lovey and Uncle Stash and hated the way they clung to each other like driftwood, forgetting Ruby and me.

"I remember my cousin Zuza and my cousin Velika, young and

beautiful. Just a little older than me," Uncle Stash sighed. (I loved how Uncle Stash could say things as if he'd never said them before.) "Zuza is the most beautiful girl in Grozovo. Velika is the best dancer. Cousin Marek was only seven. Such a funny boy. Fast runner. My father said if Marek comes to Canada, he might go to Olympics."

"I wonder if he ever thinks of that," I said. "How different his life could have been?"

"Sometimes he does," Ruby said, answering for him. And herself.

"Different," Uncle Stash said, shrugging. "But better? Only God knows."

"Stash, you can't be saying that Marek's life in Slovakia, working in the mines, was a better life than one he would have had in Canada!" Aunt Lovey's voice was strangely pitched.

"Who knows about a person's life? Maybe Marek comes to Canada and gets hit by the truck. Or he marries a wife who kills him with a hammer. Who knows?"

"Are you sure you want to do this, Stash? It's not too late to cancel," Aunt Lovey said.

Uncle Stash sighed again. "There's an apple tree. On the corner of the lane where I take the ducks when I'm a boy, there's an apple tree. I climb this tree. I have first kiss under this tree. With Cousin Zuza, but still, first kiss. I eat every year apples from this tree. All the children know this tree, but we never tell our mothers. We don't want to pick for pies. We want to keep secret. We want to make magic the apple tree. It's silly. I know. I can't explain."

"We're going all the way to Slovakia to find an apple tree?" Ruby asked in the quiet moment that followed.

Our wise Aunt Lovey pressed her cheek to Uncle Stash. "You," she whispered, and never said another word against the trip.

Not only did Aunt Lovey not speak against the trip to Slovakia but she threw herself into the adventure with a fair bit of gusto. She and Ruby went to the Sears in Chatham (I went along — ha ha) and bought a brand-new travel wardrobe for all of us. The travel wardrobe, I had to admit, was thoroughly practical, but the not-identical-but-close-to-it tracksuits and accessories were simply embarrassing. "We're Team Darlen!" Aunt Lovey had gushed, spreading the stuff out over the long pine table. "Yeah," I said, waving an imaginary banner.

UNCLE STASH SNAPPED a family portrait of us Darlens that morning before we left for the airport. It was the last picture on a roll. In the picture, you can see the snow clouds in the distant sky and six crows balanced on the branches of the maple where we stood. Uncle Stash is frowning because the timer on the camera seems to be taking longer than it should, and there's a deep crease between Aunt Lovey's eyes as she strains to smile. We accidentally left Uncle Stash's expensive camera sitting on the picnic table and noticed only as we were pulling out of the drive. (See? Too many portents.)

It had started snowing before we hit the Detroit/Windsor tunnel, and by the time we got out of the tunnel, Uncle Stash had to put on his windshield wipers. "It's a blizzard," Uncle Stash said ominously. Aunt Lovey laughed, trying to be optimistic. "I make a bigger blizzard when I beat the rugs!"

"Least it's not sticking," Ruby said, watching the large wet flakes splash on the cold ground. (The early French explorers had an expression for this — one they made up during their first winter in the country — *"bordée de neige."* They also made up the word *"poudrière"* to describe a blizzard.)

Aunt Lovey was checking the rearview mirror. "I just can't stand it when they tailgate," she said.

"It's slippery today the road," Uncle Stash said. And I got the chills.

Then Uncle Stash started to cough. A short barky little cough, as though he had something stuck in his throat. (He had no fever. Aunt Lovey would have seen the fever. She could see a fever from the far end of a long hall. She'd seen a thousand fevers and could always guess within half a degree, without even touching. She said she read fever in the eyes. If Uncle Stash's fever had come then, in the car, or before we left the house, or anytime before we boarded the plane, Aunt Lovey would have seen it and known it was serious and canceled the trip.) Aunt Lovey found a throat lozenge in her purse and unwrapped it for Uncle Stash, who let his wife feed him, rather than take a hand off the steering wheel. But just as Aunt Lovey let the lozenge drop, a cough roared up in Uncle Stash's throat and made his tongue snap back, launching the thing into his windpipe. Coughing, choking, he lost control of the vehicle, and we slid on the shoulder of the road. The car behind us connected with our bumper. There was an awful grinding sound. Uncle Stash was swerving and swearing. (I remember this with some terror, but it could have and should have been worse.)

The tailgater spun around a few times and stopped in the center of the two-lane highway, blocking the traffic and clearing the road for our careening vehicle, which Uncle Stash wrestled from one gravel shoulder to the other, then steered toward the center lines, and finally found his place in the right lane. It was over in a minute. Seconds. (And, of course, Ruby and I didn't see any of it, and had only Uncle Stash's and Aunt Lovey's versions to go on.)

Aunt Lovey whispered, "Girls?"

"Fine. We're fine," Ruby said. "God, though."

A few more miles with no one speaking, then Aunt Lovey turned to Uncle Stash. But before she could say anything, he said, "I'm not going back."

Aunt Lovey nodded. Uncle Stash coughed. And coughed again.

ABOARD THE AIRCRAFT, Ruby and I had the seats directly behind Aunt Lovey and Uncle Stash. The armrests, as we'd been assured, did fold up to allow comfortable (relative to traveling in a cat cage) seating for Ruby and me. The flight to Bratislava, the capital of Slovakia, would take about eight hours. Ruby had done well nausea-wise in the car (even with the near accident), having had a bolt of children's Dramamine before we left the house (we were nineteen years old at the time, but Ruby never could tolerate an adult dosage). She was in need of another bolt about an hour into the trip. Aunt Lovey searched her huge purse again and again.

"Well, the bottle couldn't get up and walk away on its own. Good God, did someone take it? Would someone steal my Dramamine?" she wondered.

"Yes," I said. "I read about this pediatric-meds theft ring in the *Detroit Free Press.* They think it's gypsies."

Aunt Lovey didn't think I was funny, and Uncle Stash didn't say anything, which should have alarmed us. He had fallen asleep while nibbling a pretzel, after insisting for weeks that he wouldn't get a wink of sleep the whole flight. If Aunt Lovey hadn't been so worried over our well-being, she might have questioned why her husband fell asleep so quickly and deeply, when it was his habit to struggle for sleep and to stay in the shallow end when he got there.

I got the window seat because we were on the left side of the plane, and Ruby complained like a child. Aunt Lovey promised we could try for seats on the other side of the plane for our next flight, from Bratislava to Kosice in Eastern Europe, where we'd spend the night before heading into the mountains for Grozovo.

Uncle Stash and Aunt Lovey and Ruby slept through most of the long, turbulent flight, but I couldn't or, rather, wouldn't. I thought something might happen on board that I should bear witness to, something that I might one day write about, but I was in a bad spot for observing. I'd have been better off on the aisle.

I can't crane my neck. It's not simple for me to move my head. What I saw, what I see, with my sister in periphery, is limited. From our spot in the back of the plane I could see only Uncle Stash's bald head pressed against the window, wrinkles sliding down his thick neck like the shar-pei puppy that Mrs. Merkel'd once wanted. (I'd overheard her tell Aunt Lovey with some bitterness that her husband didn't think a shar-pei would make a good farm dog.)

I contemplated Uncle Stash's moles. I examined his skull. I closed my eyes and tried to read his mind. After a while I turned to the dark sky, took out my notepad, and jotted some lines for a poem

I'm still working on about the night flight to Eastern Europe. (I was going to challenge myself with that poem by not referring to the stars or moon.)

It was obvious, watching Uncle Stash stagger down the aisle on his way to the washroom, his camera heavy on his neck, that his illness was more than *just a cold*. We still had another flight to endure, but at least, once we got to Kosice, we could relax and get a night's rest.

I hardly remember the airport in Bratislava. Aunt Lovey took us to the washroom, swiftly removed the catheters, and helped us freshen up in the handicapped stall. When we returned to where we'd left Uncle Stash with the luggage, he waved brightly and made us hopeful, then he started coughing again. It wasn't long before our flight to Kosice was called. I was relieved, imagining that the air in his birthplace would restore Uncle Stash, and I thought, selfishly, that a fancy hotel (Aunt Lovey said it had five stars, and we'd only ever stayed at Comfort Inns before) would revive me and Ruby.

The traveling was more stressful than I would have admitted then. Ruby was frightened and singing Christmas carols to distract herself. I pinched her to make her stop, and said I'd strangle her if she sang "Holly Jolly Christmas" one more time.

Waiting to board the flight, I saw an elderly couple on the other side of the glass partition. The wife was white haired and stooped, thick around the middle. The husband was shuffling, like he needed a cane. His hat fit strangely. I don't know why they caught my attention. The couple moved forward in line, and I realized it was not a glass partition I was looking into but a smoky mirror, and the couple I was watching was Aunt Lovey and Uncle Stash, out of context here, in their matching tracksuits. Team Darlen. It hit me, for the first time in my life, that our parents would not live forever. Leaning heavily on Aunt Lovey, Uncle Stash made it to the gate. When the immigration people asked him why he was traveling to Kosice, Uncle Stash opened his mouth, but no words came out. I thought he'd been choked by emotion. But he'd completely lost his voice.

Aunt Lovey explained to the officials that we were going to the Tatras Mountains to visit Uncle Stash's brothers' graves. Then she shot Ruby and me a look, in case one of us was thinking about mentioning Mother Darlensky's ashes.

The officials looked up from the desk and saw Ruby and me. "Twins?" one of the men asked in English as the other man prodded a woman beside him to look. "Join twins?" He laced his fingers and rose from his desk for a closer look. "Two girl. One head," he said, tapping my forehead, then Ruby's, then laughing hoarsely. There was the dimmest of lights in his pupils. He had white foam in the corners of his mouth. I could feel that Ruby was smiling politely. I couldn't, so I avoided eye contact altogether. "Yes," I said acidly. Then I remembered our detention at the border to Detroit and added a note of respect — "Sir."

On board the next aircraft, which was much, much smaller than the one we'd flown in across the Atlantic Ocean, we were amused to find that, according to our tickets, Ruby and I had seats at opposite ends of the plane. The astonishingly lovely flight attendant shrugged when we explained our situation. "Ask someone to move," she growled, before turning to address the next complainant.

Ruby was outraged by the flight attendant's indifference, but I admired the woman, with her gathered gold hair, her shimmery pink mouth, and her indiscriminate contempt. (I wonder if all women secretly fantasize, like me, about what it would be like to be an extraordinary beauty and bitchy as you wanna be.)

The passengers on this small aircraft were Slovak, with the exception of three — Aunt Lovey, Ruby, and me. They did not stare, which we found disturbing, but whispered among themselves as they cast furtive glances. I wanted to say, "Stare. It's okay. You won't turn to stone." But I wasn't so sure.

(Aunt Lovey liked to tell the anecdote about the old Slovak man at her wedding to Uncle Stash. As was the custom among the rural French in Baldoon County, the dessert table was put together by the four ladies attending the bride. Ladies who competed fiercely to present the best berry tarts, pecan squares, chocolate bombs, angel cakes, butter cookies, cherry drops, coconut crisps, and lemon meringues, arranging the plethora of sweets on elegant pink Depression glass and their granny's three-tiered porcelain. Mr. Lipsky, the old Slovak man who'd subsidized the Darlenskys' apartment when they first got to Windsor, had joined the bride in admiring the offerings on the long dessert table. After a while he sighed very loudly and, squeezing Aunt Lovey's fingers in one hand, swept his free arm over the tableful of dessert. "When one sweet there is, I know what to take," Mr. Lipsky said. "When so many there is . . ." He shrugged tragically. Aunt Lovey nodded, watching the old Slovak return to his table, weary and woeful, with no dessert at all. Uncle Stash would laugh when she talked about Mr. Lipsky and say, "Lovey, not all Slovaks are like Lipsky." And Aunt Lovey would laugh too and say, "No, hon, just all the ones I've met." And they would both say, in unison, which was too cute, "Present company excepted.")

The journey to Kosice was short but turbulent. Ruby had nothing in her stomach to heave. I comforted her, because it was in my best interest, but I secretly thought she was whiny and weak when she said she felt so sick she just wanted to die. The pilot, competing with the buzzing speakers, made an announcement in Slovak. There was a hush as the passengers turned to look at one another. "What did he say, Uncle Stash?" Ruby whispered across the aisle, but Uncle Stash only shook his head. Aunt Lovey was holding an airsick bag. I'd never seen Aunt Lovey ill before, and the single fact of it scared me more than the thought of a crash, which would be mercifully swift. (I'd been worried, since Aunt Poppy had died of ovarian cancer just before the trip, that the same thing would happen to Aunt Lovey.)

Suddenly, the left wing of the airplane dipped, then the right, then the left, then not dips but full banking dives. The banking and diving went on for some time. My ear was popping. So was Ruby's. The pressure was unbearable. (Did I have the aneurysm then, ten years ago? Did I get it because of the pressure in the cabin?) Ruby started to sing, which may have relieved the pressure in her ear but did not relieve mine. I shouted for Ruby to stop singing. *"Stop singing!"*

I was shocked when the wheels (which I hadn't felt release from the plane's belly) hit the tarmac. I was not an experienced flier, but I was sure the descent into Bratislava had not felt as wonky and perilous as this one into Kosice. I don't remember much else about the flight, except that they served uncommonly delicious yogurt.

Ruby here.

I haven't written in a while. I've had a few headaches, not bad ones like Rose gets, but bad enough that I've felt depressed for a few weeks and haven't wanted to do much. That's frustrating, because there's so much to do. But as of today, my depression is over.

Rose has been depressed too. She says she's not depressed. She says she's serene. Who calls themselves serene? Especially when they're depressed? Anyway, I can tell she's depressed because the Athens Olympics have come and gone, and I was more interested than she was. She didn't even pick up a sports page! She hasn't even checked out her Tigers! If that's not Rose being depressed, I don't know what is.

As of today, Rose's depression is over too. Or it seems to be.

I had this strange feeling when I woke up this morning that something was going to happen today. We were still asleep when the phone rang at around nine o'clock. Rose answered. She was very groggy and she just grunted, which I thought was rude. The person was saying something and Rose was grunting, and I didn't know who it was or what was going on. She put down the phone and said there was some kind of surprise and that we should get up and get dressed. She said she didn't know what the surprise was, but I didn't believe her.

She made me wait while she brushed her hair. Rose? Brushing her hair? Then she completely freaked me out by putting in a hair clip. So of course I'm thinking, whatever this surprise is, it is huge, because my sister put in a freakin' hair clip!

There was a sound on the front porch, but the doorbell didn't ring and then there were keys in the door. It was Nick. He uses his key so we don't have to get up. I was very disappointed that it was just Nick, then I saw that he was hiding something big behind his back. The surprise. He moved away so we could see, and it was — actually it's hard to describe what it was — a black leather bar stool from Nonna's rec room that Nick welded with some other parts and made into a customized wheelchair. It's not exactly a wheelchair, though, because, first off, it's a stool, but it does have wheels. He extended the length of the legs so it's at a height where I can sit comfortably or stand if I want to. And he even welded some bars around it for security, and as an armrest at the back for Rose. So Nick brought this wheel/stool/thingy into the living room, and I didn't even know what to say because I was just so surprised. And Rose was surprised too. And disappointed.

Rose can be selfish. Sometimes she forgets who we are. She forgets that we are we. Well, she doesn't forget really, she just conveniently ignores the fact that we are conjoined and does what she wants to do. She wasn't moving toward the stool thing, and I just about had to kick her to get her to step forward. I'm sure Nick was wondering what that was all about. She embarrassed me by saying, Don't buck me like a bronco! Which is what she always says when I want to go, but she wants to stay.

Finally she went closer, and we got a good look at the thing. It just made sense. It made sense to the way we move and the way we're joined and the way our weight is distributed. Nick never measured us. That I know of. So I figure he must be some kind of savant. The stool would mean that Rose wouldn't have to carry my full weight. If it works at all, it's going to make life way easier for Rose and me at a time when we need it to be as easy as possible.

I looked at Rose's face in the mirror, and she looked strange. Like she wasn't even there. I said, Thank you, thank you, thank you, and Rose said nothing. Nick must have been pissed off, because he said, Hey, I made it for you too, Rose. Then he whispered, thinking I couldn't hear, but I did hear. He whispered this — I made it mostly for you, Rose.

Rose just said, Yeah. Then she said she had a headache and we should lie down. Nick said he'd sit with us, but she said no. Then he said he'd come by later and watch us try it out. But when he left, Rose didn't want to lie down and she didn't want to try out the stool.

So we sat on the couch. She didn't want to talk. She said if I put on the television, she would blow a jet. After a while I got bored and I just watched her in the mirror.

I've said that I can't read Rose's mind, but today I think I did. I think she was remembering a long, long time ago when the doctors told Aunt Lovey and Uncle Stash that we would need to have a special double wheelchair made and that's how we'd have to get around. The doctor didn't say we couldn't walk. He said we shouldn't. He advised that we should not be ambulatory. Aunt Lovey said we were already ambulatory. Uncle Stash swore in Slovak and left the room while Aunt Lovey explained to the doctor that Rose's legs were perfectly fine and that she would continue to use them for walking. The doctor said Rose just wasn't strong enough to support me and couldn't possibly be expected to spend a lifetime carrying me around. Aunt Lovey said that Rose could and would spend a lifetime doing just that, and over her dead body would these girls end up in a wheelchair. We went back to the farmhouse, and Aunt Lovey made Rose cry, saying, One more time, carry Ruby to the creek and back one more time, until Rose was strong enough not to feel the effort anymore. It's just who we were and it's just what we did.

And now there was this stool, which Rose called a behemoth, staring us in the face, and Rose was feeling like she let Aunt Lovey down. Aunt Lovey wouldn't have been let down, though.

Rose just sat there for the longest time. Then she said, Shit! Like she dropped something. Like she just realized she lost her keys or something. It was very strange.

I asked her to try the chair, but she refused to try the chair, even when I begged. She got out her computer and made herself comfortable, not really paying that much attention to my comfort, and she started to write, which is all she ever wants to do these days. I asked her what she was writing about, and she said the trip to Slovakia, which may explain a few things about her recent depression.

Normally when Rose is writing, I don't bother talking because she'll get snippy or she won't answer me at all, but before I knew it I just flat out said, How about we leave the whole thing to the library? The whole thing. The money from the house, the farm, the land, everything. Rose stopped typing. God only knows what part of the Slovakia story she was at — there's not much of it I like to remember.

Rose said she thought it was a good idea to leave some of our estate to the library. Then she said, What about leaving the farmhouse to the Historical Society? It could be a new home for the Leaford Museum. How's that for a great idea?

(One day I heard Nick tell Rose, Don't leave anything to Nonna that might end up with me. He said whatever it was, he'd pawn it or piss it away in some bar. He said the only thing keeping him sober was being broke.)

We didn't talk for a while after we agreed about putting the library in our will and giving the farmhouse to the museum, and then I couldn't help myself and I said, I wish you wouldn't write about Slovakia because I think it would hurt Uncle Stash. The Slovaks don't come off looking so good in parts. But she said she couldn't write the story of our lives and not say what happened in Slovakia, and I guess she's right. I asked her not to include some embarrassing details about me.

She said we shouldn't be talking about our chapters anyway, but then she went ahead and said, I hope you're not writing about medical stuff. I hope you're not writing about the aneurysm. I hope you're not describing my decline. What a word to use. And besides, it's our decline. Then she said, What are you writing about anyway? And I had to laugh because I couldn't tell her.

My sister couldn't believe that I can't remember what I've written. It's not like I'm gonna go back and reread it.

Rose said she hopes that I'm not just rambling, because no one's gonna want to read rambling. She said it's really important for me to read what I've written so far because I might be repeating myself. I just laughed harder. Of course I'm repeating myself. That's what people do.

She said I should have a plan before I start to write. Like a theme or a subject. Like how she's writing about Slovakia. She said I should write down some things I know about the Neutrals and reasons why I'm so interested in the past. Oh my God — Does she want me to write an essay? She said she finds that stuff interesting, and other people will too. And she said if they don't, some editor will just cut it out.

Rose talks like she has real experience with publishers and editors, when really she doesn't. Maybe I will write some stuff about the Neutrals, though. Maybe I'll write down Aunt Lovey's story about the contest between the Indian brothers, which happened about half a mile from our farm.

I wrote the story down for composition class when I was in high school, the only time I ever got an A in English. Rose said it was cheating, but Aunt Lovey said it was fine. Aunt Lovey hadn't dictated it to me exactly. I remembered it on my own, and she said that meant I was interpreting it. That qualifies as art.

Here's the story, which I copied out from my essay (which I still think is pretty good).

Once upon a time, before electricity or plumbing or even roads in Baldoon County, there was a nation of Native Indians called the Neutrals who were traders, and who set up temporary fishing camps along the mighty Thames River. One of the camps was just east of Leaford, on the Thames. The Neutral Indians spoke a dialect close to Iroquois and were not at war with anyone.

Among this nation of travelers and traders lived a girl named Abey (which means "plant" or just "leaf"). Abey was beautiful and smart, and all the young men in the nation were in love with her. But none so much as a set of twin brothers, who were also her best friends. The twins had been in love with Abey since they were little boys, and Abey told them that she could never choose one of them over the other.

They had to decide themselves which brother would have her as his wife. Eventually it was time to marry, and the boys still hadn't chosen which of them would wed Abey. One of the brothers suggested a contest of endurance to decide who'd be the groom. A swimming competition. The twin brothers went to the widest place on the Thames River, near the bend where the church is now.

There was much cheering as the twin boys dove into the muddy brown water, as everyone had come to watch the contest. A few of the earliest settlers from farms nearby came down to the river when they heard the ruckus and stayed to see the brothers test their endurance.

The twin boys were strong swimmers and kept perfect pace with each other from one bank of the river to the other. But after fifty laps across the river, the brothers were starting to get tired.

Abey, who'd been watching the contest with interest, not knowing which brother to root for because she loved them both the same, began to worry. Another ten laps and another ten, and the boys began to wilt. She tried to call them out of the water, but they wouldn't come. It was starting to get dark.

The crowd began to cheer, hoping the race would be over while there was light enough to see who won. The boys, though slowing down with each stroke, continued to drive toward the riverbank. The crowd cheered their fortitude as Abey blushed at their commitment.

The twilight drifted away and the boys continued to swim, growing more and more tired, their arms barely rising from the water and their feet barely kicking. They made it to one bank. Then back to the other. Soon they were nothing but blurs of dark movement that the people squinted to track.

When the boys could no longer be seen, but only their movement heard in the black water, Abey cried to the boys again to please come on out. She said that she would decide who to marry. She cried that she had been wrong to pit brother against brother. She shouted to the boys that she was not worthy of their devotion, which got the interest of her peers, but the twins continued to swim, still keeping pace with each other, as could be heard in their splashing. People built fires, knowing the swimmers would need to be warmed when it was over. Some of the farmers cut back through the bush to bring oil lamps and blankets from their homes.

Standing alone in the blackness, Abey listened for the sound of her suitors breaking the muddy water. Abey shouted again that she wasn't worth the brothers' love. She shouted for them to come out of the water. Then she cried out, though it wasn't true, that she had been unfaithful. Thinking she was on to something, Abey began to shout out many terrible things about herself, all of them untrue, hoping to make the boys give up the contest and come out of the water.

The boys did not stop swimming, though. The boys did not hear Abey's terrible lies about herself. But the rest of her nation did. And she sounded so convincing they believed her and put it together that she was a very wicked person and had tragically cursed the twins. Abey heard her people in the dark, leaving her and the still-swimming boys.

In the morning, Abey sat cold and shivering on the riverbank. Her people had moved their camp in the night. She didn't need to look behind her to know she was alone. She didn't need to look at the river either, because she had heard one brother slip under, and then the other, seconds later, in the night, when only she and the moon were watching.

Abey thought she was dreaming, feeling the weight of the warm blanket on her shoulders. But when she turned around, there was a handsome white man with kind eyes offering a pretty pink peach from the palm of his hand. Abey took the peach and didn't feel afraid. She'd seen this man, waving from the riverbanks, when they passed by the summer before. She never imagined then that she was looking at her future husband.

Aunt Lovey would always pause there and say, as if it needed to be said, And that is how my great-great-great-great-grandfather Rosaire met my great-great-great-great-grandmother Abey.

Before I wrote out that story about Aunt Lovey's Indian forebear, I was talking about when Nick brought the stool. So, later, after we talked about what I was and wasn't writing in my yellow legal pad, Rose decided she wanted to eat one of the cannolis that Roz had picked up for us at the Oakwood Bakery. But the cannolis were in the kitchen, and she didn't feel like moving. I said, Let's try the stool. If we don't like it, we'll tell Nick thanks, but it's not comfortable. I was really happy when she said she'd try. It's hard for Rose to admit that she's not as strong as she used to be.

Getting me into the chair was a bit of a big deal, but that will get easier. Wheeling down the hall felt good. Better than good. Amazing. I felt like I had legs. Not like I was borrowing my sister's, but like I had my own. The vibration of the wheels on the floor shot up the steel legs of the stool and right into my spine.

We made it to the kitchen and back in half the time it's been taking us, because Rose stops so much now and likes to be close to a wall (in case she falls, I guess). We made it back to the couch with the box of cannolis in my lap and we ate. Just a nibble, really, because neither of us has that much of an appetite, but we felt much better. Cannolis can do that. Then Rose found the remote phone and called Nick and said, Come watch us try the chair.

If there were more craniopagus twins like us in the world, Nick could get rich. He should be an inventor — that's how good this stool is. Our hallway is fairly wide, so Rose and I went back and forth and back and forth in the hallway, getting faster and faster. Even Rose liked the stool. She doesn't complain a lot, but I know her back aches, worse now than ever. Nick watched us, kinda laughing, but not at us. He even clapped a couple of times. And Rose blushed.

We won't be able to use it outside on the sidewalk because bumps are a problem, which we found out the hard way. We can use it at work, though, which is where we have to do most of our getting around now, and the kids'll love it.

I am warming up to Nick, though he is still more Rose's friend than mine. I think he felt pretty proud of himself because of the stool. He went into the kitchen and made a pitcher of lemonade from a mix in the cupboard. Nick says if he drinks lemonade in a highball glass, he feels like he's having a G7 (Gilbey's gin and 7Up), which was his poison of choice. He brought out the lemonade, and there was a knock at the door, and we're all thinking, Who could that be? because we don't get many visitors.

It was Nonna. She had no clue who Rose and I were and she asked for Aunt Lovey, and she would not accept that Aunt Lovey wasn't home. Then she started crying, which just breaks your heart. To see an old lady who you love, and who has always been one of the people to take care of you, to see her crying is just the saddest thing. I didn't tell Nonna that Aunt Lovey was dead because she'd have keeled right over. But Nick had to take Nonna home. Rose and I both felt sick about seeing her like that. We just poured the whole pitcher of lemonade down the sink.

It's September 19. Late for lemonade anyway.

We sat on the porch a little after dinner. Nick was driving out of town. He was vague about where, but said he'd be back in the morning and to call Ruttle or Emergency at Leaford if there's a problem. Why be all mysterious about where he's going? How annoying! Plus, why would he leave Nonna alone, even if she did have a sleeping pill?

This is the first time that Rose and I are writing together. She's working on her laptop right now. It feels strange and kinda nice to be writing at the same time. Though we are not writing about the same things.

Rose has slowed down. Walking. Moving. Shifting. Everything. Even writing. When she first started this book five months ago her fingers flew so fast on the keys, a hundred miles a minute, a hundred pages at a time. Now she's slow. Slow, but steady. She never pauses much or stops for long. I get the feeling that when she closes her computer at the end of the night it's because she can't write more. Not because she doesn't have more to write.

A long time ago my sister said that when the book is done, so is she, so I think she's trying to give us more time by making the book take longer. Rose thinks she can control things. Like if she wears her disgusting brown sweater her sports teams will win. It's really very arrogant.

Everyone knows about the aneurysm now, and it's so much easier. Rose and I hate it when people pity our situation, but pity for dying isn't so bad. It isn't really pity anyway; it's empathy. Not everyone can relate to being joined at the head, but anyone can relate to dying.

People have just kind of stepped up for us. Really. Roz has brought a few casseroles for the freezer. Whiffer and Lutie dropped some groceries off (Rose and I had a laugh at how freaked they were about our house of mirrors). People are being nice and optimistic, which is good, because fatal is fatal, but it doesn't have to be all downhill.

This is the first time I've gone on writing after Rose has fallen asleep. She has been complaining about my snoring our whole life, and she has no idea she snores too. She says my snoring is a pig-snorting sound. Hers has a whistle at the end. It doesn't bother me. Nothing about Rose really bothers me. Nothing physical anyway.

Earlier tonight Rose and I talked a bit about things we don't like to talk about, and Rose said we should call our lawyer friend and see about a will, and that we should go to the archaeology museum sooner rather than later. And that we should bring the stool.

The stool doesn't fold up, which is a minor design flaw. But Nick's got a big enough trunk and he'll be driving us, so that's okay.

I'm excited to go to the Indian museum. We haven't been there since before Aunt Lovey and Uncle Stash passed away. There's an old man who works there called Errol Osler. He is quite a character. Always happy to see Ruby and me. We first met Errol Osler when Rose and I were about ten years old, when we stopped at the museum on our way home after some appointment with a specialist about my gut.

We've seen him just about every year since, up until a few years ago, and it was just too sad to think about going without Aunt Lovey and Uncle Stash. Plus, it would have meant the bus, and that can be a problem for me with my car sickness, which has gotten worse as I've grown older.

I remember when we first walked into the outdoor part of the museum in London. I felt this incredible déjà vu, which was different than the feeling that I've been here before. It was more like the feeling that I've been here before and I never left. Sometimes I wonder about my past lives, and if I ever lived my life as a Native Indian. Maybe even as Abey.

I do believe in reincarnation. I have dreams sometimes, and these little visions that just kind of pop into my brain, where I'm me but also someone else. I have one dream where I'm an English lady wearing an old-fashioned gown, and I'm walking in the meadow arguing with a man who's my husband, only the man is Rose. Rose — but a man. I've seen myself as a fish gutter on a ship, and nothing but black ocean as far as the eye can see. I'm working beside my uncle, and he's my best friend. But he's Rose too. And, in fact, Rose is in all my visions and dreams about lives I've lived. Sometimes she's my wife, and sometimes she's my cousin or my brother, or even my mother. I know that sounds flaky.

I was not good in school, but I remember once a science teacher saying how energy cannot be created or destroyed, and I got the goose shivers. And I still get the goose shivers when I think about energy, because that's what I think reincarnation is. I think our souls are energy, and they aren't destroyed when we die. They have memories of the other lives, but the memories are in this locked cabinet, and every once in a while the cabinet is accidentally opened and a few things fall out — the visions and the déjà vus. Rose says it's absolute horseshit when I try to talk about reincarnation with her, but Aunt Lovey always knew what I meant. Aunt Lovey said that when she was a little girl, she used to try to tell her mother about her other life and her other family, and her two older brothers. But her mother, Verbeena, just thought she'd been climbing the peach tree and had fallen on her head again. Aunt Lovey had a lot of déjà vu, and she said some of it could be low blood pressure.

When Rose and I first started working at the library, a mother came in with her twin four-year-old boys. They were so cute and so funny, and Rosie and I just fell in love with them. Their mother was very nice to us, though she was a little spooked when she first walked into the children's section and asked Rose for help and didn't quite notice, because of how Rose was standing, that I was there too. I saw right away how the mother could tell the twin boys apart, and that was because one of the boys had a large round strawberry birthmark below his left eye. The brother of the boy saw me looking at the birthmark and blurted out that he shot his brother with a bow and arrow. The mother laughed and said the child had been telling people that he shot his brother with a bow and arrow since he could talk, but he'd never even seen a bow and arrow. And when I heard that, I got the goose shivers again. What if that boy's remembering something that happened in another life? What if he's lived all of his lives with his brother? Just as I've lived mine with Rose? I believe in supernatural things, and I think that some people have extrasensory perception. And I swear to God that, when I walked into the Museum of Indian Archaeology that very first time, when I was only around ten years old, I had some kind of strange feeling. Like a weird trembling feeling and a knot in my stomach (but a good kind of knot), and this feeling that I wanted to cry (a good kind of cry).

Errol Osler came over and didn't make a big deal about Rose and me being conjoined twins; he just came over and looked at me, like he never questioned I was my own person, and he said a lot of people get choked up in churches and museums. He said people get touched in the most mysterious ways. I liked the way he talked and the way he understood how I felt.

Rose and I have always liked visiting museums. Especially the county ones. The history of this area of southwestern Ontario is very interesting because we are so close to America, yet we are not Americans. And so many things have happened between our two countries. Southwestern Ontario was one of the last stops on the Underground Railroad, where black American slaves found freedom and built whole towns and communities. Plus, there was the Battle of the Thames between the Americans and the British, where the Indians were on the British side. And the great Indian prophet Chief Tecumseh was killed right near the Thames River in Chatham. And the missionary village of Fairfield was burned to the ground by American troops. In the roaring twenties, half the people around here were involved in bootlegging. We did not have a local history class in grade school, but Aunt Lovey knew everything about the local history of Leaford and Chatham and the whole county because the Tremblays were among the earliest settlers and they passed down their family stories, which also ended up being history.

When I was putting together all the sketches I made of the artifacts I'd found over the years and updating my map of the farm, Aunt Lovey wrote out a poem for me — something about how people don't really die — something about a dead man's embers. Rose will remember it. I'll get her to write it down in one of her chapters.

So, anyway, Rose and I both like museums and we both like history, and since we're part of Baldoon County history, being craniopagus twins born during a fluke tornado, I joked with Rose that if her autobiography does not get published, she should leave it to the Leaford Museum for when it opens back up, and people could read bits of it if they wanted. She got huffy and said, You don't write a book to have bits read.

I thought bits would be better than nothing. Shows you what I know about writing.

Anyway, we're too old for Disney World, and Paris is not meant to be, but the Indian museum is a place I enjoy visiting, and it's a place I'd like to go again. I'd also like to say good-bye to Errol Osler, though I won't necessarily say it like it's final. Rose wants to visit the museum too. She's never been quite as interested in our Native history as I am, but she likes Errol. She says he's a good character study. What a way to talk about a person!

Before she closed her eyes tonight, Rose said she regretted that she has not done something heroic in her life. Well, it's not like she can suddenly climb a tree and save a cat, or go to medical school and begin some important cancer research.

But Rose has been my sister.

I think that's heroic.

A couple of nights ago, Rose set her computer aside but forgot to shut it down. In the morning, before she realized it was still on, I read a line that said something like "I could not have been more loved, but I could have loved more." I hope all her writing is not that freakin' boring.

I was saving my new blue blouse for laying out, but I think I'll wear it to the museum instead.

I made maps and wrote the location of all my finds. I sketched pictures of all the artifacts. I gave the stuff over to the Leaford Museum, but I kept the map and the sketches, and I still have them. I want to give them to Errol Osler.

The best thing I ever found was an intact pipe where the stem looked like a bird body and the bowl looked like a bird head. A crane, I think. Or a heron. I didn't find the bird effigy pipe in the fields in the spring, like most of my other Indian artifacts. I found it in the fall, when we were just sitting on the bridge to Merkels', waiting for herons. I saw the bird head poking out of the dry dirt at the top of the bank of the creek. We went down to investigate, and I think even Rose was excited about seeing the pipe because you could tell it was something old and rare. Rose kicked off her shoe, using her toes to move the dirt from the thing without destroying it, and then she curled her toes around it and lifted it up and gave it to me. (Obviously it's hard for us to bend down, but Rose is really good with her feet and toes, and her balance is amazing, especially since she's so weighed down. She's really quite the athlete, but only the people really close to us would get that.)

We cleaned the dirt off the pipe and we went back to sit on the bridge, and Rosie and I played this game of pretending we were Indian sisters from hundreds of years ago. We passed the pipe back and forth, pretending to take puffs of tobacco, though we weren't sure if the pipe was a leisure pipe for personal use or a peace pipe for rituals.

Another great thing I found was a kit — well at least I call it a kit. There was a flint, and a half-chipped arrowhead, and a round of sandstone, and a large grooved stone ready to be fitted to a handle. And a stone mortar and pestle. Errol Osler said it all must have been wrapped up in a pouch or something. I found the things within a couple inches of each other, which tells me they were together, so that's why I call it a kit, but of course the leather pouch would have disintegrated long ago. Rose and I tried to figure out what had happened and how the kit got left or lost. Rose wrote a short story about the pouch, imagining that it had belonged to a teenage Indian girl and that she lost it while running away from home to marry a boy from the Delaware tribe at Fairfield. Rose wrote the story as a diary of a runaway, pretending that she was the teenage Indian runaway, which I loved. I thought it was a really good story, and Rose was really proud of it. Aunt Lovey said it was the best thing Rose had ever written. But our English teacher gave her a D and wrote a note in red pen saying Rose was a good writer but that she should stick to things she knows. And then she wrote, It's not a good idea to cross racial boundaries when you are writing. Especially don't do it when you are writing in the first-person voice. You could offend and upset many people who have more right to tell a certain story than you do.

Rose has never been one to suffer in silence. She was steaming for most of the afternoon and whispering to me about her story all during science, so we almost got sent out of the room. At the end of the day, we went up to the English teacher's desk, and Rose challenged the teacher about her D. Rose was so mad she was shaking. The teacher thought Rose was really nervy for challenging the grade. She said things about how, even though Rose is part of a minority culture because of our deformity, she should not be exploiting other people in her writing, and that she should be telling her own stories, not those of someone else. Rose argued that it could not be someone else's story because the story didn't exist without her. But the teacher did not change her grade.

Rose is still snoring, but it doesn't bother me. It makes me love her more. I love that saying My cup runneth over. That's how I feel about Rose right in this moment. Like I can't even contain my feelings for her. Funny how that happens, that you just feel this intense love for a person because of the way they're snoring. Or the way they say your name. Also, my sister is vulnerable when she is asleep, and she does not let herself be that way in life. When she's sleeping, she feels more like my child than my sister, though I know that sounds extremely weird.

A couple of people have mentioned how well we're dealing with our situation and how optimistic and strong we seem. They say it to us, but they mean me, and even Rose knows that. Rose has not been herself. How could she be?

I think my beliefs are helping me deal with our current situation. I just know that the end is not the end. Something in me is energy and was not created and can't be destroyed. That's a fact. And something in Rose is indestructible too. So I know that I will come here again. And in some way or other, Rose and I will still be attached, like we are now and like we've always been.

I wish Rose could believe in something.

Writing

Words leak from my brain. Seep out my ear. Burble from my crooked mouth. Splash on my shirt. Trickle into my keyboard. Pool on my warped parquet floor. At least they're not gushing from my heart. Or, God forbid, my ass. I catch the words as they fall. My hands smell. And the place is a wreck. From all the spilled words.

It is mid-September, and my sister and I have been greeted by fog each morning for three days straight. The warmed-by-summer earth meets the chill of a fresh fall night, and the fog that results from their union is very dense and gray. Uncle Stash used to say it was a "fairy fog," which is mystical and beyond Mother Nature's intervention. That is where the fairies live. Not the beautiful winged fairies that advise heroes and rescue princesses, but devilish hoofed ones that cause loss and chaos. At least, that's how Uncle Stash told it. (Though I always had the feeling that the Leaford fairies were not as cunning or mean as the fairies of his Slovak youth.) Uncle Stash said you can see the fairies in the fog if you look hard enough. And they can bring you luck if you catch one of *their* eyes before they catch one of yours.

I remember when Uncle Stash first told Ruby and me about the fairy fog, walking us out to our phallic silver bus shelter on a late September day to wait for the yellow bus to take us to school. When he was a small child in Grozovo, he told us, he'd caught the eye of a fairy in the fog early one morning while walking the ducks to the pond. That afternoon he'd found a koruna on the road, which he gave to his mother. That evening he'd found considerably more meat in his soup than did his two older brothers. "It was good day," Stash said. "My mother was happy. *'Dobre klopsy,'* she said to me. Good boy."

As Ruby and I held our breath, he'd stood very still and stared hard at the yard where the mist seemed thickest. "There! There!" he said. "I caught the little bugger! He looked right at me!"

Ruby sobbed, terrified that this demon fairy might come rushing out of the fog to steal us away. But Uncle Stash petted my sister's silly head and stopped her tears and told her the fairies were not allowed to harm children, which I could see he didn't believe. He asked Ruby to give him her hand and pressed something into her palm that I didn't see. "Wow," Ruby breathed. "Can I keep it?"

I begged Ruby to tell me what Uncle Stash had given her, but she wouldn't, and to this day I do not know what it was. That afternoon Ruby got a C+ on her spelling test instead of her usual D−. And on the way home, Frankie Foyle opened the bus's back window when Ruby said she felt vomity.

That night after school we'd told Aunt Lovey about Uncle Stash seeing the fairy in the fog when he was a boy, and the koruna, and the meat, and his happy mother. I could tell by her expression that Aunt Lovey had never heard the story before. We wanted to explain how Uncle Stash had caught the fairy looking back at him in the fog that morning and transferred his good luck to Ruby, but Aunt Lovey had stopped listening. She was gazing down the long hall, where Uncle Stash was resting on the sofa in the den.

Aunt Lovey squeezed my shoulder, and Ruby's arm, and padded down the hall and hovered above Uncle Stash's still face. Ruby and I watched as Aunt Lovey kissed him, deeply. I saw her mouth the word "You." And he said it too. Then Aunt Lovey kicked the door closed with her foot and we did not see them again until dinner, an absence about which Ruby and I chose not to wonder.

No doubt Ruby has written about the stool Nick Todino made for us. We have nicknamed the thing Stooly Too. Or Two. I'm not sure — it was Ruby's idea. I didn't even know how to thank Nick for what he did. For what he's done. He says that doing things for Ruby and me is like therapy, which I find oddly unflattering. When Nick first came to live with Nonna, shortly after Aunt Lovey and Uncle Stash passed away, Ruby and I hated him. He never did much around the house (still doesn't do much by way of general maintenance), and there was the drinking. Then, one day, Ruby and I went over for a visit and were surprised by the sound of lively music pouring out the windows, and even more surprised by the trill of Nonna's laughter. We peered in the window and saw Nick dancing Nonna around the living room, with Italian folk music blaring on the stereo. When they answered the door, they were both sweating. Nonna looked a decade younger. Nick smelled of yeast. Nonna was just starting to get confused back then. She'd been shocked to see us on her doorstep. Her laughter stopped. And so did the music — like a cue.

Nick brought us into the house, explaining in his smoky voice, "It's Rose and Ruby, Mama. It's okay," he said. "You remember, Mama. You knew them since they were babies."

"It's not a monster?" Nonna whispered in Italian. The Italian word *"orco"* sounded nothing like the English word for "monster," but I knew what she was saying.

Nick shook his head. "Sometimes when you crack an egg there's a double yolk, right, Mama? You've seen the double yolk? And sometimes the cherry grows together — not on two stems, but the flesh of two, together." He laced his fingers to demonstrate. "It's like that. Special."

I liked the way Nick described our situation, but Ruby continued to be suspicious of him. I imagine Stooly has changed all that, though. She just about slobbered all over him for making it. I don't think it has occurred to Ruby that the stool was for me too.

Nick. Nick. Nick. What would we do without Nick? Nick, who pronounces the K in his name so hard it sounds like a separate syllable. Ni-*KA*. Nick's been such a help, driving us here and there and bringing us this and that. He has been clean and sober for twenty-nine days. Maybe his sponsor lives in Windsor. He's been going there a lot. It's either his sponsor or a woman. Or a sponsor who's a woman. Just about every Saturday he gets all dressed up (which means cowboy boots and a tweedy sports jacket) and heads out in his Thunderbird. He goes to his other meetings in the basement of Holy Cross Church around the corner from Chippewa Drive, but he does not wear his cowboy boots. Ruby and I think it's funny that Nick is so mysterious about his Saturday night adventures.

I wasn't feeling well the day Nick brought Stooly over last week. I wanted to kill Ruby for pushing me about trying the thing out. I thought I would puke if I stood up. I didn't want to puke in front of Nick. It may be normal for Ruby, but *I* don't puke in front of anyone. After Nick left, I had a missing-time episode. At least I think that's what it was. Ruby didn't say anything about rectal probes or little green men, so I'm guessing it was a seizure of some kind. I considered calling Dr. Singh, but he would most certainly say we most certainly need to see him, though there is most certainly nothing he can do. It's happened to me before — losing time — but not for such a long period. (I've been able to convince myself I had been daydreaming and got lost.) But this time I sensed a change in the air, and the sun had moved completely from one window to another.

I shouted, "Shit!" because I was scared and confused. Ruby was watching me in the mirror. Ruby misunderstood. She rambled on and on about how Aunt Lovey would have wanted me to try the stool and how it wasn't like giving up or giving in. I didn't want to tell her that it wasn't the stool. It was because I was nauseous. I've always been the well one and do not like feeling so damn vulnerable.

So I dragged my laptop from the coffee table and started to write because, even though the writing is killing me, it focuses and cleanses me too. I'd begun to write the story of our trip to Slovakia, but that story has become several stories, entwined and connected. And I want to write the next part in one big breath.

WE'RE GOING TO the Indian museum in London soon. Nick is bringing us, of course. And we'll be able to stay as long as Ruby wants, since we're bringing our cool new stool.

Sweet surrender.

This book isn't a book anymore. It's alive. It calls to me when I'm asleep. It chides me to be truthful.

So here it is.

I think I'm falling in love with Nick Todino.

It's Ruby here.

It's the first week of fall, but it feels more like summer. We had no jackets, and only short sleeves, from morning on.

Sherman Merkel came into the library today. I was finishing up reading circle and the kids were rammy, and Rose and I both had headaches. In comes Sherman Merkel wearing clean clothes, which was the first weird thing because we're used to seeing him in his farmer pants. He went straight for the bulletin board. The bulletin board is the reason most people without kids come to the kids' section, because the bulletin board is near the washrooms, which are behind the junior mysteries shelves.

Mr. Merkel tacked a notice on the bulletin board, then, on his way out, he stopped to say hello. Only not hello, really. He just dipped his chin and said, Girls, which is all he ever really says. Girls. Girls. Girls. Girls.

I've always liked Mr. Merkel, even though he's usually too shy for conversations. And, even today, I can't help how I love Mrs. Merkel. Even though she obviously doesn't love us in return.

Rosie and I have the strangest relationship with Mrs. Merkel. It's like we completely understand how she feels and don't take any of it personally. She doesn't even know it, but with Aunt Lovey passed away and Nonna not really Nonna anymore, Mrs. Merkel's the only mother figure we have left.

Anyway, after Mr. Merkel said Girls, he stood there for a long time and we could see he had tears in his eyes. We never saw Mr. Merkel with tears in his eyes before, and I felt pretty sure he was about to tell us that his wife had left him, because I always half expected that.

Instead, he said to us, If there's anything me and the missus can do, you girls just let us know. I realized he must have heard about the aneurysm, but I still didn't connect that his sad face was about us.

I hate when Rose talks the way she writes. She can sound so pretentious. And that's what happened with Mr. Merkel today. She said something like, We've always thought well of you and Mrs. Merkel, and we're richer for having been your neighbors. I swear to God I felt carsick.

Then the poor guy burst into tears. Uncontrollable tears. He was sobbing right there in the children's section, and all these kids who'd been running around stopped, and some of them started to cry. Then Mr. Merkel got the hiccups, only it sounded like retching. And I just thought I was in hell.

Two things. Why do you want to make a grown man cry and embarrass him completely in the children's section of the Leaford Library? And why can't you just be normal and say, Thanks, yeah, we'll let you know if we need anything, Mr. Merkel? You know?

We gave Mr. Merkel some Kleenex, but he had a hell of a time getting control of his emotions. Rose and I think a lot of his weeping was about losing Larry too. Even though that happened a long time ago.

The note Mr. Merkel put up on the bulletin board was about looking for a farmhand for the winter. Rosie and I were saying, Whoever they find, we hope it's someone who's good company for Mrs. Merkel.

She must get so lonely. Especially now that she doesn't keep dogs.

Rose confided in Whiffer that she's written quite a few pages for the book, and so have I. Whiffer said he was going to call his cousin to tell his friend's friend in publishing about Rose writing her story. Rose told him not to, because she doesn't want anyone to know about it until she's done. She says it'll jinx her. She laughs about me, but she is really so superstitious.

Rose said something to Whiffer about how she's not sure her story is very good. She said she thought it would be easier to write, and when she reads it back to herself it sounds simple. I knew that she was angling for him to ask to read it, but instead he said, Don't worry if it's not well written. It's the conjoined-twin thing that's gonna sell it or not.

When Whiffer said the *conjoined-twin thing,* Rose just about threw up. I could feel her swallowing and swallowing. Maybe Whiffer's right. But he didn't have to say it.

Nick knows she's writing this thing, but he's the only other one. If she gives it to Nick before she gives it to me, I will take that Tatranax.

Anyway, seeing Mr. Merkel standing there in the library with his eyes bright red and tears running down his face made me remember when he got the ammonia in his lungs one summer when we were little. There was this huge tanker of ammonia that he would take out in the field, and it's got this long tube thing and you shoot the ammonia into the earth, because it's good for the corn, but once in a while a farmer might pull the ammonia tube out too soon and get a burning blast of it. You can imagine how that would fry your lungs. And your eyes. And that happened to Mr. Merkel twice in one summer because the ammonia tank he was renting wasn't working right. When Mr. Merkel was crying in the library, he looked exactly like when he got blasted with ammonia. Aunt Lovey said Mr. Merkel was gonna have cardboard for lungs when he's an old man because of those ammonia accidents.

Eventually he got hold of himself, though, and why I would say something as stupid as this, and especially to Mr. Merkel, is beyond me. But this is what I said. I said, This has been a bad year for hurricanes in the southern United States.

I was just making small talk so Sherman Merkel wouldn't start crying again. I was just thinking about the news. I started saying something else about the bad weather in the South, and I wasn't thinking anything of it until Rose pinched me. Hard.

Mr. Merkel took this long inhale of breath, and I thought, Oh now, here he goes again. And I clocked the tissues so I could pass them back over. But Mr. Merkel didn't start crying when he let his breath out.

He just told us to watch the price of tomatoes this winter.

Prosim

W e touched down in Kosice at dusk, and I found hope in the soft pink sky. Uncle Stash seemed to be breathing more easily, though he was still woozy from travel and hadn't quite recovered his voice. There was a sense of calm, if not exactly peace, in the airport, in the hush of the square gray halls and the orderliness of the structure itself. There were no people whatsoever who did not appear to be Slovak, except Ruby and me and Aunt Lovey. I squeezed Ruby, but she was busy with her own concerns, having already noticed something I had not. No one was staring. There was *no staring*. No craning. No peering. Nothing. We walked down a long corridor, past quiet doughy people who would not look and would not stare, but, wearing frowns and looking down, passed by Ruby and me like we weren't there. It wasn't just odd or weird, it was frightening. Who would not stare, what kind of people would not even look, at conjoined twins?

There was no baggage carousel in the airport at Kosice. The baggage handler tossed the luggage onto an old wooden wagon and pulled it along behind us. The wagon's wheels nearly clipped Uncle Stash's heels when he stopped abruptly to have a coughing fit. A security guard, on seeing Uncle Stash and Aunt Lovey and Ruby and me in our sort-of-matching blue tracksuits, motioned for Team Darlen to follow him to a side door. The man smiled at my sister and me in a genuine way and radio-called for a taxi. "It's the best taxi I get for you," he said in English, as he opened the glass door to the cold Slovak night.

"Prosim," the young security guard said. *"Prosim."* (We would discover that the Slovaks say *prosim,* which translated means "if you please," about a thousand times a day, for the oddest reasons, in the strangest ways.)

The Slovak sky looked stained, blacker in the middle and lighter around the edges. I don't remember any stars. But there must have been stars. The bulb buzzing above the door where we stood was bright and made our skin green. Or we were green, from illness and fatigue.

We waited. And waited, and we were still waiting, long after the passengers from on board our flight had climbed into taxis at the official taxi stand at the front of the building. The handsome guard made small talk with Aunt Lovey in his practiced English. He smiled our way several more times with his ice-blue eyes. He even winked at Ruby. He reminded me of a tennis player (but without a tan), with his broad shoulders and whittled waist and strong forearms. I was watching him, making notes for an elaborate romantic fantasy, when he suddenly poked Ruby's shoulder and asked, "It can talk? Yes?"

Before Aunt Lovey could educate the blue-eyed guard, a long black taxi arrived and an old uniformed driver stepped out. The driver nodded to the security guard and bent to collect the luggage, but he was stopped by the sight of Ruby and me. He stood stock-still, the heavy suitcases stretching his long thin arms.

He stared. Briefly, but he stared. And I felt better.

The taxi was old, a late-seventies model, judging from its appearance. It looked something like an old Cadillac. That kind of wheelbase. That serious sleek. Ruby and I eased ourselves into the back as our parents climbed into the front, to share the bench seat with the driver. The cab was clean and smelled of dusty roses from the pink air freshener hanging on the rearview mirror. As he pulled away from the airport the old man pressed a button on the car's radio and Madonna started singing "Material Girl." *Hovno.*

We followed the winding road, barren fields to the left and right. I tried to find the Tatras Mountain range in the darkening sky but couldn't. Uncle Stash began to cough violently. I could not believe, when it was over and he moved his hands from his face, that he was not covered in blood. Aunt Lovey checked Uncle Stash's temperature with her palm. She counted the beats of his heart. To reassure all of us, she said, "I'm sure it's not your ticker, hon. It's just a lousy virus. You'll feel better after a good night's sleep."

Aunt Lovey asked the driver to slow down. "Please," she said. "It's so hard on the girls when you hit the bumps."

The elderly driver pulled up under a canopy near the front doors to the Hotel Kosice. Aunt Lovey and Uncle Stash slid out of the front and helped Ruby and me climb out from the back. The bamboo planters lining the path to the hotel grew clusters of twigs and cigarette butts. The air was cold and smelled like bacon. Leaford seemed not just a world away but years and decades and whole lifetimes away. I thought of how Sherman Merkel would be finishing up with the squash. Cathy Merkel'd be putting it up while we were gone. (I like it with butter and pepper, but squash makes Ruby bilious.) I was suddenly very homesick.

We could see through the large glass doors that the hotel lobby was nearly deserted. Exhausted, Ruby and I waited at the elevators with Uncle Stash while Aunt Lovey went to check in. I wished I was not so tired. I wished Uncle Stash was not so sick. I'd imagined him in these first few moments back in his homeland, his cheeks wet from the flood of memories, telling us stories about this strange world and the boy he was when he lived here. But Uncle Stash had no voice to tell stories.

Aunt Lovey appeared after a short time, jangling a set of keys, one that opened the hotel room door, another for the room's only closet, and one for the top dresser, where she'd been advised by the staff to keep our passports and cash. "This is where the diplomats and visiting hockey teams stay," she enthused as we climbed into the elevator.

There was new carpeting in the hallway of the fifth floor, which smelled strongly of formaldehyde. Ruby was nauseous from it and had to cover her mouth. Aunt Lovey held her breath and tried all three keys before she found the one that worked in the door. She pushed the door open. There were two double beds with torn paisley bedspreads mismatched to too-short floral drapes. In the corner near the window there was a pine desk, where a cluster of cigarette burns tried to hide under a large crystal ashtray but were magnified by it instead. The olive-green carpet was worn to its bones. Aunt Lovey exhaled. She needed to have a good cry — and deserved it. But she was all we had. And she had to keep it together. "Let's just call it charming," she said. "Besides, it's only for one night."

Uncle Stash moved to the suitcase, found the envelope with his mother's ashes, and propped it against the lamp beside the crystal ashtray. It sat there like an overdue bill — like a notice of reminder to us all — "Don't forget to bury me!" He sat on the bed and closed his eyes. Aunt Lovey moved beside him, gently pulling him down on the bed, at the same time folding her body against his strong warm back. "We all need a good sleep," she said.

Ruby and I found our bed and shifted our individual weight, stretching our necks and shoulders and arms, twisting our torsos, until we were comfortably arranged and ready to sleep. I breathed. And listened to the sound of my loved ones breathing around me. I thought of the following day, and the trip into the mountains to meet Uncle Stash's family. I wondered if we'd see the pond where Uncle Stash used to take the ducks.

"Aunt Lovey," Ruby whispered, interrupting my thoughts.

"Yes, Ruby?"

"The bed smells."

"I know, Ruby. Just close your eyes."

"It really reeks."

"Don't be a baby."

"I'm not."

"Go to sleep, Ruby."

"I can't."

Aunt Lovey sucked in air and said it was time Ruby and I grew up. There were going to be challenges on this trip. One day we were going to have to live on our own. Aunt Lovey said it was time to prove what we were made of.

Ruby paused. "But it smells like a person's ass."

I didn't sleep a wink that night. (Aunt Lovey didn't sleep either. I heard her sniffling behind her hands until dawn, when she rose and went to run the tub. Uncle Stash woke then, and I felt encouraged when he called out, "Lovey," and his voice had returned, husky but there.)

The breakfast room was busy and crowded. The hostess found a table for us in the back. She had seen us, Ruby and I were sure. I locked eyes with her. Then Ruby did. But there were no double takes, no shocked intake of breath, no nervous laughter. She led us to the table at the back. We walked past the rows of businessmen. No one stared. (Like what had happened at the airport. Discomfiting and surreal.) Uncle Stash's short coughing fit drew a few stares, but people avoided glancing at Ruby and me.

There were no hockey players in the breakfast room at the Hotel Kosice. I would have known. There were dozens of men in dark suits, with round faces and apple cheeks and sunken blue eyes and harp-shaped ears. Some of them may have been diplomats. But definitely not hockey players. Ruby and I were the only twins, conjoined or otherwise, in the place.

We went to look at the offerings on the buffet table. And we felt the eyes on our backs. I turned sharply, or at least as sharply as I could. And as I swiveled, I caught a fat man staring. Staring. Full on. Openmouthed. The man was horrified to have been caught. Then I realized who Ruby and I were to these Slovaks. *We* were the fairies from the dense gray fog. And they were afraid of us.

(Even though Uncle Stash was not much of a believer in things like fairies and witches, he defended his superstitious countrymen, saying, "Of course the Slovaks believe in devils and demons. First the Turks. Then the Magyars. Then the Nazis. And the Communists. Always the Slovaks must struggle to be Slovak. It must be *witches*. It must be *demons*. Who wants to blame *God?*")

After breakfast, we started off for the bus station, within walking distance of the Hotel Kosice. Almost right away, Uncle Stash remembered that he'd left his camera bag slung over the back of the chair in the breakfast room. Aunt Lovey hurried back to the restaurant but returned without the camera, just as we'd all known she would. We found the bus station, Aunt Lovey trying to see the brighter side of things, comforting, "It's just as well, hon. Sometimes you get so preoccupied with capturing a moment you don't live it."

"It's true," he said.

"Besides, maybe we can find a disposable camera at the convenience store in Grozovo."

"In Grozovo, Lovey, there is no convenience. There is no convenience store."

"Oh, how do you know? You haven't set foot there in fifty years! You think they don't have their version of 7-Eleven?" She laughed, thinking him naive.

"Just yesterday the Iron Curtain is lifted. It's Grozovo. In the mountains."

"We'll just have to see, Stash. But I think you'll find Grozovo not the same place you left."

"Maybe." You could tell Uncle Stash was thinking about that. Hard.

We boarded the bus, to find the seats cramped and uncomfortable. I shifted, gesturing to show Ruby the net of garlic hanging from the rearview mirror. "Werewolf country," Ruby said with a bad Transylvanian accent.

The driver, true to custom, did not stare at us directly. Instead, he nodded to Uncle Stash, whom he recognized as a countryman, before he opened his mouth to say *"Dobre rano."* The two other people aboard the enormous bus, elderly women, seemed completely uninterested in us at first, but we felt their eyes boring into our skulls as we roared out of town for the highway.

I recall the bus ride to Grozovo with a certain amount of terror. It was a diesel bus. Evil fumes were seeping from the tank. Or maybe the fumes were coming from the rotten garlic hanging from the rearview mirror or from the driver, who was attempting to light a cigarette while negotiating the sharp turns of graveled roads. I couldn't see her, but I could feel Aunt Lovey's tight smile, and I knew she was wishing she was home, making space in her pantry for Mrs. Merkel's squash.

An hour into the journey, the bus driver pulled off the road and parked beside a small plywood shack. The shack had been painted mud brown. A Slovak word was crudely scrawled over the door. Only Uncle Stash knew what it meant. Beside the shack was a broken picnic table, under which the ground was strewn with litter. Ruby woke up, groggy and annoyed. "Are we there? Why are we stopping?"

"We're stopping for another passenger, Ruby. Shh. Go back to sleep," Aunt Lovey said.

I glanced out the window, but no one emerged from the shack. After checking his face in the rearview mirror, the driver stood and turned and called out something to Uncle Stash. You could tell by the way the man was grinning that this was an invitation of some kind. But Uncle Stash did not smile back. In fact, he responded in a way that seemed to leave the driver deeply insulted.

Aunt Lovey sighed. "What's that all about, Stash?"

Uncle Stash shook his head, watching the bus driver disappear into the shed.

"Is he going to get the other passengers?"

"There's no other passengers."

"Well, is it a washroom? Tell me, because the girls and I will pee."

Uncle Stash shook his head, gazing out at the ridge of spruce forest.

"Why are we stopped?" Aunt Lovey turned to see if anyone else on the bus seemed concerned or puzzled by the delay, forgetting that the two elderly ladies had gotten out (fled) at the very first stop. "Stash?"

"He stops here because he stops here."

Aunt Lovey bristled but didn't query further. We were all tired and nauseous from the diesel fumes and no one really wanted a fight. We waited and waited, thinking our disparate thoughts. Finally, the driver emerged from the brown shed, then, with a sarcastic wave (or was it a brotherly wave? or a conciliatory one?) to Uncle Stash, the man took his seat behind the wheel of the bus and we were on our way again.

I don't know what I expected. I thought there might be a main street or a group of buildings or a bus station or anything at all to distinguish the village Uncle Stash had described in his stories on Slovak Night. In the middle of nowhere, at the edge of a cliff, the driver stopped and announced, "Grozovo."

Uncle Stash did not move. The driver and he barked back and forth until the driver folded his arms and Uncle Stash threw up his hands. "Come on," he commanded, launching himself down the aisle. We followed our venerable leader as the bus roared on.

There was nothing around but mountains and the view of more. The sky was white, but not close and not bright. Even here the air smelled of bacon, but of wet rock too, and pine and spruce. It was very, very cold. Uncle Stash pointed to the hill to our left and shrugged apologetically. "If he goes around long way to village, it takes one hour more."

"So?"

"Already he's late."

"What does that mean?" Aunt Lovey was baffled.

"We climb hill."

"A bus driver can't just drop people off and tell them to climb a hill!" Aunt Lovey's laughter verged on hysterical as she looked up at the steep climb.

Uncle Stash cast his eyes. "He did."

"You have to be kidding, Stash. He *left* us here?!"

"There's path through trees. There. It's not steep as it looks," Uncle Stash said.

"I'm seventy-one years old!" Aunt Lovey shrieked. "You've had a heart attack! And did he not notice the girls?! He just left us all to climb?!"

Uncle Stash repeated, "It's not so steep as it looks. I climbed a thousand times when I was boy."

Aunt Lovey snapped her fingers. "It's because you wouldn't go in the brown shack?"

Uncle Stash sighed but said nothing.

"Oh *lovely!* And now we have to climb the hill!" Aunt Lovey steamed ahead. "Come on, girls."

I loved the way Aunt Lovey just assumed my physical competence. She challenged the hell out of me. "It's freezing, Aunt Lovey," I said.

"Move faster," she replied.

Ruby and I walked up ahead with Aunt Lovey and found the path through the trees. We felt some relief to see steps and railings built here and there where the hill *was* as steep as it looked. "All right," Aunt Lovey breathed, putting a positive spin on it, "we've been sitting on our butts for two days straight. This is just what we need, girls."

Ruby and I were doubtful. We started slowly up the path.

"Hovno." The first time Uncle Stash said it, it was like a whisper. It had that "I don't believe it" quality. The second was a curse. *"Hovno!"* And again. *"Hovno!"*

We stopped in our tracks, turning to find Uncle Stash stamping on the fallen leaves. *"Hovno sračka!"* Uncle Stash shouted.

We hurried back to see what was wrong.

"What, Stash? Honey, what is it?" Aunt Lovey cried.

"I forgot my mother." He said it so dryly I nearly laughed.

"Oh no."

"At hotel."

"Oh, Stash."

We all four had a vision of that envelope propped up against the lamp on the cigarette-burned desk: "Don't forget to bury me."

"What will I tell them?" Uncle Stash could barely whisper. I watched a thick ribbon vein snake up his temple. I'd never seen him like this and didn't want to admit that he was on the verge of losing control.

"No one knows you were bringing her ashes, hon," Aunt Lovey said practically. "Tell them we buried her at the farm. They'll understand."

Uncle Stash squeezed Aunt Lovey's hand. They started back up the hill, this time together. The hill was steep but manageable, even for Ruby and me and our old parents. After nearly thirty minutes of climbing, Uncle Stash was huffing and puffing, and scarlet and sweaty. We stopped every four or five minutes to drink water from the canteens Aunt Lovey had packed. And to rest. There was nothing to look at but the dense black forest around us. I tried not to think of the Brothers Grimm and all the fairy-tale characters who met their fates in the deep dark woods. Ruby was quiet, which helped me focus. I was impressed with her restraint. After slightly more than an hour of slow and steady climbing, we reached the crest of the hill. I wished I'd had a flag to plant.

"The church," Uncle Stash said.

Notre Dame and St. Peter's and San Marco's and all of the great cathedrals of the world were reflected in Uncle Stash's eyes, but the church was only a small clapboard building painted white, weathered gray, whose roof was caked with pigeon shit. A black storm hung in the distance, granting form to the specters in the graveyard beside the church. Ruby squeezed me and made a quiet ghost sound. "Oooo." I laughed and shivered too, because I suddenly remembered Aunt Lovey's premonition. Her bad feeling. And I thought, "We've made a terrible mistake."

We stood for a moment watching the church, surprised when a smooth baritone voice struck a note. There were no lights within the building, and I'd assumed it was empty. There was no organ to introduce the choir's song, just this one man's powerful voice rising up to shake the trees. Uncle Stash moved forward slowly as the hymn continued and the rest of the choir joined in. We couldn't understand the words, but there was something familiar in the way sorrow met joy in the space between the notes.

The music drew Uncle Stash toward the church, and we followed. I thought he meant to peer into the church's windows to see if he could find a familiar face. Or perhaps even go inside and stand at the back to listen, but he turned sharply, entering the church cemetery. Aunt Lovey stopped Ruby and me from following him to the adjoining plots with the two polished stones.

"His brothers," Ruby whispered.

"I know."

I was disappointed when Uncle Stash left the plots rather quickly and returned to us dry-eyed. "Must be Cousin Marek planting flowers. Or Velika. Or Zuza," he said, pleased by the landscaping, and not struck by grief as I'd expected.

"That's good, hon." Aunt Lovey was struggling to be supportive.

Uncle Stash was smiling, still listening to the hymn inside the church. His face changed suddenly. "What day is today?" he asked.

"It's November twenty-fifth," Aunt Lovey said.

"It's St. Katarina's Day," he said.

"What?"

"Oh my God, it's St. Katarina's."

"The first of the Witches' Days," I mused, recalling. "That's why the driver had the garlic in the bus. To scare off the witches." Ruby made another spooky sound, but this time neither of us laughed.

(When we were children, Uncle Stash taught us about the Witches' Days, and all the traditions associated with the saints' days leading up to Christmas. According to folklore, from November 25 until after the winter solstice, when there is considerably less day than night, evil lurks in the darkness. And witches are everywhere. On one of the saints' days, women aren't allowed in the house until noon, because witches always try to enter homes in the morning hours and might do so in the guise of a wife. None of us had considered that we were arriving in Grozovo on St. Katarina's Day, or, if any of us did, we never dreamed the people still believed in witches, as they had in Uncle Stash's youth.)

Ruby joked about hoping to see a witch in Grozovo. But while she was laughing, I was beginning to fret about our arrival here on this particular occasion. What would these Slovak country people make of seeing Ruby and me in the flesh?

"Should we wait for church to end and see the family here?" Uncle Stash wondered.

"Oh. I hadn't thought of that." Aunt Lovey glanced our way. "Wouldn't that be a little overwhelming? The whole town must be in there." She didn't mention the Witches' Days, or her worry about what a superstitious village might make of our arriving on the feast of St. Katarina.

Uncle Stash nodded but had no answer. I hated when they did this. I wished one of them would just take charge. (This kind of thing never happened with Ruby and me. We had to be decisive.)

"I find my bearings," Uncle Stash said as he climbed the church's front steps. From there he could see the tiny village in the shallow valley below. "Come see," he breathed. "Lovey, girls, come see."

We followed Aunt Lovey up the church steps to find ourselves looking down on a pretty little village with houses made of straw and stone, a covered well in the center square, and a reedy little duck pond beyond. It was just as Uncle Stash had described it to us. "It's beautiful," Aunt Lovey said. "Why don't we go down to one of your cousins' houses and wait in the yard?"

Uncle Stash nodded but hadn't heard a word. He stood, gazing out over the village. I could see the flood of memories. But Uncle Stash's timing was bad. Sooner or later church was going to let out, and meeting the whole town of Grozovo at once, like Aunt Lovey said, might be a little too much. (Did she mean they'd be too much for us? Or that we'd be too much for Grozovo?)

Uncle Stash left the church steps. Maybe he was ashamed of his emotions. Maybe he just wanted to be alone. He went around to the woods at the side of the church. Aunt Lovey hesitated, unsure which of us it was safer to leave alone, and decided that her husband needed her, though I'm not sure that was the case. "You girls stay here," she said. "Rose. Ruby."

I felt abandoned but was too afraid, at my age, to say, "Please don't leave us here alone." It was time to prove what Ruby and I were made of.

The choir was singing beautifully inside the church. Ruby and I were startled when the doors to the church suddenly burst open. A crescendo of music, then the doors closed again. The woman who'd emerged seemed relieved, like she hadn't left but escaped. She was a girl our age, round as she was tall, in a clean tattered dress and an ill-fitting coat, so pregnant it seemed she'd go into labor any second, or should have done so two weeks ago. Her face was inflated, bloated, and blotchy. Her lips and earlobes looked purple instead of red. The young woman spotted Ruby, then me, alone on the church steps in the mountains of eastern Slovakia. She didn't appear especially frightened or even surprised — more curious. She moved toward us, squinting, as if she was certain we'd make sense to her if she just got close enough. She drew closer and closer, so close I could count the broken capillaries in the whites of her eye and feel the scratchy wool of her brown coat. The pregnant woman blinked and reached up and shocked Ruby and me by pressing her warm palm to the spot on our heads where we are joined.

"Oh my God," the woman whispered in Slovak, then lost consciousness and fell to the ground.

"Sonya!" screamed a tall man with a sharp black beard and fierce eyes (blinking red in my memory, though I know that isn't so) who exploded through the door just as the woman's skull hit the earth.

In the moment before the man lunged forward and dropped to his knees beside his fallen wife, his dark eyes found mine. He didn't look merely hateful, the way some people do. He looked murderous. And I understood his rage.

"Sonya? Sonya!" he cried.

Ruby and I backed away, watching as the bearded man found a lacy handkerchief in his wife's coat pocket and used it to stop the blood trickling from her scalp.

Inside the church, the choir finished the final processional song, and the rest of the crowd, led by the priest, spilled out of the church. They were alarmed to find the bearded man hovering over his pregnant wife and didn't see Ruby and me in their midst. At some point, Aunt Lovey and Uncle Stash must have come from around the side of the church. I caught their familiar blur in my periphery. Aunt Lovey started for the fallen woman's side, but Uncle Stash held her back.

"I'm a nurse," she said.

"You're a stranger," he returned.

The husband looked up to find Ruby and me watching from the church steps. He pointed at us with a shaking hand, saying words in Slovak we didn't understand. There was some nugget of relief in knowing that my sister was at my side, scared too. We held our breath as the crowd turned to look at us. No one gasped in horror. No one shrieked in fear. There was something in their collective quiet that made me think they'd been expecting us. Like prophecy. Or doom.

There was silence. But for the wind in the pines. Then the shuffling of feet as the country people crowded around us on the church steps, the way revelers surround a bride and groom, or mourners a casket.

The angry husband continued to stab the air with his finger, addressing the crowd, half of whom were helping with his wife, and the rest of whom could do nothing but pity him for his bad luck. We watched as the pregnant woman was revived with vinegar and cool water and sat up, leaning on her bearded husband. I felt relieved when she took a long deep breath. Her hand found the bloody spot on her scalp. She looked at the blood on her fingers and appeared to remember why she'd fallen. She turned to look for Ruby and me, but her husband stopped her, yanking her shoulders, speaking sharply. The woman began to cry.

"Oh my God," Ruby whispered.

"I know."

"Go, Rose."

"I can't."

"Aunt Lovey!" Ruby cried out. "Uncle Stash!"

Then, suddenly, a woman's voice, bewildered and astonished, cutting through the chaos. "Stanislaus?"

The sound, the word, was like a key that unlocked my knees. I turned slowly to find Uncle Stash and Aunt Lovey not a foot behind Ruby and me, where they'd been all along. (How strange that was, because I'd felt utterly helpless and alone.)

"It's Stanislaus! Stanislaus Darlensky!" the doughy woman cried. (The woman was Cousin Zuza, but I didn't know it then.)

At that, a group of about twenty people (whom Ruby and I refer to generically as the "Slovak Relations") came forward, as if they'd been sieved from the rest, to greet Uncle Stash, not like a stranger, or a prodigal son, but with something of disbelief. For a moment, Ruby and I were forgotten. We were mere freaks of nature. Stanislaus Darlensky was a ghost.

My attention was torn away from the Slovak Relations as I saw that the pregnant woman was conscious and walking, leaning on her dark-eyed husband and held at the other elbow by a man who was completely without hair. Along with the rest of Grozovo, the three were descending the hill, casting furtive glances over their shoulders and murmuring among themselves. Whoever Ruby and I were — witches, demons, angels — we'd finally come, they seemed to be telling one another, and it was Stanislaus Darlensky who'd brought us.

Uncle Stash held his hands out to us. "These are my daughters," he said proudly, as though the fact of our being was an accomplishment.

"*Dobre den,*" I greeted the relations.

"*Dobre rano,*" Ruby corrected.

The Slovak Relations regarded us. My sister and I are accustomed to the ping-pong style in which people stare upon first meeting us. Some people zero in on the spot of our conjoinment, but most look back and forth between Ruby's and my face. The very sophisticated, on first meeting us — we've met only a few sophisticated people in our lives, and then only ever in Toronto — act as though our conjoinment is not shocking or even very surprising. As if they know a dozen craniopagus twins and had their craniopagus dental hygienists over for dinner just last week. They make eye contact with us instantly. And never ask personal questions. (Sophisticated people are the worst.) The Slovak Relations did not ping-pong stare. They did not zero in on the spot of our conjoinment. They did not make eye contact. Instead, these Slovaks embraced my sister and me, one after the other, until all twenty-one were done and we smelled like them, of fresh cheese. And ham hocks. Uncle Stash smiled at Ruby and me and embraced us too.

Together we Darlenskys of Leaford and Grozovo made our way down the gently sloping hill to Cousin Zuza and Velika's house for lunch. (One recently widowed. One never married. The female cousins lived together now like spinsters.) I had not determined who among these people was Cousin Velika or Cousin Zuza or Cousin Marek. I was aware they were all watching Ruby and me from behind, thinking us marvelous. And awful.

There was no discussion about the pregnant woman. At least none that we understood. No one spoke English here. Not a phrase. Not a word. We had Uncle Stash to translate, but how frightening it must be, I thought then, to be alone in a strange country and misunderstood. And how lonely. (No wonder immigrants stay together. Uncle Stash used to shake his head about his mother, who'd come to Canada and never learned more than a dozen English words. She had Slovak friends. She shopped at Slovak stores. She went to a Slovak church. Uncle Stash thought he was a fully assimilated North American, but I wouldn't say that's exactly true either.)

I was relieved that the place where our cousins lived was closer to hill than dale. We were drawn into the large squat kitchen of an old stone house and directed to make ourselves comfortable at the rickety wooden table, which Ruby and I did by bringing two chairs of similar height together. Aunt Lovey and Uncle Stash sat beside us, and the rest, perhaps a dozen relations in all (we'd lost some along the way — mostly women who'd hurried on to put up lunch for their men), stood or slouched nearby or leaned against the table.

Instinctively, as we do in such situations (not that we'd ever been in just such a situation), Ruby and I found the natural rhythm of exploration. She leads in looking. I lead in looking. Then she. Then me. Breathe-two-three, and switch-two-three. The walls were made of large fieldstone, with mortar and straw to block the wind, but I felt a cold draft on my neck all the same. There were four cots in the corner, pushed together in a way that said this daytime roost was temporary. In another corner, smoke rose from a woodstove where the round-faced woman who'd first recognized Uncle Stash was stirring something in an enormous black pot. Aunt Lovey had whispered to me that the woman was Cousin Zuza. I could not imagine that she'd once been beautiful. I could not picture her young.

There was no washroom, or door leading to a washroom, or any door at all, except the one we came in. There was a sink with a pump faucet. Oil lamps and candles. It struck me right away that there were no mirrors in the old women's home, which made me feel cut off from my sister.

I heard cabbage sizzle in bacon grease. Cousin Zuza was cooking halushki. Slovak soul food. I was starving, watching the old crone stir her cauldron with her broom handle (okay — really it was a pot with a spoon, but you can see how I could get carried away), as the Slovak men gathered around Uncle Stash at the table to quaff their amber *peevos* and recall their brilliant youth. (I wondered when Uncle Stash would tell the relations about his mother's death, or if he already had.)

Excluding Ruby and me, there were only three other women in the room, and they were all busy in the kitchen. Aunt Lovey had been recruited to slice thick bricks of black bread and did so with the look of a scullery maid, oppressed and vengeful. As she sawed the bread, Aunt Lovey tried to catch Uncle Stash's eye, but he was enjoying himself too much to notice. He'd forgotten about Ruby and me many times before. I'd never once seen him forget Aunt Lovey. But then, Uncle Stash was not himself.

In due time, steaming bowls of halushki were served to the men by Cousin Zuza and a slightly younger pleasant-looking woman wearing a white blouse and chocolate skirt, who it turned out was Cousin Velika. Aunt Lovey buttered the bread she'd labored to slice and passed it out to the men, who didn't say "Thank you."

Ruby and I were served last, and after all the men had picked up their spoons, Uncle Stash nodded that we should begin too. It was then we saw that although we'd each been given a spoon, there was only one bowl, and we were meant to share it. I whispered to Ruby to swallow her humiliation and just eat the halushki, which was less oily than Aunt Lovey's, saltier and creamier, made with fresh curd instead of cottage cheese.

The stone house was quiet but for the clanging of forks and gnashing of teeth as Uncle Stash and the other men pulverized their dumplings and started in on fat slices of pear strudel the women set before them. I just happened to be watching when Uncle Stash put down his fork. I froze as his hand moved slowly to his chest. His heart, I thought, and couldn't breathe. But he thumped himself and belched, picked up his fork, and went back to his dessert.

There were footsteps on the stones outside. All eyes turned to watch the door swing open to the night and two men swept in by the wind, carrying three heavy sacks apiece. One of the men was very old and stooped, his teeth broken and black where he had any at all. The other man was young, our age, dark and handsome, with long eyelashes and groomed stubble. The men were shocked to see all the relations in the house, but too weary to wonder why we were there. Perhaps they'd forgotten it was St. Katarina's or thought it was Christmas all over again.

The old man's eyesight must have been poor because he did not spot Ruby and me right off. The young man did, though. And stared — boldly.

Seeing the old man with the black teeth, Uncle Stash turned pale. He rose, scraping back his chair, and went to the door.

"Who are you?" asked the stooped old man in Slovak.

Uncle Stash didn't speak right away, and I wondered if he'd lost his voice again. Then I saw that, this time, he was choked with emotion. "I'm Stanislaus," he said, but the old man was hard of hearing.

In the kitchen, Cousin Velika made the sign of the cross as Zuza wept into her apron.

"You know me?" the old man asked doubtfully.

"Yes, Marek. I know you." Uncle Stash put a hand on the old man's sloped shoulder. "It's me," Uncle Stash said. "Stanislaus."

I could wonder what Uncle Stash's work as a butcher had done to his psyche, but I could *see* what the mines had done to Marek. Cousin Marek shook his head, looking around the room, searching faces for the prankster responsible for this elaborate and unfunny joke.

"It's me," Uncle Stash insisted. "Stanislaus Darlensky."

"Stanislaus?" Marek said, shaking his head in disbelief. "Stash," he whispered, and could say no more.

And then it was Uncle Stash's turn to introduce Ruby and me.

Ordinarily Ruby and I like to rise, to look people in the eye, but I was utterly exhausted from the climb up the hill and found my legs unwilling. We waited, as Cousin Marek looked from Ruby to me, then made his way across the room to the table where we sat. He kissed the top of my head, and the top of Ruby's, which was both sweet and mortifying.

"He said, 'God bless you girls,'" Uncle Stash translated. "And welcome to Grozovo."

Marek pushed his grandson forward. "Jerzy," he said.

Jerzy was our age but looked and seemed like a man. Ruby shivered and I swallowed as gorgeous Jerzy, sexy Jerzy, *Cousin* Jerzy moved toward us. Ruby and I were afraid that Jerzy would touch our heads the way Cousin Marek had just done, and if he did we would die of humiliation. (I believe that's possible.) He didn't. And he didn't smile either, which made me trust him.

"Hello," Jerzy said.

"Hi."

"How you are?" he queried.

"Good," I said. "And you?"

"Fine. And you?"

"Good. And you?"

"Good. And you?"

It hit me that we were speaking English together, and I felt giddy at the prospect of a conversation with someone outside my immediate family.

"You come from America?" he asked, licking his lower lip, unintentionally lurid.

"Canada," Ruby piped up. "Everyone here gets that wrong."

"Everyone?"

"Yeah."

"Everyone? You know all Slovaks?"

Ruby giggled.

"What is different? Canada. America." He shrugged. His accent was thick, his voice smooth. "What is different, tell me?"

Ruby giggled again. The giggle that says "Don't ask me questions. I'm just here for show." "Well — what's the difference between night and day?" she trilled.

"Day is light. Night is dark," Jerzy answered confidently.

"What's the difference between you and the Czechs?" I shot.

Jerzy laughed, then paused to consider. "It's different the Slovaks and Czechs," he said slowly, then shrugged. "It's different."

"Same for Americans and Canadians."

"This comes from America," Jerzy said, yanking back his sweater sleeve to show the diamond-encrusted Rolex watch on his wrist.

"Wow," I said.

"Is it real?" Ruby asked.

Jerzy laughed, pressing a tiny button to illuminate the time. "Of course! How I should know time?"

"That's not what she meant," I said.

Jerzy looked back and forth from Ruby to me. "You think what she thinks?" (I thought he was asking me.)

"No," Ruby and I said at once, then, to each other, like a freak show, we added in unison, "He was asking *me*."

Jerzy laughed. "You are hilarious twins. You come on the airplane?" he asked. Then, "You want slivovitz? My grandpa doesn't mind if I take."

"How old are you?" Ruby asked.

"Seventeen. How old you are?" Jerzy asked.

"Nineteen," I answered.

"And you?" he asked Ruby.

"I'm the same." She giggled. "We're twins!"

"I know," Jerzy said blankly. "Is joke."

We were aware that it was creepy to have a crush on your cousin, even if he was thrice removed and not even a blood relative to begin with, but we didn't even try to resist Cousin Jerzy.

Jerzy went to pour slivovitz for himself, posturing, aware of our watching eyes. Ruby kept asking, "Is he coming back? Is he coming back?" I was annoyed with her for being so eager, though I wanted the same thing. Jerzy poured a shot of liquor and *was* coming back toward us, when he was suddenly seized by the hairless man we had seen before at the church. The hairless man pulled Jerzy apart from the crowd, and after a short conversation, the two fled the house without a word of good-bye or a backward glance to Ruby or me. I watched the door for the rest of the night, hoping Cousin Jerzy would return.

(I regret now that my preoccupation with Jerzy cost me my observation of Uncle Stash and his reunion with Cousin Marek. Cousin Marek must have seen his life flash before his eyes when he saw Uncle Stash standing there. The life that he *almost* lived.) There were many visitors, and each time the door was opened, Ruby and I hoped it was Jerzy, but it was only this neighbor or that, coming to glimpse the "join-together girls."

Very late, Uncle Stash and Cousin Marek sequestered themselves in a corner near the fire, stoking a political discussion. At least Aunt Lovey said it was political. "People here get passionate about politics," Aunt Lovey said. (Aren't people everywhere passionate about politics?) Cousin Marek slammed his hand on the table. Uncle Stash shouted over the top of the banging. Cousin Zuza put the slivovitz away. And soon it was time for bed.

Cousin Velika led us to our sleeping quarters, an unused shed at the rear of the main house, lighting the way with an oil lamp. I could smell the goats that were kept in a small barn fifty yards away. Inside the little shed, which was stone and mortar and drafty like the house, we found four cots, two of them pushed together to accommodate Ruby and me. The cots were plump feather-filled beds, which made Aunt Lovey recall how the mattresses were filled with dry corn husks when she was a child on the farm. "We would have given anything for feathers," she sighed.

"Sleep well," Velika said in careful English, taking the lamp and its light.

"*Dobru noc,*" Ruby said.

Ruby fell asleep right away, but I stayed awake, listening to Aunt Lovey and Uncle Stash whisper. I couldn't hear a word they said, but I suspected they were talking about Marek. Uncle Stash sounded regretful, Aunt Lovey sympathetic. Uncle Stash started coughing and had to sit up. I could hear Aunt Lovey in the dark, thumping on his back. I pretended to be asleep. Ruby really was.

When the coughing fit had passed and Uncle Stash was horizontal again, I heard him whisper, "You."

And I heard Aunt Lovey whisper back, "You."

I felt the stiff breeze from a hole in the wall and reached out instinctively to make sure Ruby's legs were covered. I touched Ruby's earlobe, our version of "You," and wished she was awake to touch mine.

I couldn't guess how long I had been asleep, or what time it was, when I felt a finger prodding my shoulder. I opened my eyes to see light flickering from the oil lamp left outside the shed door. I glanced at the cots beside us and saw in the flickering light that Aunt Lovey and Uncle Stash were still deeply asleep, groaning and snoring, respectively.

I could hear someone moving in the shed but couldn't see who it was or guess who it might be.

"Cousin Velika?" I whispered. "Cousin Zuza?"

"Shh!" came the reply.

Then Cousin Jerzy moved into my periphery. "Be quiet," he said. "Don't wake them."

I liked his concern for Uncle Stash and Aunt Lovey. "Why are you here?" I asked in a whisper.

"Shh. Wake your sister. Can you wake her?"

I pulled on the skin of Ruby's abdomen. Pinching just enough to get her attention. She opened her eyes, groggy and confused, to find our handsome cousin hunched over our pushed-together cots.

"It's me, Ruby," Jerzy said.

"Hi," Ruby squeaked.

"Shh," I whispered. "Don't wake up Aunt Lovey and Uncle Stash."

"Okay."

"You want to have adventure?" Cousin Jerzy asked.

"Yes," Ruby and I said together, then pinched each other, like we do.

"Come with me," Cousin Jerzy whispered, offering both arms to help us rise from the cot.

"Okay," I said too quickly.

Cousin Jerzy helped Ruby and me off the cots, comfortable handling our conjoined proportions, as if he'd known us all our lives. He'd already found our coats in the darkness and was helping us into them as he hustled us outside.

"It's good adventure," Jerzy encouraged as he led us down the black path.

"My shoes," I said, realizing I was wearing the pink wool slippers with the pom-poms that Nonna'd made Ruby and me for the trip.

Jerzy hushed me, hurrying us down the muddy lane. "It's our secret, this. Okay?"

"Okay," Ruby said. But I knew Ruby, and I knew that she was already having reservations about this "good adventure." She pulled at me, and I stopped. "Maybe we shouldn't," she said.

"We should!" Jerzy said. He pressed the button on his wristwatch to see the time. As if to confirm, he looked up at the moon. "Hurry," he whispered. "Let's go."

"I don't think so," Ruby said.

"You don't like adventure?" Jerzy asked accusingly.

"Yes, we do," I answered. "Yes, we *do,* Ruby."

"Well, what kind of adventure?" Ruby asked.

"Secret adventure."

"Maybe we better ask Aunt Lovey and Uncle Stash," Ruby said.

"Oh," Jerzy said sneeringly. "I understand. You are grown-up girls, but you are like *little* girls. I understand."

"No, we're *not,*" I protested, suddenly eager for this good secret adventure Jerzy was promising us. We were nearly twenty years old. We were not children. We were *not.*

"Let's go! *Prosim,* let's go," Jerzy said, clapping his hands.

"All right," Ruby said with sudden daring, "let's go."

I saw a glint of metal on the road ahead but didn't make out that it was a truck until we were close enough to smell fuel. Jerzy rushed us toward the truck, opened the door, and helped us climb in the passenger side. I arranged Ruby beside me in the darkness, startled to feel the heat of a body at the wheel. I shrieked in surprise, because I hadn't seen the driver inside. I looked out the corner of my eye but could not make out the person's face in the dark.

"Wait for me," Jerzy said to the unseen driver. "I have to get her shoes."

My feet were freezing in the wool slippers.

Our cousin disappeared. The driver, grunting words in Slovak that we didn't understand, turned the key in the ignition and jammed on the gas. In the faint green glow of the old truck's dashboard, I strained to see his face. The outline of his profile became clear, and I shuddered to see that it was the bearded man whose pregnant wife had touched our heads and fainted on the steps of the church.

I nearly fainted myself.

"Rosie?" Ruby whispered.

"It's okay," I said.

"Where's Jerzy?"

"He's getting my shoes."

"But why'd we leave without him?"

"Maybe he's coming in his own car," I offered.

The headlights on the truck were so sharp and low they seemed to slice the road. The man was breathing through his nose like a bull, wet and rattly. As we careened down the hill with the bearded man at the wheel, the story began to crystallize for me, as in a work of fiction, when you realize there's only one direction for it to go. I saw with perfect clarity the events leading us all to this place, and saw in my crystal ball what would happen next.

The bearded man had taken his poor young wife home after church, where she'd gone into labor and died giving birth to their stillborn baby boy. Now, with his present gone, his future not to be, he wanted revenge on Ruby and me. I busied myself with the next plot point in the mystery to ease my panic, glad that Ruby had not seen the driver and didn't know it was the bearded man. I did not know how to tell my sister that we were about to die.

The driver jammed on the gas pedal again, muttering. The woods were so black we might have been traveling in space. My feet were frozen. We made a sharp turn down another road. I clung to the dashboard and Ruby clung to me as we rocked over potholes, the back tires skidding in mud.

The moon appeared from behind a blanket of clouds, bathing the dense forest in its glow. I wondered if the bearded man would leave us in the forest to die or kill us right away. I didn't know what to root for. I felt the truck begin to slow down. The driver turned down another road, at the end of which was a short stone house where burned a single oil lamp in the small front window.

The bearded man brought the truck to a stop in front of the stone house.

"Whose house is this, Rose?"

"Shh," I said, and could say no more, as the driver had disappeared from his place beside me and reappeared at the passenger door. Ruby saw him full face in the moonlight. He must have resembled a demon. "Rose?" she choked.

"Don't be scared. Okay?"

"Okay."

"You're not alone."

"Okay."

"Don't be afraid."

"Okay."

I felt Ruby reach for my ear as the man grabbed at us, unsure which one of us he should be holding to expedite our removal from the truck.

We made our way to the house. Beside us the bearded man's heavy boots made no sound at all, while in my pom-pom slippers I clomped and lurched down the pebbled path with my sister on my hip, feeling every inch the monster I saw in his eyes.

The man opened the door and guided us inside, not roughly, but not gently. There was a faint smell of ammonia. The interior of the cottage looked much like Velika and Zuza's home, except that this house had another room, with its door ajar, and there a second lamp was burning. No movement or sound therein.

I felt that I might vomit and considered backing out the door. The bearded man came around from behind us, standing directly in front of Ruby and me. Without a weapon in his hands. I wondered if he planned to strangle us or pummel us to death with his huge hands. Instead, he just regarded us, looking from my face to Ruby's, in the ping-pong style to which we've grown accustomed.

When the door to the second room creaked open, we all turned to find the hairless man from the church standing there in silhouette. The hairless man was the connection to Cousin Jerzy, who'd given us up for slaughter. I shouldn't have been surprised to see him there, but I was.

The hairless man took a long look at Ruby and me before whispering something in Slovak to the bearded man.

The bearded man nodded slowly and pushed us toward the room, where we could see a bed. And in the bed, a body.

"Oh my God," I heard myself say.

"Is she dead?" Ruby whimpered, recognizing that it was the pregnant woman from the church.

I stopped at the edge of the bed, nearly weeping with relief when

I saw the woman's toe wiggle beneath the blanket. I would have been glad to see her open her eyes, but she appeared to be sleeping very deeply.

"She's *not* dead," I breathed, as if I'd brought her back to life myself.

Then Ruby saw what I only *heard* — a mewling sound — so tiny it might have been a newborn kitten or a fallen baby bird. Ruby urged me to turn so I could see, in the faint glow of the oil lamp, *two* babies swaddled tightly in soft cotton blankets, placed side by side in an old wooden cradle, both plush and pink and very much alive.

The babies could not have been five pounds each. ("My mother made a bigger roast for Sunday dinner," Aunt Lovey used to say about the preemies at St. Jude's. I found her choice of comparison rather curious.)

"Twins," I breathed.

"Oh my God," Ruby said. "Oh my God. Do they think she had twins because of *us?*"

"I guess," I answered slowly.

"But that's a good thing, right?"

The bearded man, when we found his face, did not smile at us or look at us with any expression I understood. He gestured at his friend (or brother?), the hairless man, and together they lifted the babies from the cradle.

Ruby and I stood dumbly by. I couldn't imagine (and I've spent my life imagining things) what the two men were going to do with the twin babies.

I looked into the pinched face of the baby closest to me, thinking, *"Creatura."* (That's the word Nonna used to describe a newborn. *Creatura.* "He's not to be human yet. Is not inside yet, the soul.") The newborns looked alien, with black insect eyes and noses that were barely there. (Scarce hours ago they'd breathed fluid, not air!) Round bloodless lips. Tufts of black curly hair. (I tried not to think of Taylor, but I heard Aunt Lovey's voice then, as I do now, insisting I'd later regret that I didn't look at my newborn daughter, and the truth of that is hard to bear.) I reached out instinctively, aching to hold one of the babies, offering the cradle of my arm, but the bearded man shook his head.

Instead, the man lifted the infant slowly and gently, in a way that was not frightening to the baby or to Ruby and me, and touched her tiny warm forehead to the spot where we are joined.

"Oh," Ruby said. "Oh."

The bearded man said some words, quiet words, that might have been holy, or damning. We didn't know if, in this action, he was asking us to bless the babies or demanding we lift our curse.

The hairless man raised the second baby and did the same, setting the baby's tiny warm forehead against the place where Ruby and I are joined, and waited a long moment, before arranging the twins in the cradle once again. Then he lifted his sleeve and pushed a small button on his wristwatch, and I noticed he had the same fake Rolex as Cousin Jerzy.

Where was Cousin Jerzy? And when could we go home? My feet were aching from the cold stone floor. The hairless man, having checked his watch, seemed suddenly alarmed. He barked something at his bearded friend, who looked at his watch too (another phony Rolex), then suddenly lunged toward me and Ruby and, taking me firmly by the arm, led us to the door. There was nothing of thanks in the way he looked at me and my sister. And no kind of fear. Certainly not reverence. I completely mistrusted my instincts about what was happening. I didn't know if the man was friend or foe. I'd been wrong about everything in Slovakia. I could not read these people. It was much more than not knowing the language.

The man opened the door, hurried us out into the cold, and motioned for Ruby and me to follow him to his truck. He gestured for us to climb back into the front seat, which we did. I could feel the quiver in Ruby's chin when she asked, "Is he taking us back to Cousin Zuza and Velika's?"

I would not have remembered which black gravel road brought us to Zuza and Velika's, but I was sure the one the man turned down wasn't the same. I could feel that we were driving *down* the mountain instead of *up,* to where the old cousins lived. We traveled deeper and deeper into the dark woods. I wondered if the man had an ax in the truck. Of course he did. Then, in the moon's light, I could see reeds and weeds, and it occurred to me that he was taking us to the pond.

I had the strangest sense that Ruby and I were kittens in a sack. "I think he's going to drown us" was all I could think to say.

"Like kittens in a sack," Ruby said. And I got gooseflesh.

I was thinking, as the man pulled (helped?) Ruby and me out of the passenger side of the truck, how ironic that Ruby and I were to be drowned in the same water where Uncle Stash had saved Cousin Marek. Then I saw the further irony that we would die in Mother Darlensky's birthplace, while she had died in ours. (My sister and I have shared the joint fear of drowning since we were children. I had never considered my fear intuitive or prophetic, just a hangover from what happened at the creek with Ryan Todino.)

The bearded man lit the ground in front of us with a flashlight he'd found in the truck and held my wrist as he directed us to a spot near a large jagged rock. The ground was cold and pebbly. I stepped lightly on my slippered feet. We stopped in front of the rock. The man turned us around to face the pond. The surrounding woods were silent, but I knew there were bears in these mountains. Wolves. Lynx. Otters. Mink. I wondered which would witness our murder.

The man said something to us in Slovak. *"Picovina,"* I answered. I had no idea what he'd said, but "bullshit" seemed the appropriate response.

Something caught my eye. The faint beams of a vehicle in the distance. And another pair of lights. And another. And another, chugging toward the pond.

Ruby and I knew that it wasn't Aunt Lovey or Uncle Stash or any of the other Slovak Relations. Whoever was coming, they were not coming to save us. Ruby shifted so I could see another train of lights advancing from a different direction. My heart began to beat wildly.

"Don't hold your breath," I instructed. "In the water. Don't hold your breath."

"Okay."

I was proud that Ruby didn't whimper or cry as the vehicles parked nearby. There were the sounds of car doors opening and shutting. I wondered if the villagers had brought shovels to bury us or if they'd leave us to bloat in the pond.

The bearded man who'd brought us was nowhere to be seen, but we heard him bark orders in the darkness. Whatever they were about to do, it appeared, was going to be done *his* way. He counted to three. Then there was a symphony of plastic clicking sounds from the flashlights the villagers had brought to light the way to Ruby and me. Except for the bearded man directing the people toward us, it was very quiet and organized, even civilized.

"Picovina," I muttered, because cursing made me feel in control. I felt Ruby squeeze her eyes shut as the flashlight circles drew closer. Ruby didn't cry or even whimper. I hadn't expected this strength from her and wondered about its origin when I felt my own ebb in proportion.

I kept my eyes wide open. I wanted to face the twenty flashlights (that's what I'd estimated) and glimpse just one soul. Whatever they were executing us for being — devils, witches, monsters — I would become that thing and curse just one of them for real.

No one spoke. At some point the clouds moved away from the moon again, and I noticed that all of the shadowy faces were female. They were, every one of them, looking directly at my sister and me with their round blank faces. One of the women, an elderly lady I remembered seeing on the church steps, croaked out something to the crowd. The bearded man (I knew from his voice that he was behind us) called out something in return. (It sounded contradictory, but to me everything sounds contradictory in Slovak.)

I squeezed my sister, baffled when the crowd quietly formed an organized line in front of us. The women did not immediately begin to drag us toward the pond as I'd imagined. They appeared not to have stones in their hands or any other crude weapons of murder. The first woman in line stepped forward, pressing a photograph into my hand, whispering something I didn't understand. I couldn't see the photo clearly and couldn't begin to imagine why this stranger was giving it to me. Then, without warning, without asking permission, the woman reached up to touch the spot of our conjoinment. Ruby and I reared back. I was shaking with fear and protest.

Ruby was brazenly calm. "You can't just touch us like that," she told the woman, who obviously did not speak English but somehow understood. The woman found the figure of the bearded man behind us and waited for an explanation.

The bearded man stepped toward Ruby and me, so close I could feel the heat of his body. His stiff canvas coat brushed up against my back as he put his right hand on Ruby's shoulder and his left on mine. However gentle his grasp, we understood that he meant to hold us steady so that the other women could touch our heads too.

"They think you are witch," said a voice beside us.

We shifted and turned and found Cousin Jerzy. He grinned and repeated, "They think you are witch."

"Take us home, Jerzy," I said.

"I will take you to Zuza and Velika," Cousin Jerzy answered plainly, "after this is done."

"This? What is *this*?"

Jerzy tossed something at my feet. My shoes.

"It's opportunity." Jerzy grinned. "Opportunity is now knocking." He made an insipid knocking sound with his tongue on the side of his mouth. "And I am to answer door. Hello."

"Why do they want to touch our heads?" Ruby asked.

"Why are they giving us things?" I asked.

"They want what everybody in world want. Luck. They want good luck." Jerzy found a toothpick in his pocket and stuck it in the wide space between his two front teeth.

"So they think we're witches because we're conjoined? They think we can bring them luck?"

"You come on St. Katarina. You come with two heads. Joined. Bang." He slapped his hands together. "You bring good luck to Sonya, so it's proof. Sonya touches your head there, and the babies don't die. Even the doctor in Rajnava say the babies will die." He shrugged, not that he necessarily believed in it, but it was a strong enough case to present.

"So what are we supposed to *do?*" I asked, looking out over the waiting faces. (There were about two dozen women there, but it felt like a thousand.)

"Just give them good luck, these women," Cousin Jerzy said impatiently. "It's to make them feel better. It's to give them hope. You understand?"

"What's the Slovak word for 'luck'?" Ruby asked Jerzy.

"Luck?" Jerzy considered a moment before he answered. "There is *stastie* and *osud* and *náhoda* and *úspech.*"

I wanted to do anything and be anywhere else. I almost wished the women had brought *shovels* instead of *hope.* I couldn't speak, though I could feel Jerzy waiting for me to lead our next move. But it was Ruby who pulled us erect. She was looking out over the crowd, taking charge. "We come on St. Katarina's Day," she started, "to bring luck to Grozovo. *Dobre stastie!*" she shouted.

The women looked at us. There was murmuring now, suspicion, growing discontent. The orderly line was disintegrating. Then someone started shouting. And the women began pressing things at us: more photographs, a pocket watch, a ring, a ceramic toad, a lock of hair. Somehow Ruby and I had gotten turned around, and the surging crowd was pushing us toward the pond.

"Sing," I told Ruby. "Sing something."

"Sing?"

"Sing!"

"Sing what?"

"Something!"

"Like what?"

The women stopped, intrigued, if baffled, by our repartee.

"Anything. A Christmas carol."

"Something happy?"

"Anything!"

"'Holly Jolly Christmas'?"

"Not that!"

The crowd was still and quiet as Ruby opened her mouth and began to sing "Silent Night," the hymn whose lyrics stop you with their beauty and brevity, even if the music's a tad sentimental. Ruby sang the song — "All is calm all is bright" — better than she ever had before — "Holy infant so tender and mild" — and made me ashamed I'd ever pinched her. Ever. "Sleep in heavenly peee-eace." My brave sister. "Slee-eep in heavenly peace." . . . Ruby.

If our life had been a Hollywood movie, Ruby's rendition of "Silent Night" would have sent the Slovak women away weeping and satisfied in their blessing, even though we hadn't let them touch our spot. As our situation was much too strange and surreal to be anything but what it was, the women quickly tired of Ruby's song and turned to Jerzy and the bearded man to see what they were going to do about our lack of cooperation.

"You have to let them," Jerzy said.

"We don't," I said.

"We're not," Ruby added.

"You have to. They paid good money."

"Good money? They paid *good money?*"

"You get cut! Of course you get cut!" Jerzy offered, but he was mad at himself for his slip.

There was no time for fury at Jerzy and his associates for their entrepreneurial atrocity. I felt Ruby looking out over the faces of the women and didn't know what to do but to follow her lead.

"Don't hold your breath," Ruby whispered as the bearded man herded the women back into line and gestured for the next woman to step forward and touch our heads.

"I can't do it," I whispered.

"You can," Ruby said. "Close your eyes."

I did.

"Think of each hand as a story or a poem you'll write one day. Imagine that the hands aren't taking something, but that they're giving something."

"Like what?" I asked, petulant.

"Ideas."

I was comforted by my sister's uncommon wisdom and made no further complaint about the strangers' hands on my head, though I can still taste the rising bile when I think of them, those women who believed they were extracting some kind of blessing from us conjoined witches.

When all the women there had touched Ruby and me, Jerzy thumped our shoulders as though we were teammates who'd just won the big game. We listened to the women whisper to one another as they squelched through the mud on the way back to their vehicles. We watched them drive away and followed Cousin Jerzy to a car nearby. I stubbed my toe on something and nearly fell. "Used to be there the old apple tree," Jerzy said. "They leave too high the stump."

On the way back to Cousin Zuza and Velika's, I was too exhausted and overwhelmed by what had just happened to think clearly or at all. Jerzy snaked along the path that cut through the forest on our way back up the hill, gloating over his success.

Our gorgeous braggart cousin explained that the villagers had been talking about the "two-faced girl" responsible for the safe delivery of not one but two healthy babies to sickly Sonya Shetlasky. Jerzy and his associate, the pregnant woman's husband, had decided to capitalize on a *relative* commodity. They charged each woman ten koruny for our special moonlight appearance, and were splitting the proceeds with the hairless man.

I was outraged. If they were splitting proceeds, how dare they consider leaving Ruby and me out? (Not that I wanted the money, but the nerve of these guys.) Jerzy understood my indignation and generously offered to cut us in on an exclusive engagement, for the duration of the Witches' Days, for appearances nightly at the pond. He felt certain they could spread the word to the neighboring villages. It occurred to him they could arrange some bus groups from nearby Rajnava and Kalinka.

He counted out a number of koruny from his pocket and stuffed them into my palm. It didn't matter, he told us, if we were witches, or even if we believed in witches. We'd already brought good luck to

Grozovo. The rest, the truth, was irrelevant. He parked in front of Cousin Zuza and Velika's and said we shouldn't answer right away, but think about it.

I looked at the koruny in my fist, feeling strangely like I'd earned them. "You should move to America," I said.

"But I'm Slovak," he answered. And that was all.

We watched the rising sun cut pink ribbons in the clouds over the church at the top of the hill. The sky promised a better day. Jerzy and Ruby talked about American movies, and though I couldn't leave, I wandered away, knowing there'd be hell to pay when Uncle Stash and Aunt Lovey found out where we'd been and what had happened at the pond. (We were too old for punishment but endured Aunt Lovey and Uncle Stash's disappointment for our remaining days in Slovakia, and that was hell enough.)

The day we left, I put the koruny Jerzy had given me in Zuza and Velika's Bible.

I RECALL FEW of the details of the return flight to Detroit. One moment we were standing in the short line at the airport in Kosice *not* being stared at, the next moment we were ensconced in the backseat of the maroon Impala, savoring the blackness in the long tunnel back to Canada. Then we were easing into the passing lane of moonlit Highway 401, astonished by the deep blanket of snow that the radio said had fallen within the past twenty-four hours. You just don't see snow that deep in late November. I thought Leaford might have been still in our absence, pining for our return. But life had gone on, hugely and splendidly, without Ruby and me.

It's Ruby.

This will be a short chapter because we are late for work. Rose made me be perfectly still for nearly ten minutes while she put on that lipstick I gave her for our birthday. Now that her skin is getting paler, the color seems to suit her better, or maybe I'm just used to it. I'm glad to see she's taking an interest in her appearance. It's about time. But I hate being late for work.

We have a school group from seventh grade coming in today, and we are nervous. I will admit it. Rose will not. But why else would she be taking ten minutes to put on lipstick? First, the school group is from an all-girls' private school in London, and girls can be quite scary. Especially so many. And if they go to an all-girls' private school, they're usually rich too. A dozen rich twelve-year-old girls is really very scary. The other thing that is in the back of our minds, but something that Rose and I don't talk about, is that these girls in seventh grade are about the same age as Taylor is. And, for all we know, one of these girls could *be* Taylor.

One time, a few years ago, a class of grade fours from Oil Springs came in, and there was this one girl where something about her reminded me of me. There was something about the way she moved and the curve of her eyebrow and her lips and high cheekbones, and I said something about it to Rose. We managed to get closer to the girl and had a good look, but Rose said it wasn't her daughter because she would have known. She said she'd have seen some recognizable light in her eye. And then, in bed that night, she said, Don't do that anymore. Don't point out girls who might be Taylor.

I was embarrassed that Rose had to point out that what I did was sort of cruel. So I made fun of her for being so touchy about it, since we were pretty sure Taylor was adopted by someone in Michigan and wouldn't be walking into the Leaford Library anytime soon. I wish I hadn't done that.

Nick is driving us to work today. He has been very helpful lately.

Rose wants me to ask him what he got sent to jail for. I'm trying to work up the nerve.

Home Again, Home Again

It was after two o'clock in the morning when we pulled onto Rural Route One on our return from Eastern Europe. Ruby was fast asleep, but I was recording for the future, the way writers do, all that had happened in Grozovo, elaborating and extrapolating, and already altering a few of the minor details. Driving through Baldoon County's familiar darkness, where the sky was high and filthy with stars, Aunt Lovey glanced in the direction of Merkels' cottage. "Something's wrong," she said. Then, as if she'd just heard a cry for help, "Turn in, hon. Turn in to Merkels'."

Uncle Stash yanked on the steering wheel, adrenaline coursing through his veins as he snaked up the lane that veered sharply up a second road to Merkels' driveway, wondering why our neighbors' house was lit up like a Christmas tree. Sherman Merkel came racing out the door when he heard our car. He didn't question why we were back from Slovakia nearly a week early.

"She's in there doubled over," he said, breathless. "Truck went dead," he added by way of explanation. "I been waiting for the ambulance, but I don't think they can find the house."

It could be hard to find a country house in the daytime if you didn't know where you were going. (Now every house has a post out front with a number on it for quick ID in emergencies, but ten years ago there was nothing for the driver to see.) In the night it could be impossible to find a cottage like Merkels', set back so far from the road and beyond a thicket of trees. And especially because the Merkels' access lane was not the same as ours.

"How long you been waiting?" Aunt Lovey asked as she hurried out of the car and rushed toward the house.

"Half an hour. More. I don't know. I called three times."

I didn't hear any more as Uncle Stash pulled the car door shut. From the car, Uncle Stash and I watched shadows moving in front of the windows. Neither of us spoke, but we must have been thinking the same thing: how fortunate that we'd driven by when we did.

The door opened and Mrs. Merkel, looking whiter and thinner and taller than when I'd seen her last, staggered through it. Aunt Lovey and Mr. Merkel held her steady as she pressed a blood-soaked towel between her bandy legs.

"I need the car, Stash," Aunt Lovey said, taking charge. "Sherman's gonna drive us in. You wait here with the girls. I'll get Cathy settled at the hospital and come back to take you home."

Uncle Stash nodded, climbing out of the driver's seat to allow Mr. Merkel the spot, and hurried to help us out of the backseat.

"Ruby," I said, "wake up. We're at Merkels'."

"I'm awake. Is Mrs. Merkel going to die?"

Uncle Stash held my arm, guiding Ruby and me through the deep snow to the slippery front porch. Given that we had seen Mrs. Merkel with the blood-soaked towel, we were not surprised to open the front door to find a circular pattern of blood near Mr. Merkel's farm boots and a trail of blood drops leading down the small hall to the kitchen at the back of the house. Like animals, we followed the trail and found, on one of the kitchen chairs, a fair quantity of blood. If you were skilled in crime-scene investigation, you might have known how long the blood had been on the chair by the way it had soaked into the cracked wooden seat. There was a cup of tea in front of the bloody chair. Steaming tea, which suggested it had just been made. Mrs. Merkel was practical, and she'd learned in the cruelest way a person can that panicking wouldn't change a goddamn thing. So she'd asked Sherman to make tea while she slowly bled to death at the kitchen table.

There was movement behind the long curtains that hid the canning. A scuttling on the floor. Uncle Stash reached for the broom beside the fridge. "Little *kurva* prick," he said, striding toward the fluttering curtain. If he'd been able to kill a mouse in that moment he might have felt some relief from his disappointment, or guilt, or fear, or whatever he may have been feeling.

"You'll wreck her sheers!" Ruby shrieked when he raised the broom. And, thank God, Ruby stopped Uncle Stash from swatting at the curtains, because it wasn't a mouse who bounded from behind the drapes but a little puppy. A little mutt with huge brown eyes. Uncle Stash picked the puppy up by the scruff of his wiry little neck, asking, "What we gonna do with you?"

"We have to take him home!" Ruby cried.

"That's fine," Uncle Stash said.

"He's too little to stay in the barn!"

"All right," Uncle Stash said.

"He can stay in our room!" Ruby whined, not quite realizing that Uncle Stash wasn't fighting her about taking the dog home.

We didn't rise when we heard the car in the driveway several hours later. "Fibroid the size of a cantaloupe," Aunt Lovey said when she opened the door.

I don't pretend to understand what happened between Uncle Stash and Aunt Lovey and Mrs. Merkel. But I'll never forget Aunt Lovey's compassion in that moment, the way she dropped her coat and went to him, shielding him with her arms, and kissed the tears from his red cheeks. "She's gonna be fine," she said. Then, "You."

The little pup, who was curled up asleep on my lap, woke from his nap and, seeing Aunt Lovey, jumped down to the floor and trotted over to heel at her stocking feet. She looked down. "Cute. Real cute," she said sarcastically.

"We're taking him home, Aunt Lovey," Ruby said.

Aunt Lovey puckered her lips but didn't say a word.

It was morning by the time we arrived at the house, and a brighter day than I'd seen before, with the sky high and blue, and the sun glinting off the flat crusted snow so the fields looked like silver lakes. I hated the crows for landing, strutting around on my illusion. We weren't expected back until the following week, and with Mrs. Merkel bleeding from her uterus, Mr. Merkel hadn't plowed yet or shoveled a path to our door, and the farm was hardly recognizable, so completely covered in snow. It seemed, with all that had happened, that we'd been gone for years instead of days.

Each winter our country road froze and heaved, shifting and lifting the earth into a patchwork of valleys and ruts. Uncle Stash bumped the car over the ruts but could not pull into our driveway, where the snow had drifted. So he stopped in the middle of the road and we abandoned the car with the keys in the ignition in case Mr. Merkel (or the county plow guys) came by and needed to move it. We understood we were supposed to walk the rest of the way to the house and didn't think to question or complain. Aunt Lovey tucked the little puppy (whom Ruby and I called Scruffy) into her coat and held him there against her breast, like a precious sleeping infant, as she trampled the unspoiled snow.

We hadn't slept well in days, and in the last day not at all, but none of us was ready to retire. Aunt Lovey busied herself with the puppy, holding him to her neck as she warmed a can of chunky beef soup for his lunch. (I could not bear to watch Aunt Lovey loving that dog. It wasn't just incongruous to see her with the animal, it was embarrassing the way she treated the thing like a baby. And yes, I was insanely jealous of their instant amity.) Uncle Stash, though Aunt Lovey had begged him not to, found the shovel and his toque and went out to clear a path in the snow. Ruby turned on the television, and I opened my computer to write a letter to Taylor, which began by describing our trip to Slovakia and ended with a tidal wave of regret that I never knew her, and she'd never know me.

In the days that followed, it became clear that Scruffy had eyes only for Aunt Lovey, who did nothing to dissuade his attachment and, in fact, encouraged it, feeding the animal from her plate at the table and letting him sleep on a towel at the foot of her bed. Aunt Lovey had transformed overnight from an animal-liker into a Scruffy-lover. When she thought no one could hear, she called the pup Baby. I think she let him suck her thumb. When Uncle Stash said he was jealous that the dog was taking all her affection, Aunt Lovey just laughed and said, "Well, it's only for a couple of weeks."

Much as Ruby and I hated Aunt Lovey's attention to the dog, it was the barking that really drove us crazy. Hush up, Scruffy! Hush up! We must have said it a million times. Scruffy *was* like a baby, barking whenever Aunt Lovey left the room. Barking at the crows from the window in the den. Barking to be let outside to pee, then peeing on the floor just to show he was boss. Near the end of the second week, we were eager to get rid of the dog, to have Aunt Lovey to ourselves again and a little peace and quiet.

I overheard Mr. Merkel tell Aunt Lovey that his wife had asked to have her fibroid pickled. Where she'd put *that* jar up, I didn't care to wonder. Ruby thought it was disgusting that Mrs. Merkel wanted to keep her tumor, but I understood her fascination. I wondered if Mrs. Merkel wanted to examine her fibroid to prove to herself that it did not have hair or teeth or eyes, and was not another child of whom she'd been robbed.

There were complications from the hysterectomy. On the day she was to have been released, Mrs. Merkel had another hemorrhage. It was winter and a slow time on the farm, so Mr. Merkel spent his days at his wife's bedside, reading aloud from books borrowed from the library or just sitting there saying nothing at all. Uncle Stash brought plastic tubs of macaroni salad from the grocery store, and the two men talked about the Red Wings and their hopes for the Tigers' draft. Aunt Lovey cut her volunteer hours to spend more time with the dog. I was writing a flurry of poems then, so who else but Aunt Lovey was gonna walk the damn dog? Sherman Merkel'd made a big deal of thanking Ruby and me for looking after Scruffy, and we never let on it was really Aunt Lovey who'd grown attached.

By spring, Mrs. Merkel was out of the hospital and recovering back in the cottage, but was too feeble to care for the energetic pup, and by then she must have known it wasn't *her* dog anyway. To Ruby's and my exasperation, Mr. Merkel asked Aunt Lovey to keep Scruffy for a while, which we knew meant indefinitely, and there'd be no end to his infernal barking.

Ruby pointed out to me then that, however indirectly, she and I had saved Cathy Merkel's life, for if we hadn't gone with Cousin Jerzy that night in Grozovo, we might not have caused all the trouble in the village, and Uncle Stash might have found the home he was searching for and would not have used the snowstorm as an excuse to leave early. We would have stayed in Slovakia, and Cathy Merkel would have bled to death at her kitchen table. We wondered if we might elicit gratitude or further scorn from Mrs. Merkel if she knew. I thought the odds were even.

However indirectly, I think Ruby and I did save Cathy Merkel's life. But if we're responsible for saving Mrs. Merkel, aren't we equally responsible for all that happened because she lived?

"All that happened" started with a puddle of pee. Not the first puddle of dog pee on the kitchen floor during Scruffy's protracted stay (Aunt Lovey constantly had the ammonia out to clean what she called piddle) and not the last. It was spring. The lilacs bloomed a week early, and Aunt Lovey had gone out to gather an armful of the fragrant deep purple ones, because Uncle Stash liked those best. She was arranging them in the milk-glass vase passed down from Verbeena, and hadn't paid attention to Scruffy's barking, and hadn't noticed him piddle on the old linoleum floor. Aunt Lovey called us in for dinner, and walking through the door, Uncle Stash slipped in the pee. He fell forward instead of back, taking his full body weight on his right knee. I could smell the sickening-sweet purple lilacs when Ruby and I pushed through the door and found Uncle Stash on the floor, howling in pain.

The kneecap was fractured, tendons torn, ligaments damaged. Uncle Stash would never recover from the fall. He couldn't take a step without a cane and got vertigo when he walked on wet grass.

He couldn't conquer three stairs, forget a whole flight, and, the worst of it, being it was his right knee that was injured, he could no longer drive a car.

"Take away a man's car. Cut off his *chuj*. It's the same," Uncle Stash told Aunt Lovey when he thought Ruby and I couldn't hear. "Such a nice drive, that Merc." (Uncle Stash had just finished re-tooling a used Mercury Marquis and had driven it only a handful of times.)

Later, Ruby and I had watched Uncle Stash at the long pine table, addressing a letter to Cousin Marek. I asked if he'd mentioned his misfortune with the pee, and the knee, and Dr. Ruttle saying he can't drive anymore. Ruby said the Slovak Relations would proba-bly blame *us* for his bad luck. Uncle Stash laughed about that, then let his head fall into his hands and wouldn't look at Ruby and me. I was confused by his weakness, not just his physical failure but his lack of ambition. He was the strongest person and the bravest man. How could he fold like that, just because he couldn't drive a car? Ruby reached out to touch his arm and said, "Aunt Lovey cut fresh asparagus for dinner."

Uncle Stash looked up. I thought he might regard us, shaken by the enormity of our challenge, and realize that his own was quietly bearable. (You see that kind of thing on TV all the time.) He didn't, though. Instead, he smiled at Ruby, tolerating her pity, and said, "You don't understand what it means to drive car, Ruby. You don't understand."

Ruby and I knew, before it was said, that we could not spend an-other season at the farmhouse, before the stairs, and the wet grass, and the getting from here to there became too great a burden on our crippled Uncle Stash. Aunt Lovey announced one day, shortly be-fore our birthday, that it was time to move to the bungalow. She'd said it simply, but with such an air of finality that the idea took my breath away. *Move to the bungalow.*

I knew that, one day, Ruby and I would live in the bungalow. I imagined us there, like Zuza and Velika, the spinster sisters of Chippewa Drive. I never thought Uncle Stash and Aunt Lovey would live there with us. I never imagined our lives would play out this way.

"There'll be all kinds of benefits to being in the city. You just wait and see," Aunt Lovey said.

"Okay." I hadn't meant to sound sullen.

"I hope you're not going to sulk about it, Rose. Not everything is about you."

(An aside: If we'd known this would be our final year in the farmhouse, what would we all have done differently? Aunt Lovey might have spent more time at the long pine table. Smelled the flowers more deeply and more often. Eaten more just-picked tomatoes and corn. Trampled longer through the bergamot with Scruffy at her heels, feeling like the young mother she never was. And Ruby? That's easy. She would have wanted more time in the fields looking for her arrowheads and bone sucking tubes. Uncle Stash would have taken more photographs. There must have been an angle or two that he'd missed. Some interpretation of the farm that was his alone. What would I have done differently? I would have listened more intently to the hum of the earth, observed more closely her rotation. Tried harder to find Larry Merkel's bones.)

There was no discussion of bringing Scruffy to the bungalow. Scruffy was a chaser: crows, cars, squirrels. He was a country dog and could never have survived the confinements of Chippewa Drive. So he was returned to Mrs. Merkel in an uneasy reunion, like a philandering husband skulking back to his wife. We left them on the bridge over the creek, barking and waving. Aunt Lovey was dry-eyed walking through the field on the way back to the Mercury, a composure I credited to all her years as a nurse.

That was the last time we saw Mrs. Merkel, with or without the dog.

Rose was feverish last night. We're not sure why. She took some medication and the fever was gone this morning, so we don't think it's brain related. Probably just something she ate. She's lost her sense of smell, and she's been craving the weirdest things lately. She doesn't seem to be able to tell when something's gone bad. For the last few weeks she's been craving caraway bread. Probably because of writing about Slovakia.

Rose hasn't been herself. She has been unusually talkative. I'm normally the talkative one, but I've been quiet lately and I don't really like how we've reversed our roles. It's just that Nick seems to be around all the time now, and they have a lot in common. I don't have much in common with Nick. Actually, I find him sort of annoying, though I can't put my finger on exactly what it is that annoys me. Of course I'm jealous that Rose is paying so much attention to Nick. It's not romantic attention. He's old and not Rose's type. Anyway, I'm pretty sure he has a girlfriend in Windsor. The cowboy boots on Saturday nights are a dead giveaway.

Rose and Nick talk about books. Listening to Nick, you'd think he had read every book ever written. Guess a stint in the can makes you literary. He was in the Kingston Penitentiary. I assume Aunt Lovey and Uncle Stash knew why Nick was in jail. Nonna must have known. Nonna must have told them, but they never told Rose and me. Uncle Stash and Aunt Lovey never met Nick. He didn't come around to care for Nonna until after they'd passed. Nick's boy, Ryan, has spent some time in Kingston too. Nick didn't even raise him, but he ended up a criminal.

Nick and Rose talk about sports too, which I prefer to the discussions about books and authors, which make them sound pretentious. At least when they discuss sports, they have passion and original opinions.

It seems in some ways that Nick is filling the place of Uncle Stash. Maybe that's what I don't like about him. Maybe that's what I'm jealous about. Because Nick can fill that place for Rose. But not for me.

Nick and Rose talk about Nonna too. And sometimes I join in those conversations. Nonna's on the waiting list to get into the care home near Rondeau. The place is on a cliff near the water and it looks like a mansion. Lots of windows and a view of the lake.

Nick came over last night and the two of them went on and on about the World Series, as if they never talked about it before. I've never been a big baseball fan, and I wouldn't admit it to Rose, but I liked watching the World Series this year. Especially the American League Championship between the Yankees and the BoSox. The BoSox haven't won a World Series since the team was cursed by a fan way back in the old days when the owners sold Babe Ruth. Uncle Stash would have loved this series. He would have sat there with Rosie, drinking *peevos* and slamming his fist on the table. He'd have been shaking his head and just admiring the hell out of the BoSox pitcher who played with a messed-up ankle. He would have jumped out of his seat watching the Sox do what no team has ever done before, which is to come from behind when they're down three-zip. Everybody believed the Sox were cursed. I don't even care about baseball and I believed it. Rose believed. Uncle Stash sure believed.

After Nick left, I thought Rose would want to write, but she didn't even open her computer. Instead, she wanted to talk. She was asking me questions about how I see my life — like, Is my life a series of little dramas, stories within a story, or does it feel more continuous, like something long with a suspenseful plot? I've never thought about my life in any particular way. I definitely don't think of my life as a bunch of little stories. Or suspenseful, though I guess it is. Guess everyone's is, really. I'm just living. I don't dwell on my past. I don't worry about my future. I'm just trying to be at peace from one moment to the next. That's the way I live my life and that's the way I think about my life. I stayed awake all night figuring that out.

I'm trying to be supportive about Rose's writing, but I'm still thinking about the odds of anyone ever reading this thing. Maybe Roz would want to read it. Nick. Not Nonna. Even if Nonna were still Nonna, she wouldn't want to read Rose's life. She watched us grow up. She knows all the good parts, believe me. Nonna liked romance books. I wonder who Fiodor was? She's been asking for Fiodor. Fiodor. Nick said he thinks it was a boy from her village in Italy. Before her family moved and she married Nick's father. (Rose acts like it's such a tragedy that Nonna is calling for Fiodor. She's imagined this whole romance for Nonna. Why does Fiodor have to be a lost love? Fiodor could be the kid who killed her goat. Or the boy she told us about who could suck spaghetti up his nose.)

Nick was telling Rose how he read about these monks who have a tradition of making beautiful mosaic art with poured colored sand. When it's finished, they let the wind blow the sand mosaic away. When I said what a waste of time, Nick said that art isn't a product. It's an experience. Which sounds like something he read. Nick does metal craft in Nonna's garage. He makes sculptures and hangs them all over the place. I think he probably learned how to do this in jail, but I'm not about to ask. Not like he could, because they wouldn't be everyone's cup of tea, but he doesn't even try to sell them.

Nick is currently reading the great philosophers, which makes me roll my eyes. He says the philosophers all say the same thing — work hard and do right but don't worry about outcomes. He said we have no control over what happens. Which I guess makes some kind of sense. He's full of quotations, if you know what I mean. You can see why Nick and Rosie are friends.

Still, it was very cool that Nick made us the stool, which is definitely making our life easier. We thought we were going to have to quit at the library because Rose is having so many headaches and not sleeping, but now with the stool the pressure's off her back a little. The kids would be so disappointed if we weren't there for story time. They can be little buggers, but I do like children a lot.

Mr. Merkel came into the library yesterday to check on his notice for help on the bulletin board. He couldn't believe that no one had pulled off one of the little tags with his telephone number. There are a lot of people in Baldoon County who are unemployed, but farmwork is hard and not too many want to be farmhands, especially in the winter, when there's not much to do and what you do you do in the cold.

Rose is still writing the story about what happened in Slovakia. She has been writing that story for three or four weeks. It seems to be driving her crazy. She is writing so slow now I don't know if she's managing a page a day.

Basically, the trip to Slovakia was pretty freaky. There were some good things, but, really, we all should have listened to Aunt Lovey and not gone. Uncle Stash would have enjoyed the trip much more on his own. Maybe he would have found what he was looking for instead of spending the whole time defending Rose and me. Why spend four weeks writing about a bunch of misunderstandings and bad feelings? There are so many more good and happy things in our lives.

Rose said she doesn't feel like she's done a good job describing how scared to death we were in Grozovo when that lunatic took us to see the woman with her twins. And about what happened after, when we thought the old ladies were going to drown us in the pond. She asked me if Jerzy was really as sexy as she remembered him. He was. Sexy and creepy at the same time. Kind of like Nick.

Rose is also worried she hasn't done a good enough job describing Aunt Lovey and Uncle Stash. She said when she's done writing about the Slovak trip, she's going back to the very beginning of the book to find a better way to introduce our parents. She asked me how I'd describe Aunt Lovey. Not what she looked like but who she was. And right away I thought of something that happened just after our family moved into the little house in Leaford. Rose and I came home from a visit to the library one day to find Aunt Lovey in the backyard with a can of blue latex and a roller, painting the mattress from our bed. She was sweating like crazy, with one hand on her aching back, rolling this awful blue paint over the pee and blood and puke stains on our old mattress. Rose and I started laughing when we saw her, though the truth is I was a little worried because I was thinking, maybe she was getting Alzheimer's like Nonna next door. We asked her what she was doing, and she said that our new mattress had come from Sears that day and the old one had to go to the curb, and she couldn't put our mattress at the curb for all of Leaford to see with pee and puke and drool stains. To me, that just says it all about Aunt Lovey.

It's harder for me to think of just one thing for Uncle Stash. For Uncle Stash, I always think of him being handsome. Even when he was older and his hair was gone. One day Uncle Stash took Rosie and me to the park and he was taking pictures of tree bark or something when someone called out, Hi, Stan. We knew it was a guy from work because all the butchers at Vanderhagen's called him Stan. Funny thing was, Uncle Stash hid his camera when he turned to see the guy and waited until the man was gone before he started taking pictures of the tree again. I remember on Slovak Nights when we were little, Uncle Stash would talk about when he was a boy in Slovakia. Things like what happened on St. Ondrej's Day when Uncle Stash and his cousin Velika did this superstitious thing of pouring molten lead into ice-cold water. The lead hardens fast and your future is decided, depending on what shape the lead turns into. The ritual was usually done by the village girls, who could see the face of the man they were going to marry in the shape of the cooled molten lead. Velika wanted to know if she would marry Boris Domenovsky or Evo Puca. Uncle Stash was teasing her, because he knew she hoped the lead would look like Evo. She was slowly pouring the liquid lead from her ladle and was just about done when Uncle Stash accidentally knocked her arm. Two blobs of lead dropped into the water instead of one, which they both knew was a very bad omen. Cousin Velika and Uncle Stash argued over what the two blobs meant, and even whose future, Cousin Velika's or Uncle

Stash's, was being foretold. The very next day Uncle Stash's two older brothers were killed when a mine shaft collapsed. Uncle Stash was usually one to laugh at superstition. Rose and Uncle Stash liked to roll their eyes when Aunt Lovey and I talked about extrasensory perception or ghosts or past lives, but then Uncle Stash would tell his story about the blobs of molten lead and you could see he was dead serious. He completely believed in that. Same way he did with the curse on the BoSox.

Writers and Baseball

I t's easy for Nick to say it doesn't matter if my story is ever read. He says, "Just that you wrote it, Rosie, let that be enough." But I want more. So much more. I want this collection of words to transform themselves into visions of Ruby and me. I want to be remembered like long-ago friends.

Immortality?

Oui.

Conjure me.

RUBY HAS NO enthusiasm for baseball, no matter that history was just made. Hollywood could not have written a better ending to this baseball season, but Ruby's hardly noticed. Still, she hasn't complained about all the baseball nights with Nick. My sister and I have been so accommodating with each other lately. Would that we could have lived *every* day thinking it might be our last. (She doesn't object to baseball. I don't object to poached eggs. How's that for give-and-take?)

Our Tigers didn't have their best season ever, but they're a young club and hold tons of promise. I just about lost interest in baseball this year until the American League Championship. I guess I've been preoccupied. This World Series has reignited my passion, though. I realize that I have totally believed in the curse on the Boston Red Sox. (Say the two words "Bill Buckner" to any sports fan, and you'll see by their face that everyone believed in the curse.) So what course of events changed fate? Why was the curse broken? How? We'll never know.

Watching the baseball with Nick has made me miss Uncle Stash. He would have loved to be sitting beside Ruby and Nick and me watching the Red Sox take this extraordinary victory. (Actually, Nick wouldn't have been here. Uncle Stash would not have liked Nick. I don't think he would have allowed Nick in the house. He wouldn't have wanted him near Ruby and me.)

Euphoria. When the Sox won, I felt euphoria. It's quite a thing to feel euphoria. And quite another to share it. I don't think a lot of people experience the feeling. The athletes surely do. Especially the victors. And the fans do too. That's why we buy the merchandise! Euphoria! When the Sox won, I had this quick flash of heaven. And heaven was the den in the old farmhouse, with the orange shag and the big TV, and there is Uncle Stash, dressed in his undershirt, drinking *peevos,* smoke billowing from his pipe, cheering for Johnny Damon and Big Papi. Euphoria.

After the game, after Nick left, something strange and remarkable happened. We were in bed and I'd closed my eyes and was nearly asleep when Ruby said, "Ernie Harwell." (Ernie Harwell was the broadcast announcer for the Detroit Tigers for forty-two years and he retired just a few years ago. The thing that is strange about Ruby saying the name Ernie Harwell is that I had been trying to remember his name the whole night. I couldn't ask Nick because I didn't want him to think I was an idiot for not remembering Ernie Harwell's name — or worse, worry because he feared my memory lapse was because of my aneurysm — so I didn't say a word, but it was bothering me all night. I could hear his distinctive voice. I could see his face — even though he was the radio *voice,* he was still recognizable, but I couldn't recall his name.) Ruby heard the question in my mind, and either pried Ernie Harwell's name from some department in my brain that was not available to me or remembered it on her own, which is even more remarkable.

Ernie Harwell used to start off each Tigers' season by reciting from "Song of the Turtle." I remember Uncle Stash would whisper it, along with Ernie Harwell, but instead of saying "the time of the singing of the birds," Uncle Stash would say "the time of the *sinking* of birds." Uncle Stash and I listened to Ernie Harwell describe as many Tigers games on the radio as we watched on TV. Ernie Harwell makes me think of being in the garage with Uncle Stash. Oil. Steel. Cursing in Slovak at North American cars. Ruby complaining because she hates cars and baseball. When Ernie Harwell retired, I mourned for Uncle Stash all over again.

I remember, one winter, Uncle Stash was driving us to the White Oaks Mall in London, where Pierre Berton was signing autographs. It had started to snow on the way there. I hate driving in the snow. Ruby was doped up on Dramamine and deep asleep. Uncle Stash cursed when a transport started to tailgate our Impala. "Don't crawl up my arse, you *kurva* bastard." (*"Kurva"* means "whore," and it was a word Uncle Stash used for drivers of any gender or denomination. There were the *kurvas* who cut him off, the *kurvas* who raced him at the stoplights, and the *kurvas* who crawled up his arse.) "We have to turn around," he said.

Uncle Stash turned off at the next intersection and drove through the snow to Thamesville, where we'd wait out the storm before heading back to Leaford. He mistook my silence for despair over not getting a signature on my copy of Pierre Berton's latest book.

"My Rosie Girl," he said, glancing at me in the rearview mirror. And nothing could have sounded sweeter, because he said "My Rosie Girl" only when we were alone (when Ruby was asleep — or pretending to be). And when he said it, there was a look in his soft brown eyes that made me think I was his favorite.

"Don't be sad about the signature," he said.

"I know," I answered. I wanted to scream at him to watch the road.

"When I was young man in Windsor," he began, and much as I

loved to hear stories from his past, I was truly afraid of the icy road to Thamesville and of dying young.

"It's really coming down," I said.

Uncle Stash looked through the snow, which had formed into little bullets that were blasting the windshield. "I put the snow tires last week," he said. "It's not gonna be an accident, my Rose. Don't be afraid."

I found myself mesmerized by the snowflakes in the foreground and the red taillights beyond as Uncle Stash told his story, one I'd never heard before, his voice trailing off from time to time as if he'd forgotten he was telling it out loud, to me.

"The first summer I am in Canada, I go to Detroit with the boys from Mr. Lipsky's apartment building. There is Joseph, and Miro, and Dusan, and Stevie. Five. We go to Briggs Stadium to see Tigers play Yankees. We go early because it's day for autographs, and we want to get autograph from Tigers. Anybody will make us happy. Hoot Evers, Eddie Lake, Billy Pierce, Dizzy Trout. We don't dream to get ten autograph. Just one. So it's okay we get to Briggs Stadium. We go inside. Is so big. So exciting. We go to where people are waiting to get autograph. The line is very long. We wait in line. We wait in line. We wait in line. In front of us is boy, younger a little. This boy hears us, Miro and me, talking in Slovak. This boy is stupid *kokot*. 'Go home, Krauts!' this boys shouts. 'You lost the war, you Kraut bastards.' Stevie or Dusan says we're Slovak — not German — but now more people are hearing us talk. And two more boys call us Krauts. We're almost near to getting autograph, so I tell my boys it doesn't matter. We want to get autograph. We want to watch game. We don't come to fight. Okay. So we move to the front with our baseballs for the players to sign. But the boy says again that we are Krauts, and Dusan starts yelling at the boys. He's calling them such names, but in Slovak, so they don't understand exactly the insult. Then I see. I'm watching the players, and one of them whispers something to the other guy and they go away down the corridor to the dugout. We don't know why they are going. Doesn't matter. There's no autograph."

Uncle Stash shrugged after telling his tale. I was relieved when he didn't ask me to guess at the moral. (Prepare to be disappointed by your heroes? Never speak Slovak among *kokot* idiots at a ball game?)

He returned his focus to the hazardous road. "Aunt Lovey will be worried, we're taking long time," he said.

We watched the road. I felt Ruby purring beside me.

"Autographs are worth *hovno,*" Uncle Stash said.

It wasn't technically true. Plus, what kind of moral was that? I waited to see if there was more. There was.

"That day, at the baseball park, still we want to see game, Rose. We find our seats. Is nowhere near us, the boy who calls us Krauts. Is good game. Exciting. And when Miro go to get *peevo,* because he has already the dark beard and is the oldest to look at, it's Slovak man serving. He gives to Miro the *peevo, free,* four times he gives to Miro the *peevo* FREE, because the boss isn't looking."

"Oh," I said.

"My Rosie" — Uncle Stash laughed — "sometimes in life we don't get the autograph. But then . . ."

He was waiting, so I ventured, "Free beer?"

"Okay." He laughed. "Okay." Uncle Stash plugged his Ray Price tape in and sighed, exhausted and edified.

RUBY ASKED ME to write this bit of verse from Robert Graves. It has taken me a while to dig it up — so to speak. Ruby says it's about archaeology. I say it's about writing. I hate it when we're both right.

> *To bring the dead to life*
> *Is no great magic.*
> *Few are wholly dead:*
> *Blow on a dead man's embers*
> *And a live flame will start.*

Human Conditions

Our first year in the bungalow on Chippewa Drive was diffi-cult, but not as great or grave a challenge as our second year would prove. That first autumn, watching the neighbors in their midsize cars crush the leaves that had fallen quietly through the night, I longed for the pumpkin patch on Rural Route One, the hum of the tractor, the foul smell of the creek that separated the Merkels from us. Uncle Stash grumbled about the city and pined for the farm. (It was just Uncle Stash's knee, just one hinge on a whole won-drous body, but when it stopped working he transformed from one thing to another. Even his heart attack hadn't changed him so sig-nificantly.) His photographs took on a darker hue. We have stacks of photographs from that first year in the city, when Uncle Stash be-came even more obsessed with the crows. Black and whites of crows in midflight. Lined up on a hydro wire. Strutting atop a garbage-bag mountain in the park down the street. One crow staring cock-eyed at the camera, mocking the photographer. When Uncle Stash wasn't taking pictures of the birds, he was trying to murder them, limping outdoors, leaning heavily on his cane, firing rocks at the crows with his pitching arm, until he made a fairly decent slingshot out of Aunt Lovey's old brassiere. He never one time hit a bird. Never once, which made me wonder if he was trying all that hard. The neighbors watched him, silently, shaking their heads. They hated the crows too, but Uncle Stash was savagely incorrect.

On Chippewa Drive Ruby watched too much TV and became bored, and boring. When the cable went out one day, she was in despair. Aunt Lovey suggested she read a book, but Ruby found Uncle Stash's photographs on the bookshelf and looked at those instead. Ruby was flipping through a stack of his most recent shots, his "crowtographs" (as my sister and I had begun to refer to his pictures), and found one of a fat crow perched on a post behind Aunt Lovey, looking, comically, as though he was standing on the top of her head. We showed this one to Uncle Stash, who laughed, for the first time since his accident, because he hadn't noticed the ridiculousness of the framing before. He thought to make a card of it for Aunt Lovey's birthday.

"What words can we put, Rose?" he asked.

"I don't know."

"You're the writer. You write something, okay?"

"Something funny?"

"Yes, something funny. Because it's funny, the picture."

I sat looking at that silly photograph for an hour and came up with "Happy Birthday, Birdbrain. You really ruffle my feathers." Aunt Lovey pretended to be amused when she opened the card and, after forcing a laugh, fled the room. Uncle Stash blamed me because I should have known she'd have preferred something more personal and romantic. I think I knew she wouldn't like the card, but I was angry about losing my childhood home. I felt bereft and needed someone to blame.

Aunt Lovey was the only one of us who didn't have a chance to miss the farm. She made frequent trips down that rutty road to check the attic for bats, or the traps for mice, or the cellar for raccoons. She was really going to the farm to see Scruffy — and we all knew it. Once, when Uncle Stash tagged along on one of her errands, he came home describing to Ruby and me the way Scruffy had bounded out of the field when the Mercury turned into the driveway and how the dog had lunged at Aunt Lovey, his muddy paws smearing her just-cleaned coat, and how she hadn't scolded him or even seemed to care. Mrs. Merkel never appeared during any of Scruffy's visits, but she must have known Aunt Lovey was with him, gamboling somewhere beyond the corn.

If it was just the physical farm I longed for, I could have asked to go with Aunt Lovey to rendezvous with the dog. Ruby would have endured the car ride if she thought it was important to me. But whatever it was I had lost in leaving the old orange farmhouse, I couldn't find in returning. I'd seen that with Uncle Stash and Slovakia.

Ruby and I watched Halloween from behind the living-room window that first year on Chippewa Drive, children pulling their mothers past our tidy little house, frightened by classmates' stories about "The Girls," all grown up now but still freaky, who'd recently moved onto their street. Aunt Lovey made some excuse about the porch light not being bright enough, but I knew it'd be some time before we were accepted here as neighbors. Uncle Stash, without residue of patience since his slip in the pee, turned the lights off altogether, so no one had to wonder why the children weren't coming to the door. Ruby got sick on all the leftover Snickers.

I was trying to overcome my disappointment about not going to university by writing short stories. I was working on a book of connected stories adapted from Aunt Lovey's tales about her eccentric mother. I called it, simply, *Verbeena,* and was going to present it as a gift to Aunt Lovey for her birthday, but I was having trouble with the structure, and the blending of fact with fiction, and sensed I was imitating Aunt Lovey's voice instead of writing with my own. I destroyed whole pages in tantrums of self-doubt. I tried not to blame my sister for my restlessness.

Aunt Lovey knew I was frustrated, so she copied a Ralph Waldo Emerson quotation, found an old frame, and hung it near where I keep my computer. I was too resentful to thank her. It's still on the wall, reminding, "Do not follow where the path may lead. Go instead where there is no path and leave a trail."

Living in the bungalow on Chippewa Drive naturally made me think of Frankie Foyle, and though his basement room was gone and Aunt Lovey had scrubbed the place clean of the renters, I found myself looking for artifacts, the way Ruby searched the fields. A chewed-on-the-end ballpoint pen that had fallen in the furnace grate. An evil-smelling clothespin of a style Aunt Lovey didn't use. A sliver of soap stuck behind the vanity in the bathroom. I wanted to hold something of Frankie Foyle's and feel the vibration that Ruby talks about. I wanted to hold something with weight, so I could prove to myself that my daughter was real.

I was thinking last night, when I couldn't sleep, how to describe my feelings about my decision to give up Taylor. While even today, in this moment, I know I did the right thing, there's a hole when I glance to my left and sorrow for what I've lost. I wonder if it was the same for our birth mother and if she ever drowned, as I do, in self-pity and doubt. I've told Ruby I want to see Taylor, and I do, part of me does, but the other part (wiser part? selfless part? mother part?) recognizes that in mending my hole, one would surely appear in my daughter's life, if one isn't there already. (How cruel to leave her twice in a lifetime.)

In those first few years after she was born, I never imagined having contact with Taylor. I just wanted to look at her. If I could have seen her through a window, or caught a glimpse of her profile in a photograph, I would have been satisfied. I thought of Taylor often in that first year we lived at the bungalow. Her memory startled me when I turned the little corners of the narrow halls. That's when I started to write, every day, like a serious writer, and found some comfort in trying to make poetry of my most human condition.

While I could fill whole days reading or writing, and came to the night feeling tired and accomplished, Ruby felt small in the new house. When Christmas came, Aunt Lovey suspected seasonal depression and said we should sit in the window, like tomatoes she was trying to ripen. Ruby said the season didn't depress her, but the little tabletop Christmas tree from the grocery store must have. One day she threw it to the floor like a toddler because she'd burned a batch of Christmas cookies. Ruby didn't sing that year. No "Silent Night." No "Holly Jolly Christmas." I think she needed to hate Christmas in the new house. I think she needed to protest the change. But I was writing then and wouldn't let myself shrink.

As the year progressed, Ruby became bored with being bored and led the two of us on various excursions around Leaford. We began to discover the primary benefit of living in the city was that we found independence. We grew up, finally, and without the Herculean effort I imagined it would require. We discovered we could get around by ourselves. We could walk to the library. Take a bus to the mall. We felt less unusual being unescorted. Without our parents in attendance, people related to us differently. I noticed myself becoming more personable as the checkout ladies and the staff at the library started talking to Ruby and me individually and even seemed to pick favorites between us, instead of looking to Aunt Lovey or Uncle Stash to translate. Ruby and I began taking on responsibilities for Nonna, going to the drugstore to fill her prescriptions, making out shopping lists for Aunt Lovey to take on Tuesday afternoons. We started to talk about getting jobs.

We could not help but notice the lives of Uncle Stash and Aunt Lovey growing smaller, as Ruby and I pushed our own conjoined lives to the edge. Aunt Lovey stopped volunteering at the hospital and, worn out from waiting on Uncle Stash, started going daily to the farm. She didn't even pretend anymore that she was there to scare the bats or ensure there weren't squatters at the long pine table. She'd return to the bungalow, frowning. "I don't know if that animal is getting any attention at all! Honestly, poor Scruffy just seems *starved* for affection."

"I'm the one starved for affection," Uncle Stash joked one day and seemed his old self again — just like that. (By spring, a whole year after injuring his knee, he'd found some way to tolerate his disability and had even started taking photographs again, of things other than crows.)

Aunt Lovey had been waiting for the strawberries to ripen and was keeping vigil daily, maybe hourly. She wanted to get to the berries before Cathy Merkel did. She'd come home reporting, "The top berries are starting to turn. They're gonna be small and red and sweet this year."

Finally, Aunt Lovey returned late one June evening with paw prints on her slacks and a pint of ripe strawberries, which she'd waited until dusk to pick, allowing them to take the day's sun like a last meal. "Berries are ready," she said.

"But tomorrow we're going shopping in Chatham," I reminded her.

"Tomorrow we pick," she corrected.

"But we need clothes," Ruby added. "For the interviews."

"There'll be time to drive to Chatham after we pick the strawberries."

We'd picked the berry patch at Tremblay Farm as a family for as long as I could remember, and we'd missed strawberry season only once when we were children, when we spent a month in the hospital in Toronto, and Cathy Merkel'd put up the berries that time. We heard the whole rest of the year about how our neighbor hadn't used enough sugar in her jam. Aunt Lovey was not going to risk such disaster again.

Ruby couldn't take a Dramamine and then be in the hot field all afternoon, so my sister braved the car ride on the winding river road back to Rural Route One with the window open and the music on loud as a distraction. We'd been gone only a year, but I realized with some shame, driving on that hot, sunny, late-spring day, that I hadn't exaggerated Baldoon County in my imagination but had, in fact, understated the blinding green of the grass, and dwarfed the magnificent barns and silos, made modest the maples and pines and sycamore trees, and left unfeted the pastoral fields.

The country was a spectacle, and I felt like a fool for having undervalued her. But the house, the old orange farmhouse, I had not underestimated. It looked shabbier than I remembered. Decrepit. I don't believe in ghosts, but I could have been convinced the place was haunted when we pulled up the graveled drive. I remember looking away, not wanting the picture to stay with me. Scruffy must have smelled the Mercury coming because, before we climbed out, he was bounding out of the field to see us, or rather to see Aunt Lovey, who fed him turkey from a bag in her coat pocket. Uncle Stash laughed and took a few photos of Scruffy. Dopey face. Muddy whiskers. Unlike me, Uncle Stash and Aunt Lovey didn't blame the dog for anything.

Uncle Stash was excused from the berry patch when he complained about his knee. He'd brought his camera and six rolls of film, and seemed eager to make up for lost time with his lens. He'd pointed at the barn nearby, and the fledgling crops, and Merkels' cottage in the distance. "See, Rose, look there at the trees and the frame of the field here. There is *geometry*. There is *poetry*."

Scruffy stayed with Aunt Lovey throughout the afternoon as we picked the sun-warmed berries for her sweet preserves. (We can't bend or squat comfortably for long periods, so I sit, with Ruby balancing on her clubfeet. I reach and pull, and pass to Ruby, who holds the container and discards the duds.) I remember being struck by the excess of insects. Had I forgotten about them, or were they so much a part of the fabric of my life that I didn't see, in my periphery, the way they made the earth come alive? In the space of two berry plants I'd encountered four bees, a beetle, a dozen spiders, a grasshopper, and a thousand tiny ants. (No bud weevils or spider mites, though — that would have been *bad*.)

Uncle Stash hobbled around, taking photographs of the beauty and ravages of spring. I hated to look up and find him pointing his camera at the old orange farmhouse. Why did he want to shoot it when it was already dead?

Aunt Lovey worked tirelessly, bent over, straddling the lush berry plants, one leg on either side, as she'd done all her life, her gnarled fingers plucking the dense red berries at a pace, dumping them into the basket when both fists were full. Scruffy barked at the bugs, or simply watched, and wagged, and waited for affection. Occasionally, tried of watching and wagging, the animal would lunge at Aunt Lovey and lick her face, her nose, and her lips, in a strictly disgusting display. I wondered if Cathy Merkel would be jealous of

Scruffy's devotion to another woman. (Or would the recompense be understood?) The dog's licking and barking irritated Ruby and me and reminded us why, among other reasons, we didn't miss the mutt. We worked our way through the berry patch, picking, eating, shouting, "Hush up, Scruffy! Hush up!"

We never went into the house. Not even to pee. Neither Ruby nor I wanted to go inside to witness the peeling wallpaper or hear the wind whistle through the empty rooms or smell the smell of long-dead mice. (Plus, what if I was wrong about ghosts?) I was eager to get away from the farm altogether and, having picked the strawberry plants clean for the day, begged Aunt Lovey, "Let's hurry up and go to Chatham."

We were heading for the Mercury when Uncle Stash noted something about the color of the sky and said he wanted to stay to snap some twilight photos. (It never occurred to me that he might go over to see Mrs. Merkel. I was sure their attachment had been severed.) Ruby and I needed some professional clothes for our upcoming interviews — drugstore clerk and secretarial assistant among them. (Our intention wasn't to share a job, but to work part-time at individual ones.) We agreed to come back for Uncle Stash in a few hours.

Uncle Stash loaded the flats of just-picked strawberries into the front seat instead of the trunk, where some motor oil had spilled days earlier. Before we climbed into the car, Uncle Stash suggested that we invite Nonna over for a barbecue. Steak and ribs. And whitefish for Ruby. Aunt Lovey decided we should stop by the Oakwood to get cheese buns and cannolis, since we were going to Chatham anyway. Scruffy jumped up on Aunt Lovey to lick her face one last time. Ruby and I made fake vomiting sounds, which inexplicably made Aunt Lovey laugh. We were having a good time. It had been a difficult year, but spring had sprung, and the berries were luscious, and we had, each one of us, evolved.

Aunt Lovey, having helped us with our straps in the backseat, gently moved Scruffy out of the way with the toe of her shoe and settled herself into the front. She managed to shut the door, but Scruffy went around and jumped at the Mercury's grille, barking as if to say, "Don't go. *Don't go.*" She laughed at his persistence, but Ruby and I were impatient to leave. Even when Aunt Lovey turned on the motor and revved the engine, the dog kept barking and would not move away from the front of the car.

Instead of being annoyed with the annoying dog, Aunt Lovey just smiled, unbuckled her seat belt, and maneuvered out of the Mercury, striding back to Uncle Stash, who hobbled to meet her halfway. Ruby and I shifted so we could take turns watching them in the rearview mirror. They were laughing. Could have been about anything. They were laughing hard, a hand on the other's shoulder, like good friends of the same sex. Scruffy started barking ferociously, which seemed to make them laugh even harder. Aunt Lovey kissed Uncle Stash on the mouth and gave him the bag of turkey from her pocket. Weak and fickle, and just a dog after all, Scruffy chose to stay with the food.

Aunt Lovey was still laughing when she climbed back into the car, and still laughing when she started driving down Rural Route One. Watching the rearview mirror, she described the scene to Ruby and me. "Uncle Stash is waving. Scruffy just jumped to get the turkey. Ouch! That was his groin! Oh dear. He's all right. Maybe not. Yes, he's fine." She sighed, still watching. "He's such a ham."

Her voice was soft and far away. In the reflection of the rearview mirror, I saw the eyes of a young woman, fair and freckled, stunning in her white satin gown with a hundred pearl buttons down the back, floating down the ninety-foot aisle of Holy Cross Church to marry her handsome Slovak. I don't believe I ever loved my Aunt Lovey more than in that moment. And I don't think I'm making that up.

Aunt Lovey looked away from Uncle Stash and returned her eyes to the road, where two fat black crows were picking at some carrion. Instinct possessed Aunt Lovey to swerve. She hit a rut in the road and lost control of the car. The Mercury flew in the air and came down hard, nose-first in the deepest part of the drainage ditch. Ruby and I were strapped into the backseat with the harness Uncle

Stash had custom-made and bolted to the frame. We were in the air. Then we were not. It happened so fast. Ruby and I never spoke a word to each other in the moments after the crash. Or in the hours and days after the accident. We didn't speak any words at all, not for a very long time. And to this day we have never spoken about the accident, the details of what did or did not happen. I tell myself that Ruby's eyes were squeezed shut and that she didn't watch Aunt Lovey slam against the windshield and snap at the neck, then clang against the steering wheel like a ringer on a bell. It was all over in a matter of seconds, the way accidents are. Aunt Lovey was perfectly still. And so was I. And so was Ruby.

The strawberries, which had been stacked in baskets on the seat beside Aunt Lovey, were tipped over, strewn about the dash. Their fragrance mingled with the smell of fuel and the mustiness of the ditch. At first, the air was so still and quiet I thought I might have gone deaf. But the crickets and cicadas, whose day we'd rudely interrupted, resumed their communication. And bees began to buzz. And I saw, in my periphery, a muskrat sniff the window of the Mercury, lured there by the berries, then frightened off by Ruby and me.

I was struck by how fast Uncle Stash made it to the car on his bad leg. And impressed that he didn't have his cane when he opened the door. Uncle Stash didn't brush away the strawberries or mention them at all, though he must have seen them and smelled them when he climbed into the front seat. He looked into the backseat at Ruby and me, and then beside him at Aunt Lovey.

I don't know if I spoke or if Ruby did, but one of us said, "We're okay."

He could barely catch his breath. "Girls. Good. Girls.

"But you," he whispered, laying his palm gently on Aunt Lovey's back, "you are not okay, my love. Are you? Are you?"

Uncle Stash stroked Aunt Lovey's back as a worried father would a sick child. "My Lovey. Oh, my Lovey." He pulled Aunt Lovey's head from the dash.

I wonder now if he was torturing himself, or fortifying himself, or assuring himself, by forcing a look at her mangled face. A crash lasting only seconds, not even at highway speed, yet her nose was horribly broken, her cheek shattered, blood at the cave of her nostril. Something clear dripping from her ear.

Uncle Stash made a sound. An indescribable sound. Not a cry, smaller than a cry, barely audible, but a sound that held such horror and such grief I wanted to cover my ear in case it came again. The sound did come again. And again. And I realized it was me.

"Shh," Uncle Stash said. "It's all right, Rose. Girls. Shh."

Though I don't believe in such things, I thought I saw something like radiant heat, or a wisp of smoke, rise up from Aunt Lovey's body and hover over Uncle Stash before dissipating. I imagined the wisp was her soul remaining briefly to say, "I love you. Good-bye." I think it kissed my cheek.

I held Ruby tightly, as she clung to me, not trembling, or sad, or even afraid. We were none of the things you'd think we'd have been. We were quiet and present. We were strong. In the distance, we could hear the sound of the truck starting up in the driveway at Merkels' cottage.

"That's Sherman," Uncle Stash whispered to Aunt Lovey's broken body. "He's coming now. It's okay, he's coming."

Uncle Stash turned to look at Ruby and me in the backseat. His voice was quiet, unwavering. "Sherman will take care of the farm. You understand?"

Ruby and I paused before we answered, pondering what he meant, because we knew he meant more than he'd said.

"Yes," Ruby and I said together.

"Yes," Uncle Stash said. And then again, this time to Aunt Lovey, "Yes."

Ruby and I watched Uncle Stash arrange Aunt Lovey's body against the berry-stained seat. He tried several times to put her floppy head right and, when finally he did, pressed his cheek to hers. There was no space, no hint of light, between Aunt Lovey's skull and Uncle Stash's. I was pondering their conjoinment, when Scruffy began to bark for the first time since the accident. We heard Sherman Merkel's truck peel over the ruts in the road and finally stop at the spot where we'd crashed.

I have some vague memory of Ruby and me standing in the mud outside the Mercury, while Aunt Lovey and Uncle Stash were still inside, Mr. Merkel using a sensible tone, trying to lure Uncle Stash away. The car didn't look so bad — a smashed front fender, a slightly bent frame, and I understood why Mr. Merkel had been so shocked when he looked inside. I don't think he'd expected to see anyone dead.

In the days that followed, I found myself wishing that Mr. Merkel hadn't pulled Uncle Stash from the wreckage of the car. In spite of their imperfect union, their different interests and language and culture, Uncle Stash and Aunt Lovey shared an essential vein and should never have been separated. After the funeral Uncle Stash spoke only a little. He would not eat at all. He stared at the dark bedroom wall, waiting. If Uncle Stash had remained in Aunt Lovey's embrace after the crash, I think he could have willed himself to death instantly. Instead, it took a week. Some people will understand that Ruby and I were relieved to find him gone one morning. How cruel it must be for a man to live past his soul.

It's Ruby.

I feel like I need to apologize every time I write that I haven't written more. Or that I haven't written longer. Or better. Do real writers do that when they write?

This isn't even technically my book, but if it got turned down because my part is so shittily written, then I would feel really bad.

Still eight weeks till Christmas, but there was already a tree up in Dr. Singh's office. A real tree that smelled like pine. Made me think of Christmas at the farm. Rose and I haven't bothered with a Christmas tree since we moved. There's no room to have a decent tree, and I can't stand the little artificial tree that sits on a table that we've got in a closet somewhere. My opinion is, Why bother?

Our Christmas shopping is done. We got Nick to take us out to Ridgetown last month, and we bought books for everyone on our list and signed the books with personal sayings. Parting thoughts, I guess. I was feeling a little sentimental when I was signing to Roz and Nonna, but I don't think I wrote anything stupid or embarrassing.

Dr. Singh was blown away by the stool thing Nick made and the way Nick adapted it for us. I swear to God I think Nick Todino blushed when Rose started telling Dr. Singh about some of the metal craft Nick has in Nonna's garage, even though she hasn't really seen any of the stuff he's done over the last few weeks.

I love Toronto. Nick drove us down Yonge Street after our appointment yesterday. The lights were pretty magical. There was a movie shooting at the Royal York Hotel on Front Street. There was a fat Santa and a bunch of kid extras, and two beautiful actors in love, and they were all dancing to some Motown song. Then snow started to fall, fake snow from this giant machine with a crane and a fan, but it looked good. If you framed it with your fingers, blocked out the lights and the camera and the bald director, the scene looked almost real. I'm sure it will be heartwarming in the movie.

Nick parked so we could watch the movie shoot for a while, which was very nice of him because he seemed bored. Of course Rose couldn't see what was going on, but she didn't complain about stopping. I described what was happening, and Rose tried to sound excited, but she is not as good an actor as me. (I might have tried to go in for musical comedy, singing and acting.)

Dr. Singh can't do anything about Rose's blindness, which we already knew, but Rose doesn't blame me for asking Nick to take us to see him. I guess I was just hoping for a miracle. Maybe she was too.

Rose reminded me of Aunt Lovey when she was trying to be optimistic. She can make out shapes, and light and dark. And all these years writing on her computer have made her fingers remember the keys. She can finish her book. That's really important to her.

The light has been bothering Rose. Especially lamplight. Nick replaced all our lights with soft low-watt bulbs, but it's still too bright for Rose. The television gives her a terrible headache, so we haven't turned it on in a while. (No hockey this year because of the lockout, but I bet Rose would have suffered the television if her Red Wings had been playing.) We don't put the lights on at all in the evenings. Just candles. Rose says we're living like our old-maid cousins in Slovakia. When Nick comes over in the evenings, which he insists on doing every night now to tuck us in like babies, he teases Rose about the candles and asks her if she's trying to get romantic with him.

Rose is still writing every day, for hours at a time, slower than she was writing when she first started losing her sight. She's kept her failing vision a secret for a long time. From me anyway.

We have been talking a lot about the past. And laughing a lot. Both of us are a little punchy, like when you're really, really tired and everything seems funny. Like when we were kids and couldn't fall asleep, and Aunt Lovey would stomp down the stairs and she'd be really seriously mad at us for still being awake, but we'd just burst out laughing the second she walked out of the room. Rose feels like the best, best friend lately. I don't know if that's because of her blindness or the way dying has changed us.

Nick drove us to London last week to the archaeology museum. If you go there and think that you're lost in suburbia, don't worry, you're in the right place. The museum is at the end of an eighties subdivision and it seems totally out of place. But this is the site where, five hundred years ago, a group of Native people made a home. It's not that they chose a weird place for the museum — it's the actual site of an ancient village. But life goes on and rises up around the past. We were the only car in the parking lot, which was great. A huge relief because this meant we were gonna be able to hang out with Errol Osler and not be stared at by school groups and have to answer a thousand questions. (Not to be bitchy, but sometimes we're just not in the mood.)

The outdoor part of the museum, the longhouse (my favorite part), is closed for the season, and normally that isn't a problem because Errol Osler lets us in with the key, but when we got inside we discovered that Errol's on a trip to China. There's a graduate student working there, but he didn't know where the key was. At least, he said he didn't know where the key was. The graduate student had a name tag with the word Gideon, which is an unusual name. Nick asked the guy where he got his name. You could tell the guy was trying to be polite. At first he said he got the name from his father, who was insane, and then he laughed at his joke, which was not really a joke. He said his mother named him after her grandfather, no big story, but he gets asked about his name a lot and it kind of drives him crazy. I understood just how he felt. But Nick looked insulted. Gideon is a guy our age, just a little taller than Rose and me, with a very slight build, like a girl.

Later, Rose said Gideon was a whisper of a man, which I thought was a good, but sort of insulting, description. What man would want to be a whisper? I didn't realize then that she couldn't really see him. He was just a dark blur to her. I asked her what kind of man Nick would be if she thought Gideon, the graduate student, was a whisper. She took a breath like she was going to say something, and of course I thought she'd say Nick was a shout, then she didn't say anything. And I waited and she went back to her computer. I think she's having little seizures. Dr. Singh said she might.

This graduate student knew about Rose and me because he had grown up in Glencoe, which is a small town where the train still stops, just about halfway between London and Chatham. Gideon even called us by the right names, which you'd think everyone would because I do not look like a Rose, and my sister does not look like a Ruby, but there you go. He made a remark about the stool Nick made, which I think Nick took the wrong way.

And then Gideon really set Nick off by saying he should have angle parked. There's a huge sign in the parking lot that says you have to angle park, but there was no one else in the lot, so Nick didn't angle park. Nick said he was not going back out to angle park his goddamn car in a goddamned empty lot. Then he called Gideon *professor*, which I don't think he liked.

I was trying to be a peacemaker and I asked Gideon if we could go out to the longhouse, because Errol always let us out there during off-season. That's when he said he didn't know where the key was kept. But Nick didn't believe him. And Nick was getting steamed, so Rose started talking to Gideon and asking him questions, and it turns out Gideon is related to a historian from Baldoon County and he's a writer himself, and he's writing a book about the Neutral Indians along the Thames River.

How's that for bingo?

It's not like Rose to blurt things out. I'm more the blurter. She usually has more self-control. But she blurted out that she was writing her autobiography and had been wishing she could meet another writer. So Rose and this complete stranger, whose face it turns out she couldn't even see, started talking about writing, which you can imagine was pretty boring. I shared a look with Nick, which was funny because Nick and I just don't share looks. But we did. And his look said he was bored too. And jealous. I know I was not reading that wrong.

Once Gideon and Rose had talked for a while about things they had in common — like not knowing other writers — and once they had shared how hard it is to work in a vacuum, they didn't have much left to say. So that's when I started talking about the farm and told Gideon about the Indian camp, and about all my finds in the fields, and the collection at the Leaford Museum, which he'd heard about but hadn't seen, because he's been living in Nova Scotia. He has only found flints and fish-bone pins and pottery shards in his excavations. Never found an effigy pipe. Never found a bone sucking tube. He was listening to me like I was some expert, which made me want to be some expert. Maybe I'm not intellectually lazy after all. Maybe I'm just lonely for someone with similar interests. So the four of us, Nick and Rose and me and Gideon, walked around this big empty museum together, Rosie and me using the stool, with Nick and Rose whispering about something I couldn't hear, and Gideon and me talking like a pair of university types. I felt about ten feet tall.

After we got home and Nick was gone, Rose made some joke about our double date with Gideon and Nick and we laughed so hard, these giant snorting laughs. But like I always do, I started worrying that the aneurysm was going to burst. We kept on laughing anyway. We haven't laughed like that in a long, long time. Since the squirrel in the kitchen, I think. It felt good. At some point, while we were still laughing, I stopped worrying that the aneurysm might burst and started hoping it would.

I didn't know last week that Rose couldn't see the artifacts at the archaeology museum. She hadn't told me she'd gone blind. I asked her point-blank if she told Nick before she told me. She says she did not, but I'm not sure I believe her. For the past few weeks Nick has been staying until after I fall asleep. Rose says they're just talking.

Rose was getting tired when we were walking around the museum, so Nick helped us into a room and arranged some chairs so we could sit down. Gideon went to get water from the staff room. I couldn't see exactly, but I would have sworn I caught Nick reaching out to hold my sister's left hand. I felt her face flush with blood. And her heart started to beat faster. She claims, because I asked her, that Nick did not hold her hand. And that there's nothing going on. But when I think about it, in the last few weeks I've felt her blush more than once. And I've felt her heart racing when Nick is close by.

When we were getting ready to leave, Gideon gave Rose and me each a spirit stone that he scoffed from the gift shop. Mine had the whale for courage, and Rose's had the ram for wisdom. (Or have I got that wrong?) Then Gideon asked me, nervous, like as if he was asking for a date, if it would be possible for him to see the old farm on Rural Route One, and if I could take him on a tour and show him where I found stuff. I told him I would try to get a hold of that lady from the Historical Society to open up the Leaford Museum where my collection is, but who knows.

Rose says I answered yes too fast about him visiting Leaford. He's coming on the bus next week. Nick grumbled about it, but he's gonna pick Gideon up at the bus stop in Chatham and drive us all out to the farm together.

I've been thinking we're going to spoil everyone's Christmas if we die too close to the holidays.

Rose would kill me if she knew I just wrote that.

Love Poems

I have written many poems. I thought one or two of them were good. I don't know anymore. A long time ago I wrote a poem about a kiss. It wasn't one of my best. Not a line from the first draft survived, hardly a word comes to mind. It's no longer stored on my computer hard drive. I altered it. Deleted it. Then rewrote it completely, and deleted it again. Then another attempt, and another, and another, jettisoned to some unredeemable place. I thought the poem could not return, but it did, like a rash, appearing one day in my handwriting on a yellow legal pad at my wrist. I've returned to the poem in my mind, over and over through the years, until it's become an enemy and something I want to conquer. I've suspected that my struggle with the poem is due to the fact that I'm obsessed by the act of kissing, because I've never been kissed myself. Maybe I've pressured the kiss with my reverence. Maybe a kiss *is* just a kiss.

Tonight, after Ruby fell asleep, I asked Nick to kiss me.

If you had told me a day ago, or even the very second before I blurted it out, that I was going to ask Nick Todino to kiss me, I would have said you were crazy. But there it was, out of my mouth and hanging in the air.

"Will you kiss me, Nick?"

I didn't give him a chance to answer, needing first to explain that the request was for purely artistic reasons. I wanted to experience the kiss, to know the sensation of a mouth pressed to mine, so I could return to my poem and ask it for surrender. I explained to Nick that he should think of the kiss as a favor for a friend. I told him I didn't expect, or necessarily want, a romantic, or passionate, or even sexual kiss. (You and I know this is not the whole truth.)

Nick didn't answer. My heart began to thud when I realized my mistake. Nick would *not* kiss me. How could I think he *would*? Now I'd ruined everything. (Of course I heard echoes of Ruby asking Frankie Foyle to kiss her and loathed drawing the parallel.)

I reached out to take Nick's hand, but he pulled away. He didn't leave the room, though, which I found odd. I could feel Ruby asleep beside me and was glad she didn't know what I'd done, how I'd humiliated myself.

"Nick," I ventured.

He said nothing.

"Nick?"

He paused a moment more, then stood and walked toward the door. I heard the light snap off and shivered involuntarily, sensing, tensing, in the dark. Still another pause, and then footsteps, not receding down the hallway as I'd supposed, but returning to the bed. I was afraid Nick might shout at me. Or kill me in some psychotic rage that I'd triggered with my unseemly request. (I still don't know what he went to prison for!)

"Nick," I began again, but he made a *shh* sound and put his hand gently over mine. I didn't say another word. I didn't want to ruin whatever fantasy he was composing of who I'd be, if he bent to kiss me. He leaned in and I felt the rush of air as he swooped over me to look at Ruby. To make sure that my sister was not just pretending to be asleep. He moved back toward my face and hovered there for a moment. I don't know if his eyes were open. I assume they were not.

The kiss was not as I'd written in my poem, not at all as I thought it would be. Not starry. Not sweet. He tasted salty. Smelled of meat.

Ham. And it was not the sensation of heat I felt but *fire,* surely, where his lips touched mine, thirty-seven times in all, on my chin, nuzzling my soft cheek, that spot near my hairline below my ear. He left burn scars where he kissed me. Raised scars I can feel today with my fingertips. Whoever Nick was imagining me to be (I know he wasn't kissing *me*), I must have been beautiful and very sexy. I must have had long, silky hair and heaving breasts and a sumptuous mouth, because he desired me (*whoever* I was in his fantasy). That fact was undeniable.

He kissed me, over and over, warm lips pressed to warm lips, tongues meeting, then just lips again, gentle sucking of lower lip, then licking of upper, no grinding of groins, no concentric circles, and yet, after a time of this sublime kissing, I found myself in the grip of a most surprising quake. (I read somewhere, when I was a teenager, that the French call an orgasm *"le petit mort"* — the little death. I asked Aunt Lovey, who I thought, being a French descendant and a nurse and a reader, would understand the metaphor on every level, but she'd bristled. "Well, French *Canadians* do *not* call it *that.*") I wanted to tell Nick, because I thought he'd be pleased, but I was too afraid to break his reverie and still wanted his mouth on mine.

Convulsions, contractions, like a *sneeze,* I'd heard a high school girl say once on the bus. Nick stroked my arm, as he kissed me once more, and again. Ruby whined in her sleep, and Nick suddenly stopped and pulled away, as though he'd been caught doing something very, very bad. Ruby didn't wake. But Nick didn't kiss me again. I couldn't look into Nick's eyes and was grateful for the dark, so he couldn't see mine. He stood and left without a word. I could not breathe, still reeling as I was, from my *petit mort.*

MELODRAMAS MUST BE written at night, as the moon and stars conspire to seduce the imagination to go farther, harder, higher, longer, faster. *Yeah, baby.* It's not too much. It's never too much. You might imagine that the fantasy I had after Nick left was a sexual one, but it wasn't. It was as narcissistic as any sexual fantasy, as driven by ego, but Nick Todino wasn't even in it. Maybe melodrama is too tepid a word to describe a fantasy that involves Ruby and me not dying, but having the aneurysm miraculously disappear and going on to be guests on an American television show to promote my surprise bestselling autobiography. In a dramatic turn, we're reunited with my adopted daughter *and* our lost mother on national TV. After our appearance on the show, my daughter, and our mother, and Ruby and I decide to get a house together in sunny California, where we live in harmony, despite the preponderance of estrogen.

(I know. I know. Even for a fantasy, it's a little over the top.)

Blame it on the moon.

What homage to *fromage*.

Tomorrow morning we're going to the farm with a fellow called Gideon, a whisper of a man we met in London at the Museum of Indian Archaeology whom I know Ruby has told you all about. Gideon asked if she could give him some quotes for the book he's writing about Neutral Indians around the Chatham area, and if he could use some of her site maps and sketches. She just about peed her pants. She did *not* just about pee her pants when I asked if I could quote her in *my* book. It made me jealous. Imagine that.

I'd been thinking how nice it would be to meet another writer, so I was delighted to meet Gideon, who's had a few journal articles published and wrote a column at the weekly paper in Chatham for a while. (He said he's seen us at the Leaford Library before, but I don't remember him.) He and I started talking about writing, and I felt like I did in Slovakia when I realized that Cousin Jerzy was speaking English — someone *understands*. And, like countrymen in a strange place, we became fast friends, right there in the gift shop, and began a candid discussion about our respective tasks. Gideon described how he wants to ignite a passion for the past in his readers. I could feel his excitement as he talked about his subject, and his deflation when he admitted he was struggling with his nonfictional narrative. He said he wasn't sure about the structure or the tone. He said he was still trying to find a way in. And here I am, trying to find a way out.

Nick is driving us all out to the farm. I'm nervous to see him, and excited. I wish I'd never kissed Nick. Or never stopped. What is he thinking? Is he sick about it? Will he even show up in the morning? If he does, I suppose there's some advantage in not having to confront a person's expression.

Ruby and I can't walk the furrows with Gideon to point spots out directly, not that I'd remember a single location. (We need the stool just to get to the bathroom now. My balance is poor. And Ruby probably wrote about how we had to leave our work at the library last week, and about Roz breaking down and how Lutie had to take her home.) But we'll be nearby if he has any questions. The lady from the Historical Society, who it turns out has been quite ill, finally called to say go ahead and let ourselves into the museum.

There's been a key under the front mat this whole time.

Dead Men's Ember

I feel like a schoolgirl writing in her diary. "We went out to the farm today and drove in the front seat. Nick held my hand the whole way there. I thought Ruby saw, but she didn't. Or what if she did? I wonder if he'll kiss me after she falls asleep tonight. Should I ask him? Will he kiss me again if I don't ask him? He's coming in an hour! What do I do? Oh my God!"

The fall has been warm. The villainous sun stole into September and drained the world of its color, the way it bleached a square in the orange shag carpet in the den. The leaves stayed on a full three weeks too long. And the maples went gray this year instead of scarlet. The oaks a shade of putty. The willows a concrete color. And the birch speckled gray, like stone. I missed the fiery sienna, the burst of saffron, the explosion of orange. The leaves turned gray, along with the cars, and the streets, and my gray self, and my gray sister in the blurry gray mirror.

The shades of gray are gone now too. It's really only dimensions of dark I see. I've been without my vision for a few weeks, but I didn't tell anyone at first. Not even Nick. I haven't meant to be a martyr. I've just been uncharacteristically optimistic, hoping I might have a reprieve. Like the leaves. Instead it appears there's some pressure on the optic nerves, which is related to the aneurysm. Or not.

Today was the first day I felt a chill in the air. A northeasterly wind assaulted me when I opened the door. I felt Ruby grip my shoulder, afraid I might lose my balance and fall. "Cold," I said, and that was all.

I couldn't tell by his tone if he regretted what happened last night. "You're gonna need gloves" was all Nick said. He helped us to the car, which he'd warmed up for a full ten minutes before knocking for Ruby and me. Even if he hates me, and hates what happened between us, I am thrilled to be near him. And I don't care how pathetic that sounds.

Ruby was excited about showing Gideon the farm. She thought it was not out of the realm of possibility that he might find something in one of the fields or near the creek if he walked that way. If she could have, she would have planted an artifact in his field of vision the way she used to do for me. Bless her cotton socks.

Nick had packed the backseat with extra blankets, foldout chairs, thermoses of hot chocolate and of tea, and a cooler with *sang*wiches, leaving just enough room for one person. "The professor can sit back there," he'd said.

Then, strange thing, we got into the car, and Ray Price was crooning on the stereo. Ray Price. Why Ray Price? If Nick had read this book, if ever I had told him about Uncle Stash's fondness for Ray Price, I might have thought it was romantic. But I hadn't told Nick, and Ruby surely wouldn't have. I felt myself flooding with warmth, and I remembered the watering can in the bathtub, how Aunt Lovey used to wash our hair when Ruby and I were children. I felt the two of them beside me, perfectly, like love. Maybe Uncle Stash and Aunt Lovey were coming to the farm, I thought. Or maybe it was God.

At the bus station in Chatham, Nick wanted to stay in the car, but Ruby insisted we wait on the platform, like *civilized* people. I felt Ruby stiffen when Gideon stepped off the bus in Chatham.

"Something's wrong," Ruby whispered.

"What?"

"He looks mad, or in pain," Ruby answered.

"Must be that pole up his ass," Nick said.

"Be nice, Nick," I begged.

Ruby was right. Gideon was in pain. And mad too. He explained from behind the stack of blankets in the backseat, as we drove the winding river road, that he'd twisted his ankle, racing to answer a knock at the door that morning, and had been handed a notice to vacate by his landlady. He complained that the place was a dump and said he was lucky to be out of it, but was in despair about where to live, because of the deadline on his book and his inability to write it. He described the black mold on the tiles in the bathroom shower, and wondered if the spores had damaged his brain, and if that's why he felt foggy when he sat down to write. (I never thought of that — blame the spores!)

Ruby surprised me by asking Nick to take the long way around Big Bear Line, because my sister doesn't usually like to drive a foot farther than she needs to. Then I realized it was because she didn't want to pass the site of our accident. I was glad for her forethought. I'd lost my own.

I couldn't watch the landscape roll past, but I could imagine it, and even with the windows closed I could smell it — the death of this present season in the rich black loam, stronger as we got closer to home, but behind the scent of dying the sweetness of spring, and the green smell of summer, and fall and winter again, and the fusion of all the seasons that ever were, and ever will be, uniting in the earth and air around us.

Finally, I knew, by the certain pattern of ruts in the road, that we had reached Rural Route One. Nick put his hand over mine, weighty and warm. I felt like a bride as we pulled into the driveway of the Leaford Museum. I imagined that my wedding ring was antique white gold.

I was relieved that I was spared the sight of the old orange farmhouse across the road and kitty-corner to the museum. I noticed that

Ruby chose not to look either. I shudder to think what's become of it and prefer to keep a picture of the place not from now, or from our last visit, or even from ten years ago, but from long before our tenure here, before the pine table and the deadly consumption. I like to think of the farmhouse in its first incarnation, with the backdrop of trees that were clear-cut for crops, Rosaire and Abey eating peaches on the porch.

"Is Mr. Merkel around?" I asked. The Leaford Museum is built on a slight rise. You can see the farmhouse from there, and the Merkels' cottage too.

Ruby paused. "I don't see anyone. Looks like the truck's there, though."

Gideon decided he wanted to see Ruby's collection in the Leaford Museum before he ventured out into the windy fields with her map.

There was much ado getting Ruby and me arranged in the stool from the trunk, and we needed more help than usual maneuvering the uneven walkway that leads to the museum porch. Once there, Nick bent to collect the key from under the mat, and we all went inside.

I breathed the dust, inhaled the past, and felt Ruby's heart flutter beside me.

"Oh," Ruby breathed. "Oh."

"You found all this?" Gideon asked, incredulous. "Without equipment? Without digging?"

I felt Ruby blush.

"*You* found *all this?*"

Ruby took a moment, and I felt her scanning the length of the cases. "Yeah," she said, sounding somewhat astonished herself. "*I found all this.*"

We hadn't been to the museum since Aunt Lovey and Uncle Stash died. Like me, recalling the splendor of the farm less than brilliantly, I think Ruby had forgotten how hugely impressive the artifacts were, stretching from wall to wall, like the pages of a book telling some wonderful tale.

"That's some collection," Nick remarked, and I swelled with

pride, realizing that all this time Ruby had been climbing her own mountain and had long ago reached the summit. "Quite a legacy. Quite a gift."

I felt Ruby blush. "Yeah," she said. "I guess."

For all the chattering Gideon had done in the car, he'd fallen silent, gazing upon the collection of Indian artifacts arranged on plum-colored velvet in the wide glass cases. I couldn't see the displays, but I felt Ruby lead us to the vast assortment of things she'd found, the mortars and pestles, the curved ax handles, the grinding stones, the beads of wampum, and I heard Gideon's deep mouth breathing as he moved slowly from object to object. With each exhalation, he seemed to be muttering, "Wow."

"Want me to say what everything looks like, Rosie?" Ruby asked, careful not to sound pitying.

"No," I whispered.

I could feel that Nick had moved away from us and walked to the other wall of the museum, in the direction of the life-size enlargement of Ruby and me, at three, under which the sign reads "Rose and Ruby Darlen. Born joined at the head on the day of the tornado — July 30, 1974 — at St. Jude's Hospital, Leaford. Rose and Ruby are one of the rarest forms of conjoined twins — craniopagus. They share an essential vein and can never be separated. In spite of their situation, the girls enjoy a normal and productive life here in Leaford. Picture taken by Stash Darlen, the girls' uncle."

Like Ruby and Gideon, who were wandering in their way, and Nick, who was still studying the photo, I wandered, the way people do, to a more thoughtful place in my mind, unburdened by the laws of gravity. This wandering took me on a journey across the road to the old orange farmhouse to recall once more, as I have in these pages, my life with my sister attached to my head. I crossed the bridge that stretched over the creek, where I could see Ruby and me sitting on the edge, my legs hanging over, swinging a little. Just a couple of sisters waiting for a heron. I moved a little to the right, and glimpsed my daughter there too, a specter sitting with her back to mine, dangling her long legs over the side of the bridge, elegant in spite of her teenage posture. "Good-bye," I whispered. She looked over her shoulder and smiled. I wandered farther through the fields. Nothing stirred but the mice at my feet as I wandered in circles, lost in the corn. I confess I was looking for my mother. Then, out of the fields and back to the creek where we were baptized and nearly drowned, I looked down and saw Larry's red truck in the muck, and was struck by an impulse to rescue it. I felt the rush of warm water on my head, and wondered if I might faint for real. I flailed my arms, reaching out for Nick.

But Nick wasn't there.

"Whoa!" Gideon cried, stumbling beneath our conjoined weight, not accustomed to handling our proportions the way Nick is after all these many months.

"Sorry," Ruby and I said at the same time.

Nick was quickly at our side. He took our weight from the wispy man, saying, "What the hell, Rose? What the hell?"

"Just a little dizzy. It's gone now," I lied.

"Maybe we should go," Nick said.

"No," Ruby and I said in chorus with Gideon. Which was funny.

The feeling of dizziness stayed with me, and that's why I did not believe when I saw her face in the window that I was seeing what I saw. I was certain I was seeing an image from my imagination. Blurry, and in color, Cathy Merkel's face.

"Mrs. Merkel?" I said to myself.

"What?" Ruby asked.

Nick swiveled to see where I was looking. There was nobody at the window.

"I think I can see, Nick," I said, but just as I said it, a wash of gray, like a wave, like a cloud over the sun, covered my field of vision once more.

When I heard her voice, I assumed it was part of the same hallucination. It's tiresome to be confused. (Poor Nonna.) And terrible to be blind.

I don't know if Ruby saw her first, or if Nick did, or Gideon. The men wouldn't have known who she was. And, at any rate, wouldn't have known her name.

"Mrs. Merkel?"

No response.

"Mrs. Merkel?" I asked, because I *felt* her presence, and I was assured of my sixth sense now, just as if I could hear her or see her. (I continue to debate myself over my vision of her at the window. Something my pressured brain constructed? Or did I regain my sight, even briefly, and could I again?)

"I didn't recognize the car," Mrs. Merkel began, her voice sounding hollow in the large quiet room. "The lady from the Historical Society asked me to keep an eye. So I thought I better come over and see what."

"It's Nick's car," I said.

"I'm Nick," Nick said. I felt him thrust out his hand and heard Mrs. Merkel clear her throat. She was uncomfortable with such a gesture, I knew. Mrs. Merkel greeted people, men and women, Uncle Stash, even her own husband, without a smile or a word, but with a subtle dip of her chin and leveling of her eyes.

"This is Gideon, Mrs. Merkel," Ruby said. "He's a friend of ours from London. He's interested in the Native stuff."

"Hi, ma'am," Gideon said, though I'm guessing he barely looked away from the dusty cases of rare artifacts. "Look at the carving on this bone sucking tube," I heard him murmur.

Ruby and I had never embraced our neighbor and didn't expect to do so now. We also did not expect her to mention my aneurysm or express her sorrow about our imminent demise. We certainly did not expect Cathy Merkel to cry, the way Sherman Merkel did in the children's section of the Leaford Library.

"She started when she was about seven years old," Mrs. Merkel said, not like a proud mother, more matter-of-factly.

We hadn't expected her to say that.

"My husband said she could see things he couldn't," Mrs. Merkel continued. "He said she could see things no one could have seen. Like she was some kind of a divining rod for these things."

I felt my sister blush. "It's true," I said.

"I just looked hard, that's all," Ruby said. She was trembling. Maybe it was pride.

"Sherman's digging a new shed in around the same place you found the cooking pots and whatnot," Mrs. Merkel said.

"Oh," Ruby said.

"Next week."

"Oh," Ruby said again.

I could feel and hear in the squeaking floorboards Gideon move beside us, shifting his weight from foot to foot. "Wonder if I could help, ma'am? Can I help your husband dig?"

There was a long pause, as Mrs. Merkel seemed to be sizing the small man up. "S'ppose. What about you, Ruby? You like to come out and watch Mr. Merkel dig?"

"Sure," Ruby said.

Gideon, realizing his enthusiasm might have been off-putting, mentioned casually, "The truth is I'm a professional, ma'am. I could assist, just in case anything historically significant —"

"Mrs. Merkel," she said. "Call me Mrs. Merkel."

"I could *assist* your husband, Mrs. Merkel. I could give you my number and you could call me in London. Or I'll give Rose and Ruby my number, and you can call them to call me."

I felt Nick twitch beside me. He didn't like Gideon. He seemed to have sniffed him out, like prey. Nick couldn't think Gideon was a threat. Or a rival. Nick could *not* be jealous of Gideon. No matter what I'd imagined about the way he kissed me. And yet when Ruby, in a stroke of genius, remembered that Sherman Merkel was looking for a farmhand, and that Gideon had just lost his apartment, Nick cleared his throat beside me, as though he was holding back a protest.

So anxious was Gideon to meet Mr. Merkel and win the job of farmhand (and access to the rich-in-artifacts fields) that he suggested they go speak with him right away. Ruby and I needed to go home to rest anyway. And Mrs. Merkel said it was fine with her. I was worried that Ruby might feel thrown over, but she seemed fine as we made our way back to the car.

Gideon and Mrs. Merkel walked with us, pausing to say goodbye. "You'll be there, right?" Gideon asked Ruby.

"I will," she said brightly.

"You're not gonna get on a writing jag and keep her away, right, Rose?" Gideon joked with me. "Promise, right?"

"Writing jag?" Mrs. Merkel sounded curious rather than astonished.

"Rose is writing her autobiography," Gideon explained.

"Really?" Mrs. Merkel said and moved closer.

"How many pages have you written, Rose?" Gideon suddenly asked me.

"I don't know," I said. "I stopped counting at four hundred." (Such a *lie*.)

"You must be nearly done," he said.

I did not see the logic.

Mrs. Merkel must have seen that I couldn't see, no matter that I was trying to focus my eyes on the spot where I thought hers would be, but she didn't comment on my blindness. "I'd like to read it when you're done," she said. I couldn't tell if she meant to be sarcastic or encouraging.

"I'll send you a copy of it," I said. (Not a lie.)

I didn't expect Mrs. Merkel to smile at me or kiss me or touch me in any physical way. And she didn't. But she did lean in and whisper, "I'll help. Anything you need. I'll help you and Ruby." Her voice was so tender I questioned my ear.

"Thanks," I said.

"Anything," she repeated.

"Thanks," I said again.

Mrs. Merkel left us, and after a moment, I could hear Gideon's receding voice as he described to our old neighbor his childhood farm in Glencoe, and his life growing up as an only child. At some point, waiting for Nick to get the stool arranged in the trunk before he helped to ease us into the front seat, we heard the sound of laughter. Ruby and I gripped each other. Though we'd never heard the sound before, Ruby and I both knew it was Cathy Merkel's laughter. Gideon hadn't said a single funny thing in the hours we'd spent together. In a million years I couldn't imagine how he'd made that poor woman laugh.

Nick started up the car, and when he was sure Ruby couldn't see, he took my left hand. "Sure you don't want to see the old house again, Rosie?"

"No," Ruby and I said together.

We rode home in silence, Nick squeezing my hand.

Ruby fell asleep.

"Will you keep driving, Nick? Will you just drive around for a while?" I asked.

He didn't ask where I wanted to go. He just kept driving the river road, the one the Indians called *Eskinippsi,* the one that curves and loops and seems to flow back into itself. Once around to the bridge. And back again. And again. And looping and again, like a needle in a groove. We drove until I felt the sun retreat, and I worried that Ruby would get cold.

"It's time to go," I said.

"I know," Nick replied.

He turned down the road that led back to Leaford.

"Will you come over tonight?" I asked.

He grunted in the affirmative and we drove in silence, his grip on my hand growing tighter with each city block toward the bungalow.

It's Ruby.

Wow. Where to begin. Or end.

We went out to the farm today with Gideon and Nick. We got into the Leaford Museum, where we found out there was a key under the mat this whole time! We weren't there for as long as we thought we'd be, though, because Rose needed to come back home and rest. Nick packed blankets and food and everything, but that's life. That really is life. You're just not always in a place for as long as you thought you'd be. Good thing Nick was prepared, but I hope all that food doesn't go to waste.

I was a little embarrassed and a little proud about the fuss everyone made over my collection of artifacts. I didn't remember that there were so many specimens, and so many rare things, and so well preserved.

Last week Gideon looked at me like I was some kind of expert. Today he looked at me like I was a genius. While I was looking at the things, which I'd forgotten the Historical Society had mounted on this really pretty purple fabric, I saw my whole life flash by.

I was remembering the farm, walking the fields in the spring, Aunt Lovey saying, Don't let Mrs. Merkel see you — it'll make her think of

Larry. I told Gideon the idea about making our old orange farmhouse into the new Leaford Museum. He got really excited about that.

And then — I guess it's not that weird or coincidental because she does live across the road — Mrs. Merkel came into the museum. Rose said it's appropriate that Mrs. Merkel should appear again near the end of our lives, since she was there at the very beginning. Rose said everything comes around again, some things more obviously than others.

Rose says the book is done.

So I'm writing to say good-bye.

Rose said a life story should be like a life, too short, no matter how long a person lives, and not sewn up, but joined up, the end joined up somehow to the beginning. Besides, we can't sew things up at the end, the way you might if the story wasn't a true one. Rose and I realize that we'll likely never know the truth about our own mother. Alive? Dead? Name? And we'll likely never find Rose's daughter, Taylor, or even see her face in a picture. That's just a reality. Just, like Rose says, part of our story.

It turns out that Rose is done, so the book is done, instead of the other way around. She said whatever it was she wanted to say, she's said. And the stories she wanted to tell, she's told. She said it's like a feeling of being full. You don't always know, until you try to put the spoon in your mouth, that you just can't take another bite.

She hasn't written much about our years in the bungalow. And — I know because I asked — she's left out some good stories about things that have happened at our work. And about Verbeena. She said that when she started writing this book she never thought about the ending, but I don't believe her. I think she's been writing her final chapter all along. She's not calling it *Autobiography of a Conjoined Twin* anymore. She says the story is more than the title says, more than just the story of us, but she hasn't thought of anything better yet. We laughed, remembering how Aunt Lovey said if Rose ever wrote a story about her life with me she should call it *Double Duty*.

We talked about the things we want to do with the time we have left. Gideon thinks if my collection of artifacts is moved to another museum, I should help pack the things, and I would like to do that. I would like to hold those things in my hands again and close my eyes and imagine myself five hundred years ago, grinding maize, smoking my turtlehead pipe. I trust the vibration of objects. Rose trusts her words on a page.

One thing Rose didn't tell you, because she doesn't know, is that I was looking at Mrs. Merkel in the Leaford Museum today and I had this weird déjà vu, and then I had this vision of me and Ruby and Nick and Gideon and Mr. and Mrs. Merkel at the cottage, ringing in the New Year. I nearly laughed out loud to think it, but found myself trembling. Stranger things have happened, though. Look at Rose and me.

Rose says, now that her book is finished, she's just going to put it in a box. She said she doesn't want to think about the book anymore. She says she doesn't care, but I'll bet she'll haunt Nick to read it, or maybe Roz or Whiffer. (I wonder if he's still connected to the friend's friend who knows a publisher in New York?) I can't imagine a writer spending so much time arranging words on a page and not caring if someone had a look.

Rose says she just wants to spend time with Nick. Maybe edit a few old love poems.

I cannot believe I am choked up to write this last bit.

I never expected to feel like you were so real, but that thing Rose said about writing to a friend, it really stuck with me, you know?

We're not leaving right away. But we won't see you again before we go.

I'll miss you.

I'll miss you, and I'm not just saying that.

Writers & Readers

My sister, Ruby, has always been cold, especially her hands and feet (Raynaud's, it's called, a circulatory problem), while I have always been warm and have hated to be overdressed or seated near a fireplace. When Ruby and I were little, she used to put her delicate hands inside my shirt, on the skin of my back, or sometimes my tummy. Her clubfeet she'd press to my thighs. She'd giggle and tease, "I'm taking your warm, Rose. I'm taking all your warm." I never minded, and never protested, because I felt that while she was taking my warm, I was taking her cool.

In the end, I want Nick to be right. Just that I wrote the book, I want that to be enough. I'm printing this whole thing up tonight, for the first time since I started writing. I'm not going to read it again, but put it in a box, and let the gods decide its fate. If ever these words and sentences and paragraphs and accumulated pages from this story of my life find the eyes of a reader, this chapter is for you. It's the second chapter I've written today. And the last chapter I will write.

I have an urge to apologize for my mountain-climbing metaphors while begging patience for one more. Because, my friends, I can see the summit. It appears bitten, scalloped white against this azure sky. There are other people there too. And not all of them writers.

Everyone says "Don't look down," but I did look down, at where I've been, how far I've come, how high I've climbed. Where I thought I'd made a single trail in the snow, I've made a thousand, blighted by debris, the bits of me I've left behind. And tools I didn't even know I had. My ax wedged between the rock and the hard place where I'd been stuck for so long. My gloves in a crevice, way back there, where I'd camped in that little cave. A boot down that direction, nearly covered over by the snowfall last night. A tube of lipstick glinting in the sun (which must belong to Ruby). The story of me, of Ruby and me, of Aunt Lovey and Uncle Stash, and the Merkels and the others, it's hard to let go.

It's hard to let go.

It is night. Cold. The air from the furnace grate makes the room feel drafty instead of warm. I kick an extra blanket over Ruby's legs. Nick has come and gone and I'm still blushing, or have a fever. He *kissed* me. He did kiss *me*. With the lights on. Looking straight into my eyes. We did not declare our love for each other. We did not promise anything beyond the moment. We just kissed. Not a dry, chaste kiss, but one that was moist, and openmouthed, and warm. It should be carved somewhere on a tree: "Nick kissed Rose." I don't feel sated, though. I want more.

Ruby and I talked for a while after Nick left. She's writing in her yellow pad this moment. About today? About the Leaford Museum? About Gideon? Is she saying good-bye? Usually I can read her mind. Not tonight. And it's just as well. Technically — I sound like my sister — we've agreed to terms and conditions about our individual final chapters. We're in agreement about the whole rest of our lives.

All those years ago, when Uncle Stash was building our elaborate metal bus shelter at the end of the lane, I asked him impatiently when he was going to be finished. He laughed and said, "People don't finish, Rose. People stop. To finish is to say okay, now it's right, never I'm going to change it. To stop is to say okay, it's not perfect, but I have to go to something else."

You hold this book, our story, in your hands (let me fantasize it's in hardcover with a brilliant jacket design), now with considerably more pages on the left side than on the right. Like you, I've been there a thousand times. We both know, writer and reader, like the proverbial sand in the hourglass, the seconds on the shot clock, the story is over.

I returned to the first chapter of this book, which I haven't read since my last crisis of confidence. I might alter it now to read: I have never looked into my sister's eyes, but I've seen inside her soul. I have never worn a hat, but I *have* been kissed like *that*. I have never raised both arms at once, but the moon beguiled me still. Sleep is for suckers. I like the bus just fine. And though I've never climbed a tree, I've scaled a mountain, and that's a hell of a thing.

One more change I might make is to say that I wouldn't live a thousand lives, but a million to infinity, to live the life I've lived as me. I am Rose Darlen of Baldoon County. Beloved sister of Ruby. The world's oldest surviving craniopagus twins. Aunt Lovey and Uncle Stash were right. How lucky Ruby and I have been to be "The Girls."

And there it is, where it's been all along, the title I've been looking for.

The end, taking me back to the beginning.

The Girls.

Acknowledgments

Thanks to Michael Pietsch, my publisher at Little, Brown and Company in New York. Special thanks to editor Judy Clain, who steered me in this direction.

I would like to thank my editor, Diane Martin, my publisher, Louise Dennys, my publicist, Sharon Klein, and the talented team at Knopf Canada/Random House of Canada Limited for their enthusiasm and commitment.

I would also like to thank my agent, Denise Bukowski, who read pages early on and gave me confidence and good counsel.

Thanks as always to my husband, my children, my parents, my brothers and their families, the Rowland family, and my husband's family. Special thanks to Dennis and Barb Loyer, and Wilfred and Trudy Loyer, for sharing their stories.

I consulted numerous works while writing this novel and wish to cite a few that were especially helpful: *Conjoined Twins: An Historical, Biological, and Ethical Issues Encyclopedia* by Christine Quigley; *The Two-Headed Boy and Other Medical Marvels* by Jan Bondeson; *One of Us: Conjoined Twins and the Future of Normal* by Alice Domurat Dreger; *Entwined Lives: Twins and What They Tell Us About*

Human Behavior by Nancy L. Segal; *Psychological Profiles of Conjoined Twins* by J. David Smith; *Millie-Christine: Fearfully and Wonderfully Made* by Joanne Martell.

Finally, my thanks to the people of southwestern Ontario, gracious hosts who continue to indulge my imagination.

About the Author

Lori Lansens has written several films and is the author of the internationally acclaimed novel *Rush Home Road*. This is her second book.